The
BROTHERHOOD
of the
RED NILE

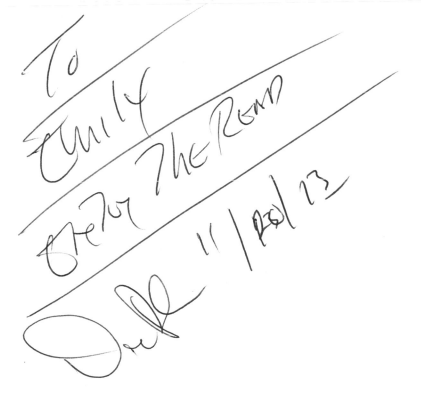

To Emily
Go For The Road
11/20/13

The BROTHERHOOD of the RED NILE

A Terrorist Perspective

DAN PERKINS

The Brotherhood of the Red Nile
A Terrorist Perspective

ISBN: 978-1-4582-0688-6 (sc)
ISBN: 978-1-4582-0687-9 (hc)
ISBN: 978-1-4582-0686-2 (e)

Library of Congress Control Number: 2012921423

Lightning Press
Totowa, NJ 07512
www.lightning-press.com

Printed in the United States of America

1st Printing: 12/12
2nd Printing: 2/13
3rd Printing: 9/13
4th Printing: 11/13

DEDICATION

To my sister Kathy Baughn, who quickly learned how to read my manuscript with the misspellings, typos, and poor grammar. She would read and then send me a text message saying "summors," which is IM for "send me more."

To my wife, Gerri, who has been an author's widow and avid reader, in spite of the mistakes; she was an objective critic, and through it all she encouraged me to go for it. She always asked, "What is your objective in writing this book?" She was the first to say, "This is really good." She has been my wife for forty-four years and has always supported me in whatever I wanted to do because she knew that if I were happy, she would be happy.

FOREWORD

I want to remind the reader that no matter how believable you think this story is this is a work of fiction; <u>it is not real</u>. Some of it is based on facts, such as places, food, and other things. All the rest comes from my mind. I have tried, to the best of my ability, to make this book real, exciting, scary, and believable all at the same time. But it is not true—nor is it possible.

A great deal of time was spent in researching to get the names of the people appropriate to their native cultures. The names are fictitious, and any name that is the same as that of a real person is purely coincidental. The core cities are real, but the locations used in the cities are not real. I paid careful attention to the food and the phone numbers and addresses used in the story. All the technology is real. Most of the technology referred to in the book is available over the Internet.

I can find no evidence of a group called the "Brotherhood of the Red Nile," at least not yet. It is clear, however, that there are terrorist groups that want to attack the United States. The attacks suggested in this book are a matter of fiction, but this book is about as real as today's headlines and as scary as tomorrow's. Fasten your seat belts: you're in for an exciting and scary ride—full of possibilities, twists and turns, and surprises. At the end you may be asking yourself, "Is this fiction? It seems so real!" Keep track of how many times you say to yourself, "I didn't see that coming!" I hope this is one of the best thrillers you've read in the last five years.

Enjoy!

Dan Perkins

Acknowledgments

THANKS TO:

My son Matthew, who helped me test all my crazy Internet ideas

My friend Bob who is a Professional Engineer,
who acted as my sounding board

My editor, who was scared reading the book but gave
me invaluable advice and encouragement

The Big Arts Center on Sanibel Island for offering the writing class;

Nancy Daversa, the teacher at Big Arts, who
unleashed whatever, was inside me;

All my friends and family who read and encouraged me to go forward.

Jane H who graciously spent her time in proofing
this work and made it even better

CHAPTER I

Flashing Orange Lights

JOHN BOWMAN USUALLY, AS THE saying goes, "slept like a log" most nights, but that night he didn't. He sensed lights flashing. When he finally opened his eyes, he was startled by the intensity, color, and contrast of the orange against the white walls. The fears of the unknown made him hesitate before putting on his robe and slippers and creeping down the stairs. The intensity of the lights grew to the point that his head began to pound as he got closer and closer to the massive bay window in the living room.

When he reached the window, he peered out and looked up the street. Some of Bowman's neighbors had already congregated there. Was that crime scene tape? The evening must be warm. None of the neighbors were wearing jackets. He'd just go see what was happening without changing his clothes, even if he did feel a little silly going out in his robe and slippers.

He strolled down the driveway. *So that's what night-blooming jasmine smells like.* For a time, the sweet smell of the jasmine calmed his fears. He'd never understood why Sarah had planted these flowers. They were never awake to smell them. His slippers slapped against the cobblestone driveway and sidewalks, sounding like a small cap gun going off. The noise seemed to startle the neighbors gathered over at the Ridley House. They gathered more tightly together.

He expected to see his town's name on the truck standing in front of the house. Instead, it read, *Department of Homeland Security*. Why would Homeland Security be in the neighborhood? Who had called them? What were they looking for? Tall Trees was an upscale, gated community with friendly, patriotic people who had, to the best of John's knowledge, never even seen a police car in the development.

As he approached the tape, he asked long-time resident Julie Borden if she knew what was happening. She didn't know, but she'd seen people in very strange-looking protective suit leave the truck and go around the back of the house.

Two nondescript white cargo vans with no markings on their sides approached without fanfare or flashing lights. The van doors swung open, and two men rushed out of each one—at least Bowman thought they were men. The strange-looking suits made it difficult to tell what they were. Each team took a gurney and raced into the house. The inside of the vans looked more elaborate than the best emergency squad vans in Springfield. The stretcher-bearers' suits looked like heavy-duty protective suits—the kind people wore around chemical or biological contamination sites—or when working with deadly bacteria. John pulled his robe tighter.

Just as quickly as the men went in the house, they came out with the two stretchers, each with a body bag strapped to it. Could that be Mike and Mary Ridley? It couldn't be. He'd seen them both last night around six o'clock as he was taking Chandler out for his evening walk. He'd stopped and chatted, and the Ridleys had both seemed fine.

Bowman glanced back toward the house. *Where is Chandler? Why isn't he barking?* The Jack Russell was a light sleeper. He usually barked at anything out of the ordinary. Bowman wanted to go back and check on the dog, but he felt drawn to the Ridley House. He had to stay and see what was going on.

Where were the local police? All the agencies were supposed to be cooperating since September 11. If Homeland Security was here, why weren't the police? Bowman reached into his robe pocket and pulled out his cell phone to call his brother-in-law. Jim Whittles was a good friend and an excellent sheriff. John, Sarah, and Jim had grown up together in Springfield. Jim would know what was going on. Springfield wasn't a very big town.

He flipped his phone open. No signal? There was a tower just behind the development. He'd never had any problems before. None of the neighbors had a signal, either. How could all the cell phones from all the providers are out of service, all at the same time? There was a dish on top of the Homeland Security truck. Were they blocking all the cell service? Why would they *want* to block the service?

Ten minutes later, the dish on the truck went down. Cell service returned. Bowman dialed Whittles cell number, and a groggy Jim answered the phone. Bowman filled him in, but Whittles didn't seem to know any more than he did.

"I'll come check it out. Give me twenty minutes."

While he was waiting for his brother-in-law, Bowman tried to talk with someone from Homeland Security. Everyone in the special suits ignored him until one of them saw the police car coming up the road. Then he took off his helmet to talk to them. He told the onlookers to go home and that everything was under control. They were in no danger.

Sheriff Whittles got out of his car, sipping a cup of coffee as he walked toward Bowman and the man from Homeland Security. He introduced himself to the man without the helmet and asked why they were in his jurisdiction without having at least notified his department. The man said they'd intended to notify him, but things were happening so fast they needed to get here and secure the site before they alerted any local authorities.

Whittles was calm and asked the representative what, exactly, was going on.

The leader responded that his section chief would be here shortly, and he would explain what was going on as best he could until then. "I can't speak to what happened here."

Bowman piped up and asked who was in the body bags.

The leader wouldn't answer.

Whittles asked the team leader, "Do I understand that bodies have been removed from the site?"

The team leader did not answer.

Bowman said, "We all *saw* the white vans come in, and empty stretchers were taken into the house. Then they came out very quickly with body bags strapped to the stretchers."

Whittles asked, "Is this true?"

The team leader said he couldn't answer the question.

"Look," said Whittles. "If I don't start getting some answers quickly, you might just find you and your whole team under arrest and sitting in my jail."

At that moment a black sedan with no markings pulled up, and a distinguished-looking man stepped out of the car and started walking toward Sheriff Whittles. He introduced himself as Frank J. Williams, the section chief. In reality, Williams was the undersecretary in charge of terrorist activity (TA) for the Department of Homeland Security. "I tried to reach you this evening, but your office said you'd gone for the day, and I didn't want to leave a message; I wanted to speak with you in private. Is there a place nearby where we can talk?"

Whittles responded, "Well, we could go back to my office."

"I'd like to stay close to the site for a while longer, if you don't mind."

Bowman piped up, "my house is just down the block, and you could use his living room. Sarah and the children were asleep in another part of the home, and they could have privacy and not disturb his family." So the three of them left and went to Bowman's living room to talk.

Williams questioned Whittles about the appropriateness of Bowman being in the room. Whittles responded, "Bowman worked for the state attorney's office and was a senior investigator in the criminal decision. After they explained as much, Frank Williams had no problem with Bowman participating in the conversation.

Bowman asked, "Do you want coffee and how do you like it," and they both said yes and black. Bowman left to start the coffee and returned to the living room, closing the sliding doors behind him. Bowman knew the smell of fresh coffee would wake Sarah, so he went back in to turn on the exhaust fan in the kitchen to blow out the smell of the coffee; he didn't need Sarah asking questions. He returned once more and sat on the oversized leather couch while Whittles and Williams each sat in one of the two red leather, wing-back chairs that faced the couch. Frank started off by saying that Homeland Security had been following the activity of an al Qaeda terrorist group in Syria. "There has been a significant amount of traffic by this group, looking for any of the twelve missing Russian suitcase dirty bombs."

Whittles interrupted. "Aren't those the suitcase atomic bombs that were stolen from the Soviet Union after it was broken up and all those countries were spun off?"

"The same," Williams replied.

Whittles responded, "But I thought that was years ago; haven't they all been found by now?"

"Not all of them. The problem is that over the years, some have been found, and those that were found were deteriorating and becoming very unstable. Nitro was leaking out of the sticks of TNT."

"So what does that have to do with Springfield, Tall Trees, and the Ridley house?"

"We suspect that the Ridley son is a member of the terrorist group that smuggled one of the few remaining suitcase bombs into the United States. We also think that this group's intent was to explode the bomb in a major city when the president was visiting."

Whittles and Bowman eyes widened. They said almost in unison, "Not Michael!" Bowman said that, "I have known Michael since Mike and Mary adopted him as an infant, and he had always been kind, gentle, and never even had a discipline problem growing up. He excelled as a student in high school and had won a full scholarship to the University of California at Berkeley as a science Major."

Bowman, only half-wanting to know and dreading the answer, asked again about the body bags. Williams responded that the bags did not contain Mike and Mary's bodies, but in fact contained the bodies of some of the members of the terrorist group with which Michael might have been working.

Chapter 2

The Brotherhood of the Red Nile

I N A SMALL VILLAGE NEAR the town of Al-Mukharram in western Syria, the council of the Brotherhood of the Red Nile met for the first time to discuss their plan of attack on the United States. This rural and very small town had a population of about 9,000, but that population was spread far and wide. It stood about 200 miles northeast of Damascus and had a fairly mild climate this time of year, with a high temperature of about 65 degrees.

The meeting site was a building across from the citrus grove, northwest of the village square, such as it was. The building was plain and had few markings on it that would make it stick out as a planning site for a terrorist group, or any kind of group, for that matter. The leadership council came by car, truck, and motorcycle, and some even walked. They all entered the building through a rear entrance and left their footprints in the dust and dirt on the first floor. Once inside they went to the metal stairs and climbed to the second-floor meeting room. The council was made up of five men—the leader and four lieutenants—and underneath these five were more. Some of them in the lower tier had been members of al-Qaeda but had spun off because they felt that al-Qaeda was no longer the organization most committed to the destruction of America.

The discussion today was to begin the process of exploring what they could do to bring the mighty America to its knees. The leader's name was Mohamed el Sargon. Sargon, Assyrian for "king," was well suited to his role as leader. He started the meeting with a prayer asking for wisdom and guidance to carry out their mission.

As the meeting came to order, Sargon said to the panel, "First we must discuss the previous attacks on America and why they failed. We must be diligent and detailed to see what mistakes were made and how we can attack America with great success. Our attack has to be so devastating that it will take decades for America to recover. During the time it will take America to recover, we will dominate the world. So let us begin with the discussions of the failures of the attack on September 11, 2001. What was the first mistake al-Qaeda made?"

Among his audience, hands went into the air, and a heated discussion began.

Chapter 3

Washington, DC Today

THE TERRORIST UNIT OF THE Office of Homeland Security was abuzz with discussions concerning the possible threat from the Brotherhood of the Red Nile. In a very large conference room, representatives were gathering from Homeland Security, the FBI, CIA, NSA, and the Secret Service. Everyone was waiting for Frank J. Williams to enter the room. Some at the meeting were actually wondering why they were here until Undersecretary Williams made his opening remarks.

"Ladies and gentlemen, we are here today because of a real threat, that if successful, could bring down America. I know that we are all concerned about threats to the safety and security of the United States, but based on what we have been able to pick up in Internet traffic, a new al-Qaeda–type terrorist group is being formed somewhere in Syria, dramatically different from al-Qaeda. We believe that it is possible that this group has purchased former Soviet Union suitcase dirty bombs and plans to use them against us. We know that Russia cannot account for twelve of these bombs.

"Other al-Qaeda–type groups have acquired one or more of these bombs, but because of their age and deterioration, they would not detonate. Intelligence tells us that the Brotherhood has been in contact with people in the nuclear weapons project in Iran to update, stabilize, and make these bombs more powerful and effective. Make no mistake: this threat is real. We are taking it very seriously, and so should you. The survival of our country is literally at stake."

Williams took a sip of water and silenced his audience with a wave of his hand before continuing. "I was in the small town of Springfield, TX, last evening, and one of our contaminant teams found two people dead in a house and the remains of an empty suitcase bomb buried in the backyard. The owners of the house were not in the house, but we found two bodies that have since been identified as members of a different terrorist group whom obviously had one of the missing bombs. We think the two people who were killed were trying to get their hands on the new super dirty bomb and were killed by members of the Brotherhood of the Red Nile. We are having the empty case examined by our forensic lab to see whether any modifications were made to the bomb. We want to try to find out whether this was an older version of the new generation of dirty bomb.

"We hope to have the analysis sometime today and will forward the information to you by secure e-mail. To the best of our knowledge, we don't know what the target is in the United States, so we are asking for your full cooperation and that you send us any Internet traffic that is out of the ordinary that might tip us off to where they plan to use the bomb or bombs. Make no mistake: this group is well financed, and every member has made a life-and-death commitment to destroy America. I'll go back to Springfield in the next day or so to speak to the people and the local authorities, so if you have any information, please call first. Now, if you will excuse me, I have to make a report to the President and the cabinet."

CHAPTER 4

Meeting in the Oval Office

FRANK WILLIAMS HAD TO TAKE a car to the White House, as it was too far to walk from his office at Homeland Security. As his car turned off Murray Lane, where his office was located, and headed for Pennsylvania Avenue, he could feel the tension building in his body. He was on his way to his first face-to-face meeting with the President, and he was the messenger who had to tell the President of the United States that the nation could be facing the most serious threat to American security since September 11, 2001.

As his unmarked car pulled into the White House driveway, he could feel those butterflies in his stomach. He got out of the car and went into a side door that led him to a corridor that looked like the length of a football field. As he walked closer to the Oval Office, the hallway was lined with Marines holding rifles at the ready. He was shown into an anteroom to wait for the President to call him in for the meeting. The room was small but very comfortable, and, sitting down, he wondered how many other visitors had sweated it out, waiting to talk to the President to discuss the possible end of America.

When he was called into meet with President, Nathan Jordan, he entered the Oval Office and saw that not only was his boss, the Secretary of Homeland Security, Mark Simons, present at the meeting, but also the Secretary of Defense, Robert Hamilton, and the National Security Adviser, Fred Markel. Williams started the discussion by telling those assembled about the new terrorist group. He told the President that he didn't have a great deal of information, but based on the chatter, this group had to be taken very seriously. Williams told the President that he was trying to get assets on the ground that could gain more information about the group. He also told the participants about his visit to Springfield the night before and the discovery of an empty suitcase bomb case and two dead terrorists in the house.

At that point President Jordan asked, "Let me ask: do we know where the contents of the bomb case are at the moment?"

Williams replied, "No, sir. We are trying to trace the radioactive marker in the bomb, but we can't get a signal." Williams waited to see whether the President or any of his advisers had any additional questions, but there was silence. Williams didn't know whether that was good or bad. He proceeded with his report.

He told them that it appeared that there had been a struggle over the bomb between competing terrorist groups, and whoever had gotten the bomb had killed the two people found in the house. Again the President asked, "Do we know for sure that the Brotherhood of the Red Nile was involved in the murders?"

Williams replied, "No, sir, we do not. We only suspect they might be involved." In an increasingly agitated mood, the President, asked, "Do we know the other terrorist group involved in the shoot-out?"

Again Williams answered, "No, sir."

The President asked, "Then what the hell *do* we know?"

As Williams continued to deliver the bad news that he didn't have answers to the President's questions, he could feel his armpits sweat, and he hoped it wasn't leaking through his suit coat. Nathan Jordan reminded everybody in the room the that he had been elected on a campaign promise to do everything in his power as President to keep Americans safe from terrorist attacks. "I am *not* going to have America attacked on my watch, its that clear? I don't care what it takes to stop this attack, but stop it we will, Am I clear on this?" Everybody said, "Yes, sir."

The President was a fair man and didn't blame Williams for the threat, but said that he wanted to be in the loop at all times to make sure that they were doing everything in their power to protect the country. "Whatever you need in resources, I want you to contact Markel. He will see that you get whatever you need."

Williams told the President that if he wanted, he could personally give him a daily briefing or it could be in his daily terrorist threat report from National Security Advisor Markel. "I want to be kept informed of any important details, and the Terrorist Threat Report will be good enough for now. Should you have something of a more urgent nature, you can call the White House, and I will see you immediately." The President seemed to have cooled off a little. "Anything else to report?" Williams did not, and the meeting disbanded.

As he entered the anteroom, Williams hoped he would get more comfortable in the Oval Office and not sweat so much in the future. Especially if he was going to be spending as much time there as he feared he was.

He headed back down the long hallway, soaking wet from perspiration, and began to wonder whether he smelled because of all the sweating, for he had not had a shower yet today. When he got to the end of the corridor, he looked out the door, and his car was waiting for him to take him back to his office at Homeland Security. After the car left the White House grounds, he opened the bar in the car and took a good, hard swallow of straight bourbon.

On the ride back to his office he realized that he had been gone three days and had not spoken to his wife Ellen. She worked at the Social Security administration and was a "lifer," as she often said. Ellen had maintained her figure and was very attractive. She always looked well dressed and loved to go out on the town. At the same time, she was just as comfortable having a few friends over for a BBQ.

She was very comfortable with herself and her husband Frank. The two of them had been married almost twenty-five years and were planning their silver wedding anniversary celebration and trip next year. By all signs possible, they loved each other very much. Williams had worked for the CIA in Langley before being offered a job at Homeland Security shortly after the agency was being set up. Frank and Ellen tried to spend as much time together as they could. They were the type of couple that believed that you had to work at being husband and wife. That's not to say that they never had disagreements; of course they did. But over the years they had developed some simple rules that they followed in their relationship. Never go to bed angry with the other. Never forget each other's birthdays, or anniversaries, and lastly and most important, if Frank was to be gone more than three days on assignment, he had to touch base with Ellen, even if it meant just a quick "Hello, I miss you, and I'm thinking about you."

Unfortunately they couldn't have children, but they enjoyed their nieces and nephews when they were around. They ate out regularly, and their favorite, any time of the year, was 1789 in Georgetown. It was a restaurant that had been in DC a long time and looked like it belonged in Dickens's London. The food was excellent and the service superb.

As the car pulled into his building, he wondered how he would tell her about the threat. Frank and Ellen shared everything, and Frank knew that, no matter what he told Ellen, she would keep his secret. He got out of the car and went to his office. His office was on the top floor of the building and he had a great view of the Mall and the original Smithsonian castle. Williams loved history and spent some of his lunchtimes, when he could, in the various museums on the mall. As he was approaching his assistant's office down a corridor longer than the one at the White House, he asked his secretary Marie, "Can you please get my wife on the phone?" "Right away, sir."

Marie had come over with Williams from Langley, and she was a very competent person. He could rely on her to get the work done, regardless of the time it took. She liked her work, and she liked working with Williams. She did think it strange that in all the time she knew him, nobody ever called him Frankie; they always called him Frank. They had worked together for fifteen years, and she knew him quite well. She knew how to read his moods and his body language. For instance, she could tell today, by the way he was walking, hitting the heel of his shoe hard on the floor, almost as if were taking out his anger on the floor, that something very, very serious was going on.

In the past, Williams would confide in her when he thought he needed a second opinion on whatever he was working on at the moment. Marie was tall, about five feet ten, with medium-length, naturally blonde hair, turned up at the ends, and very good-looking. So much so that she attracted a great deal of attention from all the men in the office, regardless of marital status. She was the secretary to the second-in-command of Homeland Security and earned an excellent salary, as her pay grade was as a GS 9. With her income she could afford nice clothes, which she enjoyed. To her, dressing for work meant no jeans or pants in the office. Several years ago, she bought a Georgetown row house and had it furnished so well that it looked like it could be the centerfold in one of those home-decorating magazines.

She knew that Frank was in love with Ellen, and she never made any advances toward Frank because she knew it would go nowhere. Marie respected Frank's love for Ellen. Plus, she loved her job, she loved the relationship she had with both Frank and Ellen, and, all in all, she knew she had a great life. She often wondered about a husband, but the longer she went without one, the more she concluded she didn't really need one. Little did she know that things were going on in the Middle East that just might change that wonderful and comfortable life she'd had forever and for which she'd worked so hard.

CHAPTER 5

Syria

SARGON WAS WAITING FOR ANSWERS to his question about September 11, 2001. One of the team members interrupted and asked Sargon how he'd come up with the name of the group. Sargon responded that the Nile River was the mother of all men, and she sent out her children from the red banks of the river to conquer the world. "We are going to conquer the world as brothers from the great Nile, and that is how I came up with the name."

His team leaders had been pondering the question about mistakes made and were ready to tell Sargon what they thought. The council had five members. Sargon was the head, and he had personally recruited the other four team leaders and many of the men who reported to the team leaders. In putting together his leadership council, he was looking for very specific talents and experience. He had a good idea as to what he wanted to do, but he needed them to pull off what might be the largest single terrorist attack in the history of the world. This attack would be carried out against the most powerful nation the world had ever seen.

Sargon wanted to bring down the United States of America single-handedly, and he believed he could. Many other terrorist groups, including Osama bin Laden's, had done nothing from which the United States couldn't quickly recover; he hoped his team would see his vision and that together they would come up with the master plan to destroy America.

The members of Sargon's team were one Syrian, one Russian, one Iranian, and one Israeli. The Syrian, Adad Al Assad, was a graduate of MIT in the United States, specializing in computer science. Assad was married to a Syrian, with two children, and had a software and hardware business in Syria that supplied productivity software to businesses in the Middle East. He was successful, with a very nice house, servants, and two cars, and his children went to an expensive private school in England. Sargon hoped that Assad would help him figure a way around all the security on the Internet to accomplish his goal.

The Iranian, Cryus Jaiari, was a graduate of the London School of Business. He was not married and had no job. He was borrowing money to live on from his parents and needed a job to pay for his basic needs. In order for him to get to the meeting, he had had to walk and hitchhike. He was not sure why he was there, but Sargon knew that in order to evaluate the options, he needed to understand the economic damage that each option could do to the US economy. His goal was to find the option most devastating to the United States, and that might not mean body count alone, but billions if not trillions of dollars.

Next, from Israel, was Mordecai Hagal, a weapons specialist. He wasn't a student of handguns or rifles, and, for that matter, he didn't know much about tanks or airplanes. What he did know about was nuclear bombs. Mordecai had worked on the Israeli nuclear weapons program but had left the program because he felt that the leadership of his country had lost its backbone and was giving away his country to placate the United States. He tried to changes things in Israel but got nowhere; he felt that the pressure from the United States forced them to make all the concessions that put his country at serious risk. On Israeli TV, he watched the prime minster being humiliated by the president of the United States, who had left their meeting to go have dinner with his family.

He was ashamed to be a Jew and an Israeli and wanted to do something to knock the Great America down to where it really belonged—a Third-World country. Mordecai was a big challenge for Sargon: he had to explain to the rest of the team just why he had brought a Jew into the Brotherhood of the Red Nile.

Last, but not least, was Oleg Barbolio from Russia, whose contribution to the cause of the brotherhood was money: something very special indeed. Oleg's uncle was Viktor Antipova, and he was a very wealthy independent oilman—one of the wealthiest men in Russia. Despite that, he was on nobody's radar; he had made his money quietly and then spread it all over the world. Before his great wealth, he was in charge of non-ballistic nuclear weapons security. When the old Soviet Union was breaking up, he was put in charge of securing many nuclear devices, and the twelve suitcase nuclear bombs in the arsenal were particularly near and dear to him. At one time, he had all twelve bombs in his possession in a vault out of the country. Over the years, he had sold some of the defective bombs to secure the money to build his oil empire in Russia. Oleg's uncle had no love for the United States; he thought that America was truly an imperialistic country that didn't care about anybody but America, no matter how much money or food they gave away. America took whatever it wanted, regardless of the outcome of stealing the world's resources.

Oleg was a petroleum engineer and had spent fifteen years working for the various oil operations of his uncle. Over time, he had done every job, from working on deep-water drilling platforms to running an oil refinery. He knew the oil business.

Sargon repeated his question, and Jaiari spoke up as he looked at Osama bin Laden's plan. "It was not a long-term plan; it was one event, or more correctly, a series of events that produced no real long-term change in America. The damage that was done had no long-term real impact on America or its economy or, for that matter, its people. Many Americans today have forgotten what really happened in most of the events, including the September 11 attack.

"Sure, the building of the memorial at ground zero was full of conflicts; it took a long time to agree on a plan. The clash of the special interest groups over what should replace the Twin Towers was an example of lost focus, for both America and bin Laden. I recently read that the museum of September

11, when completed, will be the most expensive museum ever built. And most people don't know that Con Ed, the power company in New York, had turned off the power to the grid around the World Trade Centers shortly after the first tower came down. The result was that the power company isolated the damage.

"Another mistake bin Laden made was that he spent too much time on the drawings of the buildings, thinking that if he brought the towers down, he could shut down the financial markets and in turn the American economy. He spent little time on the redundancy that Wall Street already had in place, and in fact, they brought the markets back in line in just over a week. Yes, it is true that several thousands of people lost their lives on 9-11, but 3,000 out of over 313,000,000 was a nonevent."

They all thought in silence for a moment after Jaiari spoke. Soon he continued. "If we are going to bring America to its knees by affecting the economy, we have to do it not by blowing up buildings, but by impacting all Americans, regardless of income or position." At the moment, Jaiari didn't know what that might be, but he hoped that further discussion by the leaders of the Brotherhood would in fact come up with an idea that would impact America in a way that bin Laden could never have imagined or executed. The Brotherhood was beginning to come together around the idea of finding a way to diminish America as a global leader and making Islam the dominant power in the world. Sargon was pleased.

CHAPTER 6

Back in the United States of America

As WILLIAMS WENT INTO HIS office, he called on the intercom to Marie: "Please have Ted Baker come and see me as soon as he can, and what happened to my call to Ellen?" Marie replied she would call Baker immediately, and she had called Ellen, but she was not in, so she had left a message.

Williams started to look through the huge stack of paperwork on his desk that had accumulated in just three days. One of the things that had changed since 9-11 was the enormity of the amount of paper everybody had to send to everybody else. Just as he was finishing the first run-through of the stack, Baker knocked on his door and asked permission to come in. Williams got up and closed the door and then he turned to Baker and filled him in about the Brotherhood.

"Last night we had a team in Springfield, Texas, at an upscale neighborhood where one of our special teams found two dead terrorists in a house, and outside the house we found the case of a former Soviet Union suitcase bomb. In the case we also found a significant amount of nuclear material. It appears that there was a gun battle over the case, and the contents were ripped out and taken away."

Baker's mouth flopped open. "Do we have any idea what happened to the bomb?"

"No trace."

"Do we know whether the Brotherhood was involved with the theft?" As Baker asked him questions, Williams had a flashback to his meeting with the President and all the questions he couldn't answer; he started to sweat again. This time, however, he took off his jacket to cool down.

As he filled Baker in about the Ridleys, the intercom rang, and Ellen was on line one. Williams told her he didn't have time to talk and suggested dinner at 1789 at 7:30. "I'll get our usual table," she said, and they hung up, after telling each other they loved one other.

Williams turned to Baker and apologized. "We need to find out what happened to the Ridleys and as much as possible about Michael Ridley their son. Here is the phone number of the local sheriff; give him a call. I don't know how much help he will be, but I met a neighbor by the name of John Bowman who can probably give you more on the Ridleys and Michael. Before you call the sheriff, give the university a call and see what you can find out about Michael. Get back to me as soon as you can on any information you develop. I have to brief the president once a week and give him any new information in the daily terrorist briefing.

"Ted, I want you to be very careful about this assignment. You will report directly to me and only me. All information will go to directly to me by e-mail or phone, and only on a secure line, understood?"

"Yes, sir. Sir, might I ask one question? How serious do you think this new terrorist group is about hurting America?"

"In a word? Very."

CHAPTER 7

Near Al-Mukharram, Ninety Days Earlier

J AIARI CONTINUED THE DISCUSSION WITH his brotherhood members about what else went wrong with the 9-11 attack. "The second attack was to be on the capital city of Washington, DC. More specifically, bin Laden wanted to fly a plane into the Capitol or the White House. He did strike the Pentagon but didn't take it out of commission. The second attack was poorly thought out; the one plane could not take out the Pentagon, so it was a waste of time and resources. Finally, his plan called for a plane to crash into the Capitol and take out the elected officials. Again, poorly thought out, because he did not properly estimate the will of the American passengers on the plane that was intended for the Capitol. The one plane may have damaged the Capitol, but would not destroy the building or the will of the people of America.

"When President Bush went to ground zero, he rallied the American people and its resources to find the Taliban members and Osama bin Laden and destroy them, to retaliate against them for the innocent Americans who were killed by the attack. Knocking down buildings is not the way to break the will of the American people; in fact, it does just the opposite."

Mordecai broke in and asked a question. "If you don't destroy the buildings, then how do you destroy their will to fight?"

Sargon stepped in and said, "We will get to that question soon enough, but we must hear from each of you—your objective analysis of what al-Qaeda did wrong."

So Jaiari continued. "If we are going to attack America again, then we must figure out what type of attack will have the greatest impact on the will of the Americans. One thing many of the leaders of the Taliban and al-Qaeda should have learned is that if you kick a sleeping dog, you must be ready to defend yourself for the vicious outrage and attack that will come against you when the dog wakes up. If we look at what has happened to the power of the Taliban over the last eleven years, we can see that the organization was ill equipped to deal with the concentrated efforts of the Western world to crush its movement. The success has not been in the Western world, but in the Middle East, with the casting out through rebellion of those governments influenced by the Western world. Egypt's Arab Spring is just one example of the change in the Middle East that will eventually alter the influence of Islam throughout the entire world."

Chapter 8

Ted Baker's Office

Following his instructions from Undersecretary Williams, Baker made two calls. The first was to the admissions office at UC Berkeley to inquire as to the activities of Michael Ridley. When he called the admissions phone number from the school website and introduced himself, he was transferred to Julia Brown, the director of admissions for the university, who said she would get back to him as soon as she could.

Baker's second call was to Sheriff Whittles office in Springfield, and he was told that the Sheriff was on a case. The dispatcher said she would try to contact him immediately and asked whether this had anything to do with the disappearance of Mike and Mary Ridley the night before last. He replied, "I can't really discuss that with you. I'm sure you understand," and he hung up the phone, thinking what a pain it could be to deal with big cases in small towns.

Almost as quickly as he hung up, his other line was ringing, and when he answered, it was Julia Brown from Berkeley.

She began, "Mr. Baker, Michael Ridley was admitted and registered to come to the university starting August two years ago, but the records show that he never came to classes. I can't find any record that he has ever come to school for the last two years. I do have some other things to check out, but my guess is that we will find he never actually came to UC Berkeley. If I find anything different, I will let you know."

Baker hung up after asking for a photocopy of Michael's Berkeley ID, which Julia Brown said she would send right over. Baker decided to walk down the hall and see whether Williams was in his office. Marie said that Williams was away but should return shortly. Baker looked impatiently at his watch; he could feel things happening already. Somewhere, wheels were turning.

Chapter 9

Springfield

Sheriff Whittles was out at the Ridley house, trying to figure out what had happened to Mike and Mary. He also wanted to know who was in those body bags and where they had been taken. He wondered why no one had tried to contact Michael at school. Sheriff Whittles didn't think Williams had been entirely forthcoming with all the details as to what had happened at the Ridley house the night before last.

He walked into the front door of the Ridley home and called the office to speak with his deputy, Ed Rains. When he got hold of Rains, he told him to call Berkeley and try to reach Michael and find out whether Michael knew what was going on at his house, and if so, whether he had any idea where his parents were.

Despite the fact that they lived across from his sister and Bowman, Whittles had never been in the Ridley house, so it was all new to him. He brought a camera to take pictures, much as he would have done at any crime scene. He wasn't sure this was in fact a crime scene, but for now he was going to treat it as one. The first thing he did was walk through the whole house, to get a feel for what the Ridleys were like. He had learned at the police academy that a person's surroundings could tell you a great deal, sometimes even more than talking to them might.

His initial observations were that most of the furnishings were upscale and most likely expensive. Attractive modern art was on most of the walls throughout the house. He noticed rich-looking hardwood floors in every room, including the kitchen. After he had walked through the bedrooms, the bathrooms, and the rest of the house, he started back to the main entrance and then it came to him: everything was perfect and in its place. It was almost as if the house had never been lived in. He asked Detective Edwards, who was working with him, of his impressions of the house, and he agreed, with no prompting. The sheriff went back through the house and started taking pictures.

Meanwhile, Edwards found a door in the kitchen that led down to the basement, but it was locked. He looked around the kitchen to see whether he could find a key. He noticed a key ring on the wall just to the right of the desk. He tried all the keys and nothing worked, so he decided to try his lock pick. They did not have a search warrant, so Edwards was a little hesitant to pick the lock, but he decided that it wasn't the first time he'd broken the law to gain information, and they needed to get into that basement.

He took out his lock pick set, but just when he found what he thought was the right set, the sheriff came and was looking through the lens of his camera when he saw Edwards begin to try to open the door. Through the lens of the camera, he saw that something was not right. He yelled at Edwards, **"Stop**!" Edwards was startled, and he jumped back from the door, dropping the lock picks on the kitchen floor.

The sheriff pointed to a very fine wire wrapped around the doorknob: a booby trap. He had been a Marine and had served in Kuwait, and he'd seen some of the traps the Iraqis had left for them to deal with in their searches.

"Let's get somebody out here from the bomb squad before we do anything more to that door." Before the sheriff could call and ask for help, he received a call from Rains.

"Sheriff, I called Berkeley just like you asked, and they put me through to the director of admissions, Julia Brown. It was strange."

"What was strange?"

"I was the second law enforcement person calling today about Michael Ridley. The other was someone from Homeland Security, but the strange thing is that Michael Ridley was registered at the school, but he never went."

"What do you mean, never?"

"He never showed for all of the last two years."

CHAPTER 10

The Brotherhood of the Red Nile Meeting Room

J AIARI FINISHED HIS OBSERVATIONS ABOUT what was done wrong on September 11 by Osama bin Laden and in turn al-Qaeda. It was thorough and well-presented and excellent material for thought. He turned to Sargon so that others might express a different opinion.

Sargon asked his fellow Syrian, Adad Al Assad, for his observations about the attacks. He thought for a moment and then said, "Jaiari's observations were on point, and from a tactical standpoint, Jaiari's point was that Osama's focus was too small. All the attacks that al-Qaeda had carried out before 9-11 and even those, such as they were, after 9-11, always focused on *things*—buildings or ships—some*thing* has to be destroyed to show the power of al-Qaeda.

"Look at the attacks on the entirety of the United States from cyberspace. One hacker from China, over the Internet, can compromise American credit confidentially with identity theft. Millions of credit card account numbers, social security information, and other private data has been compromised over the Internet. The American Pentagon, of which al-Qaeda knocked out one small section of an outside wall in its attack, is under constant bombardment though the Internet. Hackers are trying to break into the Pentagon computers to get top-secret information. The funny thing is that most hackers don't want the data from all of these organizations; the challenge is to try to get into the systems.

"Bin Laden had to send his messages to the West via videotape to Al Jazeera for broadcast. The picture quality was poor, and his communications technology was very dated; perhaps he wanted the picture quality to be poor so as to make it more difficult to locate him? But green screen technology would have kept him hidden forever; by his changing the backgrounds, nobody would have been able to tell where he was recording his messages.

"There were and are now even more ways to produce very high-quality video and yet at the same time do it in such a way as to hide one's location. Sending your messages by mule does not put you in the best of light on the world stage, and because he had what initially seemed to be great difficulty in hiding himself, he had to move constantly—or that is what we were led to believe. I used the word 'seemed' because when he was found, he was right in the open and apparently had been there for many years. One thing that always confused me was the amount of time bin Laden was free. Remember that he had a $25 million bounty on his head, and he remained alive for almost ten years after 9-11. I have often wondered whether the American government left him alone on purpose."

The Brotherhood nodded at Assad's comment, and he continued. "Many of his important leaders who were responsible for day-to-day activities were killed, and yet he remained alive beyond all of them; why? Was it perhaps that the US government needed to project to the American people somebody to hate, as a rallying point? When he was no longer useful to the government, it was time to eliminate him and close that chapter on al-Qaeda terrorism. Perhaps Washington found that he had outlived his usefulness, and he became more useful to the president if he were dead.

"The Arab Spring became more of a threat to the US than bin Laden, and the US government needed to send a signal to the Islam groups in the Middle East: we can take your leaders out whenever we want, so don't go too far with your rebellion. We have to have a better connection to the masses in whatever we decide to do than al-Qaeda did. I believe the Internet and places like Facebook and Twitter will be the way to communicate whatever it is we plan to do to America."

Sargon thanked Assad for his observations, and he turned to his team and asked them what he thought might well be a question that was even more important than what they would do in America: "Who do you think will be leading the attack against us for the United States? I want to hear from Mordecai and Oleg before we get to that question, but begin to think: *Who is your enemy?*"

Chapter 11

Frank Williamss Office at Homeland Security

WILLIAMS RETURNED FROM A WALK down the hall to the kitchen to get a cup of coffee. Marie said, "Baker needed to see him right away. It seemed like just seconds before Ted was standing and Williams was in his office. Baker closed the door and spoke.

"Sir, I called the university as you suggested, and I spoke with Ms. Julia Brown, the head of admissions at Berkeley. Michael Ridley was indeed enrolled at Berkeley but never showed up for classes for the last two years. She had a forwarding address of 1621 Boxer Ave., Morristown, New Jersey. No phone."

Williams thought for a second. "I want you to go to FBI. Do you have a contact there you can trust?" Baker nodded. "Call that person and arrange an in- person meeting outside the agency office and tell him this is a matter of national security and you need to find out all he can about the house in Morristown and the entire Ridley Family of Springfield, Texas. I also want you to call Sheriff Whittles of Springfield and see what he can tell you about them.

"One last thing. In my meeting with the president, I said that we were trying to get assets on the ground. I need you to contact all of our agency partners and set up a meeting for tomorrow to discuss getting assets on the ground in Syria. I want to find out who we are working against and what resources they have to bring to bear against us. And especially, who is the leader of the Brotherhood of the Red Nile?"

CHAPTER 12

Springfield, the Ridley House

BAKER CALLED SHERIFF WHITTLES OFFICE, and after a few moments heard a voice say, "This is Sheriff Whittles."

"Sheriff, this is Ted Baker, from the Office of Homeland Security. Undersecretary Frank Williams asked me to call you to update you on what we have learned so far about Michael Ridley. We called Berkeley, got a forwarding address, and are trying to put together a profile of both Michael and Mike and Mary Ridley. Any help you can give us about the Ridley family would be very helpful."

"Well, Mr. Baker, we also called the school, and, while we didn't get the forwarding address, we did get the information about him not attending school. In fact, the school told us that you had called first. As for the Ridleys, I can't find anything. We don't have any idea where they are at the moment. They haven't used their credit cards; they just seem to have disappeared off the face of the earth."

The sheriff paused, wondering how much more he should say. "I'm at the Ridley house right now. We found something very strange in the house, and I have called the bomb squad to come and take a look before we go any further. I'll let you know what happens after they get here, and if we can safely go to the basement, I will tell you what I find."

"Call me on this cell phone, and make sure you talk to me. Whatever protocols you have in your department to deal with national security issues, please start them immediately. This is getting more serious than we'd like."

CHAPTER 13

Syria

SARGON HAD INTRODUCED MORDECAI HAGAL to the group as an individual who was committed to the objectives of the Brotherhood of the Red Nile. He knew that it would be difficult for the other team leaders and their team members to believe that a Jew could turn on the United States. So the challenge before Hagal was to convince the team that he was committed to the Brotherhood and its objectives.

Hagal decided to face the issue head-on by saying to the group what he knew it was already thinking. "So how can you trust a Jew not to sabotage whatever it is we decide as a group to carry out against the United States? Let me tell you up front—I understand your concern, and I know it will be difficult for me to gain your trust. I expect to earn it slowly, but I *will* earn it. I will show you that I can make a meaningful contribution toward our goals.

"Sargon has asked each of us to review, from our perspective, what bin Laden and al-Qaeda did wrong in their attacks against the United States. I believe that the use of conventional weapons, not the ultimate weapon,

35

limited the impact of what al-Qaeda was trying to accomplish. He blew up buildings and used rubber rafts full of explosives to try to sink destroyers at sea. In many cases, he strapped bombs to humans and sent them into town squares or buildings as mules that die along with some number of civilians. While the explosions were spectacular to film, in many cases civilians were given warnings about the impending bombing. The only significant departure was the attacks on September 11 in the United States; however, he was still blowing up buildings or at least trying to blow them up.

"The only thing the American population knew was that two planes hit the World Trade Center, and one hit the Pentagon. The fourth went into the ground and never hit its target. If you were in America at the time, what do you think had the most initial impact on the government and the general American population: the number of planes that went down or the number of planes that they didn't know about? The fear of the unknown is sometimes greater the reality itself. What bin Laden didn't plan on was how to leverage the fear of not knowing whether more planes were coming. So how did the American government react to the planes crashing into buildings and not knowing how many more might crash? They grounded all planes and gave all aircrafts a time limit, or they would be shot down.

"Look how quickly the fear that gripped America on Day One and continued for a few days, at most, then turned to anger and the demand for revenge. Those people who brought down that airplane in the farmland of Pennsylvania were in fact the real heroes of September 11, and the American media blasted that story over the airways for a good while. The media drove the America people into frenzy about wanting an eye for an eye and more.

You are asking yourself what can Mordecai Hagal bring to this team? Well, for most of my life I was a believer in Israel. I was educated in the United States and have a PhD in nuclear engineering from MIT. After I completed my education at MIT, I was recruited to go to Israel to work on the Israel nuclear weapons project. I was responsible for the development of nuclear power stations, but undercover we were building what we called defensive nuclear weapons.

"My objective was to give to Israel the ability to have a deterrent, so its neighbors would respect the sovereignty of Israel. After the Second World War, both the United States and the Soviet Union developed nuclear capabilities. As the arsenals grew, each country had the ability to destroy the other many times over. It was that same ability to destroy each other that kept the bombs from being sent.

"Now with Iran working to build its own nuclear capability, I became convinced that the concept of mutual destruction as a deterrent was not going to work in this case, and that the American government will thus be responsible for the elimination of Israel via the weapons of Iran. To the best of my knowledge, since the founding of the country, the United States has been the protector and defender of Israel, but no more. My country will disappear, and I blame the president and the United States government for allowing it to happen. I hope you can sense my anger, and it is this anger that is driving me to join the Brotherhood. You see if we can destroy America, then perhaps my country can survive."

Chapter 14

The Ridley House, Springfield—Today

THE BOMB SQUAD ARRIVED AT the Ridley house, and Sheriff Whittles hung up with Baker. The leader of the bomb squad, Sergeant Jerry Kelly, came into the kitchen and found the sheriff. The sheriff took out his ballpoint pen and pointed to the wire around the doorknob. After careful examination of the wire, Kelly saw that the wire went through the door just past the lockset. Next, he studied the hinges to see whether there was any wire around the hinge. He went into his tool kit and took out a magnifying glass and a pair of tweezers.

He could see a very fine wire wrapped around the hinge, and he used his tweezers to see whether he could move the wire. Before he touched the wire, he told the sheriff and the other deputies to leave the room and that perhaps it would be best for them to leave the house altogether. He told them that the wire around the doorknob and the hinges might be connected, and that he might break the circuit and cause whatever was behind the door to do whatever it was supposed to do next.

So Whittles sent out all the deputies, but he stayed with Kelly. The next move was to try to protect Officer Kelly should there be a bomb behind the door. Kelly went to his truck and brought in a bomb blanket to drape over himself and Whittles to protect them against flying chucks of wood should the bomb, if there was a bomb, go off. The door was oak, and if it exploded, the door would splinter into shards that would be very dangerous because they could cut through doors, walls, and other things in the house—including people. Just as he was reaching with the tweezers to touch the wire, the sheriff stopped him and said, "Wait."

Whittles led Kelly out of the kitchen and into the dining room. He wanted to check something out first and asked Kelly to follow him. The two of them went outside and walked around the house, looking for a basement door or windows. They'd made their way around half the house when they found a typical basement window. Whittles shone his flashlight to see whether it was locked, and it was, but it was a simple lever lock—the kind where you just turn one portion into the other. They could easily break the glass and crawl through the window and then they could see what was behind the door.

Kelly lay down flat on the ground and crawled as close as he could and looked through the window. He took out his Maglite and looked very slowly and carefully around the window. He didn't see anything around the frame. Next he tried to see whether he could shine a light on the back of the door, but the door was all the way on the other side of the basement. As he was beginning to turn away, his eye caught the lock, and he noticed a faint line going into the lock.

He couldn't be sure, but it looked like the only basement window might also be booby-trapped. Kelly sat up, put his hands and arms around his knees and put his head on his hands.

The sheriff asked, "Kelly, what the heck are you doing?"

CHAPTER 15

Frank J. Williams's office, Washington, DC

TED BAKER WAS BACK IN Williams's office to report on his phone call with Sheriff Whittles and decided that he could hear a great deal of commotion in the background, which might mean that there was more to the story than what the sheriff was telling him. He decided he'd give the sheriff a few hours and then call him back to find out what had happened. He'd made contact with his friend at the CIA, and they were having drinks that evening.

Williams was worried. "We have to keep this under very tight control, and we have to let the smallest number of people in on what could be going on so as to have no leaks. A leak about a new terrorist organization that's planning a significant attack on the United States with a nuclear device would scare the public unnecessarily, with nothing for us to say.

"Find out from John Bowman in Springfield where Mike works and, if Mary worked, where she worked. After you get that information, call their employers and get all the information you can. Call all the banks in the town and see what you can get on their bank accounts. Check with the credit bureaus and see what credit cards they had and get the past three years of transaction data. Call the IRS and tell them we need all the tax returns for the family for the last ten years.

"While you're having drinks tonight, you need to start the ball rolling on what resources we have in Syria that we can quickly tap into to find out more about the Brotherhood of the Red Nile. If he identifies assets, then we need to find out who the handler is and how we make direct contact with that handler. We need to know as quickly as possible that the leader is of the Brotherhood, and we need to find out what we are working against. What do they have? And how are they going to use it?"

Baker, who had been hoping for a nice evening on his own, rubbed his eyes and sighed and headed to the restaurant.

CHAPTER 16

Springfield, at the Ridley House

SHERIFF WHITTLES AND SERGEANT KELLY were on their bellies trying to figure out what to do about the wire in the window. They needed to get inside. As Kelly studied the window, he could not find the wire attached to the glass or the window frame. It was possible that there was a pressure switch inside the window frame in addition to a possible switch in the window latch. They could possibly cut out the glass in the frame and get in without opening the window or turning the lock. But it was also possible that the glass had a pressure-sensitive sensor attached, and when the glass was cut, the pressure would change and could set off all the explosives in the house, if there were any.

Kelly said, "It's a high-risk maneuver, and I think a robot should do it. The robot could hold the glass cutter, and you and your crew would be well back in case of an explosion." He went to get a robot from his truck, then came back and expanded the artificial hand to install the glasscutter he intended to use to remotely. While Kelly was working on installing the glasscutter, other members of his team were laying down plywood to give

~ 42 ~

the robot a level surface to sit on while taking out the glass. In the other hand of the robot, he installed a suction cup that would hold the glass in place while he cut the glass. It was now midafternoon and getting warm. The heat was not your typical, unyielding July and August heat in Springfield, but it was still warm. The sheriff thought, *perhaps the heat is coming more from the tension than from the sun.*

Soon, Kelly had the robot ready, and he asked the policemen to clear all the neighbors away from the house. If anyone had a cell phone, Kelly wanted it turned off, as well as all the police radios. He would allow one deputy, stationed with the cars parked 500 feet away, to have his cell phone on, so if something bad happened he could at least call for help.

Once the people and the cars were moved far enough away to block possible oncoming traffic and were out of signal range, Kelly started the robot. Sheriff Whittles looked at the robot with its tread instead of wheels and thought it almost looked like a toy you would find at FAO Schwartz. Kelly used a bomb blanket over some heavy timbers that had been laid down to make a wall to protect Kelly and Whittles. Kelly started the robot and advanced it to the window. He raised the arm with the suction cup. No explosion. Next, he started to raise the arm with the glasscutter and placed it on the windowpane. No explosion. He began to rotate the cutter on the glass when all of a sudden—

Chapter 17

Syria and the Brotherhood Meeting

Oleg Barbulio sat and listened to the three other members of the Brotherhood leadership review Osama bin Laden's mistakes in his attacks on the United States. Barbulio was a university-educated mechanical engineer who had spent most of his post university life working his way through most of the Major segments of the oil business. Barbulio's uncle, Viktor Antipova, had taken over raising Oleg after the boy's father, who was in the Russian army, was killed in Afghanistan. Oleg considered himself a pragmatist about most things and looked at bin Laden's and al-Qaeda's mistakes in a totally different way.

He reviewed on the Internet all the attacks made by al-Qaeda from an engineer's standpoint. The most spectacular attack, he felt, was the planes flying into the Twin Towers in New York. He understood that bin Laden spent months going over their blueprints, trying to understand the mechanical structure of the buildings to try to find their weakest point.

Once bin Laden discovered the buildings' target point, his next step was to try to figure out what he could use to deliver the impact and in turn bring down the buildings.

Barbulio observed that the impact of the planes on the towers was spectacular television but had little impact outside of New York and said as much. "As pointed out earlier, the exchanges opened for business within a short period of time. Americans became weary of the coverage, and the television networks soon went back to regular programming. So the September 11th attacks did little to change many Americans' lives, and al-Qaeda became a new focal point for retaliation along with all Middle Eastern citizens of Islamic descent.

"I know al-Qaeda wouldn't like what I'm about to say, but I truly believe that al-Qaeda basically took a peashooter against a steel-reinforced giant. The way to bring the giant down is to find a way to cut through his armor and let him bleed to death. If you keep all help away, the giant can't heal himself. He will in effect bleed out and die.

"We have to think about how we can do something that will numb the American people so badly that they will think there is nothing they can do, and their will to survive, recover, and respond will be forever broken. Whatever we do, we must create a fundamental change in America and leave no doubt that Islam will be the world's greatest power because the world will know we brought down America and that we can take down China, Russia, anybody, whenever we want."

In the dark and dusty room, the Brotherhood was growing more and more confident, nodding and smiling excitedly now.

CHAPTER 18

Old Ebbitt Grill, Washington, DC

BAKER WAS SITTING AT THE Corner Bar of the Old Ebbitts Grill in downtown Washington, DC, across the street from the Department of the Treasury. He had scheduled to meet John Seacrest, who was with the CIA, at 6:00 p.m. for drinks and conversation. Williams told him that he was to give Seacrest as little information as possible about what was going on, but he could tell Seacrest just enough to enlist his help. "Don't lie to him, but you don't have to tell him the whole truth, either." Baker had found himself asking, "What *is* the whole truth? I don't know it enough to tell it."

As he was pondering that, Seacrest tapped Baker on the shoulder. They reminisced for a bit, and Baker asked, "How long has it been since the last time we had drinks?"

Seacrest thought about it for a moment. "I think it was the last time Homeland Security needed something from the CIA."

"Ouch," said Baker. "You got me there, but before we get too drunk, tell me about what's going on in your life."

As Seacrest talked, Baker tried hard to pay attention, and every once in a while he would say "Really?" or "That's great!" Eventually the bartender came by with two martinis, and they each picked one up and took a good swallow.

"Ted, it's really nice to see you again, and if I can help Homeland Security, I would like to, so what can I do for you?"

"I don't know a great deal at the moment and that is why I need your help. When I say we don't know a great deal, I mean we have very little information. Here is what we think we know for now. As best we can tell, a new terrorist group was formed in Syria three months ago. We believe they have a meeting place near the town of Al-Mukharram. We don't know what they are planning to do. We need to know whether CIA has any assets on the ground in Syria that could help us gather intelligence on the group: who the leaders are, how they are financed, what they are planning to do, photographs of the leaders, anything that can help. I know this sounds like a shopping list, but we are in the dark, and frankly, I'm very concerned. These people represent a new generation of terrorist, and I'm seriously concerned that we are a generation behind."

"So what can I do to help?"

Baker was glad that Seacrest had said what can I do instead of "What can the CIA do?"

"Let's get something to eat, and we can talk about what you can do to help America."

Chapter 19

Ridley House, Springfield

Sergeant Kelly couldn't tell whether the glasscutter was actually cutting the glass. The servomotor that was turning the arm made a noise. Kelly could see that the cutter had just about finished its circle cut, and when it finished the glass fell out and there was a hole in the glass, but no explosion.

The sheriff had a shooting scope that he had taken off one of the sniper rifles in the back of the SWAT truck, and he used it to look at the window to see whether anything had happened to the wires when the glass fell out. Everything was quiet, and they waited to see whether there might have been a timing device.

When a few minutes had passed, the two of them came out from under the bomb blanket and crawled on their bellies up to the window. The sheriff pulled out a bigger and brighter Maglite that he had taken from his police car, and he shone it through the glass. The kitchen door was still too far away to see, even with the brighter light, and they had no idea what was there. Kelly took out of his pocket a small, round mirror similar to the one you would see in a dentist's office, except this mirror had a telescoping handle on it. He took the sheriff's light, and as he passed the mirror through the hole in the glass, he used the mirror to reflect the light back on the window frame and lock. He could see the wires and followed the wire from the lock to find it was just hanging in space, not connected to anything. As he did the same thing on the wires into the frame, he saw that they too were not connected to anything else.

Feeling a little better about the house and the strange wires, Kelly lay on his stomach and reached through the hole in the window and slowly turned the lock. When it was unlocked, the window sprang open, and two pressure switches fell out of the frame and on to the basement floor. Again, nothing happened.

Kelly pushed the window in and lifted it off the hinge and brought it through the frame and put it on the grass next to him. He slowly stood, sweat soaked. One of his men from the bomb squad brought the biggest bottle of cold water he could find, and Kelly and the sheriff drank it. Once they had rehydrated themselves, they approached the window and used the sheriff's light again to see what they could see in the basement. The light barely illuminated what appeared to be a map on the wall. Kelly looked down toward the floor to see whether there was anything on the floor that he might trigger if he slid through the window to get into the basement, but he couldn't see anything. He asked Whittles to double-check, and the sheriff confirmed that he didn't see anything. Kelly stripped down to his T-shirt and a pair of running shorts he had in his truck, because the window was not large enough to let him through with all his gear on. Kelly and the sheriff put on a set of headsets so they could talk with each other. With what seemed like a ton of communications equipment on his back, Kelly started through the window.

CHAPTER 20

Old Ebbitt Grill, Washington, DC Later that Evening

BAKER HAD ASKED FOR A quiet table for Seacrest and himself so they could talk in private. He chose the Old Ebbitt Grill because it was sure to have a significant mix of people from various agencies in Washington, and he thought it might well be safer to talk in the restaurant than in either of their offices. Baker remembered what Williams said to him about security, so he felt comfortable that the two of them would be lost in the crowd of the busy restaurant. Seacrest was an old friend. They had been in the same class at West Point, and both went to work at the CIA after graduation. Baker had worked in special OPS, while Seacrest worked in counterintelligence.

Once Baker went to Homeland, they did not see each other as much, but they did keep in touch with phone calls, e-mails, and an occasional lunch or dinner. Ted knew that John could be trusted, but he just wasn't sure how far, none of their discussion could be written down or shared with anyone at CIA without first discussing it with him. Baker signaled to the waiter, who came over and took their order. They both ordered twelve-ounce sirloins, medium, Caesar salads without anchovies, and baked potatoes with sour cream and bacon bits. They ordered two more martinis, dry with a lemon twist. When the waiter had left, Ted felt they had some time to start the discussion before the salad arrived.

"Let me make this short and to the point. We believe that a new terrorist group called the Brotherhood of the Red Nile was formed at least ninety days ago to devise a plan to attack the United States. This group is much more sophisticated than al-Qaeda. We believe the group is also much smaller than al-Qaeda and so more mobile. We are not sure whether they have left Syria or whether they are perhaps already in the United States.

"We are giving this threat the highest priority; every resource that needs to be used is being called up. However, because we do not know a great deal about the Brotherhood, we have to be careful about how many people we involve. For now we are calling this situation 'Project Springfield,' and for the purposes of our communications, we will just use the word *Springfield*. What we need from you is a list of any CIA assets, their handlers, and contact information that you might have in Syria. We would like more specific information as to how close you have assets to the town of Al-Mukharram, which is in western Syria. We think they've been meeting in an unmarked two-story building next to a citrus grove outside the town."

The waiter brought the salads, and they both started to eat. "Ted, these sound like really bad guys, do you think they are more dangerous than al-Qaeda?"

"That's what my gut says, and for the first time since September 11, I'm really scared."

CHAPTER 21

Springfield

KELLY TURNED DOWN THE VOLUME on his headset and pulled out his flashlight to see whether he could find a light switch. He saw a pull chain hanging from a bare bulb light fixture in the ceiling and walked over, using the flashlight to scan the floor for anything that might trigger an explosion. He didn't see any trip wire, so he slowly pulled on the chain with his eyes closed. Nothing happened. No light, either. He pulled again, still no light.

Kelly pushed the talk button on his headset and asked whether someone had turned off the power to the house. "If someone has turned off the power, then leave it off. I just need to know if we turned off the power, or if someone else did." Whittles got on his radio and asked all his deputies whether anybody had turned the main power off in the house. He also asked Kelly's team members, but none of them remembered turning off the power.

One deputy who was there at the scene the night before when Homeland Security had been, said, "They did go around the back of the house. I can't recall seeing any lights on last night while they were here, either." Whittles relayed to Kelly that his best guess was that Homeland Security had turned off the power. Kelly wondered why Homeland Security would turn off the power and leave the kitchen door wired to a booby trap. He thought to himself that he'd have to look into that once he got out of the basement.

Kelly turned to face a large concrete block wall covered with some kind of a map. He turned on his flashlight and could tell that it was a map of the United States. Perhaps two dozen circles were scattered all over the map. He clicked on the headset and told the sheriff.

Whittles said, "Be careful, in case it's booby-trapped, but see if you can get it off the wall and hand it to me." Kelly used his flashlight to illuminate the area around the map: no wires attached to the map or the frame. Kelly pulled the map slowly off the wall and then rolled it up into a tube and passed it through the window to Whittles. The sheriff took the map and moved away from the house to unroll it.

After a few moments, he said, "This looks like a target map that people might use to figure out the best places to attack America. This is a war map."

Chapter 22

Syria, the Brotherhood's Meeting Room

Sargon thanked all the members of his team for their insights about what went wrong with 9-11; he said the information was critical to the next stage of the planning process. He went to the wall and pulled down a cover and revealed a map of the United States. He said to them, "This is our target. We can't attack all of the United States, but we can select targets that, if attacked successfully, will have much greater long-term impact on America.

"We must now plan using the famous American saying about the five *W*'s: Who, What, Where, When, and Why, and I'm adding an *H* for How. We have seen the impact of the attack on the World Trade Centers. The attack brought the buildings down and did shut down the world markets for a short time, but the long-term impact, as you have all said, was minimal. If we truly are going to bring down America, then let's not think in terms of mere buildings. I would like to start the discussion with the *H*: how are we going to do this?"

Oleg spoke up. "It seems to me that we have two very powerful weapons. The first is fear, and the second is the source of the fear: the two suitcase nuclear bombs we have. We must build our attack around those two weapons. We have the two bombs, but they are not very reliable. Most of the other ones that came from the old Soviet arsenal never exploded."

Sargon spoke up and said, "Mordecai, it's your turn. What do you think about Oleg's comments about the ineffective nature of the bombs?"

Mordecai agreed and said, "If we could get in contact with the Iranian nuclear people through Jaiari, then we can take our bombs to Iran and they can stabilize them and increase their power and reliability. I suggest we take one bomb to Iran and stay with it while they work on it, and then we can modify the one we have here, or wherever it is, and then we would have two very effective bombs. What is the likelihood that the Iranians would cooperate?"

Jaiari said, "I think there is a great deal of hatred in Iran for America, and they will like the idea. I can find out in a few days whether they are interested."

Sargon said he would like to have Jaiari make the calls. "We will reconvene in two days, then. We may well know by then when the decline of America can begin."

Chapter 23

The Ridley House Basement

WHITTLES TOLD KELLY, OVER THE headset that the map he retrieved was a map of the United States, with targets marking around at least twenty cities all over the map. Kelly told the sheriff that he was going to head to the stairs to see what was behind the kitchen door.

As he reached the first step, he used his flashlight again, looking for trip wires, but didn't see any. He started slowly and deliberately climbing the stairs. One step closer, and he saw a pile of sticks of dynamite. He did the math and realized that if they went off, there wouldn't be anything left of the house, and certainly not of him.

He began to sweat as he took another step, slowly, because just then he saw that the massive amount of dynamite was sitting on top of a larger drum. He was at an odd angle climbing the stairs, so he couldn't see the entire drum from where he was. When he took the next step, he could see the entire drum, and the writing on it: ammonia fertilizer.

It wasn't the drum, but what he saw at the base of the drum on the landing that made fear and panic take hold of him: a timer, ticking off with a few seconds left. He clicked on his headset and yelled, "Everybody down!" and just as he finished his sentence, a fireball came out of the basement window and every other window in the house almost at the same time. Within seconds, the entire house came apart. From the last tick on the timer to the initial explosion, Kelly thought about his wife and kids, and less than a second later, he was vaporized.

Chapter 24

Williams's House,
Washington, DC

FRANK ARRIVED JUST IN TIME to pick up Ellen and head to 1789, their favorite restaurant. In the car, Ellen could see the worried look on Frank's face; the last time she had seen it was after he finally got home on September 13, 2001.

"Can you tell me what is going on that has you so worried?"

Frank looked at her and said, "After we eat. Right now I want to talk about happier things like what I'm going to have for dinner with my best girl." The rest of the way to the restaurant, the car was silent. Ellen reached to turn on the radio, but Frank gently pushed her hand aside and said, "I need the quiet for a while."

They arrived at 1789, the valet gave Williams the parking ticket, and they headed inside. They dropped off their coats and the maître d' welcomed them back and directed them to one of the best tables in the house. He presented them with a menu, and Frank ordered a J&B Scotch and water for himself and a glass of the house chardonnay for Ellen.

As they looked over the menu, Frank asked Ellen how her day was, and she responded that it had been about the same as usual, nothing special except for a strange man who came into the office and wanted to know how to apply for social security. Frank asked, "What was strange about him?"

Ellen replied, "I asked whether he had a social security number and he said no. I asked if he was from the US and he said no, he was just visiting from Sudan. When I asked if he had a job in America he said no. Then I asked why he was applying for Social Security. He said that he saw on TV that you don't have to work to get unemployment, and if that runs out, you can get Social Security. What a great country! You don't have to work, and the government pays you not to work."

Frank chuckled a little, and Ellen was glad to see a smile back on his face. She knew that Frank had an important, high-level job in the government, but he rarely acknowledged that he was in fact second-in-command at Homeland Security. Frank knew he wanted to talk to Ellen about the last three days, but the restaurant was not the place. Instead he said, "I have a new assistant; his name is Ted Baker. He is from Langley, where he specialized in Special Ops. He's twenty-nine years old and very sharp; he was well trained. Were we ever that young?"

"I know what you mean; I have a whole bunch of new staffers at Social Security, and I don't think I ever had a waist that small." Ellen laughed.

Frank seized the opportunity to say, "Ellen, you are one of the most attractive women I have ever seen. I thought that when I met you twenty-seven years ago, and I still believe it to be true today, even after almost twenty-five years of marriage. Speaking of silver wedding anniversaries, have you given any thought as to where you might like to go for our anniversary next year?"

Ellen smiled. "I just read an article in a travel magazine written by Arthur Frommer, and he says the best place for a great vacation is Sanibel Island, Florida. I sent away for some information on the place, so when it comes, we should put it on the list. It's nothing fancy, and it's right here in the States, so no hectic traveling."

The waiter came, and they ordered the duck and the pan-seared grouper. Frank held his drink aloft and said, "God bless America and long may she live as the greatest place on the world." As he sipped his drink, Frank thought, *I hope it actually remains the best place to live.*

CHAPTER 25

What's Left of the Ridley House?

WHITTLES WAS LUCKY ENOUGH TO drop behind the temporary plywood wall and cover with the bomb blanket just as the flames shot over his head. When he fell to the ground, he put the map beneath him to try to protect it as much as he could. If the blast killed him, he hoped that his body would shield the map and keep it from being destroyed. The blast was so strong that the windows in most of the houses in the neighborhood were broken. The Ridley house was strewn all over the development, and some of the houses received a direct hit from some larger sections of the house.

When things got quiet, Whittles just lay there, and the first thing he thought about was not the fact that he must be alive, but that Jerry Kelly must be dead. When he thought it was safe, he slowly pulled the blanket off him and was amazed at the debris that was on top of him. Yet he was unhurt: not even a scratch. He checked the map, and it was undamaged.

Next he stood and looked at what was left of the Ridley house and surprised of how little was left standing. He knew that Sergeant Jerry Kelly would not be found, and the intensity of the fire drove him farther and farther away until he was back with his men.

He checked with them, and they were all fine—a few cuts, but nothing serious; Kelly had saved their lives by having them stay back. Sheriff Whittles could hear the fire truck sirens and along with them the EMS trucks racing toward what was left of the house. He decided to take the map back to his office before he opened it, and he would call Baker after he went to tell Kelly's widow about her husband's death.

As Sheriff Whittles was leaving the site and heading to Kelly's house, one question kept rolling over in his mind: could Homeland Security be in any way responsible for the bomb? If so, why? If not, then why hadn't they told the sheriff the house was booby-trapped? As the sheriff pulled into the Kelly's' driveway, his mind shifted to how was he going to tell Kelly's wife about her husband. He knew he would get two questions: Who did it and why? The sheriff had no answers, but he would get them, regardless of who was involved, and answer those questions for her.

CHAPTER 26

Old Ebbitt Grill

B AKER AND SEACREST FROM THE CIA were finishing their steaks and continuing their discussion about what Seacrest could do for Homeland Security. Before Seacrest could answer, Baker's cell phone rang, and it was an instant message from Williams: *WQSTTV.com*.

Baker told Seacrest he needed to step way for a moment, but that he wanted to continue the discussion, for it was important. Baker went to the men's room and typed in the URL, and the TV station's website came up. It was live at the scene of an explosion in Springfield at the Ridley home. Baker was stunned, and he froze for a moment, thinking about what he needed to do. When his focus returned, he knew that, while this message was important, he had to finish the conversation with Seacrest.

He pulled himself together, took a deep breath, and went back to the table.

Seacrest asked, "Something important?"

"Aren't they all? So back to the question, it would be nice to know who the leaders of the Brotherhood are and as much as you can find out about their structure and, if possible, who is funding them."

Seacrest swallowed hard, looked Baker right in the eye, and without blinking said, "Yeah, and people in hell want ice water. The broader the net, the more people I have to involve, and you said we have to keep this tight. If we don't have assets on the ground, I will have to move assets, and I can't move assets without involving more people."

Baker replied, "We might be able to get you authority directly from the director of the CIA."

"Well, if that could happen—and I don't know how it can—but if it could, my rough guess is that we could get back to you in two days. Is that quick enough?"

Baker thought about what he'd just seen on the news and worried that it wasn't.

"Does that mean I will start getting data in two days?"

"I think that is possible, but you must understand that, as of right now, I don't know what assets we have, so my guess could be way off."

"Can you figure out by noon tomorrow what you can accomplish on your own without involving anyone else?"

"Yes I think so."

"How serious is this problem?"

"Based on what we knew at the moment, and I realize that it is still sketchy, this group of terrorists is more sophisticated and many times more dangerous than al-Qaeda. The brotherhood could be a threat to the whole nation—not just one city. "

CHAPTER 27

1789 Restaurant

FRANK AND ELLEN WILLIAMS WERE just about to get their dessert
when his cell phone rang for the first time the entire evening. He had
a text message from the office that a bomb had exploded in the Ridley house
in Springfield. The bomb disposal expert Sargent Jerry Kelly had been
killed in the blast. He did not look at the whole video; he had seen enough,
but he forwarded it to Baker with the attachment to call him on his cell in
about an hour. He would also want a report on his dinner with Seacrest.

After Williams hung up, Ellen turned to him. "Anything wrong?"

"Let's have our dessert, and we'll talk later." They ordered a chocolate
lava cake with French vanilla ice cream and decaf cappuccinos. They had
had a wonderful evening and started to plan their anniversary trip for the
following year. Soon they were on their way home, but Ellen could still see
in Frank's face that he was worried about something, and she hoped that
he would confide in her when they were lying next to each other in bed that
night.

She knew that the longer Frank went without talking to her about a problem, the more it ate at him. By the time they pulled into the driveway, it was ten o'clock. When they got into the house, he said, "I need to make a phone call from the study." Ellen knew that when he told her that, she needed to go upstairs, and that when he was finished, he would come up to her and most likely tell her what was going on. So up she went.

Frank picked up his secure cell phone and called Baker, who answered on the second ring. They filled each other in on the Ridley house and the dinner with Seacrest, and immediately after Williams hung up, he dialed Sheriff Whittles cell phone number.

"Are you all right? Were any of your other men hurt?"

"Mr. Williams," said Jim Whittles tired voice, "thank you for your concern. We lost a good man, and the rest of us escaped with a few scratches from the flying debris. It appears that a bomb made of dynamite and a fifty-five-gallon drum of ammonia fertilizer were set off by a battery-operated timing mechanism, and my bomb specialist didn't see the timer until it was too late. He was a good man with a wife and two small boys."

"Is there anything I can do for you or for Mrs. Kelly?" asked Williams.

"I don't know of anything at the moment, but could I ask you a question?"

"Anything, and I'll do my best to answer."

"Well, Mr. Williams, we found a trip wire in the door going to the basement: do you have any idea how it got there, and also do you have any clue how all those explosives got into the house without your team seeing it?"

"As you know, I was never in the house. If you remember, I met you outside and then we went to the Bowman house, and I left and got on the plane back to DC. But I promise you this: I will look into it and get back to you as soon as I have anything. Anything else?"

"Oh, there is one other thing that might be of interest to you: just before the explosion, Kelly handed some kind of map to me out the window. As best I can tell, it looks like a map of the United States with a bunch of red circles on it. Would you have any interest in looking at it?"

Williams felt his heart rate explode, and he began to sweat like he had that morning in the Oval Office; only this time it was a different kind of fear. He paused, for he didn't want to overexcite the sheriff. What were the local procedures for the protection of evidence?

He thought for a moment and said, "Sheriff I don't know if the map is of any value to you or us at the moment. Could we contact you in the morning about sending a map expert to Springfield to give us an opinion on what it means?" Williams already knew that an expert would be on a plane first thing in the morning. This could be a real break in the case; this was most likely the Brotherhood's target map for the United States.

He hung up and immediately called Baker to arrange for a map expert to get on the earliest morning flight there was.

CHAPTER 28

The Brotherhood Meeting Room, Two Days Later

SARGON CALLED THE MEETING TO order, and he asked Jaiari to tell them what he had learned. Sargon already knew what Jaiari was going to tell his teammates, for Sargon had a contact on the Iranian nuclear project who had told him that they were excited about the opportunity to work on the dirty bomb project. Sargon did not disclose how or where they intended to use the bombs, and it was the truth: he did not know where or even when they were going to attack the United States, but he knew it would be soon.

Jaiari stood up and said that he had contacted his friend in the nuclear program in Iran. He told them that they only had one bomb, and that, like the ones before it, it had not been very stable or reliable. He wanted to know how much it would cost and how long it would take to stabilize the bomb and make it reliable and, if possible, more effective, which meant greater impact over a wider area. His response was that, depending on the condition, it would cost about $2,000,000 and take about two months to repair and renew the smart bomb.

He went on to say that he told his contact that money was not a problem, so how soon could he start working on the bomb? His contact wanted to know whom they were going to use it against. Jaiari had hedged, and his friend had smiled. "We have a pretty good idea, so we can start immediately."

With that, Jaiari turned to Mordecai and said, "What do you think about the cost and the time frame? If we give them one, can you fix the other one so they will both be ready at the same time?"

Mordecai responded, "I have not seen either, so I can't assess the level of deterioration. Is it possible for me to see them, so I can tell you what I think?"

Jaiari turned to Sargon. "Is it okay?"

Mordecai asked, "How far are they from here?"

"Not far," Sargon smiled. "Can we get the money to fix both bombs?"

Oleg said, "I don't think that would be a problem. If you give me a few minutes, I will make a phone call and ask for the $4 million, if that is okay?" Oleg knew that $4 million was pocket change to his uncle. In fact, they had talked about how he was going to be an extremely rich man as a result of this attack on America. Neither knew what was going to be attacked, nor did they know what the long-term impact might be, but they knew that once the target had been picked, they would figure out what would the best way to make billions of dollars. They could have spent time speculating on the size of the opportunity, but they agreed it would be a waste of time. Let Sargon and his team, including Oleg, pick the target; there would be plenty of time to figure out how they were going to make money afterward.

After a few minutes on the phone with his uncle, Oleg came back into the room. "The money will be wired to wherever you want it, Sargon."

"Excellent. I will give you instructions at the end of this meeting." Sargon called the four of them back together around the table and said, "We have to figure out how we are going to get the first bomb to Iran and, second, how will we get the similar parts to rebuild our bomb. Because of the size of the bombs, which are a little larger than an oversized suitcase, the bomb needs to be stabilized so that it can be kept from excess movement.

The bombs are old and leaking some radioactive material and perhaps some of the nitro-explosive. Most people don't know that radioisotopes are corrosive, almost like acid. If we can secure the bomb and severely reduce the amount of the movement, the better the chance that it will not leak.

"I suggest we use the most common vehicle in Syria: a plain white cargo van, with no markings on it. It will not call attention to the van, and the van will disappear in the city streets. The bomb can be strapped into place, and the movement will be severely restricted. Once the bomb has been stabilized in Iran, it will be safer and easier to transport back to here."

"We have one of those cargo vans right now. What else would we need to get?"

"I think we would need about six heavy-duty wool blankets and, say, about six adjustable tie-down straps. Also it would be helpful if we could get a van with a high output air-conditioning system. The air conditioning needs enough output to keep the van cool. Fortunately for us, we are in the cool season, so the heat will not be a big problem. Whoever is going with the bomb will be reporting back to Mordecai on a daily basis about what modifications are being made to the bomb they have, so he can change our bomb."

Jaiari spoke up and said that he thought that he and Adad should move the bomb and report back. "Mordecai can't go for two reasons: first, he is an Israeli, and if the Iranians found out, we'd lose him *and* the bomb. Second, Oleg is an engineer, and he can help Mordecai in repairing the bomb we have here. Adad is a businessman, and he travels freely around the Middle East, and his passport will show that he has been in all the countries in the Middle East, and the stamps on his passport will get him through security without any inspection. Perhaps the white van should have his company logo on it, and it should carry some office supplies and computers in boxes? The boxes can be stacked in such a way as to hide the bomb. He can have a dummy manifest for goods to be delivered to prominent companies in Iran. The border crossing is something his company vans and trucks do all the time. The border crossing we pick must be one frequented by Adad's company trucks."

"Does anybody have any questions or concerns about the plan to get the bomb to and from Iran? With no comments or questions, let's get started. By the way, Mordecai, you wanted to inspect the bombs?"

Mordecai responded, "Yes, I do. You said they were close?"

"They are right downstairs in this building."

Mordecai went downstairs, and the team carefully lifted the bomb onto the top of the table for Mordecai to examine. As he unbuckled the straps, he saw the guts of the bomb, and he made a quick assessment of what he thought he might need to make the conversion. "Based on what I see here, if we had the right parts and a team, we could rebuild this bomb in just a few days. I think the message from Iran that it would take two months is bogus. I have a friend named Ishtar who can probably get me the parts I need in a few days."

He looked at the expectant faces. "We can do this; we can rebuild this bomb to match the other one being rebuilt in Iran. And then we will have two bombs with which to attack America."

CHAPTER 29

Williams's House, Arlington, Virginia

FRANK FINISHED HIS PHONE CALL and left the den. He spent many a long day in that private room. Ellen rarely bothered Frank while he was in his office. If the door was closed, she knew it was something important, and Frank was not to be disturbed. His love for history that drove him to the museums on the mall was reflected in his special room. His bookshelves were loaded with first editions of books written by people who had lived from the founding of the nation to Operation Desert Storm.

On the walls were photographs of him and some very famous people in history, while others were photographs of leaders over the years. His favorite was a pardon signed by U. S. Grant. Frank was especially fond of Grant as a person and as a leader. He thought Grant was a man of great integrity. When Grant left the presidency, he had been conned into forming a brokerage firm called Grant and Company. His partner, the "Company" part, swindled money from the clients without Grant knowing. When Grant found out, he promised to pay back all the lost funds, and he did.

Frank found great comfort in his special room; he felt that the room and all the collections from the past inspired him to the best he could be for Ellen and for America. He felt in his heart that this next challenge might well be the greatest of his life. Frank turned out the light in the office and walked toward the stairs that would take him upstairs to Ellen. As he hit the first step, he thought of a young man he had never met, but who had given his life for his country: Sergeant Kelly. His step was a little slow, but he knew that he needed to get to Ellen before she went to sleep.

As he reached the top of the stairs, he noticed that the light was still on in their bedroom. He walked down the hallway and peeked into the room to see whether Ellen was still awake; she was in the bathroom brushing her hair. Frank stood in the bedroom looking at Ellen. He thought how, after almost twenty-five years of marriage, she was still a stunning-looking woman. Over the years, he had often wondered how he had ever convinced her to marry him, but somehow he had. As he studied her shape, he noticed, yet again, how she was very much a woman; she had the right curves. Ellen turned to look into Frank's eyes and saw a sadness she had not seen in years.

"Get ready for bed and come hug me; I need to be held tonight."

Frank changed his clothes and brushed his teeth and got into bed. They both slid to the center of the bed and Frank put his arms around Ellen and caressed both of her breasts gently in his hands; he like doing that because she was a handful, and they both enjoyed it. When he held her that way he could hear a low purr from Ellen. She loved to make love with Frank, for he was a caring and gentle lover who never rushed her, but just as important was his holding her in his arms in bed.

When Frank held her this way she felt the most secure in her relationship with Frank. She had friends who told her that their husbands rarely snuggled anymore and the lovemaking was less and less frequent. Ellen knew that their lovemaking had diminished in frequency, but when they did make love, it was wonderful. The hugging took on greater importance to her, as they got older; she felt that, as long as he wanted to hold her, it would all be okay.

"I know you hate to talk about serious things just before sleeping, but I need to tell you one thing. I couldn't tell you a whole lot before, because I didn't have a whole lot of information, but then I received an instant message at the restaurant tonight. It directed me to a TV station website in the town I was in yesterday. The story was about a house that was hit by an explosion. A young bomb squad sergeant was killed when the house exploded while he was trying to disarm a bomb in the basement.

"The Sergeant was thirty-two, with a wife and two small children. His name was Kelly, and I never met him, and yet there is a part of me that feels that he may well have just saved the United States from a devastating terrorist attack."

"How serious is this possible threat?"

Frank replied, "Perhaps the greatest ever." At that, he pulled Ellen as close as he could to him and said, "I love you."

CHAPTER 30

Springfield, Sheriff Whittles Office, Next Morning

THE WHOLE SHERIFF'S DEPARTMENT WAS very sad at the loss of Sergeant Jerry Kelly the day before. There were a lot of red eyes in the office that morning; one of the questions being asked was, "With no body, what type of service will there be for him?" Sheriff Whittles decided that he needed to send out an e-mail to the staff with the information that he had at the moment. He sat down to write.

"To the staff of the sheriff's department of Springfield. It is with great sorrow that I write to inform you that we lost one of our brightest and best officers yesterday. Sergeant Jerry Kelly was killed in the line of duty at the Ridley house while trying to disarm a bomb. While the exact details of the service have yet to be worked out, please keep him, his wife Helen, and their two sons, Michael and Sean, in your prayers.

"We are committed to expending all the resources necessary to find the killers and bring them to justice. I encourage you to speak to all your contacts to see if we can find leads as to who perpetrated this heinous crime."

The sheriff pushed the Send button and then swung his chair around to his safe and opened it to reveal the map. Just as he laid it on his desk to open it, his phone rang. Whittles answered the phone; it was Connie, the front desk receptionist.

"Sheriff, there is a woman here who says her name is Megan Brown and that she is from the Department of Homeland Security. She says that you are expecting her."

"Tell her I'll be right out."

Whittles put the map back in the safe and went out front to meet Ms. Brown. He extended his hand. "Ms. Brown, I'm Sheriff Whittles; welcome to Springfield. I wish it could be under happier circumstances."

"I heard about the explosion and the loss of one of your men. I'm very sorry for you, your department and his widow. Sheriff, one of my specialties is reading maps. Homeland Security has an entire unit that deals with maps of all kinds from all over the world. Maps can tell us a great deal about the people who had the maps and in many cases what they were planning to do, using the map. Have you looked at this map?"

"No, not really. I was able to save it from the fire, and I brought it here and locked it in my safe. It has been there all night, and only I know the combination to the safe."

They went to the safe and put on special gloves to reduce the number of fingerprints on the map. The sheriff cleared his desk and unrolled the map. He was more interested in Ms. Brown's face when he spread out the map. An expression of fear came across her face, but she controlled her emotions well.

At first glance, there were at least twenty red circles on the map; some were large, and some were small. The circles had been made with a red Sharpie. She studied the map a little more closely and saw that the twenty cities circled were the twenty largest cities in the United States. There were no other Sharpie markings on the map. She did notice that Christopher Saxton had made the map in England; she knew that Saxton was a famous English mapmaker. This did not appear to be a special map, but much like the kind you would find in a gas station in America.

"I understand from Mr. Williams that you want to keep this map as part of your investigation into the bombing. Is that correct?"

"Yes, that is correct. It appears that the bomb was set up to destroy the map should somebody come across it. What do you think?"

"Sheriff, it is hard to say at the moment, but I would like, if possible, to take this map back with me today and have our full team review it to see what they think. I know that you want to keep it as evidence; I might have a way to solve this problem. I propose that I take high-definition digital photographs of the map. We can print them out on your printer, and we can agree on the twenty circles, and we will do so in front of a judge. We can circle the twenty cities just as they are on the map and then we could have the judge put his seal on the back to certify its authenticity. I will take the map back with me and we will run it through our team, and we will let you know our thoughts, and when we are done, we will return the map to you. Is that okay with you?"

Whittles thought about it for a moment and said, "I want to check with my DA, but I think it will be fine."

After the photograph was taken and certified by Judge Symington, the sheriff handed Ms. Brown the map and asked, "Do you think this map is important?"

"This map may well help us save the United States."

CHAPTER 31

Langley, Virginia

SEACREST SAT AT HIS DESK looking at his computer, where he had just opened a top-secret file. The file provided the last known location of all the CIA ground assets and their handlers throughout the world; it had cell numbers and last-known addresses. John knew that if the list were to get into the wrong hands, it would mean that the assets would be tracked down and eliminated. Most of the work that had been done in acquiring the assets took place after the September 11 attack. The brutal attack by al-Qaeda had galvanized the information gathering process. Up until that time, the Clinton Administration had set down rules that had severely restricted the exchange of information on terrorists and the groups they belonged to. It was difficult to get the rules of the house changed, but at least for a while under President Bush the flow of intelligence increased, and many plots were foiled, and American never knew about what could have happened.

When Obama and his team took over, things reverted in many ways back to the way they had been during Clinton's time in office. New administrative orders again made it more difficult to get information on what was happening. As Seacrest looked at the maps and the locations, he knew that the data might be six months old or older, so he wasn't sure about what assets he really had on the ground. The city of Homs was the closest, with two possible assets, and Damascus, a much larger city, with half a dozen assets, but Homs was closer.

The contact in Homs was named Massri, and his last address was 17 Clock Square, Unit 27. The phone number listed was 011.963.11635-1758. John did not have a secure phone, but the conference room had a secure landline. He went to the front desk and asked Lisa if anybody was scheduled to use Conference Room Q. Lisa checked the logbook, and nobody was scheduled. Seacrest figured out the time difference: it would be about 12:30 in the afternoon in Syria. He asked Lisa if he could have the room for the next hour, and she said, "Until somebody of a higher rank tells me different, it's yours."

Seacrest went into the conference room, picked up the receiver, and heard the security click. He dialed the phone number and was told by a recording in both English and Arabic that the number had changed. He wrote down the new number and tried it. The phone rang several times, and finally, when he thought it would go to voicemail, a voice said, "Ahlan?" which means "hello" in Arabic. Seacrest couldn't just say, "This is Seacrest from the CIA and Langley," so he had to find a way to let Massri know who was calling and what he wanted done, in case the phone was bugged.

So he said, "My name is David Billah, and I'm from Damascus. I was given your name as a possible contractor who could help me with a building project. I have a farm near Al-Mukharram, and I have a large storage barn next to my citrus grove that is used to store harvested fruit. The barn has two stories and the second level was damaged severely by a storm, and I can't store my oranges until the roof and one of the sides is fixed. If you are interested in the contract, I assume you will want to go and look at the building to assess the damage before you give me a price."

Massri responded, "How soon do you need an estimate?"

"The crop is nearly ready to harvest, and if I can't get it stored quickly, it will be lost. The sooner you can get there, the better it would be."

Massri responded, "I will try to leave in the morning. The best number to call is 963.11687-3951; call me tomorrow afternoon, as it will take me a while to get there."

Seacrest hung up and waited a moment and called the cell phone number Massri had given him, and a new voice came on the line: "Massri Construction, "may I help you?"

"I just had a phone call with Massri about a job and that I was to call him on his cell phone to see whether I had more details about the contract. We didn't discuss the price because he needs to see the job first and then quote a price. I forgot to ask him whether he wanted to be paid in Syrian pounds or American dollars."

The person on the line said, "American dollars would be fine. Would it be in cash or a bank transfer?"

They decided they would have to wait and see how big the project was and how much it would cost before he decided how to pay. He would call back tomorrow and see what the estimate was if he didn't hear from Massri regarding the price before then.

Seacrest was confident that Massri had gotten the message: a contract was being let by CIA to go to near Al-Mukharram, find the citrus grove near town, and look for a two-story building. He needed to know who went into the building and, if possible, what they were.

He went back to his office and called Baker to inform him that he had a contact in Homs who would be at the building tomorrow. He hoped to hear from his asset by late tomorrow.

Baker was pleased; he would inform the undersecretary immediately. Just before he hung up with Baker, the section chief of internal security appeared at the door of Seacrest's office with two armed guards.

"I think you need to hang up that phone and come with us now."

On his end, Baker could hear shouting and then the line went dead.

CHAPTER 32

Williams's Office, Next Morning

BAKER WAS WAITING OUTSIDE WILLIAMS' office for him to arrive to tell him about his phone conversation with Seacrest and its abrupt ending. Williams invited him in and ordered two coffees from Marie.

Baker filled Williams in on the phone call and guessed that Williams would have to call the director of the CIA, Martins, and fill him in and get his full cooperation about what Seacrest was doing. "We can't afford to have Seacrest in a cell somewhere while the on-the-ground asset in Syria is doing his job and then can't get in touch with Seacrest to report."

Marie brought in the coffee and set it down in front of each of them and then she turned to Williams, who asked her to call the office of Fred Martins, the director of the CIA, in Langley. "Oh and Marie, tell his office that we must use a secure phone connection."

"Yes, sir, right away." As Marie left the office, she could only recall perhaps two times that undersecretary Williams had used the secure line in all the time she had worked for him.

"We have two other issues that we have to deal with. First, Megan

Brown is on a plane with the original map and is expected here around 11:30 this morning. Second, and perhaps of greater importance, we have to find out what has happened to Mike and Mary Ridley and their son Michael. We have an address in Morristown, New Jersey, and I'm thinking we might want to bring in someone to help you keep all the balls in the air. I know you think that you can manage it all, but we just can't afford any slip-ups or any leads left undone. Do you have any ideas for a person to add to the team?"

"If I may, sir, do you want someone from HS or would you be willing to bring in someone from another agency?"

"We don't know the magnitude of the threat yet, so I want to avoid any speculation that could lead to a leak and scare the bejeezus out of the whole country. So, if at all possible, I would like it to be someone from HS."

"I know of a new employee who came to us from the Marine Corp and worked at the Pentagon as an assistant to the chief of intelligence. I have had the chance to work with him on a couple of minor projects, and he seems very thorough and committed to protecting the country. I would like you to meet with him today, and if you like him, we would give him the assignment of the Ridley family, and he would start with the house in Morristown. He and I can work with Ms. Brown and the rest of the forensic team."

"Is there anything I should know before I meet with him? What's his name?"

"Sir, his name is Omid Rahimi, and he is American born, from parents who legally emigrated from Iran thirty-five years ago when the Shah was in power. He understands the culture and language of the Middle East, and I think he would be an excellent addition to the team, but I want you to meet him first. If you like him, do you think you will have to ask the secretary to agree with the selection or can we make him the offer immediately and have him get started on the Ridleys?"

"Ted, I will run it by the secretary, but I think he will go with my judgment; the worst that could happen is he is a spy for the Brotherhood, and we are all dead or wish we were."

Baker sort of smiled and left the office to find Rahimi.

CHAPTER 33

The Brotherhood Meeting Room

ADAD PULLED UP TO THE warehouse, and the big corrugated door rose and shed a bath of light in the room. The team leaders turned to see Sargon standing next to one of the bombs.

"Let's get this thing loaded and on its way to Iran."

First, they unloaded all the materials that Adad had brought to hide the bomb. All four of them picked up the suitcase and were surprised by how much it really weighed. They struggled to get it into the truck, but they finally got it in, not without some tense moments. As they were carrying it across the building, they ran into a stack of wooden pallets and took a chunk out of the suitcase. Adad taped the broken piece with some packing tape that had his company's name on it, and they decided to wrap the tape around the suitcase, just to make sure something didn't fall out on the trip.

Next they began to pack the office supplies, paper boxes, and software neatly around the bomb. When the bomb was completely sealed, they wove it into a cargo net to hold things in place, and it looked more open, as though they were not trying to hide anything. Adad and Jaiari checked their paperwork to make sure they had all the papers they would need to cross and recross the borders. They checked and made sure they had the chargers for both of their cell phones so they could communicate with Mordecai about what was happening with the changes being made to the bomb.

Sargon warned them that they could not return without the new bomb. As soon as they got to the site in Iran, they must call Sargon to tell him that they had arrived. Each day they would call Mordecai at 5:00 p.m. local time and report as to what was done to the bomb. They would also report what new parts were used to increase the reliability and power of the bomb. Last, they must tell what parts and supplies were needed so they could start repairing the bomb. Sargon made this next point very clear: "One of you must be with the bomb at all times. It can never leave your sight."

"I want to hear about your route to Paleto, but first I want all of us to reconvene upstairs for an important meeting." Adad locked the van, and they all climbed the stairs together. They quickly took their seats to listen what Sargon had to say.

"Adad and Jaiari you are heading out on a long and dangerous journey, and you will be together until your mission is complete, and you return to us. I want to take advantage of this time for all four of you to help us make the decision as to what plan of action we will take against the infidels in America. As you cross our homeland and into Iraq and finally Iran, I want you to come up with your own target and a rationale on how the attack will take place and your projected outcome. Keep in mind when I asked each of you to analyze the mistakes Osama bin Laden made with his plan. I want you to think about what could go wrong with your plan. When you return, we will all meet, and each of you will present your plan to the rest of us, and we will ask questions to challenge you and your thinking, looking for holes. Once we have completed the review process, we will then take a vote for the project or projects we want to carry out. I do not want any of your discussions shared over cell phone or the Internet. Oleg and Mordecai can meet here or any place in the area, as long as it is private, and talk about your plans. I want each pair to put forth ideas and then have the other person challenge the target and the plan. When we meet again, we will have one plan from each of you to review. Now, Adad, tell us your route to Paleto."

"Our route is to head north toward the Turkish border and then turn right and follow the border to the point where it runs into Iraq. We will cross the border in the town of Tail-Kushik. With the best of conditions, the travel time is about twenty-two hours, so we will not make it in one day. Most of the road is desolate, and you can easily fall asleep at the wheel so we have make contact with one of our team members, and we will spend the night near Al Mosul. There is an industrial park outside of town that will have sleeping accommodations, a place to secure the van, and showers and food.

"It is important that we keep up the appearance of delivery people for our company. We have fresh uniforms with the company logo on them that we will change before all border crossings. We have manifests for companies in Iraq and Iran that we can use at border crossings. We expect to cross the Iran border near the town of Beyuran e Bala and then on to the town of ZanJan, from where we will depart to deliver the bomb to the Iranians.

"After we have checked in, we will immediately go to Paleto to drop off the bomb. Then each of us will take twelve-hour shifts with the bomb. The team member with the bomb will be responsible to make notes of what activity is taking place with the bomb. If parts are replaced, then a list of parts will be sent by text message to Mordecai so he can get the parts and modify our other bomb.

Sargon told all of them "I have hidden in the van a GPS locater beacon that is tied into my cell phone so I can see your progress as you go and return." Adad says, "I will contact Sargon when we cross the border to Iraq and again we cross the border into Iran. I will send Sargon a text message when we are at the nuclear facility. Jaiari has determined, based on his discussion with his contact at the nuclear lab, that it could take at least two weeks to rejuvenate the bomb, perhaps longer, depending on its condition. As soon as I get a realistic assessment, I will send Sargon a date. That date will be the date we expect to leave Paleto and return to home base.

"Upon returning home we can lay out our plans to bring down America using our new weapons and make Islam and its nations a world power."

CHAPTER 34

Williams Office, 12:00 P.M.

Megan Brown was sitting in a chair outside Williams's office waiting for him to return from a meeting with the Secretary of Homeland Security. Williams was asking Simons to call Martins of the CIA to get Seacrest released and given full freedom to work on this project. He stressed that it had to happen now, because Seacrest was expecting a call later today. He would get right on it, he said, but he suggested to Williams that he needed a briefing on all that was going on.

"I'll have Marie contact your secretary and set up a time within twenty-four hours."

With that taken care of, Williams started down the hallway toward his office. As he arrived, he saw Ms. Brown sitting in a chair and not looking very comfortable.

He approached Megan and extended his hand.

"I'm sorry I'm late; I had a meeting with Secretary Simons; would you please come into my office?" He held the door open for Ms. Brown and followed her into the office, closing the door behind him. "So, Ms. Brown, how did you like Springfield?"

"Sir, I didn't get a chance to see much of it, I landed and went to the sheriff's office and talked about the map and how we could get possession in a way that would satisfy the local DA and the sheriff. The sheriff brought in a local judge to certify that the picture was a true representation of the map that I was taking back to Homeland Security. I promised that when we finished with the map, we would return it to the sheriff."

"Have you looked at the map, Ms. Brown?"

"No, sir, I took a quick look at it in the sheriff's office before I took the picture and placed it in a transport tube."

"Then let's have a look, shall we, Ms. Brown?"

They went over to Williams's conference table, and she handed him a pair of disposable gloves. She also put on a pair before she took the map out of the case and laid it on the table. It was as she had seen before; it was not a map made in the United States, but one that came from London. The map was unusual because most maps of the United States were maps of North America; this map was just the United States, with the typical side map of Alaska and Hawaii. They both studied the map and could clearly see twenty circles drawn around twenty cities in the United States. They went over a list online and found that, sure enough, nineteen of the twenty cities were in the top twenty, but the last city was not in the top twenty or even the top thousand. What could terrorists want with a city that small?

"Is it possible that that circle is a mistake?"

"I don't know, sir, but give my team and me a couple of days, and perhaps we can figure it out for you."

"Ms. Brown, based on your instincts at this moment, what is this map telling you? Would it be possible to hit all twenty places at one time?"

"Well, sir, that would depend on how many people is involved. We think there were twelve to twenty terrorists involved in the high jacking of the planes in Boston. If you wanted to attack all twenty of these cities, and you want to use something other than planes, figure four to six people per city. So if you were going to attack all twenty cities, then you would need between eighty and one hundred and twenty people to carry out the attacks. Sir, what if the map is a list of potential targets; maybe they used this map as a shopping list of what cities they might *want* to target, and, as they reviewed the targets, they eliminated some so that they are really looking at something less than twenty? If that were true, they would need a much smaller force to accomplish their mission."

"Brown, do you really think these people could destroy America as we know it?"

"Anything is possible, sir, even the destruction of America."

CHAPTER 35

Williams Office, 1:15 P.M.

AGENT BROWN HAD JUST LEFT Williams office when Marie called him on the intercom to tell him that Major Omid Rahimi was there to see him. As the door opened, Williams stood up and went over to shake Rahimi's hand, inviting him to sit down.

"Major," he began, "we are in a very difficult position in terms of a possible threat against the United States, and I need experienced people to fill in some of the holes in our team. You have been recommended to me by one of my senior analysts, Baker, for the position. Will you take a moment and tell me about yourself?"

"Sir, as you know I'm a Major from the USMC on special assignment to HS from the Pentagon. Before joining HS, I was an assistant to the G-3, the head of intelligence at the Pentagon for three years. I was the G-3 for the First Marine at Camp Pendleton, California. Before that I served as Battalion Commander of the 3rd Assault Amphibian Battalion in Operation Desert Shield."

"I can see by all the combat ribbons and medals that you have been a brave American fighting for the protection of America and the American way of life."

"Sir, I like to think that I have done my best for our country."

"Major, do you or any members of your family have any contact with people in Iran? We are dealing with a new terrorist group that has been formed in Syria. We suspect that this group, known as the Brotherhood of the Red Nile, has at least two suitcase dirty bombs. We also know that a total of twelve bombs are missing from the old Soviet arsenal, and we believe that some have been sold to other terrorist organizations, which tried to use them and failed. The closest country that has or is building nuclear capabilities is due east of Syria, and that country is Iran.

"Now, If The Brotherhood had the bombs, and they knew that there was a good chance they might not work, they would want to make sure that they would work. Not only do they want them to be reliable, but also they would want the technology to make them even more effective. So if I have a resource that had contacts in Iran that could help us, it would a very good thing for us."

"Sir, I apologize. Sometimes people look at my last name, my appearance, and they assume that I'm an Arab, and they become nervous. But even so, I do not know anybody in Iran, I have never been there, and being very frank with you, I don't even know if I have any family left in the country. But sir, if I get this position, I assure you that I will meet with my parents and see if they have any friends or family left in Iran and try to figure out how I could contact them to see if they can help in any way."

"Excellent. You get the job. The conversation with your parents is important, and I will want you to have it. Right now, major, we need you to work on locating Mike and Mary Ridley and their son, Michael. The house they lived in was located in Springfield, Texas. You may have heard the buzz around the office about this huge explosion in a home in Springfield, Texas, yesterday?"

Rahimi nodded.

"Baker will be able to give you more details, but right now we need to find out what has happened to the Ridley family. You will report directly to Baker, but I may call you from time to time to discuss your perspective. We have one lead, a house in Morristown, NJ, and I will want you to go there before you go to Springfield. In Springfield, I want you to interview as many people as you can to try to find out where the Ridleys are and then find them, the quicker the better. Any questions?"

"No, sir. I will go right now and look for Mr. Baker to get started. Sir, I apologize but I do have a question: how seriously do you take this threat?"

"It seems that everybody I talk to today wants to ask the same question. All I know today, and as I told the president yesterday, is very little, but my gut tells me that this group is more to be feared than any other group we have dealt with since September 11. So to answer your question the best I can: we need as much intelligence as we can, because I think things are in motion that, if left unchecked, could have serious consequences for all of us."

CHAPTER 36

Langley, Virginia

SEACREST WAS RELEASED FROM DETENTION and went back to his office to try to help save America. Though he was isolated for just a few short hours, he was very uncomfortable and was glad to be free. He still had about two hours before he expected to hear from Massri, so he decided to go to check out Google Earth to see what he could of the possible meeting site of the Brotherhood. The CIA no longer needed a great many of their own series of spy satellites, except in a few rare cases, and in those cases it was cheaper to use camera-equipped drones that could be remotely controlled and could fly to a specific site. Google Earth was a good way to find a site and then decide what other assets should be deployed to see what was there.

Seacrest remembered that Google Earth was updated once every three to five years, depending upon the density of the population. He knew that the area around Al-Mukharram was probably one of those places that was photographed every five years, if not less. As Seacrest was moving the Google globe to find his city, he saw the citrus grove north and west of the city, and he also saw the storage building where the meetings were supposed to be taking place. It didn't look, at least from the satellite image, like there was much cover for Massri. He did notice a water tower with a platform around it, but he couldn't tell whether or not it was a working tower. Perhaps he could set up an observation post in the citrus grove? Another possibility, which might be more dangerous, was that he could go right to the building and knock on the door. When somebody answered the door, he could present his card and tell them that the building owner was Mr. David Billah and that he had been sent to inspect the building because of some storm damage several months before. He could say that Mr. Billah was concerned about getting his citrus crop in the storage building so processing could begin. While Seacrest was thinking about all the things that could happen, the secure line rang.

"David Billah. How may I help you?" There was a pause and then he heard the female voice from Massri office respond. "Mr. Massri wanted you to know that he has seen the building, and it is as you say. Two walls on the first floor have some damage, but a greater amount of damage is on the second floor. Two walls there are damaged, and the roof has some damage. The floor on the ground level is designed as citrus storage and processing unit, and seems to be intact no damage. As far as he could tell, neither the storage boxes nor the processing equipment have been brought in as yet. It appears the only thing he could see on the first floor were two large, old suitcases and few small office supply boxes. He will spend more time outside assessing the damage, and he will call you probably by 2:00 p.m. tomorrow; will that time be satisfactory, Mr. Billah?"

He responded, "When you talk to him again, ask him to report tomorrow how long it will take to complete the job and give me a written report." Seacrest hung up the phone and then dialed Baker's secure phone to report what he knew about the citrus grove thus far.

When Massri reached the site, he could tell there was not much cover—certainly not enough to use a telephoto camera. He walked through the grove and did find a rather large stack of hay that was easily in range of his lens and would give him shelter; he could shoot all the pictures he wanted without giving away his position. He knew that he had to be quick about it, because he needed to get back to Homs for the call. As he started taking pictures, he noticed that there were no weapons. No rifles, no pistols, no IEDs, nothing. If these were bad guys, where were all their weapons? He panicked a little, wondering if he had gone to the wrong place: had he been taking pictures of just simple men, and not terrorists?

The cargo van came into view, and he saw the name on the side of the truck. Why would an office supply truck be at the processing building of a citrus grower? Why are they loading only one of the two very large suitcases? He watched through the telephoto lens and saw that they were packing boxes all around the big suitcase to the point that the boxes covered it. They used floor straps to hold the suitcase down and then, the boxes that covered it were held in place by a large, open-weave cargo net, as if to say that there was nothing there but office supplies. The real cargo was the suitcase, Massri realized, but where was it going? What was in the suitcase that had to be hidden?

CHAPTER 37

Springfield, Sheriff Whittles Office

W HITTLES HAD JUST FINISHED A phone call with the president of the deputy sheriff's union to discuss the plans for the memorial service for Sergeant Kelly. It would be this Sunday, at St. Patrick Roman Catholic Church on Main and Sycamore, in downtown Springfield. He turned to his computer and began to compose an e-mail for all the employees of the Springfield sheriff's department and the police in the surrounding communities, since they had called the department wanting to know the arrangements.

He told his employees that the service would begin at noon, and all officers not assigned to duty would report in full dress uniform to honor the loss of Sergeant Kelly, and to show respect for his wife and children. He hit the Send button, and as he swung his chair around, he saw the camera he used to take pictures at the Ridley house. He took out the SanDisk flash memory card and put it in the reader slot in his printer. As he waited for the images to pop up, he got a phone call from the receptionist, saying he had a phone call on line two from Major Omid Rahimi of Homeland Security in Washington, DC.

Whittles picked up the phone and in a rather flat voice said, "This is Sheriff Whittles. How can I help you?" Major Rahimi introduced himself to the sheriff and said that he was on Temporary Duty (TDY) to Homeland Security from the Pentagon.

"What type of Major are you?"

"I'm a Marine Major, sir."

"Hoo Ah, Major."

Omid was a little startled, but with a smile on his face he replied, "Hoo Ah."

"You're a Marine from where?"

"Well, sir, I started out as second lieutenant in bravo company First Reconnaissance Battalion, in the First Marine, in Camp Pendleton, California. I moved up the ranks and position until I became the G-3 head of intelligence for the Corp. I was sent to the Pentagon to assist the G-3 for the Department of Defense."

"Were you deployed?"

"Yes, sir. I had three tours in Operation Desert Shield and spent some time in Iraq and Afghanistan. And you, sir?"

"I was a Gunnery Sergeant in Operation Desert Storm and was given a field promotion to second lieutenant. I mustered out of the Corp and went to college on the GI bill to study police work, and I came to Springfield as a rookie deputy, and like you, Major, I worked my way up the ranks to become sheriff. Perhaps we could share a beer and swap a few Marine stories some day."

"Well, sir, that drink might be sooner than you think. Sir, I was brought over from the Pentagon to help Homeland Security figure out what happened, not only at the Ridley house but perhaps more important what happened to Mike, Mary, and Michael Ridley. I have a lead on a possible location that I need to check out, and I was hoping to come to Springfield to meet with you after I finish that lead. I want to meet with as many people in Springfield as possible to give me some insight into the Ridley family."

They arranged to meet on Thursday or Friday, after Rahimi checked out the New Jersey lead, and then Whittles said, "Major, I'll look forward to seeing you, but before we hang up, I wonder if I could ask you a favor. Just before the house blew up, I was walking through it, and I took a lot of pictures; they are the only thing left that shows us what the house looked like before it blew up. I just started to look at them and something seems to be missing; could I e-mail them to you, and if you could look at them on your way here, then we can talk about them when you arrive?"

"That's fine, Sheriff, but what's wrong in the pictures?"

"I don't want to color your judgment, but it's what's missing from them that bothers me."

Chapter 38

Ms. Brown's Lab

"THERE IS A PROBLEM WITH the size of the map. With letter or legal-sized documents, the best way to discover the fingerprints is through the cyanoacrylate fuming method. In this process you basically have a chamber into which you put the paper or anything that will fit, and you heat the equivalent of super glue to a gas state and release it into the chamber. The gas fumes settle on the paper or whatever is in the chamber, and the chemical in the fumes attaches to the fingerprint oils, if there are any on the object. After you suck out the fumes, you can see the fingerprints and then use the normal process to lift the prints and then process them through the computer files.

"The map is about four feet by six feet and can't fit into their chamber without being cut into sections. Cutting the map into sections may destroy other evidence that is on the surface of the map. The other concern is, if they cut the map in sections, will the courts accept the pieces as the original for the purpose of evidence?"

Megan called her colleagues Penelope and Derrick over to the map to have a discussion about what other options they might come up with to try to use the cyanoacrylate fuming method without destroying the map. They both agreed that the fuming method would deliver the most fingerprints.

Megan agreed and said, a little frustrated, "If we can't find a large enough place to put the whole map, then we can't run the fuming process."

"So," Derrick said out loud, "we need a place large enough to put the whole map in and have the ability to circulate the fumes to cover both sides of the map, correct? How big a chamber would we need?"

"My guess is that it would have to be at least 50 percent longer and 25 percent wider than the map. That would mean a chamber that was nine feet long and at least six feet wide." Penelope and Megan agreed. "Then the chamber has to have the ability to have an airtight seal and a way to get the fumes in and out, right?" Again the women agreed.

Penelope burst out, "A submarine!"

"Good concept, but a little expensive, and I don't know where we could get a sub on short notice. How about the sub bases at Groton Connecticut? We could call the base and ask if we could borrow a sub for a few hours."

"I have no doubts that we could make that happen, but what would happen to the inside of the sub if we release the fumes? It would have super glue fumes on every surface. We could just seal off one room to conduct our experiment. Maybe the base has a decommissioned sub that we could use?"

"That idea has something going for it. Wait a moment, we need a chamber we can pressurize, fill with the fumes, and then take out the fumes and have a chamber large enough to hold the map, right? A decompression chamber used by divers who get the bends from coming to the surface too fast would work. They put the diver in the chamber, seal it, and increase the air pressure and then slowly decrease the pressure so the lungs can adapt to the change in pressure. They have to pump in oxygen so the person can breathe while he or she is in the chamber. I think they call them hyperbaric chambers, and sometime they have them in hospitals."

"Let's do a quick Google search and see if any clinics or hospitals in the DC area have hyperbaric chambers." As Megan was speaking, Penelope was already on her computer doing a Google search and found that Georgetown University Hospital had a chamber.

Megan called the number and got hold of President Kerr, the head of the hospital. She explained who she was and what she wanted to do and how quickly she needed to get it done. Kerr explained that he didn't know the schedule for the use of the chambers, but if she would hold, he'd find out. Before he put her on hold, she said, "You cannot tell anybody what we are going to do; in fact, when we run the test, we want the least number of people involved. We will bring a person into the hospital on a gurney with an oxygen mask and take them directly to the hyperbaric chambers."

Kerr checked the schedule, and Megan thought again. "It's two o'clock now, and we will be at the emergency room of the hospital at 5:30."

"What help will you require from us for whatever you are planning to do?"

"We need the name of the technician who will be working with us."

"Let me check again," the president said. While she was on hold, Megan said to Derrick, "As soon as I get you a name, I need a background check, fast."

The president came back on the line and said, "The name of the tech is Roger Barrington."

Derrick was already running the background on Barrington, and while the data was processing, he said, "So who's on the gurney? I'll flip you for it."

Penelope said, "I'll flip you for it, and I call heads."

CHAPTER 39

1621 Boxer Ave., Morristown, New Jersey

BAKER HAD NOT HEARD BACK from his contact, Special Agent Allen Tinker, about the house in Morristown. He was just about to pick up the phone and call Tinker when his phone rang.

"Tinker, I was just getting ready to call you to see if you had any information on the Ridleys in Springfield or the house in Morristown?"

Tinker had some information, but not much yet.

"Homeland Security has a Major Rahimi, from the G-3 section of the Pentagon, and he will be working with them on this case. He is looking into the house in Morristown and the Ridley family in Springfield. I will give him your contact information, and the two of you can speak. We have a briefing with the president at four today, so Agent Tinker, any information you can give me now would be helpful."

"We have the house under surveillance, and, as of this morning, we have seen no one enter or leave the house. The mailman is dropping mail in the mail slot in the front door, but we have not seen anybody come to the front door to pick up the mail. We have not approached the house, not wishing to scare off anybody who might also be watching the house. Our local agent has made discreet contact with the Morristown chief of police, Bob Poling, advising him that the house on Boxer is under our surveillance, and not to approach our agents in the car parked near the house. We have also discussed with Chief Poling the possibility of a search warrant based on national security and a possible terrorist threat against the United States. We may need a judge to issue a search warrant on the basis of unspecified national security concerns." Tinker asked whether the chief knew a judge who would cooperate with what he needed. He said. "It could be arranged." Then Poling asked if Tinker needed any more help on the ground, "no, not right now."

"We need to see what, if anything is going on in that house, but without blowing our cover. We have come up with an idea that will give us a chance to look into the house and maintain our cover. We have contacted the local gas company and asked for a meter reader uniform for one of our agents. He will put on the uniform and go to the house. He will knock on the front door, which will give him the opportunity to look in the front door. When no one answers, he will go around to the back of the house and look for the meter and then go to the back door and knock. This will give him the opportunity to look in the back door and see what he can see. With no response, he will walk around the other side of the house, taking every opportunity to look in all the ground floor windows to see what he can see without being too obvious.

"Our gasman will have a second set of eyes, for in his collar will be a remote controlled camera with which to take pictures, plus he will have a mini earpiece so that the people running the camera will give him movement directions so as to get the best possible pictures. We will be sending out our gas man at around two o'clock today, and as soon as I get the images of the inside of the house, I will call you back."

"Tinker, if you do not find any signs of life in the pictures, will you get the warrant tomorrow?"

Tinker responded, "This is your show, you tell me when, and we'll get it done. I expect our man to be in Morristown by late tonight; what is the best way to get ahold of you?"

"Have him call me on my cell phone, and I'll call him back and set up a meeting place."

Tinker hung up and called the local agent, Jonathan Walters, about the plan for the gasman. Jonathan told him that Special Agent Edward Townsman would be playing the role of the gasman. Townsman was an experienced undercover agent, and he would do well. He would call Tinker as soon as they had something to report.

Walters hung up and went to meet Townsman at the PSEG division office on Morristown Road. When he arrived, he went into one of the service bays and met Townsman, who was already dressed for the part. He had a PSEG car and would drive to Boxer Avenue and park the car on the corner at the end of the block, so it could be seen in any direction. He would start on the 1500 block of Boxer and go from house to house, knocking on doors or ringing doorbells and asking to read their gas meters. He made sure to establish a pattern of going around the house if no one answered, so when he did it at the target house it would not seem suspicious.

As he approached the target home, his breath quickened, and he began to sweat a little. Townsman slowly walked up the front steps of 1621 and walked to the front door. He knocked and pushed the doorbell. Since there was no response to his knocks or to the doorbell, he leaned toward the door so the camera could see inside the house and was told in his earpiece to move to the side and slowly walk toward the back. As he walked around the side of the house, he could see that he was not tall enough for the camera to see into the windows, but he was tall enough just to barely see into the rooms. All the windows were dark, so he couldn't see anything. He didn't want to appear to be stretching to see in the house, so he looked as best he could. He went around to the back of the house and noticed that, like the small front lawn, the back yard had been mowed recently.

He found the back steps and walked up but found no doorbell, so, like before, he knocked loudly on the door and shouted, "Gasman, here to read your meter!" No response. He leaned in to let the camera see what it could see, if anything. He waited a moment or two and, receiving no answer, he walked around the other side of the house and looked in as best he could. He climbed the front steps to knock once more on the door, and, as he reached to turn the knob, a shot rang out.

CHAPTER 40

Ms. Brown's Lab

MEGAN BROWN AND HER TEAM had three hours before they had to leave for the hospital and the fuming of the map for fingerprints. They had no idea how long it would take in the hospital chamber to fume the map fully. They decided to take the entire supply of compound they had in the lab with them to make sure they could complete the process. In the meantime, they wanted to examine the map for other types of evidence.

Penelope pored over the map with the largest magnifier they had in the lab, starting at the upper left-hand corner. She'd hand any samples to Derrick and he would bag each sample and label where it came from on the map. They had a very short time to cover the map, and they decided that working in pairs was the most efficient way to do it. In the time remaining before they had to leave for the hospital, they had to complete both sides of the map.

While they were hunting on the real map for hair samples and skin cells, along with dust and dirt samples, Megan was studying the digital image of the map on the largest monitor they had in the lab. She kept gazing at the twenty red circles, looking at each one of them as a possible terror target. She would then make a list of facts about each city, other than the population, that might make it an enticing target. She did a search on the Census Bureau data, and she found that the total population of the twenty largest cities in the United States was just over 32.5 million, out of a total population of over 313 million people. So the twenty largest cities held only just over 10 percent of the total population. Granted, the greater metro populations held more than the cities alone, but how much more? Brown surfed a little more, drilled down, as they say, and found that if you included the greater metropolitan area around the Major cities, your concentration would be over one-third of the total population of the country. Is it possible to have a coordinated attack on the twenty largest metropolitan cities at one time? How many people would it take to attack all twenty cities? *That seems like a question for the Pentagon, not us,* Megan thought to herself.

By that time, Penelope and Derrick had found hair and dirt samples and glue samples at the corners, but no skin cells, yet. Brown went back to her digital image of the map and remembered the conversations in the panic of 2008. Back then, there was a great deal of discussion about banks and companies being too big to fail; was there something about these cities that made them too big to fail? She asked herself why nineteen plus one? Is the one more important than the other nineteen? Then she thought, *I ranked the cities thinking largest to smallest. Could I be wrong, and there is another order, like west to east or east to west or something totally different from the way we are thinking? Have the nineteen been compared against the one? What is so important about the one that it is in with the other nineteen? How many of the nineteen have been attacked or are cities where known plots have been foiled?*

Time was running out, and they still had to pack up the map and the chemicals to fume the map. Soon they headed downstairs for the waiting ambulance. The ambulance was under cover in the parking garage, and Penelope, who had lost the bet, lay down on the gurney and tucked the map case next to her. Next they placed an oversize oxygen mask on her face and lifted her into the ambulance. They taped IV bags to her arms, and off they went to the hospital.

The plan upon arrival was to rush through the emergency room and go directly to the Hyperbaric Chamber Suites. Derrick had looked up the floor plan of the hospital and found that the suites were located on the third floor. As the ambulance sped, with light flashing and sirens screaming, they raced across downtown. The fastest route to Georgetown Hospital was to take Rhode Island Avenue West until it fed into M Street. Next they needed to take M Street to Wisconsin Avenue. The trip across northern DC took under twenty minutes.

They pulled into the emergency room and shouted, "Extreme case of the bends! We need the Hyperbaric Chamber Suites on three, which way to the elevator?" They rushed to the elevator, Penelope on the gurney with Megan and Derrick in hospital scrubs on each side, pushing her into the elevator and not allowing anyone else in with them. They stopped on two, but they told people waiting, "Emergency, please takes the next elevator!" The doors opened on three, and they ran out of the elevator and down the hall to Suite One of the Hyperbaric Chambers, where they closed and locked the door.

Inside the suite, Roger Barrington was waiting for them. They quickly explained who they were and why they were in the suite.

"I didn't think you would be coming in with such fanfare."

"We're sorry about all the dramatics, but we didn't know any other way."

"Here is the chamber. I think there is plenty of room for your map. I was thinking that you'd want to do both sides, so I found some metal wire shelves in the storage room that we can lay on the bed in the chamber to allow the fumes to circulate around the map. How much space do you need to have beneath the shelf to get the circulation you need?"

"About six inches of air space, at the least."

"I took a bunch of magazines from the waiting room that we can use to lift the shelf unit off the platform."

"Great thinking! Now, how do we introduce the chemical to create the fumes?"

"The chamber has a smaller chamber that creates an air lock that we can open without changing the pressure inside. We pressurize the small chamber to the same level as the large chamber and then we can open the interconnecting door. We set in the heated chemicals and then when we open the inside door to the chamber, the fumes will flow in. Inside the main chamber are fans that circulate the air in the chamber, so the fans should do a nice job of circulating the fumes."

"How long will the map have to stay in the chamber?"

"It's hard to tell, but when we begin to see the first fingerprint, my guess is that the rest will happen very quickly. That we have a very large object, compounded by the fact that we are trying to do two sides, may extend the time in the chamber. We will monitor the developments, and when we see the fingerprints start to appear, we will time the interval until the second one appears. Knowing the time interval, when we see no more prints developing, we will wait that amount of time and if no prints develop, we are done. We will purge the chamber and then balance the pressure and take out the map. We will carefully wrap the map and be on our way back to our lab to lift the prints."

"Let's get started," Megan concluded, but she was still thinking about the relationship of circle one to the other nineteen and what kind of danger our country might be in if they attacked *any* of the nineteen? Does the one circle do something that affects the other nineteen? Do the nineteen do something together that the number twenty doesn't do? The longer she thought, the more questions without answers she came up with. The truly nagging question was could they find them before they tried to destroy America? *God, I hope so, I really hope so.*

CHAPTER 41

Williams Office, 2:00 P.M.

ILLIAMS WAS WORKING WITH MARIE in preparing the first briefing booklet for the president. He had a meeting with President Jordan, Simon's head of Homeland Security, and Markel, the National Security Advisor, at four o'clock in the president's conference room off the Oval Office. Williams had just spent the last twenty minutes briefing his assistant Marie about what had been going on, and she was sitting at the conference table in shock.

Williams concluded, "The president expects, and so does the nation, for us to do the best possible job to protect the country, and I'm going to do everything I can to save this country. I know that may sound hokey, but I believe what I'm saying. I need your perspective that what I'm saying to the president and his advisors is clear and to the point. I want no misunderstandings about our message.

"If things were to develop to the point that something has to be said to the country, the message will come from the president, then FEMA and HS would take over, along with the Pentagon. Right now, we have to prepare briefing books for the meeting with the president to let him what we know and don't know. I think it has to be in bullet form so he can clearly see what is going on, and we must do so without editorializing, at least for now. So what we don't know could probably fill pages of questions and be very distracting to all concerned. We have already agreed on a weekly briefing through the National Security Advisor, as we get more clarifying data.

"After this meeting, I will be hand-carrying our reports to Markel. I want the reports stored in the safe in my office, and I want the combination changed so that only you and I will have the combination. I want you to type the reports and load them to a flash drive, and that has to be stored in the safe too. After you have finished transferring the file, I want it deleted from your computer.

"We will only discuss the contents of the report in my office; nothing is to be said about the 'Springfield Project' in e-mail. Also, no details of our report will be discussed on the phone. Is that clear?"

"Yes, sir."

"Any reports that we get from Baker or his team members are to be stored in the safe. So then," he read, "Presidential Status Report Project Springfield.

"Known:

"We found a map in a house in Springfield; that map was transferred to HS and is under close examination for fingerprints and any DNA samples in hopes that the evidence from the map can tell us who has been in contact with it. The map has twenty red circles drawn on it, and nineteen of the twenty cities are the nineteen largest metropolitan regions in the country. The twenty cities appear to be marked as possible target cities. (Marie, we should include a copy of the photograph that was taken of the map by Ms. Brown.)

"An explosion destroyed the house that held the map shortly after the map was recovered. Sergeant Kelly of the Springfield sheriff's office bomb squad was killed in the explosion. The residents of the house—the Ridley family—Mike, Mary, and Michael are missing. The son, Michael, was enrolled at UC Berkeley but never showed up for classes in the last two years.

"Michael Ridley, the son, left a forwarding address in Morristown, New

Jersey, and we have an undercover team right now working on getting into the house.

We have a special agent from the G-3 of the Pentagon, who is on his way to Morristown and then to Springfield to work with the sheriff on trying to find out what happened to the Ridley family. One of my assistants is working with the CIA and an asset on the ground to try to get some photographs of what we believe to be the meeting site of the Brotherhood of the Red Nile, and as many members as he can get. We hope to have those images later today.

"Once the map has cleared forensics, we will put another team on the map to try to figure out the meaning of the twenty circles. At the moment, we have no assurance that the map and the Brotherhood are in fact related, but given that two terrorists from another group were taken out at the house, we believe the map may be related at least to one of the two groups.

"The nineteen circles on the map encompass 30 percent plus of the entire population of the United States, or over 110,000,000 people. In our previous meeting, we stated that we thought they might in fact have two of the dirty bombs from the old Soviet Union stockpile of nuclear weapons. Our initial assessment is: if one of those bombs were to be used in any of those nineteen population centers, that city might become a ghost town, like Chernobyl. The higher we go up the list of Major cities, the greater the problem we would have with relocating any significant number of the population.

"We have alerted all listening posts for any traffic that might be related to the activities of the Brotherhood of the Red Nile. Lastly, Mr. President, we have kept the circle of people working on this project decidedly small. As we get a better understanding of the scope of the potential attack, we will add necessary personnel. For now we must keep a very tight lid on the potential problem because we do not want widespread panic in the country.

"Mr. President, I'm sure you can understand that if information got out that twenty Major metropolitan areas in the United States were targeted by a new terrorist group, the panic in these cities would be devastating. One hundred million people trying to get out and go somewhere else might be just what the terrorists are attempting to accomplish. The dirty bombs are not so much weapons of mass destruction as much as they are weapons of fear."

At this point, Marie turned to Williams. "Wait, there is more here than you told me just before we started. Are you sure this is the kind of information I should know?"

"Marie, we have worked together a long time and over the years I have shared just about everything I have worked on with you, regardless of how top secret it was, I have always trusted you, and I have no reason not to trust you now, do I?"

"No."

"Well, this may be the most serious threat we have ever faced as an agency or perhaps even as a nation. This information is so sensitive that any leak could cause a panic throughout the country. I trust you, and that is why I'm having you help me with the briefing book. Before you make copies of this report, please call the office of the president and confirm my four o'clock appointment and see whether the list of attendees is still four, including me, and let me know what they say. Please make the number of copies required and give them to me in plain, unmarked, brown envelopes. Also, please arrange to have my car here at ten to four so that I can get to the White House."

"Anything else, sir?" "Thank you for being here and helping on perhaps our most important work. That's all."

Williams sat down and saw that Marie had left him with the after-action report from the HS team at the Ridley home in Springfield. As he began to scan the report, he looked for a section on the disposition of the bodies that were removed from the house and taken away in the white medical units, but there was nothing in the report about the bodies being taken away by HS. If *we* didn't take the bodies, then who did, and why? What did they do with the bodies? He called Marie on the intercom. "Get me Baker right away, please."

CHAPTER 42

Morristown, New Jersey

TOWNSMAN REMEMBERED SLOWLY WALKING UP the front steps of 1621 Boxer Avenue, and he remembered knocking on the door, and nobody had answered. He was left-handed and glad he was, because the knob was on the right hand side of the door. When he reached with his left hand, it put the bulk of his body past the doorframe. When he turned the knob, he found that the door was not locked; it swung in, and just seconds after, a loud bang went off and a hole the size of a basketball was blown in the middle of the front door. Townsman dropped to the floor of the porch, and a whole team of FBI agents came running to the front porch to see whether Townsman was hurt and to see who fired the shot.

They approached the house carefully and shouted to Townsman, "Are you hurt? Can you see the shooter?"

Townsman responded, "Just a flesh wound to my right arm and shoulder. There's too much debris on the porch for me to see from this angle who's inside the house."

The agent in charge, Cain, motioned for part of the team to go to the back door and try to break it down. Part of the team in the front of the house crept alongside the house and crawled onto the front porch under the window so they wouldn't be seen. They used a long-handled mirror to look into the area behind the front door, but just as they began to look in, a second shot was heard at the back of the house.

Special Agent Cain yelled on his headset, "Everybody all right?" He got a call back: everybody fine they had used a broom to push in the door.

Back on the front porch, a team member crawled back to the corner of the porch and stood up outside the window frame and out of range of the guns to try to look in to the house to see if he could see the shooter or shooters, but the window was covered with black film, so he couldn't see into the room. The agent called to Cain and told him about the film. The team at the back of the house checked the windows and found them covered with the same film.

Cain sent agents around both sides of the house and had them check the side windows. Both teams reported back that all the side windows were covered with the same black film. One of the team members came toward the right side of the house from the neighbor's yard and crawled onto the porch and reached out for Townsman's right leg; he told Townsman that he was going to pull him slowly off the porch under the window. He had to stay down below the window frame and push himself away from the door with his good hand and arm. The agent got Townsman off the porch to safety, and Cain left one agent at the rear, undercover, and one protecting the front. He talked the rest of the agents back a safe distance from the house to discuss their options in attacking the house.

Over his radio Cain heard that Major Omid Rahimi from Homeland Security was en route and to wait for him before proceeding. Cain rogered back but asked for EMS to come down Boxer from the 1500 end and then look for an agent in an FBI jacket for directions. Within about five minutes—though it seemed like half an hour to Cain and the team—Rahimi arrived.

Rahimi introduced himself to Cain and asked for an update. Cain told him that an officer was shot, but not seriously, and it appeared that the same gunman who shot out the front door just moments ago had also shot out the back door. Cain told Rahimi that all the lower windows had been covered with black film, so they could not tell what they were up against in the house. Rahimi said to Cain, "If at all possible, we have to take whoever is in that house alive; I need to talk with them about something very important."

Cain responded, "The best way to get the person or persons inside alive is with stun grenades. We have grenade launchers in our truck and I propose to fire four grenades simultaneously into the house, two on each side. We will fire one grenade in one of the two lower windows on the first floor and one on each side on the second floor. My men will be standing by with ear protection, and within a split second after the stun grenades go off, they will bust into the front and back door and begin to look for the suspect on the first floor.

"The team will split upon entering the house and move quickly to the second floor, looking for other suspects. While the suspects will be in some pain for a short time, they will not be in any real danger from the blasts. However, Major, if they are fired upon, my men will return fire, but they will do everything in their power not to kill the suspects."

Major Rahimi agreed with Agent Cain's plan, and soon the teams were loaded and in position. They got the signal from Cain to fire, and as close to perfect as possible, all four grenades broke their respective windows, and the sound was frightening. Within seconds of the blasts, the two teams charged the front and back doors and were in the house. The first team saw nobody, and the second team exploded up the stairs and went from room to room, also finding nobody. The second team returned to the first floor to join the first team and signaled to Cain: "First and second floor secured, but wait until you see the inside of this house." As the team examined the rooms on the lower floor, they saw that the stun grenades had exploded with such great force that all the windows in the house had been blown out.

Cain and Rahimi came into house, and as they walked through the front door, they saw a shotgun locked into a bracket, tied and aimed at the front door with a cord and pulley tied to the trigger of the gun. A similar mechanism was attached to the back door. As they peered into the living room, dining room, den and kitchen, they saw a similar system tied to each lower window, and all were armed, cocked, and ready to shoot anybody who tried to come in a side window instead of the door.

Cain and Omid went upstairs and in one of the bedrooms they found a map on the wall. This was not a map of the United States, but rather a map of the Middle East that included Syria, Iraq, and Iran. On the map was a route marked in red from Syria to a point in Iran called Paleto. On the table were stacks of papers that Rahimi gathered up. He put gloves on and put the papers in a case for safekeeping; he would look at them in closer detail later, on his way to Springfield. Both Cain and Rahimi began a slow search of the house. Cain asked his men to disarm the window guns but to use gloves so as not to smudge possible fingerprints. He instructed them not to touch anything else and that after they had dismantled and disarmed the weapons, they should leave the house. A FBI forensic team was on the way to collect evidence and clear the house. Cain called over his radio to see how agent Townsman was feeling and was told he would have to go to the hospital for a few stitches.

As Cain and Rahimi collected papers, they found correspondence from UC Berkeley addressed to Michael Ridley. The envelopes had not been opened, and they found a telephone bill for a cell phone in Michael's name; the bill showed the number of the cell phone and the numbers called in the last billing cycle. They also found a checkbook in Michael's name for a bank in Springfield, which Rahimi put in his case along with the phone bill. They found other papers, but Rahimi didn't have time to study them all. He stacked those papers and put them in another envelope and gave them to Cain with the following order: "I want you to send all these papers to the FBI evidence lab in DC, and I want them tested for DNA and fingerprints. I want all results to be hand carried to the office of Homeland Security and personally handed to Ted Baker. Do you understand?"

"Yes, sir."

"Then do it now; your team can secure the site until you get back. One other thing: please let me know the condition of one very lucky, left-handed FBI agent Townsman."

As Rahimi got into the car to go to the airport for his flight to Springfield, he asked himself, *Why is the city of Paleto, Iran, so important?*

CHAPTER 43

En Route to Paleto, Iran

ADAD AND JAIARI HAD BEEN on the road north from Homs for several hours, and they had spent most of the time getting to know each other better. Adad told Jaiari of his wife, Haped, and his two children, Yaman, a boy, and his daughter, Rima. His son was ten years old, and his daughter was six. He loved his children and would have done anything for them. Mohammad had provided very well for Adad and his family—so much so that Adad had shared his wealth with many poor families in Homs. His wife was a beautiful woman with whom he had been in love from the first day they met over twenty years ago.

His son had been asking him recently about what it was like when he and his mother got married. Yaman asked, "Is it true that the groom and the ring bearer take a shower together the night before the wedding?"

"Why do you ask?"

Apparently, the mother of a friend of his was remarrying; her husband-to-be wanted him to be the ring bearer, and he was concerned about taking a shower with his potential stepfather.

Jaiari laughed at the story. "What did you tell him?"

"I told him it is symbolic, and they are sprinkled with water; they don't really take a shower together."

Jaiari asked Adad about his business and how it got started.

While Adad was very proud of his business, he was reluctant to talk about it. "I came out of school, and I noticed that as oil went up in price, more and more people were starting businesses to help support the needs of the oil companies. They needed computers and software and office supplies. I didn't see anybody meeting the needs of all these startup companies, so I said to myself, *Why not me?* I bought a used truck and had it painted on the side, just like this one, and I would buy all the stuff I needed over the Internet, and I would go around and take orders for supplies and then, when they came in, I delivered to the customers all over the Middle East.

"As my business grew, I opened warehouses in almost all the countries where I was doing business. By then I was buying in bulk and having shipments sent to all my warehouses. I could then take orders in one center and ship to clients from the closest warehouse to them. I charged a shipping charge and made a nice profit off the shipping charges. My business continued to grow, and I became a wealthy man.

"Over time I saw how the West treated our people, and I grew angrier and wanted to do something about it. I wasn't interested in joining al-Qaeda, so when Sargon approached me about the Brotherhood, I gave it a great deal of thought. I prayed, my wife and I talked about it many times, and finally I decided to join and try to do something about the way we are respected and treated in the world. So enough about me; tell me *your* story."

Jaiari was born in Tehran of middle-class parents; his father was a London-educated surgeon who met his wife in London. They were married and moved back to Iran. Almost from the beginning, she didn't like Iran and all the restrictions that had been placed on women when the ayatollahs took over after the fall of The Shaw. She became so frustrated and disgusted that she took her son and went back to live in London.

"We lived in a free and open Iranian neighborhood in London. Her family had money, so I went to private school with other Iranians, and when it was time for me to go to university, I decided that I wanted to study economics. I got my undergraduate degree in business from Oxford and won admission to the London School of Business for my master's degree. I graduated from college, and I was sure I could change the world.

"While I was in school I had no idea of the real world, so when I finished my schooling and went out to try to find a job, I was surprised that there were none. I became disenchanted with the time I had spent in college because they didn't teach students about the real world. I met some people who were from all over the world, and most, like myself, were highly educated but could find no work. As we began to explore why this had happened, we concluded that it was the fault of the imperialists in the United States. Part of the problem was all those bad mortgage loans they sold all over the world, though in the scheme of things, that was small. But even more important, they exported in a big way, to many countries around the world, the idea of 'buy now and pay later.'

"The whole world was living beyond its means, and when it was time to pay for the loans, nobody had any money to make the mortgage payments or pay their credit cards or make the car payments. Prior to that, even in my country, people did not borrow money. If they needed something they paid cash; there were no credit cards. When President Mahmoud Ahmadinejad came to power in 2005, he began to change things. When the world financial markets crumbled in 2008, he set a new course for Iran and its role as a world leader by developing nuclear capability.

"Initially he didn't want to make bombs to use against the imperialists, but he blamed the United States and Israel for the economic collapse of 2008 and the near global depression that followed. His rhetoric became more inflamed, and the Iranian people supported him; I supported him. I came back to Iran to be with my father, and he got me involved with people who were working to make Iran strong. I got some work, spent time with my father, and met Sargon. We started talking about a new type of terrorist group that would act and think smarter; he called it his Think Tank. He was looking for somebody with an economics background, and I fit the bill, so here I am riding in a truck carrying an unstable nuclear bomb back to Iran to make it stable and more deadly, to use it against the mightiest imperial nation of the world, I just don't know when or how."

"We are supposed to be talking about what are the best ways to use the bombs; what do you think is the best way to use these bombs to have the greatest long-term impact on the United States?"

CHAPTER 44

Morristown Airport

WHILE THE FLIGHT PLAN FOR his flight to Springfield was being filed, Rahimi was looking at the papers found on the second floor of the house and taking some photographs for him to study on the plane to Springfield he forwarded the originals to Homeland Security for processing

Suddenly he stopped dead in his tracks and quickly dialed Agent Cain at the house. Cain answered on the third ring. "Cain, are you close to the house? Will you please go into the kitchen? I'll hang on until you get there."

Cain walked up the steps and into the house and said to Rahimi, "I'm in the kitchen."

"Tell me what you see."

"What do you mean?"

"Just describe what you can see all around you."

Cain described that the kitchen had a gas range, a fridge, a microwave, a cupboard, and a table with four chairs and dishes on the table.

"Stop. What dishes are on the table?"

"A plate with some food on it, a cup of coffee, and a bottle of milk."

"Is the coffee cup warm?"

Cain reached over and touched the cup, and it *was* warm.

"Look around the first floor; do you see a door to the basement?"

Cain walked through the house and didn't see a door to the basement and relayed that information to Rahimi, who told him to clear the house and stay in the kitchen. When the house was clear of Cain's men, Rahimi said, "I want you to go back in the kitchen and face the cupboard. When you get there, I want you to look very closely at the hinges on the doors and tell me if you see any wire, no matter how small, on the hinges."

Cain looked and felt very carefully and found nothing.

"I want you to look at the knobs on the door and see whether any wire is wrapped around the knobs. Anything?" Rahimi asked.

"Nothing," Cain responded.

"Does one door overlap the other?"

"Yes."

"I want you to take out your Maglite and open one door just enough to see with your light whether there is any wire on the back of the door."

Cain slowly opened the right door, and, using his flashlight, he looked at the screw in the back of the knob and saw nothing. Rahimi suggested that he open the door a little more and search around. Cain opened the door far enough to see the back of the door and saw no wires. He took a deep breath. Little by little, he opened the door all the way, and he saw no wires. He looked at the back of the other door, and there were no wires, and he opened it all the way. So now Cain could see the inside of the cupboard.

He could see bolts in the top and bottom corners of the cupboard.

"Call in some help."

Cain yelled out for some help to move the cupboard.

"Now close the doors and pull the cupboard away from the wall."

Cain and two of his men tried to pull the cupboard from the wall, but it wouldn't budge.

"Do you have a cordless drill in the truck? Get a cordless drill with a socket attachment and back out the bolts." One of Cain's men ran to the truck and brought back a drill and a socket attachment, and he fumbled around until he found the right size. The power drill with the right socket made quick work of the four bolts, and the cupboard was free. When they slid the cupboard out from the wall, they found that the cupboard was attached to the door to the basement. They checked the knob and hinges for wires and found none. They tried the knob on the door, but it was locked on the other side, so they pulled the pins on the hinges and were able to remove the door. They looked at the floor and could now see scuff marks where the door with the cupboard was closed and locked from the inside. Cain told Rahimi what they had found and that they were proceeding to the basement. The pilot approached Rahimi and said that the plane was ready, and Rahimi replied, "Just a moment."

Cain saw the light switch on the wall leading to the basement and was ready to throw the switch when his brain said, "Booby trap," and he decided to use his flashlight instead as he slowly walked down the stairs. As they reached the bottom, the team spread out to search the basement. Cain flashed his light toward the eastern wall and he saw a trunk up against the wall, and, as he shone his light on the floor, he saw scrapes in the dirt on the floor. He called one of his men over, and together they moved the trunk and saw a very large hole in the wall. They shone their light into the hole and saw a tunnel. Cain called out to Rahimi and told him what he was seeing, and they both concluded that someone was in the house when the front door gun went off; they had been in the kitchen eating. They went into the doorway to the basement, pulled the door shut, and locked the door behind them.

Cain said he would send a couple of his men through the tunnel to see where it led, and if he found anything of interest, he would notify Rahimi by text. Cain and his men could not fit through the hole in the wall with all their gear on, so they took everything off and entered the hole with just their side arms. They had no idea where the tunnel led, but they continued to crawl to the end of the tunnel. As they came to the end, they found that it was at the end of Boxer Street and opened into a drainage ditch. They could see that it had been covered over by some brush, but the brush had been knocked away by somebody escaping from the house.

Cain called for all but one of the remaining men to join him looking for something around the drainage ditch that would give them a clue to who had been there. As they stood on the road, they looked at how the brush was spread about, as if it had exploded out of the hole. Cain took pictures, and in one of the frames he saw something yellow and blue stuck in a bunch of branches. He climbed down into the ditch and was getting ready to pull the cloth free from its entanglements when he stopped and said, "Get me an evidence bag and some rubber gloves."

He waited until the bag arrived and wrestled the cloth out of the brush. When he got it free, he held it up so a picture could be taken, and it would show up in full length. One of his men took the picture, and Cain put the cloth in the evidence bag and then asked to see the camera. He scanned the photos until he found the one of the yellow cloth and wondered how a UC Berkeley scarf had gotten caught in the brush.

Cain sent the picture on to Rahimi with instant message, "found in the brush at the exit hole from the tunnel.

"Mean anything to you?"

CHAPTER 45

Four O'clock Meeting with the President

WILLIAMS HAD JUST GOTTEN WORD from Baker that he hoped to have the photos of the people within the next six hours; he also heard from Major Rahimi that the house in Morristown had somebody in it, and it was booby-trapped. The FBI had been able to get into the house with only one-man agent Townsman was slightly injured, and they had found an escape tunnel in the basement. They found a scarf from the UC Berkeley bookstore caught in the brush at the end of the tunnel. Thus, it was possible that Michael was in the house on Boxer Street.

Megan Brown had reported that their temporary fume chamber was working, and they hoped to be able to leave the hospital in two hours. As soon as they returned to Homeland Security, they would begin to process the fingerprints and the DNA samples they had collected before they left.

Major Rahimi was on a plane to Springfield with copies of papers and credit card and mobile phone statements that he was reviewing, and he should be in Springfield in about three hours. Williams had decided that there wasn't enough time to change the report, so he would give the written report and give the update orally, following up with a written copy in the morning.

Frank told Marie that he wanted his car to the White House early because he was to have a briefing before the meeting with National Security Advisor Markel to bring him up to speed. The meeting with the president was scheduled for four o'clock, and Marie had scheduled a meeting with Markel at 3:30. Williams's car was already waiting out front, and it was just after three when he left his office and told Marie that he was going home after the meeting. He asked her to call Ellen and tell her that he hoped to be home by 6:00 and that, because the weather was warm, he would cook the steaks on the grill.

Williams got in his car. "I have a 3:30 at the White House, so step on it. Flasher, but no sirens."

"Yes, sir."

Williams's car made it in record time, and he was walking through White House and down that long corridor at 3:20. He went to the side conference room, went over to the wet bar and got a bottle of water and some ice, and was drinking it when Markel walked through the door. Williams expected the sight of Markel would begin to make him sweat, but so far he was calm and somewhat confident. They both sat down at the small table, and Williams shared with him what was in the report and then the latest developments. Markel spoke. "So we are no closer to the identity of the Brotherhood leaders than we were two days ago?"

"Sir, I expect photographs of the leader within three hours, and we can work with the FBI to see if they have anything they can tell us about the Brotherhood leadership. Based on the initial visual identification of our asset on the ground, they do not look like the profile of what we would think of as terrorists. I'm not suggesting that there is a profile of terrorists, but our man on the ground saw no weapons—not even side arms. Perhaps we may be dealing with somebody altogether different than we have in the past. One thing we are dealing with is that I believe that the photos that were taken will show a suitcase bomb going somewhere. The presence of the bomb makes them a much more deadly threat.

"In the house in Morristown we found a map of Syria, Iraq, and Iran with a circle around a town in Iran called Paleto. We just got this information as I was leaving, so we have no information on the city or even enough evidence to suspect that the cargo van that left the meeting site was headed to Paleto."

Just as he finished, the door opened. The two of them went into the president's conference room, and this time, when Williams saw the president, he began to sweat. The head of HS, Simons, joined President Jordan at the table, and Williams passed out the briefing books. He went over the bullet points, but things were breaking very fast, so he then presented the information that had come in after the briefing book had been prepared.

President Jordan turned to Williams and asked whether he had all the help he needed. Williams responded, "For the moment, we're fine, but Mr. President, I would like to talk about that very question—not for now, but for later. As you know from our first briefing, we are in possession of a map of the United States that has twenty circles on it. We don't know what the circles mean. They could be targets for cities to attack or not. What we know at the moment is that there is a possibility that the Brotherhood has at least one suitcase bomb and more likely two bombs.

"That bomb, if it is a bomb, is in a cargo van headed somewhere, possibly to Paleto, Iran. We know the name on the truck to be Assad Office Supplies and Software. If it is in fact going to Iran, we should be able to track it via satellite. I have asked the CIA to readjust one of their birds to fly close to the Turkish border and see whether they can spot the van. If they can, then we can follow it to its destination. If it crosses the border into Iraq, then if it is going to Iran, it will have to head east."

"How is this relevant to you needing help?"

"Sir, it is possible that the twenty cities circled on the map could be target cities where the Brotherhood could use their dirty bombs. We know that nineteen of the twenty cities circled could be possible targets because of the greater metropolitan populations that represent almost one third of the entire population of the nation. If the Brotherhood has two dirty bombs, then they could attack two cities.

"I think we need to start to move military personnel in proximity of these nineteen cities, so that they can assist local law enforcement in moving people out of the cities."

"Do you really think the Brotherhood will use nuclear bombs against the United States?"

Markel responded, "Yes, sir, both bombs and more, if they had them."

CHAPTER 46

Brotherhood Building

SARGON DECIDED THAT IT WOULD be a good idea for Mordecai and Oleg to spend some time together in hopes they could figure out a way to trust each other and come up with some ideas about how to attack America. Sargon spent a little time with them to break the ice and then he told them he was leaving and that they needed to be back by eight a.m. the next day because the rebuild equipment would start arriving, and he would need both of them to help him set up the equipment.

Oleg said he would start. "I'm a petroleum engineer, and I worked for my uncle in the oil business in Russia. I'm not married and have no children; I'm pretty much a loner. I had some friends with benefits, but nothing serious. I went to college in the United States at Stanford and recently took some graduate courses at UC Berkeley. With all the new technology in drilling and exploration, I needed to get refreshed and updated. While I was there, I met a young man who was to start his freshman year at Berkeley but got caught up in the anti–big government protest that is typical at Berkeley.

"So I grew up in Mother Russia; my parents were part of the intellectual elite, and when I was about ten, the KGB came and took my parents away to the gulag, and I never saw or heard from them gain. My uncle Viktor Antipova took me to his home and raised me. He was not married, nor did he have any children, so he raised me as his son and provided the best he could. He was in the army in the ordinance section, and when the Soviet Union broke up, he was in charge of securing most of the nuclear weapons that were not missile-based. You may recall that I said that he sold some of the original suitcase dirty bombs and used the money to start his oil exportation company. It was the proceeds of the oil business that sent me to Stanford. I owe a great deal to my uncle, and I would do anything for him, including becoming a terrorist. If we are successful, my uncle and I expect to make more money than I could ever imagine." Oleg switched topics abruptly. "So, Mordecai, why is a Jew involved with Muslim freedom fighters like us?"

"I knew when Sargon recruited me that it was going to be a hard sell to convince the rest of the team why it makes sense to have an Israeli on the team. So you want to know my story? I grew up in the Borough Park section of Brooklyn New York. Mine was a very strict Hasidic Jewish family. I enjoyed both math and science in school, and I seemed to have a talent for physics, and I wanted to study at a great school. My grades were first in my class and, without my parents' permission; I applied to MIT and was accepted. How was I going to tell my parents? I went to my rabbi and told him what I had done—that I wanted to leave Borough Park and see the real world. The rabbi said that he would think and pray about my problem and for me to come back in a week, and he hoped he would have an answer for me. One week later I went back to see the rabbi, hopeful that he had an answer.

"He told me that to go around my parents was a bad thing for a son to do, and, while he understood my desire to want to leave and go to MIT, he needed to make a compromise with my parents. The rabbi said that he would ask my parents to let me go to school at MIT, but upon completion of my studies I had to go to Israel and work in a job that helped the country for no fewer than four years. I would have to send 25 percent of whatever I earned to my family.

"So I agreed with Rabbi Solomon Ben Isaac, and he said that he would talk with my parents and that I should not say anything to my parents until he spoke with them. My parents came home from temple and were very angry with me for a while, but they calmed down and agreed to the rabbi's compromise. So off to MIT I went, and my life changed forever. You've heard of wine, women, and song? Well I did it all, *and* I went to class. I didn't have to worry about my parents coming to visit, so within a month I had a roommate, and she was a great lover. She taught me everything about sex. Man, what a great time—sex for breakfast, lunch, dinner, and dessert.

"I would go home for visits with my family, but I couldn't wait to get back to school. My visits home were fewer and further between, and when I didn't make it home, I would send a note, but those diminished until they stopped. In my junior year, I reached out to the Israeli embassy in Washington, DC, and told them of my commitment to the homeland. They said that they would be in touch with me in the next month or two, and sure enough, they came to MIT to visit with me. They had already checked me out with MIT, and they knew I was first in my class. They very much wanted me to come to Israel and work in their nuclear program. I agreed and asked how much I would make, and they told me, and I asked, "Can I have 25 percent to my parents in Brooklyn Heights?" They said, not a problem. My parents did come for graduation, and all of us went back to New York until it was time for me to leave to go to Israel.

"But almost from my arrival in Tel Aviv, things didn't seem right. I went to work, found a place to live, and started to meet people. I was surprised at the number of anti-Israeli people who were openly talking and spreading their antigovernment ideas in Israel. The government started to give away land that had been paid for with Jewish blood in previous wars. The United States was pressuring the government to make more and more concessions—to the point that many in Israel thought we had lost our will to survive and be an independent country. In the Occupy Los Angles movement, a public school teacher—Patricia McAllister, an Obama supporter—said, 'I think that the Zionist Jews who are running these big banks and our Federal Reserve—which is not run by the federal government—they need to be run out of this country.' Nobody, including the president, disavowed her comments. The media and the politicians didn't say a word.

"We had become the whipping boy for the United States, and nobody was sticking up for us, including us. Now, we may well have nuclear missiles aimed at us in Iran. The US doesn't think that Iran will use them against Israel. America is no longer providing Israel with nuclear fusion materials to build our own weapons. I have no love for Iran, but the United States has walked away from a sixty-year commitment to guaranteeing the protection of Israel. I fear that very soon I may have no homeland to live in. I think that Iran wants to use their nukes to make Israel uninhabitable. I will deal with that if it happens, but for now I want to make the *United States* uninhabitable." Oleg looked Mordecai right in the eyes and said, "You are one very dangerous bastard."

Chapter 47

Georgetown University Hospital

THEY WERE JUST ABOUT READY to purge the chamber and head back to headquarters when Megan's phone rang. Baker was on the line, and he told her they had found papers and another map in the house in Morristown. The map and the papers were on a plane to DC from Morristown and should land at Andrews within ten minutes. He wanted to know from Brown how soon she and her team could be back in her lab. She responded that she would dispatch Derrick to get to the lab as soon as possible. The map coming out of the chamber would be fragile, and it would take two people to roll it up.

"We are ready to purge the chamber, so by the time we clear the chamber and roll up the map, we should leave here in about an hour. Derrick will be at the lab in ten minutes, and will be set up to fume the papers. If the map is too large for our chamber, we would have to use the one here at the hospital. We are already here, and the chamber is not scheduled for use until tomorrow, so we could run the map here tonight."

Baker put her on hold, and in less than a minute he was back with her on the phone, telling her that the map was approximately two feet by three feet.

"We can handle that size paper in our lab—great."

By then Derrick had already left. The chamber was finally clear, and Penelope and Megan gently took the map out of the chamber and set it on the stretcher. Then they both noticed something they didn't expect. Clearly, the fuming process had illuminated a lot of very clear fingerprints that they could lift and try to identify, but the fuming process had illuminated something else. The chemicals had raised twenty more circles on the back of the map. It looked to both Megan and Penelope as though this map was at one time on top of another map. It was like an overhead presentation where you have material written on the transparency, and then you put another page on top of the previous page, and so on. The question was: how many maps were in the presentation?

Megan told Penelope that a new map had been found in the house in Morristown, and she wondered whether it was the map underneath, whose impression was seen on their map. They would have to wait until they got back to the lab to look at the new map to see whether it had any of the same circles that appeared on the back of their map. So they gently laid tissue paper on the face of the map and then turned it over and put on more tissue paper on it and gently began to roll it up so it could go in their container.

Their plan was to change out of the scrubs into their street clothes and, with the map tube under Browns arm; they would just walk out of the suite and then out the front door of the hospital. They finished packing the tube and changed into clothes from the bag they had brought with them, and they said good-bye to their technician friend, Barrington. He stopped them and asked how to clean out the chamber, and they said, "We use 409 and a scrub brush." Megan suggested using a lot to soak everything and then to hose it down. Barrington asked who was going to pay for it. "Send us a bill."

CHAPTER 48

Seacrest Office, CIA

JOHN LOGGED ON TO HIS classified computer and saw the e-mail from Massri; he could see that there were attachments to the e-mail. He opened the attachments in a special encrypting file; he had made up the password for the file before he opened the e-mail. Seacrest waited for the images to be converted into something he could actually see and was surprised at the plain, unassuming nature of the people in the photos. Just as Massri had said: no weapons, no side arms in view, and an office supply delivery truck was all he could see. When he got to the images of the suitcase, he had no way of knowing whether it was a bomb or a real suitcase. He decided to print out the images and hand-carry them to Baker at HS. He knew that Baker was expecting the images, and John would call him and arrange a meeting. He was hopeful that somebody could tell if the suitcase was a real bomb or at least whether the case had been used for one.

He called Baker's office but got his voice mail. He gave Baker his secure cell number and waited for the call back from him. He spent the time looking at the series of photographs and saw that the team had strapped the suitcase down and then packed all the office supplies around and over the suitcase. It was obvious that they did not want people to know what was in the truck. Seacrest said to himself that they clearly would not go to that much trouble to hide an ordinary suitcase.

He set the photos aside and went to his computer and searched for Adad Assad Business systems. He found that in fact there was such a company and that it was located on Syria, in the town of Homs. He next did a Google search, trying to find pictures of Adad Assad to see whether it was in fact the same person in the photographs that Massri had sent him. Some of the first pictures were of a much younger Assad; the picture he had was of a much older man. He kept searching and found more recent images of Assad, and as he examined them in comparison to the picture he had, he was sure it was the same man. He'd need a second verification, but he was sure that he had identified one of the five men in the photo.

Seacrest had some friends at Interpol, and even though it was late, he decided to call his friend in London, Harold Wellington, a senior agent in the terrorist section of Interpol. The phone with that funny English double ring sound rang five times and a male voice answered.

"Harold, this is Seacrest from the States. Have I awakened you? I need your help."

"No problem. Go ahead."

"I'm very concerned. We are investigating a terrorist threat to the US, and at the moment we don't have a great deal to go on. I have an asset on the ground in Syria that has sent me some photos of the people we think are the leaders of the group. I believe I have figured out who one of them is, but I can't identify the other four through our files. I would like to send the photos to you and have Interpol look at the photos and see whether you can identify them. I also have another series of photos that I will send to you, and I would like you to have them looked at by your Russian section, because I think they are photos of an old Soviet suitcase dirty bomb.

"The name of the group is the Brotherhood of the Red Nile, and we think they have at least *two* dirty bombs from the old Soviet Union." For a moment Seacrest heard nothing from Harold, then, "Sorry, old man, I'm still processing the concept that a terrorist group has two dirty bombs. Do you think they will use them against the US?"

"Based on the best information we have, we don't think in their current state they will detonate. But we do believe that in the right hands they can be upgraded and made even more effective and more stable. There are only two nuclear programs in that region: the Israelis' and the Iranians'. While I know that there is a great deal of tension in the relationship between the United States and Israel, I don't see them working with Syrian terrorists in rebuilding the bombs and using them against America.

"Because of the unknown level of development of the Iranian nuclear program, I'm not sure they could repair the dirty bombs. I have no doubt that they would like to get their hands on the two bombs to use against Israel, but I think they may hate America even more and would like the great America brought to its knees. If they can take out America, then in turn America will not be in any shape to protect Israel. So by working with the Syrian terrorists, they can attack America without attacking America in the world's eyes. Helping the terrorists is a win-win for Iran."

"How soon can you send me the pictures?"

"Do you have a secure server at your house? Give me the URL, and I'll send them immediately."

"John, let me ask you one more question: do you think America can handle an attack of two nuclear bombs?"

"I think the answer to your question is that it depends on where the bombs are set off. I can think of some places that, were they attacked with a dirty bomb, we could be crippled for decades. Or longer."

CHAPTER 49

Williams's Office after the Meeting with the President

"MARIE, HAVE YOU HEARD FROM Baker? I wanted to speak with him."

"Sir, I have left him a voice mail at his office phone and on his cell, and he has not returned my messages." Just then her phone rang, and she could see it was Baker calling on his cell phone. "Sir, I have Baker calling in on the other line. Can you hold for a moment?"

In less than ten minutes, Baker was walking into Williams's office.

Williams began in a rush. "You know that I was at the house in Springfield a few days ago, and I was told by the local sheriff that we took two bodies from the house in unmarked panel trucks that, based on the descriptions of people at the scene, looked like mobile hospitals. The locals report the teams that took out the bodies were dressed in HAZMAT suits like the other members of the HS team."

"So what is the problem, sir?"

"Well, in the after action report there is no mention of us having an evac hospital, much less two, and there is nothing in the report of two bodies being taken off site. Further, Mr. Baker, the team member count doesn't *have* four additional members.

"My question is, if these were not our team members, who were they, and where are the bodies they took out, if in fact there *were* bodies taken out? Lastly, is it possible that the people in the body bags *were* in fact Mike and Mary Ridley, after all, and they were not dead, but very much alive? Is it possible that they were taken out of the house because they are somehow connected to the Brotherhood of the Nile?"

CHAPTER 50

Sheriff Whittles Office

MAJOR RAHIMI ARRIVED AT THE Springfield sheriff's department and asked to speak with Sheriff Whittles. The receptionist called the sheriff on the intercom. Whittles walked out into the lobby, hand extended to welcome his fellow Marine, and asked whether he had eaten anything while en route. "I could use something to eat. Let's go, we'll take my car, and I know just the place."

The sheriff's car stopped in front of the Stop Sign Diner.

He said, "This is the best place in town to get a good meal at a fair price. So while you're here, this can be your office and a place to eat. Have you booked a room?"

"No, sir, I haven't had a chance."

"No problem." Whittles took out his radio and called the dispatcher and said, "We need a room for our guest Major Rahimi. Will you call Mabel at the Excelsior Hotel and get him the best in the house? Tell her we don't know what time he'll be there but to hold the room."

As they walked in, Rahimi noticed that the restaurant was spic and spam clean with white tablecloths on the table. It wasn't like most diners the Major had eaten in before; the silverware matched and the glasses on the table were spotless and the chairs had cushions. The stools at the counter were classic diner stools covered in red, but they were not ripped or faded. When he and the sheriff sat down at the table, he noticed that the flowerers were in fact real and fresh and in the same vases on all the tables—no beer or Perrier bottles.

"Now let's eat. Everything on the menu is excellent; it's all made fresh, from local stuff."

"Could I get a cup of coffee first, before we order, to help clear my head?"

"Right away." Whittles signaled to Joann that they wanted two coffees. Joann was quick; she brought over two cups and a pot, which she left on the table. The sheriff reached for some cream and sugar and passed them to Rahimi, who just took the cream.

After they had placed their order, Rahimi said, "I would like everything you know about the Ridleys in some form of chronological order for as long as you have known them. Take your time, and give me as much detail as you can. I would like to know the names of their friends, bankers, where they worked, anybody you think I should be talking to who could help me figure out who they were and possibly what happened to them. We need to find out who they are and whether they have any connection to this terrorist plot.

"I also need to ask you a question on a different subject: has the memorial service been set for Sergeant Kelly?"

"This Sunday at noon, at St. Patrick's Roman Church."

"Would it be all right for me to go to the service?"

"Did you bring your dress uniform?"

"Yes, sir, I did."

"It would be an honor, Major."

Joann brought them their food, and they both dug in and wolfed it down. After Rahimi finished, he had another cup of coffee.

The sheriff then gave him as much detail as he could, about the Ridley house, the bomb, and the pictures.

"Was the camera destroyed in the blast?"

"No, I put it in my car before the explosion."

"Then let's go get it, and let's go see that house."

In about ten minutes, they pulled through the main gates of Tall Trees and were winding their way to the house. The sheriff pulled into the driveway, such as it was, and the Major was shocked. "In all my tours of duty in Iraq and Afghanistan I have never seen such utter destruction. As you described the blast, I was expecting that parts of the house would still be standing, but this is beyond my imagination. The concrete block walls are gone; has anything been hauled away for the bomb site?"

"Only the fallout that was in the street."

The Major started to walk around the site and the sheriff saw him just shaking his head as he looked at the utter destruction. Rahimi turned to Whittles and said, "Did you see the pictures of the destruction of the Federal building in Oklahoma City? The amount of explosives used here was in the same league as Oklahoma City. One has to wonder why so many explosives were used to destroy this house."

"I think they wanted no trace of anything in the house, including the map."

"You lost a man in saving the map, and his work may well have saved millions of Americans' lives. Was there something else we haven't seen besides the map? Maybe the pictures on the camera will give us a clue as to what else they didn't want us to see. Let's head to your office. I want to see those pictures."

Chapter 51

Megan Brown's Forensic Lab

EGAN AND PENELOPE RETURNED TO the lab, where Derrick had already started fuming the papers from the Morristown house and was waiting for the fingerprint search file to see whether it could find a match. The large light table in the center of the main room had the map from the Ridley House, and it was on the table with the backside up, so the circles could be seen. It was not possible to tell at first glance whether it was the same style of map that appeared on the front.

"What I can figure out is there may have been a series of maps on top of each other, almost as if it was part of a flip-chart presentation or was the impression on the map of a set of target cities, and the map we have was a second map targeting different cities in a different attack.

"If we shoot a digital image of the front and back of our map, we can then superimpose the back on the front and see what cities are circled. Perhaps we can see if we can find a link to the new cities, and that may give us something to look for on the original map that connects those cities."

The team started lifting the fingerprints that had been raised on the map front and back using East Shore's "hyperladder" fingerprint matcher. The Shore's systems would compare data from the input search print against all appropriate records in the database to determine whether a probable match existed, so, as they fed the prints into the machine, it automatically started looking for matches.

The problem was that they had a great number of prints to run and only one machine. Brown called Baker to tell him of their discoveries and that she wanted Baker to contact FBI and see whether they could help them by running some of the images they had. They could scan the images they had and send them to the FBI, which could run them for HS and send back the identifications.

She got through to Baker, who was in a meeting with Williams, and she told both of them what she had seen already. Williams told her that he would call FBI Director Ronald Wilson himself and get the permission to run the files.

Brown said, "As we review all the paperwork for the New Jersey house, my guess is that we will need more help and a different skill level, but we are just not far enough along in uncovering what all the information we have will mean to us."

Williams hung up and asked Baker, "Have you heard anything from Rahimi in Springfield?"

"Rahimi checked in, and he went to the Ridley house, and it was total devastation. The Major said he was on his way to the sheriff's office to look at the photographs the sheriff took before the house blew apart."

"Get a message to the Major and tell him that you want him to send the sheriff's pictures to Brown right away."

Back in the lab, seconds after Brown hung up with Williams and Baker, she heard a beep on the fingerprint search machine, and the image on the screen was Michael Ridley's, only the name was not.

"Oh no," she said, reading the name.

CHAPTER 52

The Van on the Road to Khanik, the Border Crossing to Iraq

ADAD AND JAIARI HAD BEEN on the road for ten hours with just one stop for gas and food. They knew that they were about an hour away from Khanik, Syria, and the border with Iraq. This was a checkpoint that Assad's drivers and on occasion he himself had used to cross over the border and deliver supplies. He did not expect any trouble at the checkpoint. So he said to Jaiari, "How do you think we should use the bombs?"

"When I looked at the al-Qaida attacks, they seemed to be more show that substance. The attack on the warship *Cole* on October 12, 2000, killed seventeen and wounded thirty-seven but did nothing to change the attitude of Americans about the threat from al-Qaida; in fact killing American servicemen galvanized the American will. The one thing that all the attacks had in common, regardless of whether they were in the United States or outside the US was that they were all small in scale. Yes, the World Trade Center bombings brought down the towers and nearly three thousand people were killed, but in a city like New York, three thousand is nothing. The jobs that were created to rebuild the site were more than the three thousand who lost their lives; it spurred a building boom at ground zero. Al-Qaeda sent their people on the planes to their deaths, for its objective they did so by convincing them that they would find ten thousand virgins waiting for them; in the United States they set up a victims fund and paid out over $7 billion dollars to the survivors.

"Clearly America places a higher value on life than we do. Because of this value for life, we must do something that will change the lives of millions of Americans for at least a generation. I have been thinking about what we could do with one bomb that could seriously impact America as a country. I have been reading about brownouts and total blackouts because of a shortage of electrical power. America can't put electricity in a boat in Saudi Arabia and ship it across the ocean and run its power plants. Electricity is vital to everything that runs in America. American homes use electricity to run everything from TVs to computers, clocks, cars, trucks, refrigeration, and probably a million other things.

"What would happen if one morning Americans woke up, and they went to brush their teeth in the bathroom, and there was no power, and the water didn't flow? They would go then into the kitchen, and there would be water on the floor from the thawing of things in the freezer. Suppose they looked out their windows, and none of the traffic lights were working? All the tall buildings in downtown had all the lights off; in fact the only lights on in the whole city we the emergency lights that were battery-operated or run off backup generators.

"So they'd go over to the TV to turn it on, except it doesn't turn on because there is no electrical power. They'd pull out their radios, looking for an emergency broadcast, but the radio station has no power to broadcast the message. They'd gone to bed, and everything was fine; they wake up, and nothing, I mean *nothing*, runs.

"Nobody would have a place to go to work; you couldn't pay for anything because the stores couldn't open the cash registers or safes. Banks would have money locked in vaults that couldn't be opened because they had timer locks, and the clocks would have stopped. The list could go on and on of all the things that wouldn't work. Without refrigeration, food would start to spoil, and within a week or so food would be in a shortage. Waste would pile up because no trucks could haul it to the processing plants or landfills. America would come to a standstill, and nothing would happen, progress would stop, and the American quality of life would disappear.

"And then the Brotherhood of the Nile would say to the world, 'If you help America with aid, you are next.' No doubt the borders to Mexico and Canada would be shut to try to prevent large numbers of Americans from leaving America to go to their neighboring countries. Some people with their own boats and planes would leave and go to other countries, but unless they had a lot of cash with them or in overseas accounts, they would have no way to pay for anything. All the people, mostly the elderly, who need medicines or oxygen to breathe would have no way to get to the drugstores and would run out of drugs; within a month or two the death rate would climb, but embalmers would have no supplies and no way to collect the corpses.

"The bodies would go uncollected and the smells would fill the air and disease would spread like wildfire. All this happened because one morning when you threw the switch, nothing happened. This is why electricity is the key to our success: stop the flow of electricity, and you stop America."

All this time, Adad sat with his eyes on the road, but he could paint the pictures in his mind as Jaiari was explaining his plan. The cold-hearted way he told the plan scared Adad for while he was working on his own plan, it was not of the magnitude of Jaiari plan. Adad was not ready to discuss how Jaiari was going to carry out the plan; he needed to begin to digest the magnitude of the devastation that was going to take place in America, and he was beginning to wonder whether he really understood what he had signed on for when he had joined the Brotherhood.

CHAPTER 53

Williams's House

IT WAS A COMFORTABLY WARM evening by the time Frank and Ellen sat down to dinner outside on the patio. Ellen had made a nice salad, and Frank did the steaks medium on the grill, and they had some sautéed mushrooms and microwaved potatoes. Frank had a bottle of Chardonnay in the fridge; normally they would have had a red, but they had felt like a white. Ellen had stopped by their favorite bakery in Georgetown, Patisserie Poupon, which was famous for their croissants. While she was waiting in line, she saw some strawberry tarts, so she bought four of them as a surprise dessert for Frank.

They sat and enjoyed their meal and each other's company. Frank and Ellen could be great conversationalists when dining with friends or business acquaintances, but when they were alone, small talk was fine. They finished their meal, cleaned up the dishes, and went back out to the porch to finish their wine.

Ellen noticed that Frank had been unusually quiet for the last few days, and she knew that something serious was on his mind. Ellen also knew that when Frank was ready to talk, he would. She was not going to rush him; she would wait for him to make the first move, as she had always done in the past.

Frank sat down next to her and put his arm around her, saying, "Ellen, I need to tell you some things, but I'm not sure I know all the words to tell you so you will understand."

"Why don't you start at the beginning, and maybe the words will come to you?"

"Do you remember the other night when I was in the den on the phone?"

"That was the day you got back from your trip to—I don't think you told me where you were?"

"I was in Springfield, Texas, working on a possible terrorist threat. There was a house in Springfield that I went to see because we thought it was a place where terrorists were hiding a dirty bomb. We didn't find the bomb, but we did find the case the bomb was transported in, into the United States.

"That night we were having dinner at 1789, and I got a message. It was a video from a local newscast in Springfield that showed the house destroyed. A local sergeant from the sheriff's department was virtually disintegrated by the bomb. What is bothering me is I never met the young man, yet I feel so depressed by his death. He is the first person to die in America at the hands of a terrorist since 9-11.

"The people we are dealing with are very bad people. We don't know very much about them, which makes it even harder to figure out what could happen. Ellen, we think they may have at least two dirty bombs in the US; I have heard of them, but I don't know much about them. My fear is that this terrorist group has these bombs and that they intend to use them against the United States. We believe they are called the Brotherhood of the Red Nile, and they were formed in Syria. They are not associated with Al-Qaeda. We have a number of people working on this case in many specialties, but at the same time we are trying to keep a lid on this because if it got out that there were terrorists in the United States with nuclear bombs, who knows the panic that could spread."

Frank got up and walked around, clearly thinking.

Ellen straightened up on the settee and said, "What can we do? We live in Washington, DC, and this region would be a likely target, so shouldn't we leave and go somewhere out of the country? Look, Frank, we have been married for almost twenty-five years; both of us have served the government for almost all of our working lives, and you especially have given a great deal for your country. We have saved some money, so why not take early retirement and get out of America for a while until this problem sorts itself out?" Ellen was now shaking and starting to cry.

Frank had never seen her act this way before; he went over to her and put his arms around her. He could tell that for the first time in their relationship she was terrified, and he wondered whether he had made a mistake in sharing with her what was going on.

She said, "I would rather run away to a deserted island and live a meager life than die in DC alone without you. We don't need a lot to make us happy."

Frank sighed. Holding her close, he said, "As long as it is in my power to protect you and our country, I have to do everything I can. I think I understand your fear, but as much as I would like to lie on the beach and look at your naked body—and believe me, I would—I have to try and not have anybody, including you, living in fear." He took his hand and pressed it against her breast, and she relaxed.

Soon she straightened up and said, "Enough of this for tonight; let's go upstairs and roll around in the sack at least we can still do that. And if you're lucky, you might just get closer than we are now."

So they walked into the house, turned off the lights, and headed up the stairs. As they climbed the steps, Frank watched Ellen walk up the stairs, her hips swinging back and forth. It was a great view, but no matter how great, he couldn't help but think about all the things he hadn't even told her yet.

CHAPTER 54

Brotherhood Bomb Center

SARGON HAD BROUGHT MORDECAI AND Oleg together to start them talking about their idea of an attack while they were waiting to hear from Iran what was happening to the bomb. Sargon and Mordecai discussed a list of items that needed to be brought into the warehouse that could be used to repair the bomb they had in their possession.

Sargon had left the building to start making arrangements for the materials that Mordecai would need to upgrade the bomb. Oleg asked, "What do you think they will do to the bomb?"

"My guess is they will replace the timer because it was mercury-based. Mercury is very toxic and was by now eating its way through the casing. I think they will replace it with a digital timer that could, if we wanted, be set off by a cell phone. The reason it is called a dirty bomb is that the gas from the heat of the explosion propels whatever is around into the air. The explosion makes the particles radioactive because the radioactive material sticks to the exploding material. Dirty bombs have mushroom cloud–like explosions, but they are smaller, so the particles that are contaminated by the radioactive material don't go as high in the air and therefore return much quicker, and they coat everything with the dirty, radioactive material.

"I think the best way to think about them is smaller versions of the bigger bombs. My guess is they will take out the old TNT that becomes more and more unstable with age and replace it with a more powerful explosive. I do think it might be helpful to you if I demonstrate how they work."

"Are you going to explode a dirty bomb here?" Oleg asked.

Mordecai responded, "Not a real bomb, but a simulation. Let's go outside, and I'll show you what I mean."

They went outside and Mordecai said, "I have two firecrackers that are the same in power. I want you to take that shovel over there and out into the middle of the parking lot. I want you to build a mound of sand out of ten shovels of sand. Next we will take the same ten shovels of sand and pile it next to the building.

"After that is done, I will use a stick and bore a hole in about the same spot in both piles of sand, and we will photograph with our phone both explosions and then we can download them on our computer to compare the difference."

Mordecai already knew the difference, but by running and recording his experiment, he could show the team members how effective his idea could be, and perhaps it would persuade them to use it. "Let's put some different-colored food coloring on the sand so we can see the patterns of its dispersal. The sand in the parking lot will be tinted red, and the sand by the white wall will be tinted dark green."

It took them about two hours to get everything set up.

"You take the pictures, and I'll light the firecrackers, so let me know when you are ready."

"Where is the best position to stand for the parking lot detonation?"

"We want to get a good view of the dispersal, so look in your phone and walk back until the pile of sand takes up only half the frame." After what seemed like forever, the firecracker exploded and sent sand flying in all directions. The original pile of ten shovelfuls of sand made a pile about three feet in diameter and two feet high. After the explosion, the pile was flat, and Oleg estimated that it spread out to about eight feet in diameter.

Oleg was impressed at how the small firecracker moved so much sand, and he was expecting similar results with the second blast.

Oleg moved over to shoot the second explosion and did his best to make sure he had the same framed image before the blast. He was ready, and that was the signal for Mordecai to light the fuse. He ran in and lit the fuse and then quickly joined Oleg at the camera. Again, it seemed like forever; the second firecracker finally went off, but to Oleg's surprise a great deal of the sand was stuck to the wall in a wide pattern. The wall was covered, at least ten feet wide and eight feet tall, with little dark-green dots.

"Now, suppose that each green dot was radioactive, and it was stuck, if not welded, to the wall because of the heat from the explosion? This entire wall is now radioactive and it could kill you if you get too close, say for the next twenty-five to fifty years. On the other hand, if you go back to the first explosion you will see that all the sand is on the ground and could easily be cleaned up by people in HAZMAT suits. It may take time for the area in the parking lot to cool down to be used again, but it will happen much sooner than the area on the wall."

"If the buildings around the blast and the area around the building for several miles could be contaminated, then the entire area would be useless for many years, as with the Chernobyl accident in Russia a number of years back, is that correct?"

"In a way yes, you are correct. The events are significantly different, but the outcomes would be similar."

"So if the building or plant or whatever was important to the livelihood of America, and after the explosion, the building and whatever was inside it would be worthless to America, then America would be crippled for perhaps generations?"

"More than one generation, many generation will be affected Oleg. All we have to do is decide which building, covered with radioactive dust, could do the most damage to America."

CHAPTER 55

Springfield Sheriff Whittles Office

THE SHERIFF AND MAJOR RAHIMI were leaving Tall Trees and the Ridley house on their way to the sheriff's office to look at the pictures Whittles had taken of the Ridley house just before it exploded. "When I took these," he said, "I was looking for any clue to what had happened to Mike and Mary Ridley, and I remember saying to one of my deputies, 'Something doesn't look right. I have not had a chance to look at the pictures, with everything else going on, so I'll be interested in seeing what kind of photographer I am."

They arrived at the station and the sheriff parked in his space, which was a distance from the front door of the station.

"Why is your parking space not near the front door?"

"Well it used to be, but I moved it because if somebody didn't like the outcome inside the building, somehow my car would get keyed and sometimes the side mirror would disappear, so it's less wear and tear on my car to park it out of direct contact with the public."

They walked into the lobby and said hello to the receptionist and headed to Whittles office. The sheriff opened his safe and took out the camera and set it on his desk. He turned on his computer, and when it came up, he removed the flash memory card from the camera and loaded it into the slot on his computer. In just a moment, images appeared on the screen. He scrolled down and saw the first image of the Ridley house and then he changed the images to four on a page. The sheriff and the Major sat there and went through the images until they came to the end, and the sheriff started over again but paused. "Does anything strike you about the pictures?"

"Mary must have been a very neat housekeeper. If Mike and Mary were murdered in the house, why is there no sign of a murder?"

"I was in every room in the house, and I took photos of all the rooms, and so far I can't find any sign of a crime." Just as the sheriff was finishing his sentence, the Major's phone rang, and it was Baker.

"This is my office. I need to take this call."

"Go ahead. I'll just go get a soda. Do you want anything?"

"Anything with caffeine, thank you."

Rahimi answered Baker's call. "I'm in the sheriff's office, and we just started going over the interior shots he took of the Ridley house."

"I just met with Williams; he was reviewing the after-action report of the team that searched the Ridley grounds and house. The report doesn't mention the two-medevac vans, and the team member count does not account for the four people going into the house with two stretchers. There is no mention of bodies being removed from the house by our team.

"The report from the neighbors, including John Bowman, who was at the house, did not mention any markings on the two vans. So the secretary is questioning whether the Ridleys were killed. If so, by whom, and if they were, then where are their bodies?"

The Major was hanging up his phone just as Whittles was coming through the door with the sodas. Omid had just talked with his office, and he had gotten a message from the undersecretary with information he was told it was OK to share with the sheriff. "Before we get back to the pictures, let me ask you: who around here would have vans with all that sophisticated medical equipment and not be EMS or fire department?"

"Well, let me think for a moment. The only place that I can think of that would have portable emergency room would be down the road in Texas City."

"What is there that would command two of these vans?"

The sheriff responded, "I guess you don't know much about the oil business; Texas City is the home of several oil refineries and, in fact, the largest refinery in the United State—the BP Refinery of Texas City. You see, Texas City is a small town, but mighty important in that about 25 percent of all the oil, natural gas, and finished product is processed and shipped in the pipelines that are in the ground that run through Texas City. These pipelines receive and send energy all over the United States. Because they are so important, they have the best firefighting equipment and medical equipment money can buy.

"I know the person in charge of the emergency medical in Texas City; let me put in a call and see if any of their EMS vans were unaccounted for earlier in the week."

"Sheriff, could you place that call before we get back to the pictures? I think Washington would very much like to know the answer to that question. If they were missing, then finding out who took them could possibly lead us to the Ridleys and the terrorists."

The sheriff made the call.

CHAPTER 56

Ms. Brown's Forensic Lab

THE PICTURE ON THE FINGERPRINT analyzer was that of Michael Ridley, but the name under the picture was Al Ishtar Hamwi. It said that Ishtar's last known address was in Damascus, Syria, yet Michael Ridley had been in the United States all his life. Brown asked her team to run the print again to see what the machine said about whom it belonged to. About twenty minutes later the machine chimed, and the picture was the same, but this time the name was Michael Ridley—last known address, Springfield, Texas.

Derrick said, "We must have a set of identical twins. The fingerprints of identical twins can look the same, but finer review will reveal the subtle differences between the two."

Megan asked, "Do we have a file on the Ridley family?"

Penelope said, "We don't have much of a file on the family or Michael; maybe we should contact Major Rahimi and see what he can find out from the people in Springfield."

Brown agreed and asked Penelope to contact Baker and get Major Rahimi's cell phone number.

Penelope called Baker, and he answered on the second ring.

"Agent Baker, this Penelope Smyth, of Megan Brown's forensic lab, and I need to ask you a question. You know that we have been working on the map from the basement of the Ridley house looking for fingerprints and DNA? We have identified an index fingerprint that originally came through the analyzer as belonging to Al Ishtar Hamwi, a Syrian living in Damascus. What is interesting is that the picture that came with the prints is a dead ringer for Michael Ridley. We thought there must be a mistake, so we ran it again, and this time the picture was the same, but the name was Michael Ridley. All we can deduce is that the two boys are identical twins. We need Major Rahimi to try to find out whether Michael Ridley is the natural-born son of Mike and Mary Ridley, or whether he was adopted."

I wonder which one didn't show at UC Berkeley: Mike or Ishtar Baker, he thought to himself. Baker came back on the line with Major Rahimi number. "I will send him a text message to expect your call."

Penelope hung up and immediately dialed the Major's cell phone, and Rahimi picked it up on the third ring. Smyth introduced herself, and Rahimi said, "I'm a little busy right now; is this important?"

"Sir, it is very important, but I'll be brief. We found fingerprints on the map from the Ridley basement and they match *two* people. It appears that Michael Ridley and Al Ishtar Hamwi are identical twins. We need you to find out whether Mike and Mary Ridley adopted Michael Ridley. If he was adopted, we are looking for when and where the adoption took place. We need to know how long the family has lived in Springfield and whether anybody knows where they lived before they came to Springfield. Anything you can find out for us would be of great help in trying to find out where the whole Ridley family is and what connection, if any, they might have to the Brotherhood of the Nile."

In a much friendlier voice, Rahimi said, "I'm with the sheriff right now. I'll see what he knows and get back to you. What can you tell me about Hamwi?"

"I can tell you that the last known address for him was Damascus, and he was classified by Interpol and the Syrian secret police, Mukhabarat, as a dissident college student who was working with the rebels to overthrow the government."

"Can you pull up his passport records to see whether a person with that name has ever come to the United States and if so, when and how long he stayed and where he went after he left the US?"

"Sir, that will take some time, but I think we can get that information."

"Call me whenever you get the information any time, night or day, and when I have more information on the family, I'll call you. Deal?"

"Deal."

Smyth told Brown about the conversation with Rahimi, and Brown told her to get to work retrieving the information for Rahimi. First, she wanted to know whether anybody using the name Al Ishtar Hamwi had entered the United States in the last two years. Surprisingly, the computer responded that someone by that name had entered the United States in San Francisco and indicated that his destination was Berkeley, California. As for the reason for the visit, he said he was going to meet his brother.

Brown then asked, "Has he left the country since?"

CHAPTER 57

Seacrest, CIA, Langley, Virginia

Seacrest was meeting with Baker at 2:00 p.m. at the base of the Washington Monument to hand over the photos his agent had taken on the ground of the van and the five people around at the site. While he was waiting to get through to Baker, he sent pictures of the five men to his friend at Interpol in London, Harold Wellington. He was hopeful that Wellington would get back to him before his meeting with Baker.

Seacrest would have to leave by 1:00 p.m. in order to make his meeting with Baker; it was now 12:00, and he would wait until 12:30. If Harold did not call, he would call him at 12:30. He had been on the phone with the satellite control center and had asked whether they had a bird in the sky over the coordinates he gave them. He described the van to them because, if they spotted it, he wanted them to follow it. He had not heard back from the satellite control center; he was batting and not very well, for he had two strikes.

He sat down waiting for phone calls and started to review the images of Adad Al Assad again. He was looking at one of most recent pictures, and he took out his magnifying glass to get a closer look at one of the men in the background. He loaded that photo on a split screen image of the photo on the ground, and he was sure it was the same person in both photos. There was a list of names of the people in the picture, and in the back row was someone named Mohamed el Sargon. The clock on his desk said it was 12:28, and he was just going to search Sargon's name on his computer when his phone rang; the caller ID said Interpol. He picked up the phone and said "Seacrest here."

"It's Wellington. Are you there, old boy? I ran the pictures of the people you asked about, and nothing turns up as bad guys, but we did get a hit on an Adad Al Assad, not for any unsavory activities, but as someone who is building a serious business presence in the Middle East.

"As for the photo of the suitcase, our Russian section says that it is most definitely the size and look of an old Soviet suitcase dirty bomb. The section chief says he has not seen one of those in fifteen years. He knew some were missing at the breakup of the Soviet Union, but nobody knows for sure where they disappeared.

"There was a rumor a number of years ago that Viktor Antipova, the Russian oil billionaire, had possession of the bombs at the end of the Cold War and sold some of them to terrorist groups, which gave him the money to start his oil business. The section chief said that if they were still around today, they would be very unstable. You see, old boy, over time the compounds in the sticks of explosives begin to separate. When they were new, they were very stable, and it took a detonator cap and high voltage to get the sticks to explode, but after all these years, a simple jar could set it off. I wouldn't want to drive around in a truck with this stuff in the back because if you hit a big pothole, you could be in for it.

"I want to send you a photo and a name; let me know if you have any information on him."

"Right-o. I'll look forward to trying to be of some assistance."

Just as Seacrest was hanging up with Wellington, he got another call; this one was from the navigation office. They told Seacrest that they had been over the site just as a random search two days ago, and the truck was there. They looked at the morning pass by the bird, and the van was still there. In their afternoon flyover it was gone. "We have some overlap of birds that are covering the Middle East, and the next satellite caught the truck heading north to the Turkish border. At that point we stopped watching. Sir, do you want us to try to reacquire the image of the van and track it?"

"You're reading my mind. Yes, I want you to follow this van. We believe it is heading toward Iran, but we can't be sure. Please keep me posted when you reacquire the van, and plot its direction as best you can."

It was fast approaching 1:00 p.m., his departure time. If he was going to take his car, he could work a little later and take the DC Metro very close to the monument. He wanted to spend some time on the face in the picture with Adad—Mr. Sargon. First, he did a Google search, and nothing showed up under Mohamed el Sargon. Next, he had an Internet connection to the Syrian internal security agency. He knew that this agency had gone through a significant amount of change, and he didn't know whether the database was still live or not. Seacrest decided to send a ping to see whether the system was running.

A ping was like a knock on the door; if nobody answered, then there was probably nobody home. On the other hand, if the ping was responded to with an ID and password request, then at least the system was still there. Seacrest looked at his watch; he really needed to go, but he decided to wait one more minute before leaving.

Time was up: he had to leave to meet Baker.

And just after he shut the door of his office and headed to the elevator, the very second he touched the elevator call button, *Ping* went his computer, requesting his ID and password.

CHAPTER 58

Sheriff Whittles Office

MAJOR RAHIMI TURNED TO THE sheriff and said, "This thing just keeps getting more and more bizarre."

"What's bizarre?"

"The map that you rescued from the basement had fingerprints all over it, which doesn't seem so unusual, but one of the fingerprints on the map was that of Michael Ridley."

"Well, I'm not really that surprised; I expected that someone in the Ridley family had to be involved. It was the Ridley house, after all, so it would seem logical that you would find Ridley family prints."

"I agree with that, but here is the bizarre twist: when our forensic lab ran the prints, the match came back with a person named Al Ishtar Hamwi. Brown, whom you met when she came to collect the map, said there must be a mistake. And when the lab ran it again, this time Michael Ridley's picture and name came up with the match. The lab ran it a third and fourth time, and every other time it came up as either Michael or Ishtar. We are dealing with a set of identical twins.

"And wait until you hear this. The lab did a Homeland Security and Transportation Safety Administration (TSA) database search for the name of Al Ishtar Hamwi, and they got a match. Apparently, Ishtar entered the United States at San Francisco Airport, and when asked for the purpose of his visit, he said that it was to visit his brother. And when asked where his brother lived, he said at the University of California at Berkeley. One more search as to when he arrived in the US showed July two years ago. The office did one more search, and the question was when did he leave the country? The response was that he had not left as of yet. So, Sheriff, how long have you known Michael Ridley?"

"I've been here for fifteen years, and I would guess he was three or four when I arrived? Would you call back and ask your lab to go back to their computer databases and see whether they can find Michael Ridley? Did he leave the country? And if he did go, where did he go? When did he return? Major, if we are dealing with identical twins, they could be using each other's passports."

"I'll call right now, if you don't mind." Major Rahimi pulled out his cell phone and called Penelope Smyth's phone number; it rang several times and just when it was ready to go to voice mail, she answered the phone. The Major explained quickly. "We need you to make a second search for Michael Ridley. Does he have a passport? Has he used it and if so when, and where did he go, and has he returned? We may have a case of two brothers freely using each other's identities. Let me know as soon as you can what you find out."

Rahimi turned to Whittles. "It appears to me that Ishtar arrived in California just about the time Michael Ridley was to start going to UC Berkeley. We know that the admissions office at the school told both of us that Michael had been enrolled but never showed up to classes. So, until my office calls back, we can't do anything concerning Michael. Let's look at the photographs."

The sheriff powered up his computer, and the lot of photos that related to the Ridley house were small thumbnails—too small to see anything. The sheriff clicked on the first photo in the series, and it popped onto the large computer screen. "I want to take you quickly through the pictures because

I want to get your overall impression. I won't tell you mine until after you have seen them, and we can compare impressions."

In all there were about fifty images, and the sheriff set them on a slide show of about ten seconds each; they both watched the screen and didn't say a word until the presentation was over. "Well, Major, tell me what you saw in the images."

"The first impression was that it was not a crime scene; nothing seemed to be out of place, no sign of a struggle."

Whittles agreed with the Major's observation. "What else?"

"This is going to sound strange, but the only way I can describe what I saw was that it looked like it was staged, like for a home magazine; it didn't look like anybody lived there."

The sheriff nodded excitedly, and just then the Major's cell phone rang. It was Penelope.

"Well, Major, tell the sheriff he needs to come and work here; he has had good instincts. We ran the search you asked for, and sure enough, Michael Ridley has a passport, and he left from San Francisco airport just about eighteen months ago and has not returned. He said that he was headed to Amman, Jordan, to visit family."

"So on the surface it appears that Michael has family in the Middle East. Amman isn't that far to the Syrian border. The question is: which Michael is using that passport?"

CHAPTER 59

On the Way to ZanJan, Iraq

JAIARI AND ADAD HAD CLEARED the border crossing; in fact, one of the guards recognized Adad and waved him through without checking anything. After about ten minutes both men breathed a sigh of relief; now they could make their way to ZanJan and good food, a shower, and a good night's sleep.

After a while, Jaiari turned to Adad and said, "I gave you my idea; now it's your turn."

"Well, I'm a successful businessman selling hardware, software, and office supplies all over the Middle East. It took me many years to build my business, but it is mine. I have expanded this business to include business development; I help startups find money and talent to grow their businesses. One of the problems in every country around the world is Internet security. Over the last few years in the United States, just as one example, tens of millions of customer account files have been hacked.

"According to a recent report, identity theft is the No. 1 crime in America and has been for the seventh year in a row. Typically, an identity is stolen or used fraudulently every three seconds. Americans spend billions of dollars a year trying to fix identify theft problems. If I wanted to attack America, I would go after the Internet. There is a new data storage concept called the cloud. Instead of storing your data on your own local server, you store it on somebody else's server. You can even store operating software in the cloud. If we said that, hypothetically, you or your company stores all of your data on the cloud and the operating software in the cloud, you are totally dependent of the reliability of the cloud to get access to your systems or your data. And the technology is changing so fast that the expense of keeping up can be prohibitive, except for only the largest companies. The demand for storage is growing exponentially. Two years ago Facebook had ten thousand servers, and they just recently said they are now up to thirty thousand.

"If we can knock out two Major data storage farms, perhaps like the one in Chicago, we can shut down the Internet. Let's use the example of both the Microsoft storage farm in Chicago and the Hewlett Packard facilities in San Antonio. We know that the Chicago operation has at least 300,000 servers on site, and, as a matter of fact, it takes three electric substations to power that operation.

"While currently in America they have over seven thousand server farms to process the data, a new approach is developing quickly. In comes the cloud. The cloud allows customers to store their data on a cloud system. Hewlett Packard, the largest computer maker in the world, is concentrating all of its cloud operations by replacing eighty-five data centers across the world, with six in the US. I think that sever farms will get larger and larger, and smaller ones will be closed. The fact that Hewlett Packard is consolidating eighty-five centers into six is proof of my concept of concentration.

"One dirty bomb at the Microsoft facility will take out the power substations and contaminate the substations, and access to the 300,000 servers will be shut down. At the same time, we use the other bomb at the HP data center in San Antonio, and we shut down one site of the HP data storage. With the fallout from the dirty bomb, you could not change out any of the servers in either location, and, while it might be true that some of the capacity could be transferred to some of the other centers, trying to move all the data would prove to be impossible, because they would have no power.

"Once the power substations are shut down, you have effectively shut down 300,000 servers for the Internet because no power means you can't run the servers, so you can't transfer the data to other centers. The contamination will prohibit working on the substation perhaps for many years. So think about the chain reaction as being like one of those fantastic domino puzzles: you knock over the first one and the momentum takes out the rest. Suppose you were a business that stored all your client files on the center in Chicago, and you come in the next morning, and you turn on your computer to do business, and nothing is there. You check more and more of the computers and—nothing. You call your IT guy, and he says the whole system is down; he tells you that he has tried to reach the data center, but nobody answers the phone. This same situation is happening all over the Internet with businesses that have not got computing capability.

"All across the United States, more and more dominoes are falling at a faster and faster pace. Thousands if not tens of thousands of businesses across the United States are frozen at the end of the first day. The dominoes are falling at a faster and wider rate on day two when other companies find they can't contact their clients at their satellite offices or factories. Banks, insurance companies, capital markets can't open and process transactions because they can't clear transactions. UPS and FedEx can't fly their planes because the programs that would build their flight plans don't work; the software is in the data center cloud.

"The government will not be able to run, and no planes or missiles could be launched or tracked. Not only will the federal government not be able to function, but also all the state and local government will not be able to provide services for the citizens of America. The impact would be devastating: think about taking the computer out of a government, business, school, or home. How do you think America could function? We could spend the rest of our journey talking about all the possibilities of the impact of using our two bombs. One other thought about the loss of hundreds of thousands of servers is that the remaining part of the Internet will eventually collapse under the weight of the missing capacity.

"If we use our two dirty bombs correctly, we could close down the

Internet in the USA. When the last domino falls, we will have shut down the Internet. If we can shut down the Internet, we shut down America."

Jaiari was quiet the entire time Adad was talking. He wondered about all the things that could happen if Assad's idea worked. "I love the concept. Initially a few people who are around the sites die when the bombs go off, but the real devastation to America comes days, months, and years later. I want to shut down America. How long to ZanJan?"

CHAPTER 60

Base of the Washington Monument

SEACREST GOT ON THE WASHINGTON, DC, Metro and took the Red Line at the Van Ness station and took the subway to the Metro Center, where he switched to the Blue Line and got off at 15th and Constitution. There was a very long and very high escalator to the street, and he could see the Washington Monument growing in height as the escalator got closer and closer. When he reached the top, John started walking toward the benches around the base, hoping to see Baker. As he came up a small rise, he saw Baker pacing back and forth because he was late.

Seacrest apologized for being late. Baker acknowledged that and suggested that they start walking, just in case either of them was followed.

"So, John, I understand you have some pictures for me of who the leadership of the Brotherhood might be in Syria."

Seacrest is taken aback at the last comment—at least the Syria part. "Do you think there might be leadership in the United States, Ted?"

"For now we are assuming that there is a team here in the United States. Williams was at the Ridley house in Springfield and was told by neighbors that four people, dressed in HAZMAT suits, arrived in unmarked hospital vans and took two bodies out of the house. The after-action report said nothing about two emergency hospital vans being on the equipment list, and the four people with the EMS vans were not on the duty roster. We have a lead as to where the vans came from, and we're checking it out now."

They walked down 15th street to Constitution Avenue, a wide, tree-lined thoroughfare in the heart of Washington. At the intersection, they turned left and saw a series of benches set back in the hedge for some privacy. They sat down and Seacrest pulled out some of the photographs to share with Baker. Seacrest showed Baker the image of Adad Assad, along with images he had downloaded from the Internet to help Seacrest identify Adad; Baker agreed that they looked like the same person. Based on the images taken, Seacrest believed that the person in the photo was the leader of the group—at least the group in Syria.

"The US now has E-Verifying, a photo-matching process designed to detect instances where an undocumented worker—or perhaps a terrorist—has obtained or created a fake immigration document by pasting (or otherwise manipulating) his/her photograph on a real document belonging to someone else to enter the United States."

"Do you know if any other countries have similar passport photo identification processes in place? If they did, then we could try to see whether the images we have can be identified through their databases."

Seacrest responded that he would contact Wellington to see what he could find out.

"What else are you trying to do to try to identify the other people in the photo?"

Seacrest said he had sent a message to the secret police in Syria, but he had not heard back from them before he left to come here. He wasn't sure that the secret police there still existed, or if it did, that anybody was working in the office. Other than that, he wasn't sure there was any way to identify the people in the photo.

"Is it possible that the reason we can't find anything on these potential terrorists is that, until this point in time, they were not terrorists? Maybe, just maybe, these people are a new breed of terrorists. This generation of terrorists wasn't trained in camps, living on hardtack and water, but rather are college-trained zealots." Baker pointed to the photo. "Look at the clothes in these photos. They're clean, well-dressed, and well-groomed men; these are middle-class terrorists."

"If the organization is being taken over by leaders who care more about the culture of the past than military actions, attacks, and the like, we could be dealing with some of the best and brightest terrorists in the world. I believe that it will be more important to them to make bigger-picture attacks than fire a bunch of bullets and see who we hit."

"Should I have our asset on the ground explore the possibility of taking more pictures? If this is the hot spot, we need all the surveillance we can get. I have talked to the bird managers, and they will reroute the birds to give me as much time over the site as they can. We have our other birds in the area trying to find the Assad Office Supply van, but again, no luck yet."

Just as Baker wanted to ask Seacrest another question, Seacrest cell phone rang; the call was from Langley, from the office of flight operations. He answered the phone, and a voice on the other end asked whether it was he and for the password. Seacrest said the password —"nine eleven forever." The voice says, "Thank you, sir, we wanted to let you know something interesting that we've discovered."

Chapter 61

Sheriff Whittles Office

R AHIMI HUNG UP THE PHONE and continued his conversation with Whittles about the Ridley family. "Based on the fingerprints, we strongly believe that Michael Ridley is from the Middle East and that he has a twin brother. We are not sure who got on the plane to Jordan, and we don't know whether Ishtar or Michael is the one in the United States."

Just as they were starting to get into some serious discussions, the sheriff's phone rang, and it was the receptionist; she said that the Texas City refinery fire and rescue department was on the line and wanted to know whether he wanted to take the call or call them back. She put the call through.

"This is Randy Martin for the RFR team; the emergency trucks are taken out on a regular basis for test runs. I checked the logbook for two of the four mobile hospital units, and they were out on a test run the night in question. We make test runs every so often just to make sure everything is in tip-top shape. Sheriff, I don't know whether or not you have rules in your department as to how equipment should be stored, but we do here, and when I went to check, the mobile hospital HAZMAT suits were not put back in the same place where they belong."

"What have you done to the trucks? Did you clean and wash the vans; did you put the suits away where they belonged?"

Rahimi was listening intently to the conversation between Martin and the sheriff.

"Yes, they seemed a little dirty and disorderly, so I had the day shift clean and store the equipment correctly."

"Randy, just out of curiosity, how many of the suits were stored improperly?"

Martin replied, "Four."

"Did they just fold them and restore them, or did they clean them?"

"Just a moment, and I'll look at the equipment logbook." Martin came back to the phone and said, "It appears that they were just folded and put back in place."

"I want you to seal and lock those vans until I can send somebody to collect those four suits. We will want to go over them for DNA evidence."

Whittles told Martin that he would be sending a deputy with a warrant for the suits.

"That's fine, Sheriff, but I did notice something unusual when I looked at the van logbooks, if you can give me a moment." They heard the sound of rustling, and Randy returned to the phone. "You see, Sheriff, we keep track of the mileage on our trucks so we know when to service them. The typical test run is about twenty-five miles, and we can see the miles when it left and the miles when it returns in the logbook. On the night in question as I said, two vans were tested, and when I compared the logbooks, both showed a distance of about 200 miles."

They did some fast mapping, and Randy said, "Sheriff, it is almost 100 miles from here in Texas City to the center of Springfield."

"Randy, you've been a big help. I'll send a deputy to pick up the suits and you can call your lab and tell them the uniforms are on their way, and for now we have other fish to fry."

Whittles hung up and called in Sergeant Franks. He told Franks about his assignment with the warrant for the suits. He also told Franks he wanted photos of Randy Martin's vans in a dark room so it would look like nighttime. Franks nodded and went out.

Rahimi tried to get back on track. "Now let's talk about the Ridley family and Springfield, without interruption, I hope. Sheriff, tell me as much as you can of your first recollections of the Ridley family."

"You know, I think the only way to get all the information we need is to go back to the house and start talking with the neighbors. I don't know enough about them. And before we go back to the neighborhood, let's go get something for lunch. I think I know the place that might just kill two birds with one stone."

"Does everything revolve around food in this town?"

"Hell no, football first, and then food, if the football team isn't playing."

It was early afternoon by the time the two men reach Fred's Taco on the corner of Market and Vine. The building that housed Fred's Taco was a relic from the past. It looked like it was built in the fifties, and nothing had been done to it in the ensuing sixty years. It had a series of six booths around the edges of the room and a few tables in the center. The tops of the booths and floor tables had been wiped off so many times that the finish was gone in many spots. The counter had the same surface as the tables, and it too looked like it was worn away, but more so, because the counter was used more than the tables or booths. The counter had stools that turned, but not all the way, and the red vinyl covering was showing white in places where people had slid on and off the seats. Most of the fans in the ceiling worked some of the time; one started and stopped on a regular basis and even occasionally sparked.

"The kids will be here soon, when school's out. I never understood why they love this place so much; it must be the food and the prices."

Rahimi looked out the window, as much as it was possible to see through the smudged pane. Right across the street from Fred's was the Springfield High School, and a sign outside the building, about the size of a billboard, read, Home of the Mighty Roughnecks. A message on the marquee mentioned the noon memorial service on Sunday for Sergeant Kelly at St. Patrick's Church.

Fred was behind the counter; he acknowledged Sheriff Whittles. Whittles introduced Rahimi and said, "We'll have two Fred's specials with a Diet Coke."

While Fred's back was to Whittles, the sheriff casually asked, "Any talk about the bombing of the Ridley house?"

"Well, some of the kids don't understand why none of the Ridleys was found. Nobody seems to know where they went. One of the neighbor kids said they saw them talking to John Bowman the night before around six or six thirty, and then they just disappeared. Some of the seniors knew Michael when they were sophomores, and they'll be in today. Perhaps you could ask them what they know. But right now it is time for Fred's famous double meat and cheese tacos." Fred turned around and brought out two plates of the largest tacos Omid had ever seen. They looked almost too good to eat.

They saw through the front window of the restaurant that school was now out, and the kids were on their way over to Fred's. Sheriff Whittles had a great relationship with the young people around town. They liked the sheriff, and he had helped some of them when they got into trouble. The sheriff went to all the sporting events he could to show support for the teams and the kids, and in turn the kids trusted him because he wasn't always on their case. If they were doing something they shouldn't be, he called them out, but he didn't tell their parents unless it was really bad, in which case he would go with the kid. Parents knew they could trust the sheriff and that he was fair and honest, with no agenda. So, as the kids walked in, he said hello to them, and they said, "What's up?" with smiles on their faces.

The kids who had placed their orders were now gathered around the sheriff, who introduced Rahimi as a fellow Marine who was in Springfield helping him on the Ridley case.

One voice from the back of the crowd asked, "Did you ever kill anybody?"

"Yes, in defending my men and myself."

The sheriff interrupted. "I want to ask you guys a question. Did any of you ever see Michael's parents at school?"

The juniors and seniors looked at each other, and someone said, somewhat uncertainly, "I can't remember ever seeing them."

One of the students remarked, "Some adults are wondering if they were in the witness protection program, and somebody in Springfield found out that they were in the program, and they had to be moved to another location in the middle of the night."

Rahimi wondered, not for the first time, whether the bodies in the body bags were not dead, but in fact very much alive, and were Mike and Mary Ridley being smuggled out of the house—not by the FBI in the witness protection program, but the Brotherhood of the Red Nile. Were Mike, Mary, and Michael part of the Brotherhood and so important that they had to be moved in the middle of the night?

CHAPTER 62

Meeting Room
The Brotherhood of
the Red Nile

MORDECAI AND OLEG WERE BACK in the meeting room and, as directed by Sargon, it was Oleg's turn to talk about his idea regarding how to bring America down with one of the bombs.

Oleg started off, "Mordecai, it's all been about oil for the last hundred years. Oil was first discovered in the United States in Oil Creek, Pennsylvania, in 1859. That discovery changed America forever and its need for oil to fuel the greatest economic expansion the world has ever seen. Finding oil in America and the thirst for more oil spurred drilling all over America made serious money for a great many people. Huge oil deposits were eventually discovered in Texas and many other areas, including Alaska. Cheap oil begat cheap energy and resulted in a dramatic increase in the quality of life in America. New processes were being developed to drill deeper to find even more oil. The opportunity to find oil outside America was being paid for by the riches from American oil.

"In 1932, in what was at the time called Persia, now Iran, oil was discovered. The amount of oil was vast, and yet Persia had no resources to get the oil to market on its own. American companies gladly offered to drill for oil and build the pipelines to move it across the country in exchange for significant ownership of the oil they found. America, in its thirst for oil, forever changed the culture of the Middle East from nomadic nations to mini clones of the big cities in America. Eventually they figured out that they had paid for all the capital development, drilling, pipelines, and transportation many times over, so many countries began to nationalize or organize outright takeovers of the oil fields, pipelines, and port facilities. But by the time they took control, their culture was lost. It makes no difference what you wear *on* your head: it is what is *in* your head that makes you, you.

"All the turmoil in our part of the world is a result of American imperialism. We have factions that want to go back to their 'roots,' as Americans say it. Yet we also have other factions that want the progress, as they see it, that money and power and oil can bring to them. In my country, we tried living under the Communist rule of Marx and Lenin, but the corruption and the bureaucracy of the government never allowed Communism to really work. As the workers saw the difference between Russia and America, the Russian people wanted to be more like America. They wanted Western everything, so a huge black market operated in the Soviet Union to fill the needs of the people. When the pressure to be like America brought down the wall and the government, we found that we had vast amounts of money underground that we could not only sell, but also yield for political power. Oil was a main source of power in Russia, and oil provided me with my education at Stanford where I became a petroleum engineer who then worked for my uncle.

"I have worked in every aspect of my uncle's oil business over the last twenty-five years and gained a great deal of experience. It is this background that has led me to suggest my project. Energy is the blood of America. If Americans can't get gas for their cars, they panic. In 1973, OPEC decided to slow down the flow of crude oil to the United States. If you owned a car in

1973, you know what happened to the availability of gasoline. Rationing—buying gas based on your last name or your house number—became a way of life, and the cost escalated. The price of a gallon of gas was thirty-five cents and went to the unbelievable price of fifty-five cents per gallon. The American and most stock markets around the world saw some of the biggest declines post–Second World War.

"But the biggest impact was a significant change in the American attitude. The arrogance was gone; it first started with anger and then moved to depression, as they couldn't do anything; they were helpless. What student of American history can ever forget the quote from President Jimmy Carter in his speech of July 15, 1979, when he was trying to deal with an end result that was causing an erosion of American pride and confidence amid a growing feeling that "America's best days might indeed be behind it." The American people were told that he would not light the national Christmas tree to save energy and that they should not light the trees in their homes and that in order to preserve energy, they needed to turn down the heat in the winter.

"I want to bring back that sense of hopelessness, and I think I know how to do it with one bomb. If you could peel back the surface of the United States, you would find fifty-five thousand miles of oil pipelines and 2.3 million miles of natural gas pipelines. You have to add to that feeder pipelines and offshoot pipelines, plus all the pipelines in the water offshore, drilling and pumping, moving oil and natural gas on shore. If you look at a map of the network of these pipelines, you will find that there is a very high concentration of pipelines in Texas and Louisiana. The largest oil refinery in the America is located in Texas, and the largest transportation network carrying crude, finished products like gasoline, jet fuel, and natural gas is located in Louisiana. In fact, it carries 25 percent of the product moved in the United States. So let's assume that we set off a dirty bomb in one of these two places: What would happen? Let's start with the largest refinery in the America. The refinery would be contaminated and unable to process crude. Because it was contaminated, all finished products would cease being made, immediately creating a shortage of jet fuel, gasoline, and diesel fuel. America hasn't built a new refinery in the US in over thirty years. The initial result is that the price of product skyrockets because they can't replace the refinery in a week.

"Next, some reporter will ask the question of some government official: If the bomb contaminated the refinery, what about the pipes that carry the product north? The official will have to say that they can't get into the site to see whether the pipeline is contaminated. They will have to shut down the pipelines until they can assess the level of contamination of the product going through the pipelines. A great number of the pipelines are above ground in proximity to the refineries. The reporter will ask, "But you said *refineries*, as if to say that more than one was affected by the blast. The government spokesman will see he is getting in over his head and call an end to the press briefing.

"Within moments, the White House switchboards will be flooded by calls from governors, mayors, and city council people wanting to know whether the government should, to be safe, shut down all pipelines flowing through the bomb site. The president has called for a special full cabinet meeting to discuss this issue. The longer the president waits to speak, the greater the fear raging across America will be. Reporters will say, people will say, "I don't want that nuke gas in my house." Other comments will be, "How can we heat our buildings and factories with nuke gas? Will it be safe to fly with so much nuke fuel on board? I've been told we generate 25 percent of our electricity from oil and natural gas. Will we have to shut down the power plants?'

"The days will pass, and the president and his advisors will have no solutions. They will have talked with OPEC, and they will not bring their tankers into port for fear of contamination. The world has no solutions, and, as predicted by President Carter, the best days of America will truly be behind it. The president of the United States is about to broadcast over the radio a message to the American people to save power.

"So by now, scientists have told him and his advisors that it may take twenty-five years before we can ever use those pipelines again. Every day that they can't pump fuel through them, they'll deteriorate, so they may never be able to use them again. He is exploring other distribution possibilities, but what to say to the people? The president will have to shut down production in the Gulf and other offshore drilling because there is no place to store the crude, and no place that can process the oversupply of crude.

"The chairman of the Securities and Exchange Commission will strongly suggest to the president that he close the market indefinitely. The chairman of the Federal Reserve Board has also strongly suggested to the president that he close the bank indefinitely to prevent a 1930s-style run on the banks. The president says, 'My fellow Americans, we have a grave situation that will require us to make great sacrifices, and therefore today I'm asking the Department of Defense to …'"

Mordecai had listened quietly to Oleg's story and said, nodding, at the end, "If what you are suggesting could really happen, then it truly would be the end of America."

CHAPTER 63

Park Bench, Constitution Avenue

BAKER AND SEACREST WERE REVIEWING the photos from Syria taken by one of the CIA operatives on the ground. Baker suggested to Seacrest that he would like to see newer pictures of the site and would like to know whether CIA birds have located the Assad van.

"If the Brotherhood has two bombs and only one was loaded in the truck, then where is the other bomb, if they have it? If possible, we need photos of the inside of the warehouse to see whether the other bomb is inside. If they have one bomb, perhaps they are holding it, just in case the Iranians decide to keep the first bomb for themselves. If they do fix the bomb, then perhaps the Brotherhood is planning to have the new bomb brought back to Syria and having somebody there replicate the modifications to the other bomb in the warehouse."

Seacrest brushed grass from his cuff and says, "My guess is that one of the two who stayed behind is that person. If they are in fact planning what you are suggesting, then we have to assume that one of the two has nuclear experience. This is not a typical terrorist pipe bomb, but a sophisticated weapon. If we get my guy on the ground to get close-ups of both men, we can start a search to see who he is and where he studied physics. I've asked my contact in London, at Interpol, to see whether they can identify any of the other four, but I haven't heard back from him; I'll follow up when I return to my office. My first priority will be to reach out to my asset on the ground in Syria and get him on his way taking pictures at the meeting site. I have a message in to the Syrian secret police, what is left of it, to see whether they can help us identify the other person standing next to Assad in the photo that I found on the Internet and who looks exactly like the person in the photos of the Brotherhood leadership. Is there anything else you need me to do?"

"Yes, I want to contact your friend at Interpol and have them see whether they can find anything on a person named Al Ishtar Hamwi. Who is he? We don't know, but we do know that he is Michael Ridley's identical twin brother and that he or Michael is in Amman, Jordan—we think, on their way to the Brotherhood meeting site. So you can send the image of Michael Ridley along with your inquiry, but use the name Al Ishtar Hamwi. Let me know anything you have, John. We need an update for the president in two days."

Seacrest took the Metro in the reverse direction and was headed back to his office at Langley and his assignments. He put the key in his door about forty-five minutes after he left Barker on the bench. The first thing he did was to go to his computer, where he saw the message from the Syrian secret service. The message was from Asu Aldiri, who said that things were a little crazy, but he would do his best to help. Seacrest wrote back, "I'm going to send you a photo. I know that one man in the photo is Adad Assad. I will circle the person I need your help in identifying. Thanks for your help." Seacrest scanned the photos and attached them to his e-mail message and pushed the Send button.

Next Seacrest dialed Wellington's cell number, and it rang and rang and then Harold answered the phone. "Seacrest, old boy, I'm in the middle of a very old scotch and a very young girl, but what do you need?"

"I'll be quick."

"Well, that's what she just said about me, and how wrong she was! At any rate, what is it you need?"

"First, did you find any identification on the photos I sent you?"

"Nothing yet."

"I'm going to send you a photo and a name, and I want you to see if you can find anything about the person in the photo. The last we heard was that he was in Amman, Jordan. Let me know as soon as possible on either project."

Seacrest sent Wellington a copy of the file he sent to Asu Aldiri with hopes that one of the two could help identify the twin brother. With those projects done, he headed toward the secure conference room and checked its availability. He found that it was available, and he placed his call to Massri. After about five rings, someone answered the phone.

"I'm David Billah from Damascus, I'm looking for Massri."

"This is he, how can I help you?"

"Mr. Massri, you took some photos, for insurance purposes, of one of my storage warehouses near Al-Mukharram a few days ago. The insurance company would like different angles, now, and I was wondering if you were available for hire on short notice?"

"When were you thinking?"

"I would like to get this claim out of the way, so could you leave tomorrow morning?"

"That is not possible. I am committed to a photo shoot until noon tomorrow, but I could be there early Thursday. I could e-mail the photos to you late Thursday night. Would that work?"

"That would be terrific. I will call the insurance company and let them know you are going to take the pictures on Thursday."

"Perhaps before you hang up, you can tell me what shots you are looking for?"

"The insurance company says that the pictures of the first floor seem to be missing a photo of an exterior wall. In the last photo a stack of boxes was blocking the wall, so we can't tell whether the wall is damaged. The insurance company wants you to reshoot the first floor from all angles inside and out. This way they will be able to assess any additional structural damage to the building. In some of the photos I noticed people at the building whom I have not seen before, while others I have known for many years. Please take closer pictures of the workers so I can distinguish those whom I have known and the new hires. Please tell the foreman I hope to be there in about ten days, if all goes well with the insurance company, to hire a crew to make the repairs."

"Is there anything else you need me to take pictures of for the insurance company? I was concerned about the harvesting equipment and how it fared through the storm."

"I have been so focused on the damage to the building, but yes, how about some pictures of the harvesters, trucks, and cars from all sides. You can use the water tower to shoot the pictures of the tops of the equipment. If you have a chance, you could turn to your right and left on the tower and shoot some pictures of the citrus grove so I could see how the fruit is doing. Let me know if you see a lot of fruit on the ground."

"Anything else you need?"

"No, thanks for squeezing me in, and I'll look forward to seeing your work the day after tomorrow."

Massri knew that he needed to take the shots from the water tower and that Billah wanted to see photos of all the people at the site. Any photos of car license plates might help identify who was at the meeting. The shot of the four walls meant that the pile of office supply boxes in the last photos blocked something Billah needed to see. Inside the building might be the most difficult, and second most difficult would be getting up the water tower without being noticed. Massri decided to leave as soon as he had packed his equipment, for if he could get there before dark, perhaps the warehouse would be empty, and he could get in and get his shots before anybody saw him. He decided that he would take a moment to look at the last set of photos and see whether he had any pictures of the water tower.

As he did, he now understood why Billah had instructed him to turn right and then left.

CHAPTER 64

Megan Brown's Lab

MEGAN AND HER TEAM HAD spent the last day going over both sides of the Ridley map for fingerprints. The found prints that belonged to Sheriff Whittles, Sergeant Kelly, and a number of other prints besides Michael or Ishtar, but several did not appear in the databases to which they had access; there were two databases that they had not run because they did not have access. The first was the FBI "Special File," and the second was Interpol in Lyon, France, which had a fingerprint file on known felons all over the world.

"I do not have the clearance to make the call to either organization, but I will speak to Baker and see if he will talk with Undersecretary Williams to make some calls to see if we can get access. I have a call in to Mr. Baker, so while we are waiting for him to call back, let's move on to the ghost images on the backside of the map."

Derrick had taken digital images of both the front and the back of the Ridley map and had projected them side-by-side on the big plasma screen in front of them. He said, "I don't know whether the ghost image on the back of our map is from a map of similar size. If the back impressions are on a different size map, then I'm not sure what we will get when we superimpose one on top of the other."

Derrick slides the image on the right part of the screen, which is the image from the back, over on top of the image of the main map. The circles on the backside of the map do not line up with any of the circles on the front.

Penelope suggested to Derrick that he flip the image just to see if it reveals anything different. Derrick flipped the image 180 degrees: nothing. Then Derrick flipped it 180 degrees, top to bottom, and none of the circles line up. He decided that he wanted to go back to the original image. One thing of interest was that one circle sat right on top of Port Fourchon, Louisiana. Why would this be so important? It didn't appear that the hole in the wall even had an oil refinery. Why would it be circled?

Brown did a quick Google search and found more than she was looking for. She read, "In 2006 an economic impact study was made for, as you say, Derrick, a hole in the wall, and the study came to the following conclusions: Port Fourchon is located near the mouth of Bayou Lafourche in Lafourche Parish, Louisiana. It is the only Louisiana port directly on the Gulf of Mexico. Port Fourchon plays two crucial roles in the US economy: one, servicing offshore rigs in the Gulf of Mexico, and two, serving as a host for the Louisiana Offshore Port (LOOP). In terms of service, Port Fourchon provides catering to 90 percent of all deep-water rigs in the Gulf of Mexico and roughly 45 percent of all shallow-water rigs in the Gulf. The Gulf of Mexico (GOM) accounted for 470.7 million barrels, or roughly 80 percent of US offshore oil in 2006. With regard to natural gas, the GOM accounted for 2.9 trillion cubic feet (tcf) of production, or 88 percent of total US offshore production in 2005. The LOOP is the only port in the United States capable of handling Ultra Large Crude Carriers and Very Large Crude Carriers. The LOOP has unloaded more than 3.5 billion barrels of oil from over 3,000 tankers from its beginning in 1981 to March 2007. The Greater Lafourche Port Commission reports that the LOOP handles roughly 15 percent of US imports of foreign oil, and its pipeline distribution connects to over 50 percent of US refining capacity. This translates into 1.5 million barrels per day (bd) of oil (1.15 million barrels of imported crude and 350,000 barrels of domestic production). Given the role of oil and natural gas in our economy, the economic significance of Port Fourchon is apparent.

"To make this simple: 50 percent of all of the refineries in the United States get their oil from this port. And 90 percent of all the oil and gas from the Gulf of Mexico comes through this port. Bottom line? You shut down this port, and you shut down America."

"What about the other cities inside circles? How many circles?"

They counted twenty, just like before. "Look at the cities on the back; *are they close to the cities on the front of the map?*" The two of them started making a list of the cities, and, while some are close, none matched.

"What did we think the first map was used for?"

"A targeting map?"

"If that is true, then what is the second map for?"

"A targeting map for different targets?"

"We believe that the Brotherhood has two bombs, correct? If you wanted to get the maximum use out of the bombs, would you target both bombs to the same type of target or would you want to have two different targets?"

Derrick responded, "Well, I might want or need to use two bombs to get the maximum effect at a big target. Let's say I want to take out a really big target, and I know that my bombs have limited range. So if I wanted to make sure that I really destroyed the target effectively, I might want to use two bombs.

"When the terrorists attacked New York City, they used two planes, one for each tower. If they only used one plane, the best they could hope for was that one tower would fall into the other and in turn take down both towers. The terrorists were unsure that the planes could in fact take down one tower. If they took out just one tower, they would have left Wall Street unharmed. By sending two planes at one target, they increased their chances of success. Look at what little damage the one plane did to the Pentagon. It took down part of one exterior wall, but it didn't shut down the Pentagon for a long period of time. I'm not sure that it shut down the Pentagon at all. It is true that Wall Street did have backup, and in a very short period of time they were back and running, so I wonder if the terrorists have looked at bin Laden's attacks and are trying not to make the same mistakes he did when he attacked America."

"I think we have to assume that each of these maps is a scenario map. I don't know how many scenarios they are playing out. The two maps we have may, in fact, not be the final target maps, but I feel comfortable telling undersecretary Williams what I think. I want you to continue to review the papers for the Morristown house and see if you can find clues to other possible targets while I meet with Williams."

"Megan, if we have identified what we think is one of the targets, then how do we figure out which of the twenty circles on the original is the second target?"

"Perhaps those papers from the Morristown house will give us a clue. And let's pray to God there aren't any other maps."

CHAPTER 65

Williamss' Office

WILLIAMS WAS GETTING READY TO prepare his next report to the president, due the following Monday. He reviewed the reports from all of his operatives and was working on their requests. He had a call in to the director of the FBI to get access to its special fingerprint file; he also asked the director to reach out to Interpol for access to its fingerprint file. Williams had Marie call Brown and tell her he was working on her request and would get back to her as soon as he heard back from the FBI director.

It seemed to Williams that his team had a great many irons in the fire, but he felt he wasn't going to show the president much progress. Unanswered questions nagged at him: was Michael Ridley in Amman, Jordan, or was it Ishtar? Where were Mike and Mary Ridley? Was Ridley their real name? Were they, as the high school students in Springfield thought, in the witness protection program? And where was the Assad cargo van with the bomb in it?

The one thing he felt reasonably sure of was that the truck, wherever it was and wherever it was going, was carrying a very unstable dirty bomb to somewhere. Williams had a thought: perhaps this was all a diversion. What if the bomb wasn't headed to the United States, but to Israel? The tension in the Middle East was very high. The world had been putting a great deal of pressure on Iran about its commitment to developing a nuclear bomb to use against Israel. Williams called Marie and said, "Get me Nava Dobias, the head of Mossad. His number is in my contact file." Dobias and Williams had worked together on many occasions, long before Dobias became head of Mossad. They were good friends and talked on a regular basis. Williams trusted Dobias to be open and honest with him, and in turn he had to be open and honest with Dobias. He knew that Dobias was one of those types of people who never answered his phone. He eventually did call back, but when you needed to talk with him, like now, he tended to be gone.

He would just have to wait until Dobias called back. So he called Baker in the meantime and was leaving a message when suddenly, miraculously, Dobias was on the other line.

Williams grabbed the phone, "Nava, my old friend, how are you?"

"I'm fine. And how about you and that beautiful wife of yours, Ellen?"

"She's well. We're planning our twenty-fifth wedding anniversary celebration, and we want you to come and bring a friend."

"When is the celebration?"

"Next June, around the middle of the month."

"My dear friend, you don't know the exact date of your wedding?"

"That's why I have a smart phone and Marie."

Nava said to Williams in a more somber tone, "We could talk about the weather and lots of meaningless stuff, but you are calling either because you need information from me or you need my help, or perhaps both. There is a nasty rumor going around about a new terrorist group call the Brotherhood of something that wants to destroy America."

"Nava, the group is called the Brotherhood of the Red Nile. We think they have two old Soviet suitcase dirty bombs they plan to use against us. I'm calling you because I'm concerned that we may be going in the wrong direction."

"What do you mean the wrong direction?"

"Nava, we have been thinking that the bombs are going to be used against us, but what if we are wrong and they are really planning to use them against Israel?"

There was a long pause from Nava, then, "Frank, what makes you think that these terrorists might be planning an attack against Israel?"

"We think it is possible that one of the two bombs they may have in their possession is being refitted to make it more powerful by expanding its range and power. As far as we know, there are only two places in the Middle East that have some level of nuclear capabilities: Iran and Israel. I know the Saudis have threatened to go nuclear if Iran gets the bomb, but for now there are only two. We think one of the bombs is currently on its way to Iran by cargo van.

"We also think the second bomb is still in Syria, near the town of Al-Mukharram, and it is being held there out of fear that the Iranians will steal the bomb and the Brotherhood would have to make do with one outdated bomb. If the one bomb is upgraded to something more powerful and stable and it comes back to Syria, we believe they will convert the second bomb. We think that in order to do this, they need somebody with a nuclear background who has recently been doing nuclear research.

"We have some photos that were taken at what appears to be a meeting site near Al-Mukharram. What I was hoping, old friend, is if I send you these pictures, could you have somebody look at them and see if they recognize anybody, and determine whether that person is or was involved with your nuclear program? In addition, as we are not sure that Israel is not the target, I will be sending you information from our investigation as I receive it. I would ask that you talk to your team members and see if they know or have heard anything about the Brotherhood or their activities. My friend, we must keep a lid on this, if I'm wrong and Israel is not the target, then a leak of the information may well anger them enough to take out Israel for not being able to carry out their plans to attack America."

"Frank thank you very much for your valuable information, I will circulate the photos immediately after we get them, and if we have anything to report, I will personally get back to you. I fully understand that one slipup on our part may well be the end of Israel."

CHAPTER 66

Springfield

Omid and Whittles waited for the kids to pile out of Fred's, but instead of going back to the sheriff's car, they walked down Main Street for about two blocks. Omid noticed a sign that said Third National Bank of Springfield. Whittles pointed out, "this is one of the two banks we have in town. Let's go talk with the president of the bank Wendell Parker."

They went through the door and greeted Mary Lou Martin, the receptionist. "Hello, Mary Lou. Is Wendell in today?"

Mary Lou said, "Yes he is. I will see if he can see you now." Mary Lou called on the intercom, and Wendell Parker, the president of the bank, said, "Send them in, please." Mary Lou showed the two of them to Parker's office.

They went through the door, and Wendell Parker held out his hand and, with a big smile, said, "Welcome to our bank. How can I help you?"

Whittles introduced Major Rahimi to Parker, who invited them to sit down and offered them something to drink.

"Wendell, I'm sure you have heard that Mike and Mary Ridley and their son, Michael, are missing. Can you check your records and tell us whether the Ridleys, including Michael, had accounts at this bank?"

"I can look and see whether they had accounts, but the details of the accounts and their activity are confidential. Let me do a quick scan on my computer." After a few moments, he found that the bank held several accounts for Mike and Mary, but none for Michael.

"I need to know how many accounts in total, so I can get the correct search warrant."

"I see five accounts in various combinations for Mike and Mary Ridley."

"Wendell, can I use your phone? You can never tell who is listening to the police radio." Whittles called the office and talked to his sergeant about getting over to Judge Symington for a search warrant.

After he hung up, he said, "We can't do anything more until the search warrant arrives. Let's go to the other bank in town and see if they had any banking relationships there. We'll be back as soon as my deputy gets word to me that he has the warrant."

"I'll be waiting," Wendell said.

Whittles and Rahimi left the bank and walked three blocks to the main branch of Citizen National Bank. The receptionist, Mary Wishborn, was sitting at her desk and obligingly called Mr. Ford's office at their request.

Whittles and Rahimi walked through the door to Bill Ford's office and were greeted with a big smile similar to Wendell Parker's. *Must be part of the training program*, Omid muttered to the sheriff.

"I'm sure you heard about what happened at the Ridley house."

Bill Ford nodded and expressed his condolences about Kelly.

"We need to know whether Mike and Mary Ridley had bank accounts with you and also whether their son Michael had any accounts at the bank?"

"Sheriff, you know I can't tell you that."

"Stop. I understand. All you have to do is tell me whether they had accounts and how many, and I'll get a search warrant."

"Fine," Ford said, and he swung around to his computer and searched for all three Ridley family members. "I have nothing for Mike and Mary, but Michael has two accounts: a money market/checking and a credit card. Michael has a very large balance in his money market account."

"Can you tell me how much Michael has in that account?"

"Not without a warrant, but I can say sizable. Especially for a college student."

Whittles again called the deputy, but this time said, "When you get the warrants, bring them to me at Citizen National first; we'll be waiting here for you, since things are closing soon."

While they were waiting for the warrants, the sheriff says, "Perhaps you can help us with another question?"

"If I can, legally, I'm more than happy to help."

"Am I correct that when a property is sold, that transaction is recorded at the property tax file at the courthouse? And if the property has a mortgage, that also has to be filed. Is that correct?"

"Yes."

"And that information is a matter of public record?"

"Yes."

"One last question, John: can you access those filings on that computer? I want to find out who bought the house that the Ridleys lived in and who held the mortgage. The address was 171 Tall Trees Drive, Springfield."

Bill Ford typed something into his computer and frowned. "Are you sure of that address?"

The sheriff gave it again, and Ford moved his fingers over the keys. "Mike and Mary Ridley don't own that home, and it has no mortgage; it was paid for in cash."

"Well, then, who owns the home?"

CHAPTER 67

In the Van, Closer to ZanJan, Iraq

ASSAD AND JAIARI HAD BEEN traveling for the better part of twelve hours and found themselves just a few miles from ZanJan, where they would spend the night. The plan was to approach the town from the north, just off Route 2. There was an industrial section at the intersection of 2 and 23 where they would stay the night. In that complex, one of Jaiari's team members had made arrangements to spend the night in a warehouse where they could pull the van inside and make it secure. They could take showers, have something to eat, and get a good night's rest before the final leg of their journey to Iran. They had agreed that they would switch off guard duty every two hours.

A considerable amount of time had passed since both men had laid out their plans for the attack, with no discussion of each other's plans. They both knew that at some point they would have to start discussing how to execute their plans, but not now.

"Do you mind if I ask you a question?"

Adad replied, "Sure, why not?"

"I could see why the other three of us might get involved in this project, but I don't understand why a person of your success and recognition is risking so much for yourself and your family. Why are you involved?"

"Jaiari, that is an excellent question, and in fact that was a question my wife asked me when I told her what I was doing. I wish there was a simple answer, but there is not one. I have known Sargon for many years; in fact, we grew up together in Damascus. We met in the primary education level and continued to lower secondary, and we finished in the upper secondary at the same time. We both went on to higher education and got degrees; Sargon got his in Syria, and I received mine in the United States.

"I studied information technology, and Sargon studied philosophy. Unfortunately for Sargon, there were no teaching positions available, so he floundered for a number of years working at anything and everything, making enough money to get by. We lost touch when we went off to college and never sought each other out after we returned. I worked in sales and was making a good living selling computer hardware and software along with office supplies; in a very short time I decided to open my first business. I was looking for a shop to rent, and at that time Sargon was a rental agent for the office I wanted to rent."

"Did you recognize each other right away?"

"Well, we had changed, and it had been fifteen years since we had been together, but within five minutes we had our arms around each other and were catching up on what had happened since university. We started talking about my business, and we struck a deal for the rent and improvements. He would keep a close watch on the build out to make sure I was getting quality materials and workmanship. The remodeling took about four months, and we stayed in close contact. I invited him to meet my wife and children, and he even joined us for *mezzeh*, a traditional meal that he had for some reason never eaten.

"In a mezzeh, you may have twenty to thirty dishes of fruits, vegetables, rice, and several different kinds of meats: a very lavish meal. After that we began to talk about what Sargon was doing away from his job. He spoke of being involved with the Free Syrian Army but found it fruitless because the American government was supporting it with arms, and the other governments were giving lip service to the plight of the people of Syria. Sargon started to spend more and more of his free time searching for information on the involvement of the US government and the private companies they had throughout the Middle East.

"The more he read, the more he became convinced that no matter what the American government said publicly about wanting change in the Middle East, behind closed doors they were making decisions on what to do based on their needs only. Let me give you an example of something he said to me recently.

"When oil prices spiked, and the price of gasoline went to over $4 a gallon during the winter of 2012, the senior Senator from the state of New York, Charles Schumer, wrote a letter to the American Secretary of State, Mrs. Clinton, asking her to tell Saudi Arabia to pump more oil so as to reduce the price of oil and gasoline at the pump in the United States. It seemed to Sargon and many others in the Middle East that America was not the home of the free, but the home of the world's biggest dictator.

"Sargon suggested that it was not only the president or the senators, but all levels of government and the private sector that were trying to be the dictator to the world. Sargon suggested that America was now active in regime change in the Middle East. They tried in Iraq and Afghanistan, and it cost billions of dollars and many lives on both sides, but when it came time for Libya to have a change, America led the way with aircraft and missiles that regime armies could not overcome. He decided that something had to be done outside the Free Syrian Army to bring about significant change in the American swagger.

"The more he talked, the more I understood and appreciated the need for someone to try to do something about American imperialism. He was developing a plan for a new organization that would not be widespread, like al-Qaeda; it would be small and quick to respond to opportunities. Sargon didn't know what he wanted to do except that he wanted the best and brightest around him to think about the possibilities. He wanted me to join his new Brotherhood as part of his think tank. He thought that I might bring a different prospective to the discussions and planning that would make the Brotherhood better, and more effective and successful. So we met and talked."

"And then?" Jaiari asked.

Adad smiled, a little grimly. "And then a person walked into his life that would bring blood to the Brotherhood of the Red Nile."

CHAPTER 68

Mossad Headquarters, Tel Aviv

Nava Dobias had just hung up the phone with Williams of United States Homeland Security and was still in shock that American Homeland Security knew about a terrorist group in his own backyard before he did. He picked up his phone and called his assistant, Ayala Sofer, and asked her to come into his office. She could tell by the tone in his voice that he was not happy. She moved quickly and burst through the door. Nava looked at her and thought, *what a combination: brains, experience, and drop-dead gorgeous.* Ayala was very tall, over six feet, with olive skin and black hair down to her shoulders. She dressed in a very understated way, but her femininity was in full display. When they first met her, most everybody was struck by her appearance, but when she opened her mouth, they knew why she was working for the head of Mossad.

Nava quickly refocused. "I want a meeting of all the section and department leaders in one hour in the big conference hall. I want the room swept for bugs constantly, up to just before the meeting starts."

Ayala asked, "But what if all the leaders are not here?"

"Then I want the second in command, and if they aren't there then keep going down the chain. I want every section represented, and Ayala, no e-mails. I want you to start making phone calls now."

"Yes, sir," she said, but she was thinking, *How in the world can I make all the phone calls and get security in the room to have it swept in less than an hour?*

In reality, that was the easy part. She made the call to the head of security, and that was done. She made a list of the departments and sections that needed to be in attendance. She split it in half and decided that she would have the section chiefs contact specific department heads to relay the message. If the department head was not present, then she could speak to his or her assistant and that person could tell the person who was next in charge to be at the meeting. Ayala got busy.

As Nava sat thinking about the phone call he had had with Williams, he was trying to decide how he was going to alert his resources without alerting the Brotherhood that he knew about them. He had to take the suggestion from Williams as serious. If in fact the Brotherhood had two nuclear bombs, and there was any possibility that they could be used against Israel, he had to be prepared, and he had very little time to prepare for the meeting, let alone a nuclear onslaught. He was thinking and writing at the same time; he was thinking faster than he could make notes. What would be the likely target in Israel? Dirty bombs, at least the Cold War type were not meant for mass destruction, but contamination and abandonment of areas that would be uninhabitable, perhaps for decades. He looked at his watch and saw it was time to go.

He walked out of his office as Ayala was just hanging up the phone.

"Time to go, sir?"

"Yes, and bring your laptop with you."

"You want me in the meeting, sir?"

"This may well be the most important meeting in the life of our country, and I want the best and the brightest; that includes you."

"Thank you, sir."

"Let's go; we're already late."

They walked quickly down the hallway, and, as they approached the meeting room, Ayala could see the security people screening everyone before they went into the meeting room. Nava and Ayala went in and took their seats in a full room. Nava decided to wait one more minute. No one else came through the doors, so Nava signaled to the guard, and the door was secured.

"Ladies and gentlemen, less than one hour ago I received a phone call from the undersecretary for Homeland Security of the United States that a terrorist group by the name of the Brotherhood of the Red Nile may be in possession of two dirty bombs that they are planning to use against the United States and possibly our country.

"Undersecretary Williams thinks that one of the bombs is on its way to Iran for upgrading and stabilization. He believes that the second bomb is in Syria and will be upgraded to match the other bomb once it returns from Iran. I will be receiving photos of the people Williams thinks are the leaders of the Brotherhood, which I will circulate to you. Williams believes that only someone trained in physics and has working experience around nuclear material could reconfigure the second bomb.

"Williams would like to know if we can identify anybody in the photos and, more specifically, an Israeli nuclear physicist who may have left our program and can't be accounted for presently."

The crowd began murmuring.

"Yes, ladies and gentlemen, one of our own, an Israeli, may be planning a dirty bomb attack on Israel."

CHAPTER 69

Brotherhood Meeting Site near Al-Mukharram, Syria

IT WAS DARK WHEN MASSRI turned down the lane to the warehouse that the Brotherhood was using as a meeting site. He stopped at least a mile from the warehouse, turned off the lights, and hid the car deep in the woods. When the car was secure, he loaded up his equipment and headed out on foot to the lane that led to the warehouse. He was trying to be as quiet as he could as he walked down the lane. He could see the building in the distance, and it appeared that only one light was on in the building.

As he approached it, he was scanning the area, looking for cars and trucks that the leadership might use to get to the meeting site. As he got closer to the building, his steps became more deliberate so as not to make any noise, in case someone he couldn't see was in or around the building. Massri looked through the night sky and could see the water tower. He now could see what Seacrest was talking about; below the storage tank was a walkway that had a railing that was enclosed and high enough that he could lie there and not be seen from the ground. If he moved to the right and to the left, he could see the entire compound, and from the right side he could see directly into the building. With the doors open, he could see the section of the warehouse that he hadn't shot in the last set of pictures.

He approached the building away from the window. This would give him cover in the darkness, and he could creep slowly along the outside wall in the shadows toward the window. Then, when he was close enough, he could peek in to see whether anybody was there. As he got closer and closer to the window, his hearing grew keener. He tried to detect whether anybody was inside the building; no sounds yet, but he remained on guard.

As he got closer, he heard a hum, like the noise of a small motor. He stopped in his tracks to listen for other sounds that might tell him whether someone was in the building. He started again toward the window, and soon he was just at the edge, where he could look inside from an angle, without having to stand at the window.

He decided to drop down below the window and crawl to the other side to see from that angle. The ground under the window had a lot of gravel, and he thought he might be making too much noise. He soon made it under but did not see anything except a rather large workbench, where the noise was coming from. The bench was too far away for him to tell what the motor was. He continued to scan the warehouse and didn't see anybody downstairs. There was a stair and railing that led to the second floor, but he couldn't see any light in the opening to the second floor.

It was late when he arrived, so it was possible that people were asleep on the second floor of the building; trying to get inside to take the pictures and not knowing whether people were upstairs would be a very high-risk maneuver. He also knew that he couldn't use his flash because the burst of light could awaken the people upstairs.

Massri decided that he would work his way around the building to the front door. If it was unlocked, then he would have to make the decision whether or not to open the door and go into the building, but for now he needed to get to the front door undetected. He remembered from his previous visit that the front door opened into the orchard; there were no other buildings outside the front door. It seemed like it took hours to get from the window to the front door, but in reality it took under ten minutes.

When he arrived at the front door, which was made of metal and had no window, he could see the doorknob in the moonlight. The moment of truth was at hand: Massri reached out to grab the doorknob and just as he was ready to turn it, he heard a faint cough on the other side of the door.

He quickly pulled his hand away from the door and slowly made his way around to the other side of the building. He walked very deliberately, and the ground under him crunched like breaking eggs with every footstep. As before, he pulled up short and had a decent view of this side of the warehouse. He looked down and, sure enough, there was a person lying on a cot right under the window. Right next to the cot was the other suitcase bomb; similar to the one he saw being loaded into the cargo van at his last trip.

Massri slowly turned and, just as he was turning, he saw a wire running out of something over to the suitcase. He concluded that it must be a power source for whatever was in the suitcase. It was the power source that was making the noise. He quickly raised his camera, and, using its telephoto lens, he could make out part of the label: *DC Generator Model Number.* The plate curved around the motor, so he couldn't read the rest of it, but clearly this motor was powering what was in the suitcase. As he turned away from the window, he could see the ladder leading to the top of the water tower. It was now about an hour before sunrise, and he needed to get to the platform on the top of the water tower before the sun rose.

He had brought some food and water to take with him to the top of the tower, for he had thought he might be up there until dark again. But he had not stopped to relieve himself, and he thought it was important to do it now, before he went up to the top. He looked around for a spot away from the building that wouldn't be detected, and when he found it, he quietly set his bag on the ground and unzipped his fly. All of a sudden he heard the door behind him open.

CHAPTER 70

Springfield

WHITTLES AND RAHIMI WERE SITTING in the office of Bill Ford, president of the Citizens National Bank of Springfield, who had been looking up the ownership of the Ridley house and has had just told them they wouldn't believe who owns the house, and who has owned it since the Ridleys moved in almost 20 twenty years ago, when the development was brand-new.

"The name on the deed is my bank." Ford was shocked and needed to look further into the detail of the transaction. He found that his bank was holding the house under a trust set up nearly twenty years ago by someone called Viktor Antipova. "This was before I started at the bank, so I was not familiar with the transaction, and I must say I don't recognize the name. Sheriff, do you recognize the name?"

"I don't think I know anybody by that name. Do me a favor and do a Google search on that name and see if anything comes up."

Ford typed in the name Viktor Antipova and the search results quickly appeared. There was even a photo of the man, who happened to be one of the wealthiest men in the world. There were over three million sites associated with the name. His biography stated that he was the holder of vast oil and natural gas reserves in both Russia and the other countries of the former Soviet Union. It also said that, before he struck it rich in the oil business, he was a high-ranking official in the Red Army in charge of non ballistic missile bases and nuclear weapons research and development. It said he lived a very lavish lifestyle and had jet planes, cars, and houses all over the world.

"Does it say where he owns homes?"

"The usual: London, Paris, Rome, Moscow, and New York. But why Springfield? While this transaction was before my time at the bank, I do remember reading about what was going on at that time. The old Soviet Union was falling apart, and many people who had money in Russia wanted to get it out of the county. The logic, such as it was, was that if I own land in the United States, and Mother Russia falls into anarchy, I can leave Russia, and I have land in the US; I can come and live here. Their logic was that if I was an American landowner, America has to let me in by going to the head of the line for immigration.

"Most of the time these land transactions were for what they call circle farms. You can see them when you fly over the States heading west; there are tens of thousands of them that are still growing crops in a circle. My guess is that Viktor decided that if he bought a circle farm, he would have no place to live because they didn't allow houses on the circle farms, only crops, so he decided to buy a house, so that if he had to come to America, he had a place to live."

"Who has been paying the taxes and other related costs for the house?"

"It looks like the bank has been making all the payments on behalf of the trust. I will have to dig deeper to find the details, but my guess is that money comes from somewhere and is deposited in the trust, and the bills are paid. So a Russian oil magnate bought a house in Springfield, but that at the time of the purchase, he wasn't an oil baron; he just wanted to have an out if Russia imploded. The billions came later."

As they were looking at the screen, Whittles deputy Dan Matthews came in with the signed warrants and handed them to the sheriff.

"For both banks?"

"Yes, sir."

"Mr. Ford, I have the search warrant to review the records and transactions in all accounts of Michael Ridley," and he handed Ford the warrant.

"Excuse me, Sheriff. Let me ask Mr. Ford to do one other thing for us before we start looking at Michael's records. Mr. Ford, can you run a credit check on Mike and Mary Ridley?"

"Do you have a social security number?"

Both men say no, but Whittles suggested that Ford could call Wendell Parker of Second National and ask him to run a credit check, because Second National had checking and savings relationships with Mike and Mary, and the banks could exchange information that they couldn't share with nonbank entities.

Ford picked up the phone and dialed Parker's private number; it rang twice. "Parker, this is Bill Ford from Citizens. I have Sheriff Whittles and Major Rahimi in my office, and I have seen search warrants for both our banks, and I know that the two of them will be heading to your bank soon to gather information on Mike and Mary Ridley. For now, could you answer one question for me? Can you run a credit check on Mike and Mary Ridley and tell me what their social security numbers are? Add one more question: where does Mike Ridley work?"

While they were waiting for Wendell Parker to get back to them, Omid turned to Ford. "Tell me about the unusual accounts that Michael Ridley has at your bank."

Ford recalled the screen and said he had two accounts, one money market account with a checking account and a credit card.

The Major asked, "What's so unusual about having a checking account and a money market account?"

"On the face of it, nothing, but what is unusual is that for the two years that Michael was supposed to be in UC Berkeley, his money market account was receiving $25,000 per month, and now it currently stands at about $600,000. How does a college student make $25,000 a month while attending school full time?"

"The checking account—how much does he have in the balance there?"

"It's overdrawn."

"Wouldn't the bank automatically move the money from the money market to the checking account to cover bad checks?"

"Ordinarily, but the two were never linked."

"Can you tell where the monthly deposits are coming from?"

"I'll have to search a little, but I'll try."

At that moment, Parker came back on the line. "I searched all the records I can see, and it appears—keep in mind I'll need to do more checking—that Mike Ridley doesn't *have* a job."

CHAPTER 71

Megan Brown's Lab

MEGAN AND HER TEAM HAD been processing fingerprints with the help of the FBI and Interpol. While the team was waiting for reports to come back, they started looking at the papers found at the house in Morristown. They were not sure what they had in front of them; in some respects they looked like sketches, and on the other hand, they looked like scribbles.

They were all on the same size paper, but each seemed to be totally unrelated to the others. They brought all the papers over to the big light table in the center of the lab for closer examination. There were twenty pieces of paper, all the same size— eight and a half by eleven. They seemed to have no clear orientation—up, down, right, or left. Brown split the papers into two stacks of ten.

"Let's start with the top of each stack. Put them side by side and then tell me what you see."

Derrick and Penelope both said nothing. Megan took away one and added the second in the stack and paired it with the first; "Anything?"

Derrick said nothing, so they continued and proceeded with the rest of the ten in the first stack. Still nothing. Every time a page was rejected, it was turned facedown, and they took the old stack and turned it over face up.

"Now, take the other stack and place the top page on the bottom. Now look at the new top page and compare it to the page on the right. Anything?"

Both said no, and they flipped to the second page.

Penelope said, "Those two look like a map. I'm not sure what it is a map of, but they both seem to go together." The set the two pages aside and continued the process for most of the day. They had to take a break every hour because the strain of trying to see something was sapping their energy. Little by little, they found matches, and by the end of the day, they had ten pairs of something. They were just about ready to give up for the day when Derrick said, "Is it possible that these maps coincide with the twenty circled cities on the big map?"

"On the big screen, I want you to put the city center maps for all twenty cities. If the effective range of a dirty bomb is about two miles, let's create an image of the downtown out two miles. Let's start with midtown New York, so look at all the landmarks in midtown now start leafing through the smaller maps to see whether we can find something that looks like midtown. Look on the small map for a landmark on the big map. We need to digitize both the maps so the scale will be the same." Megan thinks that the scale on the small maps is very different, and if they get the sections of the big map the same scale, maybe they will have a better chance of finding matches. "It will take a while to get all twenty cities in the same scale as the small maps, so we can feed the maps in the scanner and program the computer to do the scaling off the small maps. Let's go home get something to eat and a good night sleep and see what the computer has come up with in the morning."

Penelope and Derrick were reluctant to leave, but they finally agreed to go home, but only if Megan left with them. The three of them walked out the door together, but once outside, they parted company and went their separate ways.

Megan was not married and had never been married. She made a good salary and lived in a modest apartment in Chevy Chase, Maryland, close to the Metro. It took her about forty minutes door-to-door. It had been a long day and instead of going straight home, she decided that she needed a workout. For most people that would mean going to the gym, but for Megan it meant that she wanted to go shoot something.

Megan had a secret desire; she wanted to work for the CIA as a black ops agent. She had been working on her shooting ability and worked out three to four times a week, trying to get into shape so she could be tested for admittance into CIA black ops. She knew it was a long shot, but problems like the ones she had worked on that day would eventually have to have a black ops component to solve. She knew that she couldn't qualify for *this* mission, but she believed that if she could get included in the planning of the counterattack—the defense of the country, if you will—then perhaps Williams would speak to CIA and see if he could get her an interview.

She got off the Metro at Friendship station and took a cab to the Montgomery County Maryland Police shooting range. She checked in at the front desk and showed her ID, but they all knew her and waved it aside. She went to her locker and changed into shooting gear. She returned to the front desk and asked to shoot "an AK-47, please."

The scheduler called on the intercom, "Megan Brown, AK-47 to the line, shooting booth three." Police Sergeant William Quigley, who was holding the AK-47 Megan had requested, met her at the shooting booth. "Have you ever fired this weapon before?"

"Yes, sir, several times. What is the maximum distance I can shoot on this range?"

"You could press it to about 300 yards, ma'am."

"I guess I'll have to shoot at a smaller target."

"What size target would you like to shoot at, ma'am?"

"How about one the size of a full-sized suitcase?"

Chapter 72

Mossad Headquarters, Tel Aviv

Dobias finished his meeting with the section chiefs and department heads, telling them perhaps for the first time something they didn't know: that a terrorist group in Syria had nuclear bombs and might use them against Israel. He went into his office and began to think about how he was going to break the news to the Prime Minister, Benjamin Weinstock. He called for Ayala to come into his office and told her that he needed to see the prime minster as soon as possible, but the meeting should take place outside of Tel Aviv.

"Why outside the city?"

"Fewer eyes and ears."

As she was dialing the number, she was asking herself, *how is he going to have a conversation with no information? How do you build a plan if you don't know if or when they might strike?* She had one last and most disturbing thought: *How could one of our own turns on us?* The prime minister's office answered the phone, and Ayala told them what needed to be done for a meeting. Now, when the head of Mossad called the prime minster, it got attention.

Back in his office, Nava sat in his chair trying to get a handle on what he had just heard and, more important, what he needed to do to protect Israel. The expression on everybody's face when he told them was not priceless. He thought about the priority of the things that needed to be done immediately; he called for Ayala to come in with her laptop. When she came through the door, he told her to close the door and to make sure to turn off the Wi-Fi on her computer. The two of them began to develop the meeting notes that he would leave with Weinstock. Ayala thought to herself with a bit of a thrill, *this is very serious, and I have been asked to be part of this mission.*

"Let's start with bullet statements we got from Frank Williams:

Section One: Current Data

The group's name is the Brotherhood of the Red Nile.

We believe they are meeting near the Syrian town of Al-Mukharram.

One central leader and four team leaders; we do not know how many other individuals are involved.

Possibly two Soviet Union nuclear suitcase bombs

Possible targets: the United States and/or Israel

One of the team leaders may be an Israeli who works or worked at a nuclear plant.

Possible ties with Iran's nuclear program to upgrade and stabilize the bombs.

Photos of the suspected terrorists on the way to us from the United States.

For now this is all we can tell the prime minister that we know. Now we must turn our attention to talk about what we should do while we are awaiting more information." Ayala agreed. "The fact that we are already developing a plan that may never be implemented is an important part of defense."

Nava continued.

"Section Two Operational and Contingent Plans:

First step is to assemble a team that we can put near the site of the Brotherhood under surveillance; we need to know who is coming and going and what resources they have or bring to the site. I want to see Captain David Oppenheimer as soon as possible.

"Second, anybody who leaves the site must be followed; so I want a second team of about twelve people in the town with transportation so that they can follow people who leave and find out where they go and who they see.

"We need to adjust our satellites immediately to find the town and look for places that we can deploy observers in places where they cannot be seen. I want the team to be made up of twelve people with six rotating from base camp to the various observation points, and I want at least four observation points surrounding the warehouse; we may want to change the points and the size of the team depending on what Captain Oppenheimer thinks he needs to cover the target area effectively. I think the teams at the observation points should be changed every twelve hours. I want people refreshed and with keen eyes to watch with close scrutiny all activities at the meeting sites.

"This has to be a minimalist operation, meaning that everything the team needs is on their backs—no jeeps, trucks, or tents; nothing that will attract attention, and, more important, nothing that will change the profile of the landscape. If people want to look in our direction, they can't see us day or night: no fires and no lights and no smoking.

"The team will take two weeks of food and one week of water, replenishments will be dropped at night far away from the reconnaissance area. The supply depot will be responsible for communicating with Oppenheimer to fill his needs on a timely basis. One third of the team in the town will be rotated out every six days, and those who are rotated out will switch places with the team members in the observation post.

"Communications of what the observation posts see will be very important. I will have Captain Oppenheimer send me a report daily on all the activity at the meeting place. If any of the team members leave the warehouse, he or she must be followed. When a team leader enters town, a follower and an assistant will be assigned to that person. The follower will be given an Infineon XPOSYS chip, which is about the size of a single match head, and it has enough power to stay in contact with our orbiting satellites no matter where they go. The assistant must quickly find an opportunity in a crowd or someplace to attach the GPS chip; each chip will be assigned a number, and when one is planted, the assistant will report to his leader which GPS unit was attached. The GPS unit will act as a backup, should our surveillance team lose contact with the terrorist team member.

"It is very important to develop a code that can communicate information that can be transmitted quickly and securely. If it got out— even a hint that Israel was going to be attacked with dirty bombs—the panic could be catastrophic. After the satellites have spotted and filmed the meeting site and the surrounding area, they will turn to finding the cargo van. We know that it left the village two days ago, and we think it will be heading to Iran. It may have already crossed the Iraq border, but my guess is they are spending the night somewhere under cover, so our best chance is to look for the van in the morning. We have no idea were in Iran the van is headed; I think they will stay on well-traveled routes, at least through Iraq.

"We need to touch base with Frank Williams of US Homeland Security to see what has developed since my call with him, and we must share with him what we've learned."

Nava told Ayala that it would be her job to be in touch with Williams. "I want you to contact his office and set out a schedule of the frequency with which he wants me to contact him. If he has something he thinks I need to hear immediately, he should call me on my private cell phone. Contact with Williams will be extremely important, for even if the attack isn't coming against Israel; perhaps we can help protect America. Ayala, you will collect the information and get it to me and Capitan Oppenheimer and, when I tell you to, you will provide information to the prime minister's office, but you will not answer any questions or offer any opinions; that will be my responsibility. Last, I think we need to spend some time talking about the possible targets in Israel."

CHAPTER 73

Outside the Warehouse, Syria

MASSRI COWERED AS THE DOOR to the warehouse swung open and somebody stepped out. Somebody looked around and then went back in and shut the door. Massri really let go then, and it seemed that he would go forever, but he finally stopped. Most of the time he was emptying his bladder, his head was turned, looking at the door to see whether his friend had the same idea himself.

He realized that he was not going to get a picture inside the building and, while it was close to sunup, it was still dark enough for him to climb the water tower. He picked up his bag and walked quietly toward the tower; his route would take him past the front door. He took a deep breath and crossed in front of the door, and moments later his foot was on the first rung of the ladder heading up to the platform.

He swung his backpack on his shoulder and increased his speed in climbing up the ladder. Massri was constantly looking around to see whether anybody was coming or could see him climbing the ladder. He did not see anybody, so he finished his climb and landed safely on the platform. He spent a moment looking at the platform, trying to figure out what was the best vantage point in order to shoot his pictures. He was wearing sneakers, so the soft soles made no noise as he walked around the platform. He found some holes in the wood around the platform that would allow him to shoot pictures without having to stand up. The platform was wide enough for him to lie down and stretch out. All in all, it was very comfortable and gave him a great view of the compound and, depending upon whether the door was open wide enough, he might just might get an angle to shoot the wall and what was in front of it. Now all he had to do was wait and see who came to the meeting site, and also hope that no one needed to get to the tower. With that thought in mind, he looked around the entire platform to see whether he could find valves or any other control mechanisms, so that if somebody were to come up, he could hide on the other side while they worked. He looked up to see whether there was another ladder opening to get to the top of the tower and there was, but he would have to stand on the railing to get to it.

Now fully aware of his surroundings, he settled back and decided before people started arriving he would have something to eat and then sit and wait for the party to start. He had just finished the sandwich he brought and a banana, when he heard a car coming up the lane. It was light enough that he could tell what type of car it was, but more important, through the lens of the camera he could see the license plate number on the car and was able to shoot it. The car pulled behind the building and blocked the ladder to the water tower. At least for now, nobody was coming up the tower. He watched the person leave the car and, in rapid succession, shot many images of the person. He used his jacket over the camera to reduce the noise of the camera shooting. The first visitor turned around and looked straight up at the tower and Massri got a clear, full-face image; while he didn't take out the other pictures, the face reminded him of someone from the previous photos. Once the person went into the warehouse, he took a breath and went to the view screen on the camera to check the images.

The next to arrive was a large truck with two people, and they pulled close to the front door and left the motor running. One knocked on the door, while the other went to the back of the truck and lowered the hydraulic tailgate. He rode the lift to the floor of the truck and rolled out a series of cartons on a pallet that was wrapped in plastic. He loaded it on the lift and went back into the truck and brought forward another full pallet and then waited for the other person to arrive at the back of the truck. Massri continued to shoot rapid-fire pictures of the cargo and the people and the name on the side of the truck and then he stopped.

The other delivery person came to the back of the truck and he started shooting again, and this time with better light he could see that this person looked like someone he had shot before, but he was dressed in delivery coveralls. He lowered the tailgate and moved the pallet, which had wheels, through the dirt into the warehouse. Massri shot pictures of the ruts made in the dirt, indicating that whatever was on the pallet was heavy. They went through the same exercise with the second pallet to get it into the warehouse. The driver rode the lift up to the floor and disappeared inside the truck; this time he struggled to get the pallet, which was half the size of the other two, onto the lift. He finally got it on the lift and sent it down with him on the plate. When it hit the ground, the weight made a hard thud and then all three men struggled to get the pallet into the warehouse.

The driver came out of the warehouse and lifted the tailgate in place and ran around to the front of the truck and hopped in, but he was by himself; the other man stayed behind. The driver backed and turned the truck to leave, and Massri got a clear picture of the name on the side of the truck: Assad Systems of Damascus. Massri sat back on the platform and took a deep breath, wondering what it was that had been taken into this warehouse. He decided to move to his right so that he could see in the window of the warehouse, he wasn't sure what he was looking at through his telephoto lens, but he continued to shoot images while they were unwrapping the pallets and putting things on top of the bench. Some were left on the floor.

The two men walked out of sight, and both of them came back very carefully carrying a suitcase that seemed to be heavy. On second thought, they were carrying it as if, were they to jar it, the suitcase might explode.

CHAPTER 74

Outside ZanJan, Iraq, on the Way to Paleto, Iran

ADAD AND JAIARI HAD BEEN on the road to Paleto for about one hour; they had about ten hours before they reached Mehdiabad, and about six hours until they reached the border going though the town of Tolafarush. The night in ZanJan was uneventful; they rested, ate two meals, showered, and changed clothes. They checked the straps to make certain everything was secure, and they changed the shipping manifest to make sure it said they were delivering the supplies to Republic Transport LTD, in Mehdiabad, Iran.

With everything checked and rechecked, they both felt comfortable that the next part of the journey would go smoothly. Adad turned to Jaiari and said, "Sargon asked us to discuss our plans for how we would use the bombs against America; I think we should use this time to explore how each of us plans to carry out our use of the bombs on the targets we have chosen;

why don't you go first? If I remember, you wanted to take out the power grid in the United States. So how do you plan to do that?"

"America expects another attack on New York, and I plan to give them one, but not where they think it will happen. America has a great deal of security around Wall Street, so they have concentrated their forces in lower Manhattan. As we learned earlier, when the planes hit the first World Trade Center tower, Con Ed was able to shut the power to the lower Manhattan grid, in turn protecting the rest of the city's electrical infrastructure. Almost all of the power plants in the United States are part of what is called the grid. The grid moves power around as needed from low demand to high demand. If a plant has to go down for repairs, the grid manager can shift power to make up for the lost power for a short while. If you take two generating plants offline, you put more pressure on the grid, and if you take three plants offline, you put tremendous pressure on the grid to hold up. If the power plants are offline for an extended period of time, a time bomb starts ticking. If it takes all the capacity the grid has to make up for three power plants down, then no other plants can go down for maintenance or repairs. If a plant is forced to shut down, then a domino effect will shut down the power grid in the entire United States.

"We have already talked about the implications of a total loss of power in the United States, but you want to know how I would do it. Well, metropolitan New York City generates electrical power at several power stations in the city. Some plants used to be coal-fired and those are all gone; those that remain are fuel oil and/or natural gas–based plants. On the East Side of New York, there are three natural gas power generating stations almost running in a straight line from downtown to Upper East Side. These plants run alongside the East River. The river supplies cooling for the turbines, and so if we place one of our bombs at the East River power generating station between 14th and 15th at Avenue C, we can contaminate the lower plant and lower Manhattan.

"We place one of our dirty bombs in a car as close as possible to the plant in the visitor's parking lot. The driver has a choice: he can leave and do his best to get out of Manhattan or we find one of those martyrs who want to go to heaven and meet his vestal virgins as a reward for doing Allah's work. He is in the parking lot about five minutes at the most; he takes out his cell phone, and it looks like he is making a phone call. He dials the prescribed phone number that is attached to the detonator of the bomb, and the bomb blows.

"All three power plants are connected by a thirty-inch gas line, and the radiation in the pipes because of the blast may well force the government to shut down all three eastside power plants at the same time. They will have no way of knowing whether there is more than one bomb, so to be safe and to try to protect the rest of the plants, they will close all of them down. The blast will send fallout all across lower Manhattan and all the way from the Hudson River to New Jersey and across the East River to Brooklyn.

"The power company will stop the flow of natural gas to the other plants, and the coal-fired plants on the west side of the Hudson River in Jersey City will see their coal piles contaminated, and they will have to shut down those plants. The grid managers will not have enough time to react to try to bring on standby power, if they have any. The city of New York will be without power and will have lost at least six power plants, and because of the quick drop, it may well shut down the entire grid.

"The contaminated plants will be down not for a few days like in 2001, but New York City will be uninhabitable for perhaps ten to twenty years, like Chernobyl. The government will tell people after three to five years that it will be safe to return, but the physiological impact will keep people out of New York for at least a generation. The cost to rebuild the city will be astronomical, and people will ask, "Can we afford it and do we need it?" The collapse of the grid will take decades to be rebuilt. The explosion will cause the dislocation of millions of New Yorkers. Those people north, east, and west of the blast will try to get out of the city, but it will be gridlock of proportions never seen before. As the mushroom cloud spreads, more and more people will try to escape New York, New Jersey, and Connecticut. The metropolitan population of the greater New York is in excess of eighteen million people. Let's say that a significant number of them get out: where are they going to go? FEMA had a difficult time getting people out of New Orleans; imagine the challenge to relocate ten million people or more out of metropolitan New York. How do you feed them, find shelter and sanitary facilities, in such a short period of time?

"Let's assume that 100,000 people need medical attention because of their proximity to the blast site. How do you get to them? And if you could get to them, how do you get them out? Where do you find a medical care facility to handle this many people? Will the hospitals have the electrical power to care for the needy? The backup generators will run out of gas and it may well be impossible to get fuel to them.

"That takes care of the first bomb; I think the second bomb should be used at Hoover Dam. This monster generating plant produces over four billion kilowatt-hours per year, with the principal amount of power, over 57 percent, currently going to Los Angeles. The bomb at Hoover would shut down the city of LA. The traffic is bad *with* power; imagine LA with *no* power. Again, where do you put three million people who are looking for a home? The movement of a couple of hundred thousand people at one time could put tremendous pressure on other power companies, causing power failures and a further collapse of the grid.

"If we set off the bomb above the water line on the western wall of the dam near the two water intake towers, we will contaminate the water flowing through the dam. The water is filtered to eliminate all the rock and debris, but the nuclear contamination will rocket through all the water turbines before they can shut them down. It would almost be impossible to clean out all the contamination for a generation; nobody will want to take the risk to go into the power station to clean it up. In effect, four billion kilowatt-hours of power will be gone forever from this plant.

"Las Vegas will become a ghost town, as the drinking water for the town and other water needs will be contaminated and unusable. The water that normally flows out of the dam will not be able to be shut down because they will realize they can't shut the massive hydraulic doors without power. The contaminated water will flow downriver, and we will contaminate the towns and villages for hundreds of miles downstream. Hundreds of thousands of people all along the river will leave everything they have behind and flee for their lives.

"Questions will start appearing in papers—not online because the Internet will not work without electrical power. The towns that always generated their own power will drop out of the grid and protect their own. Those places that have power, which will be few and far between, will have armed guards at every entrance to the town to keep out people who would dilute the power of the town. As things settle into a routine people will start asking questions:

When can we go back and get our things?

When will the power be back on?

How can we get at our money in the bank?

Will there be food shortages?

Is the water safe to drink?

When will the schools reopen?

How soon before the hospitals are up and running?

Can I run my natural gas furnace this winter?

These are just some of the basic questions that will be asked, but after these are asked, a whole new round of questions will come. These new questions will come with anger and rage:

How did this happen?

What happened to Homeland Security?

Did the president know about the attacks?

And finally, the most important questions will be asked over and over again: Who did this and why?"

CHAPTER 75

Nava Dobias Office at Mossad

DOBIAS ASSISTANT, AYALA, HAD MADE contact with Captain Oppenheimer, and he was on his way to Dobias office. While he was waiting for the Captain, Dobias was thinking about the team he needed to put together to try to figure out what the possible targets might be in Israel for the Brotherhood and possibly their two dirty bombs.

He decided to call in Ayala to talk with her and get her ideas on suggestions for team members. Some in Mossad had raised concern about how much Nava trusted and depended on Ayala, and people wondered why he trusted her so much by having her involved. They didn't think she was a security risk, but the relationship was "different," and "different" makes people suspicious.

Nava didn't care about what other people thought he trusted her and she had always done an excellent job for him and their country. He buzzed her into his office and said to her, "We need to put together a damage assessment team. The job of the team is to try to figure out what are the two likely targets the Brotherhood will use their two dirty bombs against. So, Ayala, who do you think should be on the team?"

She responded, "You, sir, one or two rabbis, some people from cultural affairs, and Captain Oppenheimer."

"That's it?"

"Sir, I don't mean to be curt, but there aren't that many high-profile targets in Jerusalem. The larger the committee, the greater the chance for it to get out that there might be a possible bomb attacks."

Dobias door opened and the striking figure of a man in uniform walked through. He was about six feet two inches tall, had broad shoulders, and weighed about 200 pounds. The captain's uniform was full of medals and ribbons—so many that it didn't appear to have room for any more awards and you couldn't see much of the fabric. Nava invited the captain to be seated and suggested that Ayala also be seated so she could hear and record the highlights of the meeting.

"Captain Oppenheimer, I have selected you for two reasons: first, your reputation as a soldier and a leader; and second, you have been involved in some of the most secret missions in the history of the country. Captain, this mission may be the most challenging and most frustrating in your military career. For now the only notes of this meeting will be taken by my assistant, Ms. Ayala Softer. You can speak freely in front of her; so let's get started. You will report directly to me and the team that you will assemble will report to me and all information will flow directly to me. Any questions before we go further?"

"No, sir."

"The undersecretary of US Homeland Security for terrorist activities has notified me that a new terrorist group has been located in Syria. This new group is not an offshoot of al-Qaeda, but a new separate group that, like al-Qaeda, is out to destroy America, but may also have the intention of attacking Israel. The name of this group is the Brotherhood of the Red Nile. I need you to put together a team that will go into Syria and create observation posts to monitor the activities of the group. For now, this will be observation only, not search and destroy, do you understand?"

"Yes, sir."

"You will have a second team in the nearby village of Al-Mukharram that will monitor the activities of the terrorists if and when they come into the village. Team members will follow the terrorist group's leaders as long as they can but will also implant miniature GPS tracking devices that can follow a team member wherever they go. I want at least three outposts staffed with two men each. You cannot be spotted under any circumstances, so you will have to do everything you can to make your men invisible. You will have no tanks, trucks, and no mechanized equipment at your base. Your radio communications will be done at night for security purposes, and you will use a satellite phone to contact me directly.

"Any supplies needed will be dropped by aircraft a significant distance away from your base of operations, and your team will be responsible for retrieving the supplies. Any questions so far, Captain?"

"Sir, how big a force do you think I will need?" The Captain knew that Dobias was the most decorated man in the Israeli Army and he would know what to do to carry out a mission.

"I think about twenty-four should be enough, but that is your call. You let me know how many you want, and I'll get them for you. Captain, this part is very important: we believe that the Brotherhood has two dirty bombs from the former Soviet Union. We believe that one of the suitcase bombs is currently on its way to Iran, where an Iranian nuclear team is going to repair, stabilize, and upgrade one of the bombs. We believe that the second bomb is in the warehouse you will be observing. When the first bomb returns from Iran, we think the Brotherhood has a nuclear expert on their team who will duplicate what changes were made on the first bomb on the second bomb. The US believes that the Brotherhood has the United States as its first objective, but they also think it is possible that they may turn their attention on Israel. I will contact Frank Williams and let him know what we are planning.

"Captain, before you leave, I have decided that I want your input on one other issue for your assignment. By the way, we didn't talk about *when* I want you to go. I want the team on the ground in no more than three days. After you leave my office you will go directly to the satellite control center and you will scan the site where you will deploy and figure out what are the best places to deploy and your route to get to your destinations. You will also need to select a leader for the team in the village and figure out how the two of you will talk, either in person or over your cell phones, without blowing each other's cover.

"Now, back to the other issue. I need your thoughts on this question: If you had to choose two targets in Israel where you would want to use dirty bombs to the greatest effect in destroying morale in our country, what places would you destroy?"

CHAPTER 76

Frank Williams's Office

WILLIAMS WAS MEETING WITH MARIE and Baker, putting together the briefing book for the next meeting with the president. Williams wants an update of what is going on in identifying the people involved. Baker starts off by tell him of his meeting with Seacrest of the CIA. Seacrest has a person going back to the meeting site to try to get other pictures of the people involved and more pictures of the suitcase bomb.

"Seacrest tells me that he has reached out through Interpol to try to identify the people in the photographs sent to them. Harold Wellington of Interpol London is working through its Russian bureau and has identified from the photos we sent that the suitcase is the type and description of a Soviet Union dirty bomb. One of the terrorists has been identified as Adad Assad of Damascus, Syria. He is reported to be a self-made millionaire who got rich by developing an information systems and office supply company that markets throughout the Middle East.

"One other member who may be the leader of the Brotherhood is being researched at the moment to see if we can identify him. The CIA is trying to locate a cargo van with the name Assad Office Systems painted on the side that appears to be headed to Iran for retrofitting and upgrading one of the bombs. Seacrest has sent photos to his contact in the Syrian secret police to see whether they can identify the person with Assad. I think that's all I have to report. Marie, did you get it all down and do you have any questions?"

"I got it."

"I have been talking with Brown in the forensics lab, and she is trying to decipher the pages that were found in the Morristown, New Jersey home. She thinks at the moment that the twenty pages are targeting maps related to the twenty cities circled on the map found in the Ridley basement. She hopes to have some answers today.

"My last report has to do with Major Rahimi in Springfield. Omid is working with Sheriff Whittles, trying to find out what happened to the Ridley family. Brown checked the fingerprints from the map and the house and found that Michael has an identical twin named Ishtar. We know that either Ishtar or Michael took a flight to Amman, Jordan. Omid reports that just today he and the sheriff found out that Mike Ridley apparently never had a job because all the credit bureaus show no employment history. On the other hand, Michael, who was supposed to be in college, has a money market account that has been getting deposits of $25,000 per month since he went off to college over two years ago. That's over $600,000, and remember, he never went to classes. One last thing: the Ridleys don't own the home in Springfield. A Russian oil baron owns the Ridley house. Got it all, Marie?"

"Yes, sir."

Williams had something to add to the report concerning his contact with Nava Dobias, head of Mossad. "I've called Dobias to give him the information that we have obtained on the Brotherhood of the Red Nile. I told him that we have every indication that this terrorist group will be attacking America, but if for some reason that should not happen, it is possible that the Brotherhood might turn its attention to Israel."

Baker responded almost in shock: "Sir, it never crossed my mind that they might go after Israel."

Williams went on. "What if the Brotherhood finds that in order to get the Iranians to fix at least one of the bombs, they have to commit to using at least one upon Israel? Obviously, I have no proof of that type of deal, but it is a possibility and the price to fix the old bombs is so high that they don't have the money and they might have to make some concessions in order to get a bomb or two fixed. The old saying 'half a loaf is better than none' could, and I repeat, *could* be in play. I will be in contact with Nava on a regular basis to see what is developing. Nava told me in his follow-up call that they are launching a small surveillance team that will establish observation points for the purpose of just watching and reporting on what is going on at the warehouse.

"It could be possible that if the second bomb returns, we might seriously consider asking the Israelis to take out the terrorists, rather than try to land an American special ops teams to take them out. I will discuss this option with the president at the briefing tomorrow."

Baker asked, "Williams, do you think the president would seriously consider sending in American ground forces in the strife-torn country of Syria, risking an international incident?"

"If it took that action to secure America from a dirty bomb attack, I think he would. But the price America might pay for the failure of its mission could very well be the loss of Israel. Not just as an ally, but altogether," Williams replied somberly.

CHAPTER 77

Seacrest CIA Office

ODAY WAS THE DAY FOR Seacrest to follow up with the contacts that were working on his problems. His contact at the Syrian secret police; Wellington of INTERPOL in London to see if his team could identify the people in the photo he sent.

Ted Baker called and told him of Mossad plans. Seacrest knew Oppenheimer and planned to reach out to him quickly, for Ted indicated that after they left, they would be very restricted in outside contact. Seacrest was very nervous that nobody, even with all the eyes in the sky, could find the cargo van headed to Iran. Seacrest hoped that he could work his birds in conjunction with those of the Israelis to sweep the area where they were meeting and then move north and east to try to find the Assad van.

Right now, the Israeli satellites were mapping the area around the warehouse and the village to figure out the best areas for a base camp and observation posts. As soon as they finished, they would join the CIA in scouring the land for the cargo van.

While Seacrest was waiting for the callbacks from his contacts, his thoughts turned to something Baker said. Mossad was talking about possible targets in Israel. Baker had broached the subject of how they would get the bombs to America and when they got here, where they would use them. It was almost unthinkable that nuclear bombs could be used against the United States. John knew that right now, with so much unknown, it was impossible to figure out the chances of a bomb going off here. He realized that he needed to get a call in to Captain Oppenheimer, so he set aside for a moment the things he had been thinking about and focused his attention on the call to Oppenheimer. He didn't expect to get through to him on his first call, but he did get Oppenheimer's voice mail. John left a message: "David, my old friend, this is Seacrest, and it appears that we may be working on the same project, so if you have a moment before you go on 'vacation,' please give me a call."

After he hung up, it dawned on him *that if the US and Israeli governments decided to take out the Brotherhood, Mossad would likely be the group to take them out, and David would most likely lead the assault.* There was a great deal that was unknown about the Brotherhood; John remembered seeing the initial photos and had said to Baker that he didn't see any weapons. So if David Oppenheimer were given the order, they would be going after unarmed people, if you didn't count the two nuclear bombs. True, they might have two dirty bombs, but you can defend yourself unless you set them off, and if you do, you wipe out everybody in the Brotherhood and the team from Mossad and most of central Syria.

Seacrest thoughts turned back to a possible attack by the Brotherhood against the United States. He thought that the government resources had two challenges: could the Brotherhood be stopped at the borders and if not, then the more complicated question was how and where they would use the bombs. Seacrest thought that the entrance to the United States would be dictated by the weight of the bombs after they had been reconfigured. He was hopeful that Wellington and his Russian connections would be able to give him some idea of the possible weight of the bomb. "An oversize suitcase" could be a very misleading description. He saw the photos of the five men loading the bomb into the truck, and it looked heavy—very heavy. He didn't know how heavy the new bombs would be, but for now he was assuming that they would weigh about the same. So if the Brotherhood was going to bring two bombs into the country, most likely it wouldn't be by plane, unless it was by private plane. A private plane flying at low altitude could be almost invisible on radar, so a private plane was a strong possibility.

Seacrest thought to himself, *Wait a minute, a plane would be the fastest way to get the bombs into the country, and the best plane would be a diplomatic plane like an ambassador's plane.* Seacrest did a Google search about size limitations and what he found was: "The diplomatic bag shall not be opened or detained, under the Vienna Convention of 1961. The packages constituting the diplomatic bag must bear visible external marks of their character and may contain only diplomatic documents or articles intended for official use." According to the US Department of State, "This means that the words 'Diplomatic Bag' (or 'Pouch') must be clearly visible and displayed in English on the outside of the diplomatic bag. The diplomatic bag must also bear the seal of the government to which it belongs. This seal may be a lead seal that is attached to a tie that closes the bag, or a seal printed on the fabric of the diplomatic bag, or an ink seal impressed on the detachable tag." The US State Department said that packages so marked were exempt from detention, inspection, or X-ray. Such packages need only be described as "diplomatic pouches" on advance air manifests.

He read on and found something very important: *any* container could be a diplomatic bag—there were no limitations on size or shape. John stopped for a moment, and he decided that must be how they were going to get the bombs into the United States. Given all the possible ports of entry, it would be impossible for the government to cover every possible entry point into the borders of the United States. John knew that, with almost 11,000 miles of borders, there weren't enough personnel in all the branches of the government, including the military, to patrol the borders effectively.

There was some risk by sending the bomb in as a diplomatic pouch, but it might be worth the risk. Another option would be someplace along the Canadian border. The border with Mexico was fewer than 2,000 miles, while the Canadian border with the United States was almost 5,500 miles. The great expanse of the Canadian border made it a better crossing point. It might be easier to chase planes and diplomatic pouches, and moving two suitcases across an isolated Canadian crossing involved the least amount of risk and the highest potential for success for the Brotherhood.

As much as he hated to admit it, there was virtually no way, except pure luck, to stop the bombs from coming into the United States. John knew he needed to talk to Wellington to ask him to inquire of the Russian section whether the dirty bomb gave off radiation in its ready state. If it did, they could use satellites to scan the border and perhaps spot where the bomb was and then perhaps track it through its signal. John rocked back in his chair and came to one terrifying conclusion: unless we were extremely lucky, there was no way to stop the bombs from coming into the United States and being used on us.

CHAPTER 78

Megan Brown's Forensic Lab

THE FORENSIC TEAM ARRIVED EARLY next morning and eagerly went to the main computer to see what had happened. They downloaded the results, and twenty of the small maps matched with the twenty circles on the large map. A closer review of the overlay images showed that not all the maps were showing downtown, center-city targets. One of the cities was clearly New York, and the small map showed lower Manhattan, but away from the financial district.

Brown went to Google Earth and zoomed into New York City and found the exact area illustrated on the small map; she adjusted the scale and was able to lay the small map on top of Google Earth, and they matched perfectly, except they didn't see anything in the area that seemed worth blowing up. They did the same thing with the other nineteen small maps and Google Earth, and they kept coming up with target areas that didn't make sense to them. Brown said to Penelope and Derrick, "What are we missing? Is it possible that these are the targets that were eliminated?"

It might not be possible to attack twenty cities, so they went through a process of elimination to find the best possible targets. "We know that nineteen of the circles are the nineteen largest metropolitan areas in the United States, so it would make sense that if you only have two bombs, you can't bomb all twenty cities, so you have to make choices and what we might be seeing is that they reviewed these twenty places and they have decided on two, assuming they still have two bombs. But which two?"

"We can understand why they would consider New York, because it is the largest metropolitan region in the country, so New York has to be one of the target cities. So let's say that's a given; now we have to try to figure out what the second of the nineteen makes the most viable target."

"From the very beginning, you said the nineteen had commonality; the nineteen were the largest cities in the country, and yet number twenty doesn't fit with the other nineteen, so why is it in the group with the other nineteen?"

"I agree that we are missing something, but I think it has to do with the twenty circles. Perhaps they were laying out several plans for cities to attack to get the maximum effect. If we know that there are at least five leaders, perhaps each leader was asked to pick five cities and come up with a plan of how to use the bombs in each of the five cities?"

Derrick said, "Okay, so what do nineteen of the twenty have that the number twenty doesn't have? Let's look at it in a different way: what does number twenty have that the other nineteen don't have? What is number twenty?"

Penelope began, "Based on the small map, it is a very large area and the largest city in the area is—"

Brown stopped her in her tracks: "Springfield, Texas."

"You're right, it is Springfield, but I can't see anything in Springfield that a terrorist would want to blow up. It is as if Springfield is just a small version of the other nineteen, except that there is a lot of an open space in this section of the country. The nineteen have a huge concentration of people. Springfield doesn't. Perhaps Springfield's significance is that it was the center of the plot and somehow the Ridleys, including Michael, are involved. It the plot was hatched in Syria, then how does Springfield fit into the plot?"

"I don't know, but until we prove otherwise, there is some connection to the people in the house in Springfield and the people in Syria. We know that Michael has an identical twin, and either Michael or Ishtar, his twin, is in Amman, Jordan, while the other one is somewhere in America. We don't know whether he stayed there, went somewhere else, or is on his way to join the rest of the team. We also have no idea what happened to Mike and Mary Ridley, what role they are playing in this potential attack, or if those are even their real names."

Chapter 79

On the Road to Paleto

ADAD AND JAIARI HAD MADE it though the border between Iraq and Iran and were speeding toward Paleto to drop off the bomb and wait for it to be rejuvenated. Adad had turned the driving over to Jaiari and decided that he needed to tell Jaiari how he would carry out his attacks in Chicago and San Antonio. Jaiari, at the wheel, listened attentively.

"The first challenge is how do we get the bombs into the United States." Jaiari said immediately, "I didn't even think about that! What good are the bombs if we can't get them into America?"

Adad was pleased, because Jaiari had already suggested that he had thought about things in more detail than Adad had. "We also have to be concerned as to how we get them out of Syria: we clearly don't want the rebels or the government to get their hands on these bombs. I think my truck is the best way to get them to the port at Latakia and then we put them on a ship headed for Canada. We must use Poonen Shipping. I know the owners, and they owe me many favors. They have shipped my cargo many times, so it will not be a problem for them to take my cargo container.

They have also been to that port in Canada many times, so they will not be suspicious of our shipment.

"We will pack them in a cargo container that I will be sending to a computer hardware supplier who buys my used hardware and fixes them up and then resells them in Third-World countries at huge profits. We will have to work our way to the port of Rimouski Harbor, Canada. It is a small town of about 42,000 people, with a small dock. We can have them offload our container alongside the ship and clear customs. They may scan the container and then again they may not. If they scan it, all the computer equipment will camouflage our cargo.

"Looking at the map, I think we should look for a entreating the United States at White Fish, Montana. The US Customs Service says that the White Fish crossing does not operate 24/7, so we should look to enter when the crossing is closed. Once we are in the US, we need to split the team into two. One team will work its way to Chicago, and the second team will head to San Antonio.

"The Chicago team will find the server site and begin surveillance for at least five days. They will be looking for personnel changes; I think they call them shift changes in the US. The team will collect pictures of all three-power substations and assess where the best place might be to place the bomb. The second team will follow the same process in San Antonio. Once the surveillance is complete, the two teams with call each other to set a time to place their bombs and to determine the time of detonation.

"Now let's go to the server farm around Chicago. My engineer friend tells me that, in order to house 300,000 servers, it would take at least two buildings the size of aircraft hangers, probably 600 feet long by 200 feet wide and 100 feet high. If in fact there were three substations, then I would guess that there are three buildings, one building for each substation. The substations draw power from a trunk line that will feed high voltage power to all three substations. The substations provide power to run the servers, but the greatest amount of power is used to run the air conditioning to cool down the servers. If we cut the power at the mainline, we effectively shut down the power to all the farms. The bomb will make it impossible to get into the buildings for several years. The substations will have to be built somewhere else and then lines run to the facility. While the servers will not be able to run, and there will be no electricity to cool the building from the natural heat, over time the excess heat with no ventilation will destroy most, if not all the servers. As for San Antonio, we know less about the makeup of the facility, but if in fact they have consolidated eight-five centers in six in the United States, the facilities have to be almost as large as the one in Chicago. As soon as the team arrives in San Antonio, they need to get a phone book and a map and then ask gas station attendants, store clerks, and Quick Mart counter people where the HP buildings are in town. I would be surprised if the team doesn't locate the second site in less than four hours: if they don't, they aren't asking the right questions of the right people.

"These bomb placements will have to be quick, and we can't wait very long to detonate them; we may want to look for volunteers who are willing to join the Brotherhood and who want to go to heaven and meet their vestal virgins. We have to understand that if we can't find anybody to do the work for us, then we will have to do it ourselves. The time of the placement to the time of detonation has to be enough for us to get out of the immediate blast area. Once the blasts go off, there will be panic in the streets, so we need to have a safe house in each city a sufficient distance from the detonation site that we can stock with food, water, and nonperishable foodstuffs to sustain us for at least three weeks. We will be going nowhere for a period of time. I expect traffic control on the ground and in the air will come to a standstill, so gridlock will be a very big problem. All the systems that require the Internet will stop working. Interbank transactions won't work, credit cards won't work in stores or ATM machines, and these are some of the basic services that will stop, so we will need cash, a lot of cash. On a larger scale, Social Security checks will not go out to beneficiaries, pension checks cannot be processed, and the US government won't be able to pay its bills. State and local governments will not be able to collect tax revenue or pay their bills. The president, congressmen, and senators can't fly anywhere.

"The result of these two bombs is that America and Americans will become isolated from each other and the rest of the world. The world will no longer be one big family, but a group of truly isolated countries trying to survive. No more United Nations, because leaders can't fly there, and they may not even be able to talk on phones. They will not be able to launch aircraft or missiles against other countries. Jaiari, if we are successful,

America and a significant part of the world will have no choice but to revert to a different world that does not have computer networks.

"Jaiari, as I think about my plan, I often wonder: is what we are doing under my plan such a bad thing? Yes, people will die because of the disruption we cause, but people will die anyway, eventually. The real question is what will the American people do with the loss of such an important tool, and will they rededicate themselves to punish those who brought on this terrible change? Will we put Islam at risk of total eradication by our actions?"

CHAPTER 80

Springfield

"WHAT DO YOU MEAN, HE didn't have a job?"

"Sheriff, I'm telling you that the credit report came back, and under 'employment,' it says 'none listed.'"

"Is there anything on Mary?" Ford asked Wendell Parker, who was still on the line running a check on Mary Ridley. In a moment Parker told Ford, "Nope, no job for her, either." Omid asked how Mike Ridley could have lived in this town for fifteen years and have nobody notice that he never went to work? Whittles responded, "I'll call my brother-in-law, John Bowman, and see if he remembers where Mike Ridley worked."

"Sheriff, I want to talk with Mr. Bowman in person, so hold off calling him; we need to see the records on all three Ridleys first."

Omid asked Ford whether he could put Parker on the speaker phone, and while Ford was making the connection, Rahimi got up and walked over and closed Ford's door.

Omid said to the sheriff, "Do you mind if I do this part?"

"Go right ahead, Major. I'm all ears," Sheriff Whittles said.

"We will need your time and your patience to go through the records for all the Ridley accounts. Bill, I have shown the search warrants signed by the judge, and I believe he will tell you that he is honoring them for his bank."

"Yes, we will cooperate fully in the investigation."

"Wendell, I will send my deputy with the warrants for your bank to you shortly, in the meantime, whatever Major Rahimi needs, I want your full cooperation."

Omid said to both bank presidents, "My guess is that you are on different record-keeping systems. Is that correct?"

Parker said, "Our bank is on Flex Software."

Ford said, "We run Multiview.netn10."

"My guess is they are not compatible?"

The bank presidents agreed.

"Excellent. Let's start with some basics. Mr. Parker, you indicated you had an account for Mike and Mary and none for Michael. Is that correct?"

"Correct."

"Mr. Ford, you said, you only had accounts for Michael, is that correct?"

"Yes, that is true."

"Okay, can each of you tell when the first account was opened for each of the parties in your bank?"

"Michael's money market was opened on July 10, 1997, and the checking account was opened in June 2008. It was opened with $25,000."

"How far back can you go on his credit card?"

"We don't keep the information at the bank; we actually use another bank's credit card, and we put our name on the card. I would have to speak with them in the morning."

"Excellent. Mr. Parker, thank you for being so patient; I need the same deposit and transaction date for all the accounts under the names of Mike and/or Mary Ridley. I want any account in a joint name or a single name, and I want to see money market, checking, or any other account with their names on it. Do you understand?"

"Yes, Major."

"When can we see the data?"

"I think by sometime tomorrow, but it's hard to be sure, because I don't know the magnitude of the accounts. My screens only go back so far, so if the accounts went back further, I would have to search the company files over the Internet. Also, Mike and Mary had credit cards for at least ten years, perhaps longer."

"I have one last question for both of you: Is it possible to load all historical data on a computer tape reel or a CD?"

Both men agreed that it was.

Omid thanked the men and gave both men his cell number in case they had any questions or problems. The Major hung up the phone, and he and Sheriff Whittles left Ford's office and went outside.

"I don't know what the data will show, but just maybe we have saved America today. And if it doesn't turn up anything, then maybe we haven't."

CHAPTER 81

Mossad

CAPTAIN DAVID OPPENHEIMER HAD ASSEMBLED his teams and was getting them ready to deploy in less than twenty-four hours. He saw that he had a phone message from Seacrest and wondered whether he had time to return the call. He had a meeting with Dobias in about half an hour, and he had a lot to do. He decided he would call John but just spend a few moments. He dialed Seacrest number, and John picked up on the third ring.

"John, this is David. How are you? It's been a long while." "David, it has been a long time, and I hope you are well. I know you're very busy at the moment, and I'll make this quick. I have an asset currently on the ground at the site you are headed to, and if he can get out without being caught, he will have more pictures in about two days. I will get them to you through Nava as soon I get them. I want you to be safe, and if can help in any way, please call me, and I'll do the best I can. I have to tell you that these people scare me a great deal. They don't seem to be your typical terrorists. Perhaps they're the new breed of terrorists who want to destroy America for the intellectual satisfaction of knowing that they can do it. It's almost like the hackers who are trying to break into bank security systems not to steal, but to prove to themselves and to the rest of the world that they can."

"I agree with you: we have not seen anything like this before. Thank you for your offer, and be assured if I need you to bail me out, I will call. John, I have to run to a meeting to decide what the likely targets are in my home country."

John thought to himself after he hung up, *a lot more people than me need to be doing the same thing to figure out their targets in America.*

Oppenheimer was walking in the door of Dobias office when he saw two rabbis and Ayala and Nava. They were all sitting around Nava's conference table. He knew what the meeting was about, and he wanted to be with his men, but he knew his boss wanted him there.

Nava said to the group, "We all know why we're here: we need to try to figure out what buildings would the terrorists strike with their dirty bombs to bring Israel down." Nava walked over to a whiteboard that had been brought to his office and asked, "What is target No. 1?"

As if they had all read a script, they answered, "The Temple Mount."

"Then what would be the next thing?"

"The Western Wall."

"Is it possible that the Western Wall and the Temple could be taken out in one blast?"

Based on the answers from the rabbis, they had not been briefed about the dirty bombs possibly being used against their country. Nava thought the range of the bomb exploded by the Temple Mount would contaminate the Western Wall and over thirty-five churches, temples, and mosques. The one bomb would isolate the city from the rest of the country and the world. The almost three million tourists would no longer be able to come to this most holy and sacred city. Given the size of the city, a bomb would have to be placed as close as possible to the exact center of the city. The exact center of the City of Jerusalem is 31° 47° 00 N by 35° 13° 00 E.

"If we add those numbers we get 666; as we know from the Bible, 666 is a mark of the Beast. If the terrorists are going to make a statement for the world to see, I think they would place the bomb at the exact center of the old city."

One of the rabbis spoke up. "It would seem to me that this would be the natural place for us to have forces, perhaps men from Mossad that could keep vigilance on that one spot, so if a suitcase bomb is left there it could be captured, disarmed, and disposed of without alerting the country or the world until after the fact."

Rabbis Berlitz speaking for all of them turned to Nava and asked, "Do you have the manpower to cover the site 24/7 for the foreseeable future?"

"Before I answer that question, can any of you think of any other sites where it would make sense to add a bomb?"

Ayala spoke up. "I realize that the exact center of the old city has things going for it, but we believe that the terrorists have two bombs, and they may well conclude that two is in fact better than one. If we concentrate all our efforts on the center of Jerusalem, and they have a second bomb that they will use against us, then we could be safe in the center of the city while another bomb goes off in some other part of the city or another place in the country.

"My guess is that the bomb will be brought in and detonated in a very short time after placement. So finding a suitcase bomb when we have no idea what it looks like and disarming a detonation system we have never seen is not very realistic. We can use intersection surveillance cameras already in place to help us watch for the bombs, and when we see them, we can use blasting netting to try to contain the blast. We need to try to figure out where to get these nets and whether we have to send a plane today to get them. We should get six of them, and we could pile three on top of the bomb or bombs. Perhaps if the Americans can get some information as to the power of the bombs, with that information we can see how much damage we can prevent with the nets, if any."

David said, "I think this is an excellent plan and, short of taking them out before they leave Syria, there doesn't appear to be much else we can do at the moment. I need to get to my team."

Nava walked him to the door and asked him to call him when he was ready to depart. He continued, "David, the fate of Israel may well be in your hands. May God be with you and your team."

As David walked through the door, he was thinking, *are they saying the best we can hope for is* blasting nets *to save Israel? This is why I hate working with civilians.*

Chapter 82

Brotherhood Meeting Site

Mordecai and Oleg arrived at the meeting room to see the machinery and equipment that had been delivered earlier that morning. Massri, from his vantage point on the water tower platform, was able to snap several pictures of each of them as they went into the warehouse.

The equipment was still sitting where it was delivered, and Mordecai was beginning to unpack the equipment and putting it on the workbench. Oleg was helping him unpack, so it was just the two of them in the building, neither of them saying much to the other. Oleg was not sure what all this equipment was for—whether they were just going to change out the explosives. Massri saw the night guard leave, and he took a picture of the guard, just in case Seacrest wanted to see what he looked like, too. With the door open, the voices traveled up the tower very clearly, almost like a reverse megaphone. He heard the two men in conversation say that someone named Sargon was not expected until later in the day.

Massri could hear them using each other's first names, and he wrote this all down so he could report to Seacrest when he returned to Damascus. When the wind shifted, the sound quality of the conversation degraded; he also noticed that if they moved to another part of the warehouse he could not hear anything, so while he had the opportunity, he listened intently.

Mordecai said, "I would like to share with you my plan of how to deliver the knockout blow to America. Do you remember our experiment in the parking lot with the sand and the firecrackers?"

"Yes, I do; you said the challenge would be to find enough dust."

"I think I have found some dust. I realize that what I'm about to say seems like it has nothing to do with my plan, but you will see where it fits."

With that, Mordecai began to tell a story. "The year was 1961, and in the small town of Centralia, Pennsylvania, a fire broke out in the Centralia coal mine. The fire was small at the start, and they quickly tried to extinguish it, but everything they tried failed, and the fire spread. They tried to seal the mine, but there were cracks everywhere in the walls and ceiling, and if they didn't seal all the cracks, the fire would get the oxygen necessary to keep burning. As the fire spread, thick, toxic smoke and gases leaked up through the ground, and in some places you could see the coal burning yellow through the cracks. The smoke and fumes got so dangerous that all the townspeople had to be evacuated, and to this day, over fifty years later, the fire is still burning and the townspeople have never been able to go back to live in Centralia.

"In some respects it's like the people who had to leave Chernobyl, Russia, when the nuclear reactor exploded and spread radioactive debris all over the town, forcing the people to leave in order to survive. Oleg, the moral of this story of the Centralia coal mine is that once you get coal burning, as long as it has oxygen, it will continue to burn, until the fire is extinguished or the fire runs out of coal. My attack plan will only take one bomb, so that if somebody has an idea for another target for the second bomb, with both bombs, we can really do an incredible amount of damage.

"I doubt that you know that the City of New York no longer has any coal-fired generating stations left in the city, but across the river, in clear view from midtown Manhattan, in Jersey City, New Jersey, Public Service Electric and Gas (PSEG) has a coal, natural gas, and oil-fired power-generating station at Duffield and Van Keuren Avenue. This power plant has an inventory of coal; in fact it has over 50,000 tons on site that they can call on when it is less expensive to generate electricity by using coal. The thousands of tons of coal sit on top of a concrete reinforced tunnel. This tunnel has walls and ceilings that are twenty-four inches thick, made out of steel-reinforced high-density concrete. The tunnel has to be this strong in order to support the weight of the coal on top of the tunnel. Attached to the ceiling are electric feeds that slowly feed the coal onto a conveyor belt that runs the entire 300 feet of the tunnel.

"When PSEG wants to use coal to fire the boilers to make steam, the belt conveyors are turned on first, and then the feeders deposit coal on the running conveyor belt in the concrete enclosure. The electric feeders draw coal from the bottom of the pile to fill the belts that go to the plant to provide fuel to fire the boilers that generate steam to turn the turbines that generated the electricity."

Oleg said, "I understand, but so what happens next?"

Russians are so impatient, Mordecai thinks to himself. "Coal fires at 871 degrees and so we will plant our bomb in the bottom of the pile."

Oleg asked, "Are we going to dig a hole down through all the coal?"

"No, we are going to come up from the bottom. You may recall that I said they can run several different fuels, so if they are running natural gas, because it is less expensive than coal, the coal pile sits waiting. When the plant is not running coal, we will break into the plant and go down into the conveyor tunnel and install the bomb. It should fit in the opening where the coal comes out of the pile when the feeders are used to fill the conveyor belts with coal.

"I know that PSEG sprays a fire retardant on the top of the coal to prevent spontaneous combustion of the coal dust, but our explosion will come up from the inside and the bottom of the coal pile. The massive fire and explosion will burn off the fire retardant sitting on the coal pile. The bomb has to be strong enough to blow a hole large enough in the pile to supply oxygen to the burning coal. Once we hear from Adad and Jaiari as to the power of the bomb, we can figure out how big a hole we can blow in the coal pile and you, being the engineer, can figure out how long the pile can burn before it burns out.

"The concrete tunnel under the pile of coal, Oleg, will intensify the initial explosion almost like a funnel. Do you remember the parking lot experiments? The one that hit the wall showed more intensity in the pattern. The energy of the bomb will be pushed against the concrete walls of the tunnel and finding no way to escape through the wall, the power will take the path of least resistance and be forced up though the coal pile in the feeder opening where we have placed the bomb.

"The intensity of the explosion will send contaminated burning coal all over the plant area. Red hot and glowing embers of coal will rain down not only on the plant, but also for miles away from the plant. The spray of fiery coal could start fires in the plant, and for miles around houses and other buildings will burn as a result of the glowing embers hitting the roofs and burning them away. Back at the plant, the concentrated area of equipment and flammable fuel in an area should create secondary explosions in the oil and natural gas lines. The heat from the bomb will be much greater than the flash point of the coal. The coal will burn, and the ash of the burning coal will be radioactive and begin to enter the air. Shortly after the explosion, the contaminated smoke and ash will start traveling on the wind. This is the part that gets very interesting and is a potentially very dangerous situation. How does the government clean up the radioactive soot without endangering the cleanup crews?

"Think of our coal pile as a small Mt. St. Helens. When Mt. St. Helens erupted in Washington State, the plume of ash from the fire in the volcano encircled the globe in fifteen days. Now, I'm not expecting our coal pile to encircle the globe, but I do believe it could have an impact on at least a third of the eastern United States.

Because of the intensity of the flame, it will try to burn all the coal in the coal pile. It may take a long time to burn out 50,000 tons of coal, but all the time it will be spewing out contaminated ash. The plant is gone, probably forever; nobody will want to go in to try to do anything because of the danger of radiation. The idea that a coal fire is spreading radioactive material will make the governments and people panic all over the region. We have a pile of coal burning out of control with smoke and ash going in any direction depending on the wind. If the wind is blowing east, then New York City and parts of Long Island and Connecticut will be receiving smoke, ash, and possible radiation. When the wind shifts the smoke, ash and radiation could fall on central New Jersey. Oleg, think of the smoke coming out of the coal pile at the power plant as a wind sock: every time the wind shifts, the sock moves, and so every time the wind shifts, the danger shifts.

"Do you think people will want to stay in New York City, not knowing whether, when they went to work in the morning and the wind and danger was blowing away from them, and when they come out of their offices in the afternoon, the wind and the danger was landing on everything around them? I want you to try to picture this chaos. How could the government accommodate the millions of people who will want to be relocated out of harm's way in days? Oleg, what do you think will happen to the largest metropolitan population in the United States? Would you want to live there? Where could the government possibly put eighteen million people in a month, six months, or a year?"

CHAPTER 83

Nimrod Castle, Close to the Syrian Border

Captain David Oppenheimer was assembling his task force for deployment to Syria and, more specifically, the Brotherhood meeting site. He chose the Nimrod Castle section of the Golan Heights because it was the closest entrance point to Syria in Israel. David knew that he could not use traditional military garb or equipment to cross the border. If they went in as an Israeli Army unit, it would cause an international incident, and the Syrians would be shouting to the world that the Jews were invading Syria.

Fortunately, Mossad had an assortment of what appeared to be beat-up old trucks and cars that would fit in with the rest of the environment, though in reality they were well-equipped, armed assault vehicles. No military uniforms, nothing, including provisions, could look as if it came from Israel.

David had broken down the team into two units; the first unit consisted of twelve people and would be around the warehouse, commanded by him. The second unit of twelve people—eight men and four women—would be in the village, and First Lieutenant Hadar Hassen would command it. David knew this would be her first action as a team leader, but he believed her training, experience, and her work ethic made her right for the job. Hadar knew this was an opportunity for her to prove herself capable, and as a result, she hoped to get a promotion.

Oppenheimer had purposefully mixed men and women on the team for the village because he could pair them up as couples and not attract attention. All of the women looked more Syrian than Israeli. They were all young and in great shape, they had trained just as hard as their male counterparts. The entire unit would have Syrian passports, and all Israeli identifying papers would be left behind. The teams and the commanders could communicate by cell phone, if possible, and each unit would have a satellite phone only to be used when all other forms of communication had failed.

The plan was, once the teams left, they would head to their assigned destinations and would not see each other again until the mission was over, unless David wanted to shift personnel. He asked the team members whether they had any questions. He said, "We will be leaving shortly after Lieutenant Hassen and I have a review of the plan one more time, so get your gear loaded and stand by to mount up."

Hassen and Oppenheimer walked to the side of the road. He reached into his pocket and took out the miniature GPS tracking devices he had received from Dobias and said, "If one of the terrorist team comes into the town, you are to attach a GPS device to him so we can track him. I don't care what you have to do to get this device on the terrorists; I just want it done."

"Yes, sir."

"While we are en route, new photos of the terrorists should arrive at Mossad, and they will forward them to me. I will contact you and arrange to get them to you for your team so you can have some idea who you are looking for in the village. Until you hear anything different from me, you are here to observe, track, and you take no action unless ordered to by me. Any questions?"

"No, sir."

"You have enough women to make four couples, so book rooms for two people and in different hotels. During the day, no congregating, and that goes for nighttime too; for all intents and purposes you do not know each other, period. On your journey to the village, I want your team members to work out signals to be able to alert each other when there is a need to meet, and that signal has to come from you.

"One method that I have used in the past when I have been under cover is to look for a village square. In the square there will generally be a fountain, or there will be some statue, and it usually sits on a base. Find the north side of the base and mark the agreed-upon signal for a meeting outside of town. Mark the sign with chalk, and tell your people to walk by and look for the signal every day. At some point during the day you go and remove the sign.

"En route to the city, your team will agree on a password for the first meeting. You will be responsible for communicating to your team what actions will be required should the operational plans change. If I notify you that it is time to leave, it will be by cell phone. You will have to develop in advance of your arrival an exit sign. The sign can be as simple as your room window flower box. If you move a flowerpot from one side to the other, that could be a sign to exit whatever you use, just make sure everybody knows the signal. You must figure out what the symbol is before you arrive, and make sure the whole team knows what it is, so they can react quickly.

"I want you to inspect every person on your team to make sure that there is nothing on his or her person or in their baggage that can tie them back to Israel. I want you to go through their wallets, look for driver's licenses, credit cards, even a library card, and if they have photographs, review them carefully, and have someone else look at the photos to see if there is anything, I mean *anything*, that could tie them to our mother country. If there is any doubt in your mind, burn it before we leave. Look for dog tags, anything that could compromise this mission. This is very important I can't stress this enough: there can be no sign, no tie to Israel; do you understand, Lieutenant Hassen?"

"Absolutely, sir, I will check everybody down to every detail."

"Excellent, and when each of us has completed checking our people, we need to have somebody check us, and when this is complete, we can move out. I expect it will take you about seven hours to get to Al-Mukharram, and we will be outside the village near the warehouse at about the same time you reach the outskirts of the village. While you are en route, avoid any contact with rebels, military, and police even if it takes longer to avoid contact. I can't tell you how long this mission will last, but, as of now, I think we should plan for at least three weeks. Because of the length of the assignment, no letters or postcards home can be sent. I realize that it will be difficult not to reach out to our family and friends, but we just can't take the chance. And I, for one, know how much I will miss you, but when this is over, I hope to have some time together."

Hassen responded with a warm smile. "Yes, sir."

Chapter 84

Seacrest, Langley, Virginia

Seacrest was waiting for a call back from London and Syria, and he was still waiting for Massri to get back to Damascus and send him the new photos of the team members. He decided to follow up with Wellington at Interpol on the identifications of the people in the photos he had sent him several days ago. It was early enough to call Wellington, and so he dialed his number; as in the past, there was no answering machine, so it rang and rang until Harold picked up the phone. "Wellington here. May I help you?"

"Harold, how are you? This is Seacrest."

"I'm fine, except for too much Irish whiskey last night."

"I'm truly sorry about the whiskey, but I was calling to follow up with you on the photos I sent you; have you had any luck identifying anybody in the photos?"

"Seacrest, old chap, I circulated them, and nobody seems to know the people in the pictures except for one fellow."

"Who might that be?"

"While we can't be sure, it appears that one of the fellows is the nephew of one of Russia's richest."

"Do you have a name?"

"For the uncle or the nephew? I can tell you the names of both people. The nephew is Oleg Barbolio, and he is the nephew of Viktor Antipova."

"That is great news. Let me know when you get anything else."

Seacrest was ecstatic that he had more information that he could send on to Ted Baker to help him fill out the identities of the team members. Seacrest did a Google search on Viktor Antipova and found thousands of hits. His wealth came from oil that he had found in the Ukraine. Seacrest search didn't reveal that Antipova owned what was the house in Springfield, however.

Instead, he saw from the search that at one time Antipova had worked for the KGB in the old Soviet Union and had been in charge of all non missile-based nuclear weapons. There were stories that he had sold some of the nuclear devices that didn't function to raise the money to develop his oil business, but nothing was ever proven. As for the nephew, all Seacrest could find was that Oleg had worked for his uncle's oil business, but for reasons unknown, went out on his own a few years back. The article went on to say that he had been educated in America at Stanford University School of Engineering, with a specialty in petroleum engineering.

Seacrest decided to call his contact in the Syrian secret service, Asu Aldiri, to see whether he could identify the person in the photo with Assad. Somebody who was not Aldiri answered the phone. He said who he was and then the phone went dead for what seemed like a long time. Eventually Seacrest heard Aldiri voice, but he seemed a little tentative.

"Aldiri, are you okay?"

"John, things are getting out of hand here; the rebels are everywhere, and it is difficult to safely get around town, much less the whole country. I'm sorry, but I can't seem to find anything on the man in the photo with Assad. I have searched the records, and I can find nothing on him in our files. If he is a Syrian, then he doesn't have any record. I was not able to get through by phone to the newspaper that published the photo, and they have not responded to my e-mails. You might have better luck if the e-mails came from the US and perhaps from Homeland Security."

"Thank you for your help. Should you find anything out, please contact me immediately—and stay safe, my friend."

Next, Seacrest decided to put in a call to Baker to let him know what he had found out from Interpol and the Syrian secret police. He called Ted and reached his voice mail; he left a message to meet him at the Starbucks on Seventh and Pennsylvania at two, if he could make it, and to call him back as soon as possible if he couldn't.

While he was waiting for Baker to call back, he was thinking about Massri and wondering how the picture taking was going; he knew that it would be at least another twenty-four hours before he could expect to hear from him.

As Seacrest waited, he worried, and he thought that the one thing that was different from perhaps every other time the alert level had been raised to the highest level was the threat of a nuclear bomb—and nobody could say that it was because of a nuclear threat, because of the chaos in the country. Airplanes and cargo vans loaded with TNT or dynamite are dramatically different from, and in reality, less threatening than, nuclear bombs. The detonation of a nuclear bomb would have more far-reaching implications than any other form of explosive device. A bomb set off in a Major city would render the city worthless for many generations to come, in addition to the immediate loss of life.

He questioned what kind of hatred was so strong that it would use not only weapons of mass destruction, but also weapons of mass interruptions. *Are we Americans so evil that we are driving Islam to the point that they feel they must destroy our way of life and us? In order for them to preserve their way of life, they must use nuclear bombs against us? Are there other nations, which, if America falls, will take over and lead the world? Will these new world leaders be destroyed to preserve Islam, like the United States might be? Where does the killing between nations based on religion and ideology stop? We are not trying to bring down Syria in this battle, but a handful of men want to do everything they can to destroy America, destroy an entire nation. Better that five men die, and bombs are captured, than that an entire nation is destroyed. We are on the right side, the side of good, right?*

Just then his phone rang, and it was Baker confirming his coffee appointment at two. Just before he hung up, Seacrest asked, "We *are* doing the right thing, aren't we, Ted?"

Chapter 85

Meeting Site

Captain David Oppenheimer and his special ops team were traveling the back roads; such as they were, in Syria, headed to the outskirts of Al-Mukharram, looking for a small warehouse near a citrus grove.

Oppenheimer had seen the satellite maps and could tell from his handheld GPS that they were about four miles from the warehouse. His GPS told him that the town was to his left and was about ten miles away. They needed to begin to find places where they could hide their cars and trucks. The terrain was somewhat hilly, and he thought it best to separate the vehicles belonging to his team members and hides them in different hills. He told his team, which had six pickup trucks, to separate them, starting now, and putting them at least 500 yards apart. By separating them it would be more difficult to spot the trucks. In addition, Oppenheimer had desert cloth to throw over the trucks to blend them into the landscape. It would also provide shelter for those team members not manning the observation positions. The captain decided to wait until dark to select the observation posts. Through his field glasses he could make out the citrus grove, and he could see the warehouse and water tower at the end of the grove. Just as he was looking at the tower, he saw a small flash in the sun. Initially, he couldn't tell whether it was the flash of some metal in the water tower or whether it was the reflection of a sniper rifle up in the water tower protecting the people below. He told his men to stop and wait until he could figure out who or what was up in the tower.

Based on where he saw the reflection, he decided to approach the flash from the opposite direction. He figured that the sniper was probably walking around the tower, so if he came around to Oppenheimer's side of the tower, the angle of the sun would create another flash. He took cover behind a stand of scrub pine and waited for the flash, but it never came. He took out his field glasses, which were blackened so that the sun would not reflect off the glasses, and tried to see the sniper, but he couldn't.

Perhaps the reflection was off some metal on the side of the tower and not a sniper rifle? Then again maybe not Oppenheimer decided he could make his way to the citrus grove, and he moved to his left so that he could get a better look at the building and the water tower. As he moved through the grove, he was about a thousand feet away, and he decided that was close enough. He took cover behind a stand of orange trees that had branches hanging low to the ground. He found that the center of the tree was very open and gave him plenty of room to see what was going on, and at the same time gave him great cover and some juice from the oranges to quench his thirst.

With his back to the tree he cut open the orange and it was juicy and very ripe. As he sucked on the orange, he began to look around for different vantage points for his men. He took out a small notepad and made some sketches of the surrounding terrain. Just as he turned back to make a note on an observation point, another flash from the tower caught his eye. The flash wasn't as if a rifle were aimed at him, though. Was it possible that the terrorists had two snipers in the tower?

He felt safe where he was, but he was concerned about his men being out in the open. He had confidence that they were well hidden and that they would not do anything until he returned. It was now about five o'clock, and the sun was beginning to go down; soon he would have to return to his men, but under the cover of darkness was the best time to leave.

At about 7:30, two men came out of the building, got into a pickup truck, and drove away. Oppenheimer was just about to leave when he decided to wait until the snipers came down from the tower. Oppenheimer waited another thirty minutes, and nobody came down. He waited. Then, in an instant, Oppenheimer saw a leg come over the edge of the rim of the platform and reach for the rung of the ladder. Then the other leg came over, and the sniper slowly and gingerly climbed down from the tower.

Oppenheimer focused with intensity at the sniper coming down the ladder. As the sniper came into view, Oppenheimer noticed that he was carrying not a rifle, but a camera. As he reached the bottom of the ladder, he stepped off and stretched his legs. The man must have been taking pictures of the people and the site all day. But for whom? The flash must have been the sun reflecting off the camera he held in his hands, and because he was so high up in the air on the tower, Oppenheimer couldn't see the jacket the man had wrapped around the camera to muffle the clicking.

The man looked around and started to leave the site by way of the grove. Oppenheimer saw that he was headed right for the tree under which he was hiding, so in a panic, he moved. He quickly slid to his right, with his back to the approaching man. Oppenheimer held his breath as the man got closer and closer to the tree. Oppenheimer saw the man's shadow approach his tree, and he was sure the man had seen him. Oppenheimer carefully reached into his pocket.

CHAPTER 86

Approaching Paleto

ADAD AND JAIARI WERE JUST outside the town of Mahabad, the town in which they would stay while the bomb was being upgraded; it was just a short drive to Paleto, the site of one of Iran's nuclear testing laboratories, where they would take their bomb today. They would stop at the hotel Shahr-e-Ghesseh and check in and then go immediately to Paleto.

Jaiari said he needed to do most of the talking, at least until they got inside and met people who would be working on the bomb. He would discuss with them the payment terms and that one of them would be present with the bomb at all times. He would wire half the money the next day and the other half when they proved to him that the bomb was operational, and they had answered his questions about what they had done to the bomb. Jaiari would have Adad take a series of photos before they started, and would have him take photos throughout the process.

Jaiari was now having a phone conversation with the project leader and was telling him that they would be at the lab today around four p.m. As they followed the directions to the hotel, they could spot it out the windshield of the now dirty cargo van. It didn't look like a four-star hotel, but it was not a dump, either. They pulled in, and Jaiari went in to register, Adad stayed in the cargo van for a few moments. Jaiari signaled that Adad must come into the lobby. Adad turned off the engine, got out, locked the van, and headed to the lobby. As he walked through one front door he noticed that the other door seemed to be stuck.

Adad had stayed in some excellent places all over the Middle East, and it was a stretch to call this a two-star hotel. The furniture and rugs in the lobby were showing wear. The paint was chipping off the walls in places. It was clear to Adad that the tough times in Iran had taken a toll on the buildings, the streets, and the hotels. He could only imagine what the restaurants must be like.

He walked over to the sign-in desk and saw that Jaiari was having a friendly conversation with the desk clerk.

"They need to see your passport before we check in."

Adad pulled out a well-worn passport with many in-and-out stamps from numerous countries in the Middle East. The clerk made a copy of the passport and returned it to Adad. Jaiari told them that they would stay perhaps as much as two weeks, but probably not more than three weeks, though it could be less. Jaiari thought, *I guess we can't just say, "Until the nuclear team sees the bomb and knows how long it will take to rebuild it."*

The clerk showed them to the room, and it was one overlooking the parking lot, so they could see who was coming and going. The furnishings were about twenty years old, but the room was clean; the shower had running water, along with clean towels and even those small bottles of shampoo and conditioner, along with bars of soap and twin beds. They went back to the front desk and told the clerk they would take the room and asked whether they could have two keys.

There was a café adjacent to the hotel; they were hungry, and they decided to go have something to eat. With their stomachs full, they headed out to Paleto. Their hearts were just as full, with the excitement of getting one step closer to their goal—the destruction of America. When they were out of the Mahabad, Jaiari took out his cell phone and called his contact, Saeed Zarin, at the center. He waited for Zarin to answer, and after five rings he expected his call to go to voice mail, but Saeed finally answered. *This is Zarin.* Not recognizing the phone number, he didn't know that it was Jaiari calling him. When Jaiari introduced himself again to Zarin, he knew why Jaiari was calling.

"How far are you to Paleto?"

"We are just outside Mahabad, and I would guess we are another forty-five minutes from Paleto."

"Unfortunately, I do not know where to go to get to you. You go to the center of town, and you come to a square. Go around the square and take the second right, which is route 28, and head east for about ten kilometers. Road 32 intersects, and you will turn right on 32 and then go two kilometers, and you will see a plain white building on your left.

"There will be a single guardhouse just after you turn off the road; the guard will stop you and ask to see your passports and then he will want to know who you have come to see. Tell him to call me on extension 21 and ask for Saeed Zarin. What are you driving?"

"We are in a cargo van with Assad Business Systems on the side. Mr. Adad Assad is with me."

"Excellent. Before the guard will let you pass, he will look under the van for any explosives, and when he is finished, he will let you into the compound."

Nothing about looking in *the van,* Jaiari noted.

"Drive around to the back of the building and pull up to Loading Dock D, and I will help you unload your supplies."

Following the directions, they arrived at the guard gate about twenty-five minutes later, and the guard called Zarin. The guard hung up the phone. He had a mirror on a long pole to look all the way around and under the cargo van. Seeing nothing, he let them pass.

They drove around to where Zarin was waiting for them to arrive, and when he saw them, he waved them over to the far loading dock. Adad backed the cargo van into the loading dock under Zarin guidance. He stopped when told and then jumped out and hurried to the back of the van and opened the doors.

"Do you have anybody to help us unload the device? It's heavy. It took five of us to load it into the van."

"Yes, we have plenty of people. Let's get it uncovered and then we can figure out what equipment we will need to unload it."

Adad took off the cargo net and started moving the office supply boxes to the front of the van, and quickly the bomb was exposed. Once it was clear of all the boxes, Zarin, said, after looking at the bomb for a moment or two, "This is a Soviet Union model RSU-172916ZRC; I have not seen one of these in several years. Most of these were sold on the black market, but they were so old, they never worked. It is my understanding that you want us to stabilize and upgrade this to a more powerful weapon, and that you intend to use it against the foreign power?"

"Yes, we want to use it against the U—"

"Stop," said Zarin. "We are not interested in who you might want to use this weapon against; we are just being hired to fix it the way you want it."

Jaiari then introduced Adad Assad as his partner and the owner of the company whose name was on the side of the van. "The two of us have been in the van for the last twenty-four hours, and we would like to get this out of the van as soon as possible."

Zarin smiled and said, "I understand." He took out his cell phone and requested a team with a lift and transport from the D Dock immediately. While they were waiting on the transport team, Jaiari told Zarin that one of them would be with the bomb twenty-four hours a day until the project was complete. He also told Zarin that one-half of the agreed-upon amount would be wired to the account the next morning, and the balance would be wired once they were sure the work was complete.

"Whichever of us is on site will take pictures of what is being done, and no faces will be in the pictures, just the bomb. Each day you or whomever you designate can review the photos and delete any that are in any way compromising to this facility. We both assure you that we will not get in the way of your performing the job we have hired you and your team to do."

Zarin agreed, they shook hands, and just at that moment, the team arrived to unload the bomb. As the five men lifted the bomb to place it on the transport, one of the men noticed that a liquid was leaking from the bomb case. He turned to Zarin.

"We have a problem. A serious problem."

Chapter 87

Springfield

W HITTLES AND MAJOR RAHIMI PRESENTED the search warrants to both bank presidents and told them what information they were looking for in the accounts at each of their banks. They wanted a printout of all the checking account deposits and checks written, but they were particularly interested in recurring transactions, especially in Michael's account. Rahimi wanted payments to the same parties on a regular basis in the same amounts or a number of transactions to the same party to be sorted out of the report. They wanted the bank to sort out of their report any payments to the electric, water, sewer, trash, and gas companies that appeared in the account history.

As for the telephone, they were to report any amount above the average of the last twelve months, and they told Mr. Ford, "For example, if you see payment to the phone company running at about $30 per month and then all of a sudden you see a bill of $45 or more, I want that noted, so we can talk to the phone company about what calls were made to whom during that period.

"You also need to look for the cable bill, if there is one, and let us know how much the bills were. We will check to see whether they have voice over the Internet protocol (VOIP) flat rate calling. Look for cell phone bills and give us the cellular provider and phone numbers for any cell phones the Ridleys have that are active. We will also need annual reports on Michael's credit card account for as long as he has had the account. We would like to see whether any transactions took place outside the United States. We would like to know whether there were two people on the account and, if so, what was the name of the other person? Also, you indicated that he received regular monthly deposits in the amount of $25,000; we need to trace who made those deposits and where they have been coming from. By the way, when was the last $25,000 deposit made to that account?"

"Let me check that real quick for you. The last deposit was made a week ago Monday. It appears that all deposits were made on the first Monday of the month."

Whittles realized that this was Friday afternoon, and he needed to know how soon they could start getting the information. Both Parker and Ford said the same thing: we are willing to have people come in the next day and start working on what we can.

"Sheriff, please realize that we will spend whatever it takes, but both of our institutions are small, and we will be limited in what we can get by the time constraints of our clearing intuitions. My guess is we can have most of our account information by late tomorrow, but the credit card history and the transfer into his money market account will take until early next week, assuming we don't run into any glitches."

The two men left to go to Parker's office to deliver the search warrant. Ford sat at his desk and was thinking about who on his staff could be of the greatest help to him in collecting the data that the sheriff and the Major wanted; he decided to call in his VP of operations, Kristen Murphy.

A few moments later, Murphy knocked on Ford's door. She went over and somewhat nervously sat down in the chair and waited for Ford to tell her what he wanted. He explained to her about the visit by Whittles and Rahimi and what information they were looking for from the bank with regards to the Michael Ridley accounts. "Murphy, "do you think we can get a significant amount of the information that the sheriff is looking for by tomorrow afternoon?"

Murphy. stopped to think for a moment, somewhat relieved, because when she had heard Michael's name, she had tensed up. She was sure that most people at the bank, including Ford, didn't know that she still had a relationship with Michael. Mary mentioned several employees in the bank that she thought might be helpful with the project. Together they spent some time trying to figure out what they could do on their own and what had to be done by a corresponding bank. They made a list of activities and what person should be assigned to do what work.

He told Murphy. that Mr. Parker at Second National was doing the same thing; only Mike and Mary Ridley had accounts at Second National and one credit card, so Second National's work would be easier than theirs. Ford said to Murphy. "I want you to head this group for the bank. Would you be willing to do that?"

Murphy, asked, "What do you think the sheriff is looking for in the records?"

"I think at the moment they don't know what they are looking for; they are hoping that the collection of the data will show them what all three Ridleys have been doing in Springfield. We found out in a credit search that Mike Ridley never seems to have had a job."

Murphy. responded, "If that is true, then how did he pay his bills?"

"We now know that the Ridleys didn't own the home they lived in; a Russian billionaire owned it, and they just lived in it."

Murphy. asked Ford, "Who in Springfield is a Russian billionaire?"

Ford told her that he'd looked at Michael's money market account, and every month for the last two years, when Michael was in college, he was receiving $25,000, and that his money market account now had over $600,000. He never took any money out of the account.

Bill Ford sat in his chair a moment longer, and a thought came to him that made him very uncomfortable. His brain was in control, forcing out questions, and he didn't know where they were coming from.

"Didn't you graduate in the same class as Michael Ridley?"

"Yes, I did."

"Do I remember seeing a picture of you and Mike at the homecoming dance in the Beacon? Weren't you and Michael good friends all through high school?"

Murphy. was getting more uncomfortable with each question, but she kept being honest and answering "yes."

Just then a shot pierced the window of Bill Ford's office.

CHAPTER 88

Meeting Room

MORDECAI AND OLEG WERE SITTING at a table working on some measuring equipment that Mordecai would use in constructing the new bomb, based on the one they hoped they would be getting back soon from Iran.

Oleg cleared his throat. "I guess it's my turn to tell you how I want to use the two bombs. Well, as much as recent presidents like Obama and now Jordan think they can replace carbon-based fuels with 'green energy,' nothing could be further from the truth. The bottom line is, and will be for generations to come, that the world runs on oil. As a world we eat it, drink it, wash in it, wear it, and it drives our economies on a global basis. The day may come when we have true alternative fuels that can be made in your backyard to heat and cool your house, run your car, power your industries, and lift a 747 off the ground and keep it flying, but not in our lifetime.

"How I would like to use the bombs may in fact accelerate the replacement of oil. So one potential positive of our attack is that we may effect global change for real alternative energy. The vast Majority of Americans think that they have very little crude oil, and we have all heard that the world is running out of oil, but it's not the truth. America has some of the largest stores of oil, and in some cases they are richer with it than many other countries in the world, including Saudi Arabia and Russia. But for over forty years, the American government has made it very difficult to get the permits to drill and bring out the oil.

"American oil policy is based on the price of crude oil. When the price goes up to the point that Americans become angry about what it costs to buy gas at the pump, then Congress and the administration say we need to do something about the high price of oil. Then Washington says we need to do something, and Saudi Arabia pumps more oil to bring down the market price of oil, and that takes the issue off the table, and Americans complain about something else until the next spike in price. It always amazes me how easily the American people can be manipulated by the price of a gallon of gas. But what if, overnight, there really was no more oil? I have two bombs, and I propose to shut down oil and natural gas production and distribution in the United States."

Mordecai laughs. "You can't shut down oil and natural gas production in the United States with just two dirty bombs; you're crazy!"

"We'll see how crazy I am. First, I propose that we use one bomb in Port Fourchon, Louisiana. If you asked ten people on the street, zero would say they have heard of this place. However, it's important because over 30 percent of all the oil and natural gas drilled for in the Gulf of Mexico goes through this port and into distribution pipelines throughout America. If you use Google Earth and look for Port Fourchon, you will see the pipeline coming in from the Gulf and then on land you will see many storage and transfer tanks that act as holding areas for the oil and gas coming in and waiting to be put in the pipelines moving energy north. If this port is shut down, then there is no switch to throw that will move oil and gas away from there to another port. New pipeline connections would take years to complete. One possibility is that tankers can be loaded from the drilling platforms and then taken to another port to refine the crude oil. The natural gas could be compressed and liquefied and then transported by LNG tankers to other ports, but America hasn't built an LNG plant in the United States in twenty-five years, and to build several of them would take years. The drilling platforms in the Gulf that send oil and gas through Port Fourchon might just have to shut down until alternative ways can be found to move the oil and gas on shore.

"If America can't refine the crude, then perhaps America, which has been a net importer of crude oil, could become a net exporter. More oil on the market will depress the price, as OPEC and non-OPEC producers will be forced to reduce production because of excess supply. With more supply and falling demand, countries like Saudi Arabia and other oil-producing nations will see significant decline in revenues. With falling revenue, they will no longer be in a position to provide for their citizens all the things they think their people want from the West. The results will be an overthrow of the royalty government, and a new Arab Spring will erupt in all the oil-producing nations, who can no longer feed their people the buy-now, pay-later attitude imported from America.

"Set off a dirty bomb and contaminate the storage tanks and pipelines, and they will be left with no choice but to shut down the port, stop the flow of oil and natural gas from the Gulf northward. First bomb goes off, and the price of crude increases by two to one, from $110 to $220 a barrel for a while.

"At the same time the first dirty bomb is going off in Port Fourchon, a second bomb is exploding in Texas City, Texas. Yes, Mordecai, this is another city nobody has ever heard of, but it's important. Just down the road from Springfield, Texas, is Texas City, the home of the largest oil refinery in the America, as well as three other refineries. People don't know that almost 25 percent of all the crude oil that is processed in the United States goes through the four refineries in Texas City.

"In addition, the oil and gas pipelines that run through the Texas City area supply over 25 percent of all the crude oil that is processed in northern refineries and process 25 percent of all the natural gas delivered to homes, businesses, and factories in the United States. If the bomb goes off in the biggest refinery, then there is an excellent possibility that the other three refineries are contaminated and will be shut down. The debris from the explosion will land on the storage tanks and the pipelines, making all of it radioactive.

"Let's say that you are a northern electrical or gas utility company that was depending on the supply of oil and gas through Texas City and Port Fourchon to run your plants: are you going to want to import the pipeline oil and gas from either? Would you be willing to take the risk that the oil and gas you might be importing would bring nuclear radiation into your plants and the homes of your customers? Would the federal, state, and local governments allow the potentially contaminated oil and gas to flow through the states?

"A significant portion of the 55,000 miles of oil pipeline and 2.3 million miles of natural gas pipelines in the United States will have to be shut down to prevent the flow of contaminated oil and gas north, east, and west. If the pipelines are shut down, then how do they power America? The simple answer is: they don't. If the pipelines were contaminated, where would America put its imported oil? Shutting down the Texas City refineries and their storage tanks and pipelines, and the gas pipelines would initially drive up the price of oil perhaps as high as $300 a barrel. But, if former President Obama was correct that we consume 20 percent of the world's oil supply, what happens to the price of oil if American is no longer buying 20 percent of the world's oil? What if American doesn't come back to the oil markets for generations, if ever? The demand for oil will fall, and so will the price of oil, like an old Cold War Russian satellite falling from space.

"Those OPEC countries that needed demand for oil to support their economies will also see the rapid deterioration of their economies and the quality of life of their people. These people, who have abandoned their historical way of life in exchange for the government providing everything, will be lost about how to live on their own. If we truly want to punish America and drive it back to its past, then using the two bombs as I have suggested will surely bring America to its knees—along with other non-Islamic nations.

"People will ask, 'How will I heat my home in winter? How will I cook my food?' With over 40 percent of electricity generated by oil and natural gas, what parts of the country will have safe gas, and what parts will not? If the government needs to move people out of the south to the north, where would they put them, how would they move them, and how would the government feed and care for them, along with the rest of the nation? The governments—local, state, and federal—will lose tax revenue from decreased oil sales, and there will be a general decline in incomes across America. Think of all the things that won't work or can't be made because America won't have enough energy.

"It is true that the disruption will not only be in America; there will be disruptions around the world. If America falls as a world power, then those countries that are energy-independent will gain more and more power on the world stage. Because of the changes in America, the world may well be in a better position to accept that Islam is right and just and needs to rule the world. The use of my bombs could change the world forever into societies ruled by the Koran, the only true law in the world."

Mordecai says, "Okay, you may be crazy, but you're also a genius, and I hope we choose your option. An America without oil and gas will forever be changed."

CHAPTER 89

Iran Nuclear Project near Paleto

ZARIN HURRIED THE MEN TO get the bomb on the transporter and quickly wheeled it into the laboratory and then into a cold room. As soon as the door was closed, Zarin turned the temperature gauge down to 30 degrees Fahrenheit to stop the leak, whatever it was. He sent one of his lab technicians to get a sample of what had leaked in the van and on the floor of the loading dock.

As soon as the sample was collected, an absorbing agent was spread all over the damp area to suck up everything that had spilled. The technicians looked into the truck to see if the bomb had leaked in the truck they found a small amount and sucked it up with the absorbing agent. They carefully swept up the absorbing agent and placed the saturated agent in a hard plastic container and took it to the lab, where they gently slid it in the container next to the bomb in the cooler.

Zarin was working on the initial sample to see whether he could identify what the liquid was. Saeed told Adad and Jaiari while he was running tests to try to figure out what was on the floor, "One of the problems with these old bombs is the lack of stability of the explosive charge as it ages. As the bomb ages, the liquid nitroglycerin, which was suspended in a clay or sawdust, begins to liquefy and seeps out of the clay. After a few years in an uncontrolled environment, the nitro begins to seep out of the sticks with increasing speed. It's possible that all the nitro could seep out of the bomb, and people who weren't looking for it might not even notice that it was gone. The sticks of TNT in your bomb looked the same; the clay or filler did not break down when the nitro oozed away. When somebody buys a bomb on the black market, they didn't know whether or not it will work, and most of the time, they don't work. TNT, which is the explosive that propels the radioactive material, is made up of clay and a thick, pale yellow liquid, $C_3H_5N_3O_9$, which is explosive with jarring or exposure to sudden heat.

He squinted into his microscope and continued, "Newer bombs will use dynamite or some other more powerful or more exotic materials like HMX to increase the power of the bomb many times over the power of TNT. Some governments are trying to produce Octanitrocubane, which is believed to be the most powerful subnuclear explosive ever developed. The liquid we've just found is in fact a weak, diluted TNT $C_3H_5N_3O_9$. It is so weak that it will not explode."

He told them he wanted the liquid to firm up and then in a few hours they would go into the cold room and remove the remaining TNT. He was not sure that the other sticks had degraded to the point that they had no TNT left in them, so he would handle it all very carefully.

For now there wasn't much that could be done, so Zarin suggested they go and get something to eat. As they walked toward lunch, Jaiari asked if there was a place to clean up before eating.

"Let me show you."

While they went through the door, Adad said, "I'll go eat, and you stay and watch the bomb and then I'll watch the bomb, and you can eat."

Jaiari agreed and said, "Is it me or do you think they are being very hospitable?"

"I noticed that very same thing; do you think it's because they are scientists and are not involved with political issues?"

"I remember some American history when Ronald Reagan was president, and he was dealing with the old Soviet Union. He always said,

'Trust but verify.' I think for now we can trust them, but we must be diligent and to the best of our ability verify everything they are doing to our bomb. We must ask questions and take as many photos as we can so as to provide Mordecai with everything they have done to this bomb so he can match the bomb at the meeting site to this one."

As they came out of the WC, Adad told Zarin that he would go with him to lunch, and Jaiari would stay here with the bomb; he reminded Zarin that they had discussed upon their arrival that one of them would stay with the bomb 24/7 in twelve-hour shifts. Zarin didn't seem to object, so they headed to the food service area to get something to eat.

While they were eating, they talked about what they were planning to do.

Zarin asked Adad, "How have you decided were to use the bomb?"

"That really depends on how powerful you can make this bomb. The more powerful it is, the bigger the target." He told Saeed that one of the charges of the team was to come up with ideas about how to use the bomb. The entire team would hear all of the proposed uses of the bombs and then all of them would vote on what was the best use of the bomb. Adad asked Zarin to compare the power of the bomb the way it was made and with the modifications they were possibly going to make, and then tell him how powerful it would be.

"We still have to look inside the case, but if the guts are good and functional, we should be able to make a bomb about ten times the power of the original bomb."

"Couldn't you make it just five times the explosive power and five times more radioactive instead?"

CHAPTER 90

Citrus Grove

OPPENHEIMER WAS HIDING UNDER AN orange tree in the citrus grove outside the Brotherhood meeting site and getting very nervous as the sniper, or the man he thought was a sniper, approached his hiding place. Oppenheimer saw, as the man approached, that he reached into his pocket and pulled out a plastic film canister and tossed it into the tree towards him. Oppenheimer braced himself as he saw the canister roll along the ground into the tree next to him, Oppenheimer expected that there was a bomb in the canister and was waiting to go off.

He held his breath, expecting an explosion, but nothing happened—no bang. He reached down and picked up the canister and felt around the edges and he couldn't find any trip wires, so he opened the canister, and inside he found a small piece of paper and on it, the sniper had written one word: Seacrest. The other side of the paper said nothing.

While Oppenheimer couldn't see the face of the man, he could tell from his general size and shape that he was not Seacrest. He had talked with Seacrest who was in DC, less than twelve hours ago, so if it wasn't John, then who was it and why the name Seacrest on the paper? Oppenheimer took a deep breath and relaxed. All the tension came out of his body as he thought about the name on the paper. It finally came to him: the man was not Seacrest, but was working for Seacrest as an asset on the ground. He had been sent to the warehouse to get pictures of all the team members. He might even be the same person who took the original images that David had seen in the meeting with Nava Dobias back at Mossad.

If he was right, then the Americans were already involved, but what were they trying to do? Oppenheimer decided that he needed to get a closer look at the warehouse before he returned to his men. Sundown was coming fast, so Oppenheimer needed to move fast to get a quick look inside the building. He crawled out from under the tree, kept low to the ground, and moved quickly toward the building. He approached the building from the grove side because this side provided the best cover.

In a matter of seconds, he was next to the building and close to the window, so he could look into it and scan the room's contents. There were no lights on in the building, but he did have his Army-issue Maglite. He pulled it out of his breast pocket and turned it on to try to see what was in the building. Oppenheimer was scanning quickly, and his light caught the image of a very large suitcase up against the wall opposite the window he was looking into. Just then he heard somebody coming down the path in the front of the building. He turned off his flashlight and slid down below the window.

Oppenheimer heard a key go into the lock, and a person walked in and turned on the lights. Oppenheimer could see the glow coming out the window above his head and hear the person inside moving around. Then he heard the sound of the person walking up a flight of stairs. When Oppenheimer heard those steps, he counted eight and then a noise, as the man was walking around, and then he heard the man going up eight more steps.

He stood up cautiously to look; the glass in the window was not the cleanest glass he had seen, and he wondered whether his cell phone camera could capture images. He had no idea how long he had, so he would take pictures with his phone, and when he heard footsteps coming down, he would count to eight and stop and drop to the ground and get away as fast as he could. Oppenheimer pointed his cell phone and shot as many photos as he could, panning the room. He heard the first step and continued to shoot, then the second, still shooting, now the third, and his heart began to race, though he was still shooting as fast as his camera phone would allow. He heard the fourth, fifth, and sixth, and at seven steps he decided to stop and drop down and take a quick and quiet breath.

He heard the person take the rest of the steps more rapidly then, as if he were running down the steps to get somewhere fast. Oppenheimer moved down the side of the building away from the window and, just as he turned the corner of the building, he heard the window open. Just seconds earlier he had been looking into it to see what he could see. Now someone had opened that window and in Arabic was asking, "Who's there?"

Oppenheimer knew that he had to get away from the building and get to his troops. The shortest way was past the window, but he knew that if he went past the window and made any noise, he was probably a dead man. He had to make a decision: chance the shortest route and potentially be discovered and shot or killed with the cell phone full of pictures of the inside of the building, or take the longer path, which would possibly take him to the village before he could get back to his men. By now his men would start to be concerned that there captain might have been captured or dead, and the longer he waited, the higher the chance that the mission would be scrubbed. Oppenheimer made his decision.

CHAPTER 91

Iranian Nuclear Laboratory

WHILE JAIARI WAS AT LUNCH with Zarin, Adad decided that he needed to call Sargon and warn him about the leaking bomb and let him know that he needed to check the bomb at the meeting site. He had to assume that his call was monitored and that he must be selective in his words, in order to protect the location of the bomb and the names of the people involved with the project. He looked around to see whether anybody was watching, and he scanned the ceilings and walls for cameras that could be recording the call he was about to make.

Adad took out the phone and hid the dial and tapped in Sargon's cell number. The phone rang, and after several rings, Sargon answered the phone.

"I thought I would let you know that we made it safely, and we are inside the facility. The ride seemed to go okay, but when we arrived and they were unloading the boxes, it appeared that a bottle on the inside of one of the boxes had broken, and the liquid leaked out into my van and onto the loading dock floor. They needed to be sure that the liquid was not hazardous, so they tested it right away. Because it takes a while to run the tests, they decided to put the case in a cold room. I think they said it was just below 30 degrees, and the cold would solidify the liquid until the tests were done.

"I don't remember seeing any liquid on the floor of the warehouse when we loaded the van for the delivery. We expect to be out of here and making our return-trip deliveries in about five days. If it should take longer, I will call you back. Do you have any questions for me?"

Sargon said no.

Adad replayed the entire conversation in his mind and realized that Sargon had just used two words: *hello* and *no*. Adad hoped that the message had gotten through to check the bomb at the warehouse and that cold would stop the leak.

Within moments of completing his call to Adad, Sargon got on the phone to Mordecai to tell him to get to the warehouse as quickly as possible; the bomb might be leaking nitro. After he dialed the number, he got Mordecai's voice message. Sargon told Mordecai to meet him at the warehouse ASAP. Sargon then called Oleg and reached him in two rings. "I need you at the warehouse as soon as possible, and I need you to bring as many bags of ice as you can fit in your car. No questions; just do it now."

Oleg hung up the phone and grabbed his keys and a box of black trash bags and was out the door in less than a minute. On the way to the warehouse, there was a petrol station, and he remembered seeing an ice cabinet. Oleg was about two minutes from the petrol station and took a moment to ask himself, *why all the ice I can carry in my car?* He pulled into the station and asked the attendant how many bags of ice he had in the cabinet out front. They both went out front to the ice freezer, and Oleg said, "I'll take it all. I'll load, and you count." Oleg put four bags of ice in each black trash bag and tossed them into his car. After loading twenty-four bags of ice in the vehicle, Oleg paid the attendant and jumped into the car. As he was departing, the attendant said, "Must be some party!"

Oleg responded, "I hope so." He sped down the road to the warehouse and just as he made the turn into the driveway, he saw Sargon at the front door with the guard standing next to him. Oleg hit the brakes, and the car slid on the gravel, just missing both of them and narrowly missing the warehouse wall. Oleg leaped out of his car and raced toward Sargon.

"Open the car and help us bring the bags of ice inside; we need to pack the bomb in ice."

"We are packing the bomb in ice, why?"

"Because we don't have a refrigerator large enough to hold the bomb to cool it down, and it's leaking."

They continued to pack bags of ice around the bomb, and Mordecai walked through the door and asked what is going on. Sargon replied, "Grab some bags of ice from my car, and we'll talk when we're done." In about twenty minutes, the cars were unloaded, and the bomb was solidly packed in ice.

"I knew we didn't have a freezer, so ice was the only thing I could think of that could quickly cool down our bomb. When I arrived at the warehouse, I noticed a small pool of liquid on the floor next to the bomb. I scraped a sample of the liquid so we could test to see whether it is nitro."

Mordecai said, "My guess is that the long ride over some bumpy roads may have accelerated the separation. Once the Iranians get the nitro stabilized, they will remove it from the bomb, clean the case of any nitro, and put in a new explosive. But in the meantime, I know a quick test we can do to see whether the sample you found was nitro or not."

"Why do we need to find out whether it is nitro we found on the floor?"

"We will go outside and put a drop on a stone, then put an unlit match in one part of the drop and then light the other end as the match burns toward the drop, the heat from the flame will heat the stone and in turn increase the temperature of the nitro. When the flame reaches the drop, if it's nitro we will hear a big bang. The nitro needs heat to detonate so the heat from the flame will cause the explosion. If we get no explosion, then we don't have nitro, and we have no problem. If, on the other hand, we get a big boom, then we know that we have nitro, and we have to be very careful with the leaking nitro."

Sargon was concerned about the size of the explosion attracting attention to the warehouse. But the explosion would only sound like gunfire or the backfiring of a car or truck, and Mordecai assured Sargon that the explosion would not attract that much attention, though they would want to stand way back because the explosion would destroy the stone and turn the pieces of it into projectiles. "If we get too close, someone could be seriously hurt, even with a small drop of nitro. I think we need to take this out in the grove and let the trees muffle the noise and absorb the fragments."

What they didn't know was that Oppenheimer was already in the citrus grove, watching and listening and now worrying about being in the wrong place at the wrong time.

CHAPTER 92

Frank Williams's Office

Baker had briefed Frank as to the latest developments so he could prepare his briefing with the president. Baker said to Williams, "The latest development is that Mossad has sent a special ops team into Syria, and half of the team is at the warehouse, and the other half is in the village."

Williams was a little uncomfortable that the Israelis were involved, even if it was just as observers. "Why does it take twenty-four people just to observe somewhere between two and four people?"

"My guess is that if the terrorists decide that they want to attack Israel instead of America, the Israelis wanted the firepower in place to take everybody out."

"How will they determine whether they are the target, not us?"

"Sir, Seacrest of the CIA, who is working on this project with us, believes that were the terrorists to they take the bombs out of Syria, that would be a good indication of their commitment. If they put them on a boat headed for Canada, then we are the target; on the other hand, if the bombs go to someplace in the Middle East, then they are headed for Israel."

"Will the Israelis wait until the bombs cross the border before they respond?"

"I think they will wait until the bombs are on Israeli soil to respond."

"Do you think they will attack Iran because of their cooperation with the terrorists?"

"I think they will tell the United States that they have control of the bombs and will show them to the news media and charge that the Iranian government built at least one of the bombs for the Brotherhood. They will puff out their chest and make a great deal of noise, but I don't think they will attack Iran, at least not over this issue."

"Any update from our operative at the site?"

"Sir, I expect pictures later today, assuming he made it out of the site without being captured. As soon as I get them, I will send them on to you."

"And what is happening in Springfield?"

"We got the warrants to search the records for all three Ridleys at two local banks. That data is being mined as we speak, and we hope to have some insight today with more information on Monday at the latest. The day after tomorrow is the memorial service for Sergeant Kelly, who was killed in the bomb blast; Major Rahimi will be attending the service representing Homeland Security, but he will not speak. Going back to the Ridleys, sir, it's as if they have disappeared, leaving no trace or trail. We hope the data from the bank accounts will give us some clues as to what happened to them and where they are in the world. I feel if we could locate the three of them, we could fill in some gaping holes in what the Brotherhood is trying to do.

"We have not made progress in identifying the leadership of the Brotherhood. Seacrest is working with Interpol and the Syrian secret service to identify some of the people in the photos we had taken at the warehouse. We were not able to reposition the satellites to follow the cargo van, so we don't know to what city in Iran they took the bomb." Williams paused for a moment and Baker could see from the expression on his face that he had an idea that was quickly developing, so he waited for his boss to speak.

"Do we have a technology expert on staff?"

"Sir, I'm sure we have many; what type of technology were you looking for?"

"GPS."

"Let's call the chief technology officer for Homeland Security and ask him." Williams called Marie and asked, "Who is the chief technology officer at HS?" In a short while Marie came back on the line and said, "That would be John William Moore, sir. I'll call him for you." A few moments later, Williams's intercom rang: Mr. Moore was on line one.

Williams picked up the phone and said, "Hello, we have a serious problem, and we need your resources."

"How can we help you, sir?"

"I do not claim to be an expert on technology; I still can't program my DVD, so I need someone like you to help me with a question. Let's suppose that I leave my office today, and I have GPS in the car. I start the car and the GPS, and it asks whether I want to use my current location as a starting point. I respond yes, because I'm going to a place I have never been before, and I don't want to get lost. You with me?"

"Yes, sir. I do that all the time."

"When I arrive at my destination, the GPS has my starting and ending point, so my address when I started is stored in the GPS, and the arrival point is also stored. When I want to return home, I tell my GPS to return home, is that correct?"

"Yes, sir."

"When I want to go home, the GPS in my car sends a signal to the GPS satellite, and it reviews the home location and sets a course to get me home. Is that correct?"

"So far, you got it right."

"The data of home and destination is stored on my GPS in my car, but is it stored in the GPS satellite?"

"Not necessarily. You see, the GPS is receiving million of pieces of data every second; it would be impossible to store all the data from all the GPS devices in the world, but when a new place is set as a base, the satellite stores the location and then the next time it's used, it can process the request more quickly."

"Do different satellites cover different part of the world?"

"Some satellites cover wide areas, like Africa, while others may cover a section of the United States."

"So if I give you the location of a site, could we find out whether anyone asked for directions from the site in the last thirty days? If it can tell us that it did get a direction request, can it tell us where it was going to end up?"

"It may be possible."

"If I get you the start location, how long to find out whether you can get the destination?"

"Sir, I'll have to find the company that owns the satellite that covers the area and then make contact and make the request, so my guess is, at least a couple of days. Sir, I don't mean to throw a monkey wrench in what you are trying to do, but governments control some of the GPS satellites, and sometimes these governments can be uncooperative in providing information."

Williams took out a piece of paper and gave it to Baker and asked him to write down the location of the warehouse for Mr. Moore. "I hope you can help, because this is extremely important to our national security, and the lives of millions of Americans are at stake."

CHAPTER 93

Springfield Office of Bill Ford

As the window of Ford's office was shattered, a bullet whizzed through, just missing Murphy and burying itself in a painting on the wall of Ford's office. Ford leaped over the desk and and knocked Murphy out of chair and to the ground, and then laid on top of her to protect her in case other bullets came in the window. John didn't want to go to the desk and leave Murphy exposed, so he took out his cell phone and dialed the main number of Second National and asked for Wendell Parker. Bill picked up the phone.

"Parker, this is Bill Ford; is Sheriff Whittles with you?"

"He's right here."

"May I speak with him please?"

Whittles came on the line and said, "Bill, what can I do for you?"

"I'm on the floor of my office guarding Murphy; someone just took a shot at her through my office window and missed. I don't know whether they are waiting for her to move or not, but I'm holding her down to try to keep her safe. How soon can you get here?"

Whittles had already handed the phone to Parker, and he told Parker to tell Ford to stay down and try to move under the window; he and the Rahimi and backup were on the way. While they were both running back to the bank, Whittles was on his cell phone calling the dispatcher and asking for full team backup: shots fired.

Whittles and Rahimi arrived at the front door and they signaled for the bank employees to get down and crawl out of the bank and get behind one of the cruisers that were just pulling up in front of the bank. Whittles asked one of the employees as he came out of the bank the location of Ford's office and the outside window. He found out that it was in the back right of the building, so Rahimi and Whittles decided to move out to the left and work their way around the building to the back and then assess their approach to the window area.

Once all the people were out of the bank and safe, Whittles and Rahimi made their move down the front slowly to the first corner, and they carefully looked around the side of the building to see whether there were any windows; seeing none, they moved quickly toward the back of the building.

"I'm going to call and have two men sent down the other side of the building. I'll use my cell phone, because if I used my radio, whoever is out there could possibly hear the messages." Whittles made the call, and one officer stood at the front of the building and hand signaled to Whittles when the other team was headed toward the back of the building. Both teams reached the back of the building, and they could see each other. Whittles signaled for both teams to move to the other side of the street, so their backs were against the wall.

"Do you have a cell number for Ford?"

No, but he called the officer at the corner and told him to go over to the employees behind the patrol car and see whether they knew his number. Five minutes passed, and Whittles got a call back with the cell number for Ford. Rahimi got the number and dialed it from his cell phone, and Ford answered.

"Ford, are you and Murphy okay?"

"Yes. A little scared, but other than that, we're fine."

"I need your help; the window the bullet came through is on the wall where you have your back. Is that correct?"

"Yes."

"Excellent; can you see the glass on the floor from the broken window?"

Ford said, "Yes."

"Excellent; can you tell me what you see? Describe the glass on the office floor. The glass should be lying on the floor with some direction. Think of the window frame as the base of a rectangle. Is the glass scattered to the left or right or straight ahead?" Ford and Murphy both looked at the shattered glass, and they concluded that the glass was moving from the center to the right side giving a look of the shape the triangle.

"Very good. Both of you are a great help. Stay put. We're coming to get you out soon."

"The glass pattern on the floor indicates that the shot was fired from the right side of the building as we face it, and I would guess from at least the first floor." Whittles called on his cell phone and said he wanted four men to go to the building across from the bank, and he wanted two men on the second floor and two men on the third floor with weapons drawn. Whittles had the other team working with them by the building to hold its ground, and he and Omid moved along the wall of the building and were looking for windows that might be open.

Whittles heard the screech of tires and footsteps running up into the building. He listened on the radio and heard, "Second floor clear" and was expecting to hear that the third floor was clear, but he heard nothing. Whittles signaled to the team on the opposite side of the street to go into the building and go to the third floor and see what was going on.

The team left and headed to the building and then the voice on the radio said, "Sheriff, you need to come to the third floor. We found something." Whittles and Rahimi carefully turned the corner and went up the steps inside the building, hurrying up the stairs two at a time to the third floor, where they saw two of his men in the hallway and the two other deputies in the room. Over by the window the only things in the room were a chair, a large, heavy-duty cardboard box, a sandbag on top of the box, and an AK-47 sniper rifle with what looked like a high-powered scope on the rifle. Then they all noticed the one other thing in the room, taped to the window: a photograph of Murphy, with a bullet hole in her head.

Chapter 94

Iranian Nuclear Laboratory

Jaiari returned with Zarin and indicated that it was his turn to go back to the hotel and for Adad to stay with the bomb; he would be back in the morning, and they would conclude the first part of the financial arrangement. He and Adad had made a pact, and there would not be any trouble at all.

"All we will need is a cot to sleep on and a shower room when our shift is over."

"If that is what you want, then it is no problem for us to accommodate your needs."

Jaiari asked, "How long do you think it will take you and your team to rebuild the bomb?"

"That will depend on how much damage the leaking nitro did to the rest of the bomb. If it didn't do much damage, and we have all the parts to give you what you want on-site, my guess is about five to six days."

Jaiari met up with Adad and told him, "We can stay, and everything will be fine; they will find you a cot, and you can shower at the hotel or here, whatever you want, and you can eat here or at the hotel."

"We would like to see the bomb before Adad leaves," Jaiari said, so both of them went over to the window in the door to the cold room, and they could see their bomb, just to be sure. Jaiari went back to the loading dock and drove back to the hotel; it was late when he got there, and he washed his face, brushed his teeth, and climbed into bed. He set the alarm for 7:00 a.m., and he was so tired, he fell asleep quickly.

Back at the compound, nothing was going on; all the people had left for the day, and before Zarin left, he had a cot brought in for Adad to rest on during the night, should he want to sleep. Adad decided to place the cot next to the cooler; in case somebody wanted to open the cooler door, it would hit his cot and wake him. Initially, Adad was not sleepy, so he wandered around the building. He didn't know much about the science of nuclear fusion, but all the equipment looked impressive. He came across a door that had a warning sign on it that said, "Atomic matter can be dangerous." He looked around the door, and he saw a camera focused on the door, and on the right-hand side of the door was a warning signal light, like the ones that you see in the movies that spin and flash. Adad reached out to grab the handle but stepped away from the door because he had no clue what would happen if he tried open the door. He didn't want to do anything that might jeopardize getting their bomb repaired. He guessed that what was behind this door would in some way end up in his bomb.

As Adad saw all this equipment, he began to wonder what the bomb options would be for the Brotherhood bomb; he realized that in a week he and Jaiari would be back at the warehouse, and Mordecai would be replicating the new bomb they would bring back to Syria. He guessed that the room down the hall had all the nuclear material they would need for their new bomb—and perhaps a thousand dirty bombs or at least a few nuclear bombs. He believed that the material had to be developed over time. You had to make it yourself; you just couldn't go out in the market and buy the finished product. You had to have the nuclear material before you could build the bomb. The world, or at least some parts of the world, had a problem with Iran developing nuclear bombs. The leaders were concerned that, should Iran get enough material, they would build the bomb and use it against Israel and perhaps other countries that didn't believe what the Iranians believed.

As he walked the halls of the great facility, Adad remembered reading for several years now of the possible threat that Iran was building a bomb, yet it appeared that they didn't have enough for one bomb. Apparently, they had yet to produce enough nuclear material to build one warhead. *Why would they sell us the nuclear material when they are trying to make enough stuff to build their bomb?* If it took so long to make the material, Adad wondered where Mordecai was going to get the nuclear material for the bomb that he was building. Had he stolen it from the Israeli program where he worked? How could you steal nuclear material without somebody knowing? Didn't somebody keep track of all that stuff? Was it possible that he was going to buy it on the black market? If it was so hard to make, who had a surplus?

Immediately the answer hit him. The same people who gave us the suitcase dirty bombs: the Russians. They had the second biggest arsenal of nuclear warheads, and there had been many rumors suggesting that some amount of material in the Russian arsenal was unaccounted for.

As he continued his walk in the vacant hallways, he began to think about what might be the long-term effects on America and for the American people. He thought of the loss of life and human misery if his option were chosen. He did not know the other two options; he just knew his and Jaiari's options. So it was possible that the other two could be even more devastating than either of theirs. He walked down a hallway and saw more machines, not having any idea what they did, but as he turned a corner, his eye caught what looked like another cold room back in a corner. He was startled that there were two cold rooms were there more than two? He walked up and noticed that it had a solid door, but around the corner on the side was a window, albeit smaller than the one in the other cold room.

He stepped up to look in the window, and his gasp echoed down the cold cinderblock hallway.

CHAPTER 95

Warehouse Meeting Place

MORDECAI WAS ABOUT TO DEMONSTRATE to Oleg and Sargon the power of just one drop of nitro, and for his demonstration he was going to use one drop on a good-sized stone. Oppenheimer was close to the house and had a chance to get away, but with all the commotion over the leaky bomb, he decided to stay. He had two options for leaving: either by the road that led to town, or if he chose this route, it would be hours before he could get back to his men. Instead, he chose the most direct route: under the window and out into the grove and then on to his men.

It was almost dark when he struck out to rejoin his men, but just as he hit the edge of the grove, he heard the three terrorists coming, so he jumped under an orange tree for the second time in the same day. He overheard comments, and he heard the name "Mordecai" mentioned several times, so he must be the bomb expert. Oppenheimer knew what Mordecai was going to do, and he was going to be within twenty feet of the blast. Based on what he had heard, there was a good chance that the orange tree and Oppenheimer would be the worse for wear after the explosion.

Oppenheimer noticed that there was a ditch around the entire grove; he concluded that it might have been a way to get water to the trees in the dry season. If he could get there before the explosion, he would be all right. He pulled out his cell phone and sent a text message to the second in command. It read: *Need distraction toward the warehouse so I can escape. Do no damage.* The second in command was Lt. Amzi Rabin, and he received the message and quickly thought about what he might use that was loud and distracting enough. The answer was a night flare. It was loud when it exploded, and they were designed to be bright to light the ground so troops could see, and the enemy would be illuminated. He found the night flare gun, pointed it left of the warehouse, and prepared to shoot. Rabin texted back: *Night flare coming now, make your break when you see the first flash.*

Oppenheimer watched Mordecai setting up his demonstration and, just as he was ready to light the match, the flare went off. Mordecai pulled his match back, and all three men turned to see what had exploded. They saw the initial flash of the flare; as soon as David saw that all three had turned toward the flash, he rolled out from under the tree and into the ditch. He poked his head out just above the top of the ditch and saw that they were all still looking at the flare; he continued to slide down the ditch, farther and farther away from the trees and the blast when it came. He heard Mordecai ask one of the other two whether they should go back to the warehouse.

Sargon said, "No, it looked like it was far away from the warehouse, and besides, we have a guard at the warehouse who would sound the alarm if he needed help. Let's get back to your show." Oppenheimer saw them coming back to the pile of rocks; he dropped below the edge of the ditch and waited for the explosion. He heard the three men running away from the pile of stones. Next Oppenheimer heard a very loud boom—so strong, in fact, that the earth beneath him in the ditch moved. He could feel the shockwave go over the top of the ditch in a series of very loud swooshes. There was a good chunk of the orange tree in the ditch with him. The blast created a small fire, and it threw off enough light that Oppenheimer could see the damage. He was shocked that the ground was level, but the enormous orange tree that had hid him in the afternoon was cut off at ground level. Nothing within twenty feet was left standing.

The three men came back to the site of the blast, and all were pleased with the result. Oppenheimer heard one say, "My brothers, can you imagine the impact our two bombs will have on America?"

As the men walked back to the warehouse, Oppenheimer speedily and quietly moved toward his men. He had been away for almost twelve hours and was glad to see them and to get something to eat and drink. He gave his phone to Lt. Rabin and told him to send the images on his phone back to Nava at Mossad on the satellite phone right away.

Oppenheimer's team reported on the sites for their observation points, and they all reported that they had made shift changes and nothing had happened except the explosion in the grove.

He told them about the ice, the bomb, and the nitro, and then said, with a very serious look on his face, "We are very close to an old nuclear bomb that could explode anytime it wants. If it blows, you all need to keep in mind what happened to the orange tree with one drop of nitro. As much as I would like to send you home, we have to stay here because it is possible they could use these bombs against us anywhere we are."

CHAPTER 96

Bill Ford's Office, Citizens National Bank of Springfield

SHERIFF JIM WHITTLES, MAJOR OMID Rahimi, Bill Ford, and Helen Murphy were in the bank's conference room, which had no windows. They were all seated around the table, Mary with a soda and the rest of them with strong, black coffee. Ford asked Whittles, "Did you find the shooter?"

"No, but we have the weapon; in fact, it is on a Homeland Security plane headed to DC and their forensics lab to look for fingerprints and any DNA."

Whittles turned to Helen Murphy and asked her, "Do you know why anybody would want to kill you?"

"I can't imagine; to the best of my knowledge, I can't think of anybody whom I have offended or made angry enough."

"Do you sometimes have to turn people down for a loan?"

"No, I do not have anything to do with making loans."

"Have you ever had to foreclose on somebody's home or business?"

"While I have to prepare the paperwork, I don't work with, or even meet the borrowers."

He turned to Parker. "To the best of your knowledge, has any customer of the bank or employee, past or present, ever lodged a complaint against Murphy?"

"I would have to double-check her personal file, but to the best of my knowledge, no to both of your questions."

Whittles turned to Murphy, and in a calm and sincere voice said, "Mary, we need to know about your relationship with Michael Ridley."

"I'm not sure what you mean when you say 'relationship'."

"Let me try this in a different way. Mary, when was the last time you talked or saw Michael Ridley?"

Mary paused and then replied, "I saw him two weeks ago."

"Where?"

Mary asked, "You mean in Springfield?"

The sheriff responded, with just hint of anger, "I don't care about the words. Where did you meet with Michael?"

"We met in Berkeley, California, on Friday night the 21st, in a bar called Saturn Rings."

"Not counting that Friday night, how many times over the last two years have you met Michael Ridley and where?"

Mary had to stop and think, and she said, "Two years is a long time to remember."

Omid intervened in a calm voice. "I know it's hard to think back for the past two years, so let me try to help you, okay? Was it more frequently than once a month over the last twenty-four months?"

Mary thought for a moment, and she answered that it was probably more.

"Did you always meet him in Berkeley?"

Mary replied, "No, but a lot of the time we met someplace outside of Springfield."

"Why didn't he want to meet with you in Springfield?"

"He didn't want to come to Springfield while school was in session because he didn't want his parents to know he wasn't in school."

"So you knew that Michael didn't go to college?"

"Yes."

"Did Michael tell you why he never went to school when he had a free ride?"

"He said he'd met some people in Berkeley who thought he was very smart, and they offered him a job that paid very well, and he didn't see a need to go to college when he could make a fortune doing what he was doing. He could save most of his income, and when he had what he thought was enough, the two of us were going to get married and buy an island in the Caribbean and live on the beach."

"Could you see Michael's accounts at the bank?"

"Well, I'm the person in charge of all the systems, so yes, I could see Michael's account grow, and it grew by about $25,000 per month."

"Did you think that was a lot of money each month, and did you ever ask Michael how he was earning so much money?"

"I tried, and he was never very specific about it, even though I pressed for an answer."

"So you and Michael were in a romantic relationship?"

Mary paused. "Am I being charged with anything?"

"Do you think you have done anything wrong that you could be charged for?"

"No, not that I'm aware of."

"Did you believe you were going to be married?"

"Yes."

"Do you believe that Michael wanted to marry you?"

"Most of the time I think he did."

"What made you unsure?"

"Sometimes he seemed like a different person. "Were you intimate with Michael?" "What do you mean intimate?" "Well that could mean many things, what do you think of when I use the word intimate?" "Are you asking did we have sex?" "That is up to you to decide what the word means in your relationship with Michael." "I'm somewhat uncomfortable talking about our relationship but I can say we did have intimate relations and sometimes we even made love differently and then the next visit everything was the same as it was before."

"Has anything else changed in your relationship?"

"I pressed at our last visit what he was doing to make so much money. I wanted to know if he was doing something illegal. He was clearly angry with me and said how he earned his money was his business, not mine. I never saw him that angry. He scared me a little. It was as if I didn't know who he was."

"Let's change the subject: do you know where Mike and Mary Ridley are?"

"After Michael went off to Berkeley, I didn't have much contact with them. Sometimes I would see them in a store or on the street and I would wave, but they never called, and neither did I. To answer your question, I have no way of knowing where they are."

"Did Michael ever talk about his parents?"

"Not that I recall."

"I need to ask you one more question: could the Michael Ridley you saw two weeks ago be angry enough to have taken a shot at you?"

At that question, Helen Murphy began to cry.

Chapter 97

Seacrest, CIA

John was in his office when his phone rang, and it was Massri on the other end. He was sending the pictures that he took from the tower, but this time only three of the original five are in the pictures being sent. He was not able to get a lot of pictures inside the warehouse because there was a person there. He was almost discovered when he was relieving himself, and the person in the warehouse came crashing out the door.

He could hear most of the conversation between the two men, and one of them, who seemed to know the most about the dirty bomb, was named Mordecai. Massri thought that he had worked in some type of nuclear plant. The other seemed to have a slight Russian ascent, but his English was very good, and so was Mordecai's. Massri thought both had spent time in America, perhaps a long time in America.

While he was shooting pictures, he said, he saw a group of men in pickup trucks come into the area, and they hid their trucks against hills and mounds and then covered them with camouflage tarps. It appeared to him that they were a team of Mossad special ops and that they had moved in to watch what was going on. In the photos were images of an officer hiding under an orange tree in the citrus grove.

"When I finally could leave the tower and start back home, I walked past the orange tree with the person hiding under it. I had in my camera bag an old plastic canister from the time when we all used film; I took a piece of paper and wrote a single word on the paper."

"What was the word?"

"I needed to tell the person that I saw him and his team, and I wanted to use a word that, if they were friendly, they would know what it meant. If, on the other hand, they were not friendly, they would not know what the word meant."

"I'm dying to know what the word was. What was it?"

"Seacrest."

"Very funny. Are you trying to get me killed?"

"I know it's hard to believe, but a whole lot of people have no idea who you are, and if you did a Google search for your name, nothing would come up, my friend. So when you send copies of my photos to Mossad, ask if they have a team near a citrus grove in central Syria and ask if anyone got a message with your name on it."

"Anything else you need to report?"

"I was looking around the site, and in the windows I could see, but I was unable to photograph, the big suitcase item you had inquired about in our first call. I did make a sketch from memory when I had some time atop the water tower, and I have also sent you that sketch."

"Thank you for all that you have done; your information may just save the world. I'll let you know how things work out, and if they don't, I won't have to tell you; it will be in every newspaper and on every TV outlet in the world."

Just as he hung up with Massri, Seacrest got a phone call from Asu Aldiri of the Syrian secret service. "John, as you know things are in chaos here and nobody knows who is in power and who works for whom anymore. I have been trying mostly to stay alive and have had very little time to work on your pictures. But I have a friend who is a reporter for the Syrian Arab News Agency (SANA), and I sent her one of the photos with the man next to Adad Assad to see if she knows who he is. So far the best she can come with is a guess at the name: Mohamed el Sargon. She ran the name on her database and came up with nothing, and I ran it on mine, and I came up with nothing. This is the best I can do at the moment. If things settle down, perhaps I can do more, but for now this is all I have."

"I know that things are difficult and at a life-threatening time for you, but I want to thank you for what you have done for me and my country and perhaps the world. Asu, you have given me a name to go with a face, which is 100 percent more information than I had just seconds ago. I will ask all the security services on a global basis to try to help me find out who Sargon is and what threat he is to the United States of America."

CHAPTER 98

Megan Brown's Lab

B ROWN HAD BEEN WARNED THAT the AK-47 that was used to try to scare or kill Helen Murphy was on its way to her lab from Springfield and should be there in about half an hour. Omid Rahimi told her they needed to know two things: whose fingerprints were on the gun and who owned the rifle? They needed the information yesterday. There was a possibility that the shooter might be Michael Ridley or his twin.

Brown called over Penelope and Derrick to talk about the confusion over the fingerprints between the twins. "We are about to receive an AK-47 rifle that was used to take a shot at Helen Murphy, who was the girlfriend of Michael Ridley or Ishtar, or both. I want to talk about the process of identifying the differences between twins. We have to find, on a scientific and repeatable basis, a foolproof way to tell them apart. Most of the research I have read on fingerprints of twins is that the differences are small, but they are there. We have the prints we took off the big map, and that print led us to an initial determination of the identity of Al Ishtar Hamwi, and yet the second time we ran the print it came back as Michael Ridley. So let's assume the computer correctly identified the first print as belonging to Al Ishtar Hamwi; what did the computer see differently to call the second Michael Ridley?"

On a split-screen, Derrick put Ishtar's print on the left and the print that came back identifying Michael on the right. It took Derrick a few moments to load both prints. When he was done, he put the image on the big screen and Brown told him now to put the left over the right. All three of them went over the image, and even when the image was increased to ten times larger, they could not find a difference.

Brown asked Derrick to reverse the process by putting the right over the left and within seconds they saw the difference: the third loop had a slightly different radius. They reversed the slides again, left over right, and found that the top slide covered the radius in the second slide. As they looked at all other points of identification, they looked identical.

"Derrick, this is very important: was the print on the left the print that matched the print on the map that came back Al Ishtar Hamwi?"

"Yes, I'm sure I wrote down the computer code. Every fingerprint when matched is given a code for that very reason, and the second print that came back identifying Michael's print was also given a code, but a totally different alphanumeric code from Ishtar's code."

Just as Derrick was finishing, there was a knock at the door, and the courier was at the door with a package for Brown to sign for. She took it over to the big table and, along with her assistants, she carefully opened the box to reveal the AK-47 from Major Rahimi in Springfield, along with the bullet Omid had dug out of the wall.

The rifle was encased in bubble wrap, and they unrolled it to look for fingerprints that might be visible. Then they tried to decide whether they should fume it or dust it. The overall length made it impossible for them to use their fume chamber, so Penelope and Derrick decided to dust the rifle, but before they could, Brown stepped in and said, "Let's try smoking it."

Penelope and Derrick had never heard of smoking.

"We use the same chemical that we used in the big chamber in Georgetown, but we use it in this to spray the smoke over the gun one section at a time." Megan went to a cabinet and waved a device around. "It's a bee fogger, the kind they use to lay down smoke on a beehive to keep the bees calm while the keeper harvests the honey. If the fogger doesn't work, we can go back to Georgetown or try the dust; we will just lose some time, but the fingerprints will not be affected."

Brown loaded the fogger and ran it down one side, and some prints appeared immediately. Penelope lifted them and handed them to Derrick, who put them in the computer and waited for the next one to be passed over. On the first side, they lifted five prints, and all five came back unreadable. Brown turned over the rifle and put it on the other side and followed the same procedure, but this time she only found one print, which she passed on to Penelope. Finally, she turned the rifle on its back so the trigger section was pointing up, and she found one really good-quality print; she passed it on, and Derrick put it in the computer for processing.

All three sat around waiting. They waited and waited for what seemed like an hour and finally, the bell rang, and the image and name were a shock.

The name and photo was not of Michael or Ishtar, but Mike Ridley, their father.

CHAPTER 99

Paleto Nuclear Research Facility, Iran

ADAD LOOKED INTO THE WINDOW of the cooler and was shocked to see three other Soviet suitcase dirty bombs, or what looked like them, in the cooler. Was it possible that other terrorist groups had come to the Iranians seeking help in rebuilding their bombs? If they were, were they, as well as the Brotherhood, going to attack the United States? Could these groups be less organized than the Brotherhood and not really know what they were doing with such a powerful device? Why hadn't Oleg told them that his uncle had sold more bombs that were still in circulation?

Then he thought that perhaps the Iranian government was buying them on the open market and fixing them up to sell or even use themselves against the United States or perhaps Israel. Adad thought if America was being taken care of by the Brotherhood, then Iran could use the other bombs on Israel, and perhaps the Iranians should try to coordinate their attack on Israel with the Brotherhood's attack on America.

Adad asked himself another very important question: would the Iranian government sell one or all three additional bombs to the Brotherhood? Assad didn't know how much it would cost to buy the three bombs. Thinking positively, he wondered whether Oleg's uncle would invest more money in the Brotherhood to buy the three additional bombs. His mind was in a whirl, and, as made his way back to his cot, he knew he wasn't going to sleep, so he lay down and thought about the challenges and the opportunities. He still had four hours before Jaiari was to take over; that was four hours before he could tell Jaiari what he had found and about his plan. He knew that when Jaiari returned, he was going to finalize the arrangements to wire the money for the fixing of the one bomb they'd brought, and that would be the time to broach the subject about the other bombs he had discovered. But how could he be sure that what he saw in the other cooler was in fact dirty bombs?

He needed to wait until morning and the arrival of Jaiari to figure things out, but it would be a long four hours. Adad tried to fall asleep but couldn't; there were other sections of the lab that he had yet to explore. So he got up and started walking to the other side of the building. The one thing he noticed was that it was very different from where he'd just been. As he walked through a small door inside a giant set of double doors, he immediately noticed a set of railroad tracks. As he stepped into the vast room, he saw a railroad flat car with nothing on it. But on the ground were several large, round tubes; he guessed them to be in excess of five feet in diameter. The tubes were lying in a line and looked like they were getting ready to be fashioned into something else.

As he walked to the back of the building, he saw what looked like a large rocket engine and then it dawned on him: they were building a rocket. He had no idea how far along they were in building the rocket. Adad concluded that if they were building rockets at a nuclear site, they might also be building the bombs that sit on top of the rockets. He knew nothing about rockets, but he took out his cell phone and shot some pictures to share with Jaiari and the team on their return to Syria. But now he felt very uncomfortable in this place and wanted to get out as quickly as possible. He headed back to his cot to wait for morning.

Three hours later, Jaiari arrived to take his turn in relieving Adad.

They went out on the loading dock to talk. Adad told Jaiari what he had discovered—both the possible other bombs and the rocket. Jaiari said, "We must ignore the rocket and talk about their bomb and ask about other bombs they might have, and would they be willing to sell them, and if so, at what price. They know that you were here alone last night, so they have to assume that we know about the other bombs; let me do the talking and see what we can do, if anything. We do not want to do anything that would cause them to throw us out and keep our bomb, agreed?"

Adad agreed.

They went back in and were welcomed by Zarin, who asked whether they had both slept well and would they like to join him for some breakfast.

"We are hungry and would be glad to join you." They walked down the corridor toward the dining hall and made small talk. They walked in and were the only people in the room, other than the cooks.

"We need to settle our financial arrangement first thing this morning."

Zarin agreed and pulled out a binder that had the wire instructions in it, but before Zarin could hand it to him, Jaiari said, "Might I ask you a question before we conclude our transaction? We have heard that there were several bombs missing from the Soviet arsenal. Do you have access to any more of these bombs? And if you do, would they be available for sale?"

CHAPTER 100

Frank Williams's Office

MOORE, THE CHIEF OF TECHNOLOGY for Homeland Security returned to Williams's office to present his GPS findings to Williams and Baker.

"I have had an off-the-record discussion with the major GPS manufacturers, and they tell me officially that they do record the initial request, but they can only track where the vehicle is if the GPS is on at the destination. We did find the GPS company that had the system that asked for the route from Al-Mukharram to a place in Iran called Paleto, but we have no way of knowing whether that vehicle made it there or if it is still there. We will not know by GPS when it leaves Paleto unless the GPS is turned on, and they request a return trip to Al-Mukharram."

"If we think we know where it went, we can't be sure until it leaves, and it must turn on its GPS for us to see it, is that correct?"

"Correct."

"Is it possible to find out the coordinates of the last stop in Paleto?"

"Sir, we can only give you the location of the last place the GPS was on."

"How long will it take you to get the location?"

"About as long as it takes me to pass you this piece of paper across your desk." Moore gave Williams the location and Williams passed it to Baker. Baker knew he needed to adjust a satellite to look for the truck.

"Excellent job Mr. Moore!" and with that compliment, Moore and Baker left Williams's office.

Shortly after Baker and Moore left Williams's office, he asked Marie to get Dobias of Mossad on the phone right away. A few minutes later, Mr. Dobias was on line one.

"Nava, how are you?"

"Well," said Nava, "we are not making much progress. How about you?"

"We just received some images that our team took of the people and the meeting site, which we will send to Seacrest shortly. Perhaps you can help us identify who these people are? We are expecting new pictures from our operative on the ground later today, and I will send them to you as soon as I get them. We also believe we have a GPS signal that started from the town of Al-Mukharram in Syria, and the GPS was asked to calculate a route to Paleto, Iran. I will give you the location before this call ends, and you can look for yourself. We think this is the site of one of Iran's nuclear scientific centers and perhaps a location that could be building the bombs we all have been worried about since Mahmoud Ahmadinejad took power in Iran in 2005.

"But he told the world that he is developing nuclear energy to generate power, not bombs. We believe that this and other sites are offering help to terrorist groups with newer versions of dirty bombs and may in fact be a manufacturing site for their first intercontinental ballistic missile, which could carry a nuclear warhead to your country. We have repositioned several of our satellites to cover that location, and you might want to consider investigating that site both in the air and with observers on the ground. If there is going to be an attack on Israel by Iran, it will come from a location like this one. I do not think that the Brotherhood will give up on their idea of attacking America, but I do think that Iran will want to attack Israel."

Dobias had listened very patiently to the last part of the conversation while Frank told him his story. "I do want the location, and we will take a look perhaps in both the ways you suggest. We don't have enough information on the Brotherhood and the likeliness of their changing their minds about what country to attack. We have a team in place watching and listening to what is taking place at the moment near Al-Mukharram, and I will put a second team together to look at the Paleto site. We believe that they do have an older version of the Soviet suitcase bomb, but it must be degrading because we have pictures of them covering it with bags and bags of ice. That would lead us to believe that they have two bombs, one in Syria and one in Iran.

"Our biggest challenge is that we can't really do anything until the Brotherhood makes a move against us, and in reality a rocket would be easier for us to bring down than a suitcase bomb that could be in anything. It is frustrating to be watching two sites and not knowing what either group will do.

"We have to be very careful about the number of teams we put in Iran, for we have a number of teams already in place watching other possible installations. I understand you might be in a tight place, so perhaps our birds can do more of the heavy lifting, and you can save your personnel. I *do* want to tell you we have a new lead on one of the terrorist's leaders. At the moment, we only have a first name: Mordecai. We picked it up from one of our men on the ground, and we are searching the personnel records for the Israeli nuclear program to see whether they have had a person with the first name that matches ours. If we can identify the name, we can compare photos and see if we have the right person.

"Old friend, I wish there was more I could do for you; I will pass the name on to Seacrest and have him run it by his contacts to see whether he can come up with a last name."

"If you get a last name and the name matches any of the images we both have, let me know."

"Let us promise each other that if either of us picks up the movement of that cargo van, we will call immediately. The future of both our nations may be riding in the back of that white cargo van."

Chapter 101

Paleto, Iran Research Center

Zarin responded to Jaiari's question about other bombs. "We would like to suggest an exchange of your bomb for a more modern version that they think will meet your requirements in terms of destruction capability. If you agree, you could be on your way today."

Jaiari asked about additional bombs, and Saeed politely replied, "That is not possible," and simply presented the wire instructions. Jaiari took out his cell phone and sent the wire instructions to Sargon and told him that it was possible that they would need all the money today, as the Iranians were offering an already updated bomb they had in their position. The wire instructions were sent, and while they are waiting for the wire transfer to go through, Jaiari said, "Tell me about this exchange offer."

"We have acquired several of the old-style bombs on the open market, and none of them were capable of working for the same reason yours will not work. We were able to restore and significantly upgrade the older bombs, and we have a few that we use for a swap-out like the one we are proposing to you. There are a limited number of these bombs in the marketplace, and soon we will run out of replacements."

"With so few left, wouldn't you like to sell and recapture your investment and reuse the money for other projects?"

"Thank you for your concern, but we want to spread the wealth around."

Adad stepped in and asked, "Are there other groups around the world who have exchanged or purchased bombs from you?"

"That is not for me to say. The government tells us what to do; we do not transact with the parties, and I hope you understand." Zarin took Jaiari and Adad to the part of the center that Adad had found the previous night, where he had seen the other bombs in the cooler. "I have a few left, and I'm ready to go over their power and capabilities with you if you want to make the exchange. If you do, then I believe we have just enough time to complete our transaction today; is that okay with you?"

Adad felt like he was talking to a used car salesman instead of a nuclear scientist, but it was what it was.

The three of them walked through the building to the cooler that Adad had seen the previous evening. This time the cooler was unlocked, and Zarin opened the door. Adad and Jaiari could see three bombs that looked very similar to their bomb. Saeed invited them into the cooler and said the bombs were all originally made about the same time as their bomb, but the Iranian team had reconditioned the old bombs to make them more effective and much more powerful.

"What is the difference between the two bombs?"

"The old bomb could send radioactive debris between 1.6 to 3.2 miles from the center of the blast. The greatest amount of destruction would be in the range of one-half to three-quarters of a mile. The closer to the center of the blast, the higher the radiation and in turn the greater amount of time required to have the contaminated area deplete its radioactive material. These bombs were never intended to be weapons of mass destruction, but weapons of fear. If a dirty bomb went off in the center of a city, then the people in the outskirts might not have any radioactive material reaching them, but people would not want to go back into the city for fear of being contaminated, and so they would leave the entire area and it would then become a ghost town.

"Today, however, with much more powerful explosives, we can construct a bomb that has a greater quantity of radioactive material in it and as a result the range of these bombs, depending on atmospheric conditions, could be almost triple the effective range of the old bombs. With these bombs having a range of between five and fifteen miles, most of the Major cities in the world would be affected. Let's use New York City as an example: Manhattan is at its widest part is 2.8 miles across and just over eighteen miles from the tip of the Battery to Harlem, so one of our bombs set off in midtown Manhattan would make Manhattan uninhabitable for decades. The death and destruction will be concentrated on either side of midtown Manhattan. Most of the damage would be within a five-mile range of midtown, which would take it all the way to the tip of the island, including Wall Street, and well above Central Park into Harlem."

"That is impressive if we wanted to take out New York, but let me ask you a question: if you could reconfigure the bomb with all the new technology, how long would it take and how much more powerful would it be than these newly reconstructed bombs?"

"Given the size constraints of the package and the current limits on explosives, we are at max. We could try to squeeze out additional capacity, but I have no idea how much it would cost, or how long it would take to gain a small amount of capacity. I would have to check with the government to see whether they even have any interest. So for now I guess it's take it or wait to have your bomb rebuilt, and my guess is that will take many months to complete."

Jaiari said he needed to make a call, and he would have an answer for Zarin in a few moments. He took out his cell phone and dialed Sargon, telling him of the deal and that he and Adad were in agreement about making the switch. "We will have a significantly more powerful bomb that will be stable and allow us to bring America to its knees, especially if Mordecai can duplicate the new bomb." Sargon thought for a moment and told Jaiari that he agreed to the swap.

While they were waiting for the second wire transfer to go through, they started loading the bomb into the cargo van. They packed it just the way they had before, and in about an hour, the wire transfer was complete and the bomb packed into the truck. Jaiari and Adad shook hands with Zarin, got in the truck, and were on their way. Jaiari said to Adad, after they had cleared the security gate, "My friend, today we start counting the days until America falls."

Chapter 102

Ted Baker's Office

The phone rang in Baker's office, and it was Seacrest on the phone. "The van has left Paleto, and our infrared satellite says there is a nuclear device in the van. They have asked the GPS system to set a course to return to home base, and they should be there within twenty-four to thirty hours. Do you want me to call Mossad, or should we have Williams make the call?"

"I think the call should come from Williams. Is there a way we can send the tracking signal from the satellite to Williams and Mossad?"

"Yes, I believe we can. I will contact Marie, and I will get Williams's IP address, and you can ask Williams to get the IP address Mossad wants the signal sent to and then get back to me so I can set it up. I'll be back to you shortly, John, and thanks."

Baker called Marie and asked her whether she knew Williams's IP address and also to schedule a meeting with him later in the day.

"I don't want to seem stupid, but what is an IP address?"

"In order for a computer or any device like a modem or printer to work on the Internet it must have an Internet Protocol address that identifies that particular device and allows it to talk to other devices over the Internet; it is almost like a direct dial phone number for every computer."

"Thank you for explaining it to me, and I'll get right on Mr. Williams's IP address."

Baker heard a chime on his computer, and it was a secure e-mail from Seacrest; in the e-mail was a link and instructions as to what to do when he clicked on the link. Baker clicked on the link, and in a matter of moments, he had set up his computer to follow the cargo van on its way south. The arrow wasn't moving very fast; in fact sometimes it looked like it wasn't moving at all. He found himself staring at the screen, almost mesmerized by the image, but he realized that he had a great deal more to do and that he had a meeting with Williams in about thirty minutes.

Baker called Seacrest and got him on the first ring.

"The satellite tracking is the first break I think we have had."

"We may have another break: Mossad called Williams and told him that the first name of one of the terrorists is in fact Mordecai, and so there is a 99 percent chance he has to be Jewish. Mossad is checking all the employment records they have on past and present employees in the Israeli nuclear program to see whether they can find anybody with the first name of Mordecai. If we get a last name, I'll let you know, and see if it rings any bells.

"We also know that a house in Springfield was purchased by Viktor Antipova, the Russian billionaire, and the evidence is that he was in charge of all the non-missile-based nuclear bombs, including the suitcase bombs, in the old Soviet Union. Would you check with Interpol and see if you can find anything about his extended family? Was he or is he married, did he have any children, legitimate or not, and what does his extended family look like? We might find a connection from him to the Brotherhood. Let me know as soon as possible what you find out."

CHAPTER 103

Meeting Warehouse in Syria

SARGON CALLED MORDECAI AND OLEG to tell them to meet him at the warehouse as soon as possible; the van had left earlier than anticipated and, based on the travel to the site in Iran, they should be back at the warehouse in about two days. Sargon was the first to arrive, and shortly thereafter, Mordecai and Oleg arrived. Captain Oppenheimer saw all the activity and had the communications expert, Gal Grossman; turn on the Parabolic Microphone System that was good for eavesdropping up to 300 yards away.

Grossman reported a lot of background noise, but no conversation yet. All of a sudden he turned his head and Oppenheimer saw the move, which was a signal that dialogue was taking place.

Grossman said, "I can hear that one person is telling the other two that, instead of rebuilding the bomb, they traded it for a newer version and have already departed. I expect them to be here in just over two days. Once they have cleared Iran, they will call us and describe what the new bomb looks like; this will give Mordecai some time to think about what he needs to do with the one they have packed in ice. They did say that it was almost three times more powerful and yet the explosives seem to take up less space."

Oppenheimer was taking notes. Grossman heard the leader saying, "We will have to figure a plan to get the bombs into the United States and then we will spend time on deciding on the target; as for now, I think we need more ice for our bomb."

Grossman said that the one named Mordecai was headed to town to meet with his contact. It sounded as though he were saying the person's name was Al Ishtar Hamwi?

Oppenheimer would contact Dobias at Mossad to see whether he has any information on this Hamwi person. "Any information on him we need to get to Lt. Hassen in the city so she can identify him and follow him to his contact. Let's get a set of long-distance eyes on that building and see whether we can get a description of this Mordecai person that we can send to Lt. Hassen."

With things in motion, he decided he would call Nava himself and give him an update. He dialed Nava's phone number and reached him on the second ring. Sir, this is Captain Oppenheimer, and I want to report that the van has left wherever it was and is expected to be here in about two days. The one they call Mordecai is headed to the village to make contact with a person named Al Ishtar Hamwi; do you have any pictures of this Ishtar person that you can send to Lt. Hassen in the village?"

"What was the name again?"

"Al Ishtar Hamwi."

"Please hold on for a moment; that name rings a bell. One of the Americans, at least we think he is an American, is named Michael Ridley. When the US ran a fingerprint test, they found that Michael Ridley has a twin brother whose name is Al Ishtar Hamwi. I don't know whether or not it is the same person, so I will send the picture we have on both Michael Ridley and Al Ishtar Hamwi, so she can be on the lookout for one or the other. We have identified a person named Mordecai Hagel, who used to work in our nuclear program but disappeared at least six months ago. I will forward his picture to both of you, and you can tell me whether this is your Mordecai."

"Sir, could I ask you to contact Lt. Hassen, I'm concerned about calls from my phone going into the village, but you have scramblers."

"Captain, no problem. I'll get this off to her immediately, and perhaps her team can identify these two people and we can find out where they are headed and what they are up to."

CHAPTER 104

Lt. Hassen, the Village of Al-Mukharram

ASSEN AND HER TEAM HAD been in the city for three days, and nothing had happened, except that she thought she had put on a few pounds. She had been in contact with the rest of her team on a daily basis, but there was nothing to do this morning. Her phone, which had not rung in four days, now rang, and it was a text message from the head of Mossad telling her that important images were being sent to her, and after she got them she needed to contact him immediately. Her heart started to pound, for she was going to be talking not to her captain, but to the head of the entire agency, which she had never met.

She heard her phone ring again and a note in the e-mail said two images were attached. She opened the file and looked at the photos and didn't recognize the man in either picture. She immediately forwarded the two photos and asked the team members whether any of them had seen either of these two men. She did not wait for a reply; she dialed the number for the head of Mossad, and Nava answered the phone on the second ring. She introduced herself and said that she had received his message and was calling for instructions. He was very straightforward with her and said, "Find these two, attach the tracking devices given to you, and follow them—find out whom they are and what they are doing. Do you understand?"

Almost unable to speak, she replied, "Yes, sir."

"Any questions, Lt. Hassen?"

"No, sir."

"I want a report when you make contact with them; I want a report when you find out where they are going. I want a report when you confirm their names, and I want a report on what they are doing, do you understand?"

"Yes, sir," and the line went dead. After Nava had disconnected, Hassen finally took a breath.

She needed to call a team meeting, but it had to be in a place where they could talk freely and openly about what they needed to do. She sent an instant message to the whole team: any ideas of a place for all of us to meet? She waited and waited what seemed like hours to get a reply about a decent place. About half a mile out of the south end of town was an empty barn that sat back from the road. There was a back entrance, so they could come through the woods two at a time and come in the back door and not be noticed. She said that everybody should leave then and head for the barn; she wanted the entire team in the barn in thirty minutes.

Hassen had been around town by herself and she decided that she would leave by herself and meet up with the team. Walking deliberately but quickly, she left town and strode past the barn. She found a bend in the road, and that gave her the opportunity to jump off the road and double back to the barn. She arrived at the barn door, and just before she opened it, she said to herself, *Be calm, forceful, and decisive: the team is looking for you to lead them.*

She pulled open the door and, seeing all the members of her team, she said to them, "This is going to be quick. You have seen the photos of the people we are looking for; I want you to spread out throughout the town and find them and tag them with the GPS I'm about to give you. When you find them, stay with them, but send me a text message of where you are and where you are heading. Do not use your cell phones for calls just text messages if at all possible."

One of the team members asked, "Who are these people?"

She responds responded with authority, "Very, very bad people. Any more questions?" "How do we get the GPS on them without them knowing?"

"Look for an opportunity to have contact with them so you can attach the GPS. Any other questions?"

"One more, ma'am: if they leave town, how do we follow them?"

"If they take public transportation, you take it along with them; if they use a car, we will have to depend on the GPS to tell us where they are going, but be assured they are coming back here. Let's disperse and return to the village and keep a watchful eye and good luck. One last thing: when you have made contact and placed the GPS, then send me an IM."

They started to leave the building, and Hassen decided to go back the way she had come, using the main road. As she opened the door of the barn, it slammed into something—or someone—with a loud thud.

CHAPTER 105

Return to Al-Mukharram

JAIARI AND ADAD WERE ON their way back to the warehouse with the new bomb.

While they had only been gone a few days, the long drive in both directions had worn them out. Adad, who was to go back to the hotel and sleep for the twelve-hour shift, never made it back to the hotel except to get his belongings and check out, yet the owner charged them for the week. They were close to the Iran-Iraq border, and they would feel much better after they had crossed into Iraq. The border crossing went without a hitch, and they sped toward Syria and home. They both realized that they were hungry, and they found a roadside café where they stopped for a quick meal; with their stomachs full, they were back in the van headed for ZanJan and what they hoped would be a good night's sleep.

As they left the café, they decided to call Sargon and talk to him about the differences between the new bomb and the old. They guessed that he would want Mordecai on the phone, and he might not be at the warehouse when they called. Adad dialed Sargon's number, and it rang a couple of times before he answered. Adad told Sargon that they planned to stay in the same warehouse in ZanJan that they had stayed in on their trip over. Adad asked whether Mordecai was in the warehouse, and Sargon said no, he was looking for his contact in town to supply him with what he needed to fix the old bomb. Jaiari asked how their bomb was holding up.

"We have kept it very well cooled. Mordecai seems to think it is stable, and he will be able, with what we have, and his supplier contacts, to build a bomb similar to the one in the back of your cargo van."

Adad asked Sargon whether Mordecai and Oleg had developed their ideas as to how to use the bombs and in America. "Very much so. In fact, they both have compelling ideas, and I will be very interested in hearing both of your ideas when you get back. My plan is to have each of you make a presentation of your plan of use, and after all four have been presented, we will pick two and then make our final decision. Adad, can you tell me about the road you are currently traveling?"

Adad wasn't sure what he wanted to know.

"Is there a lot of traffic on the road?"

Adad responded, "Not a lot. We see a car or a truck every few minutes."

"Are there are places where you can get off the road and rest?"

Adad responded that there were.

"Then one more question: do some of these places have trees that you can pull under for shade?"

Adad again responded, "Yes."

"Do you see one coming up soon? Turn into the next pull off and park the van under the largest tree. If you do not see a tree that can give you adequate shelter then pull out and go down the road."

Confused, Adad saw a pull off and swung in under a very large date palm tree that must have had a canopy thirty feet in diameter. He pulled the van under the tree and shut off the engine. Adad told Sargon that the van was parked under a significant spreading palm tree.

"Adad, get out of the van, but as much as possible stay under the tree."

Adad got out.

"Now go to the back of the van and reach up into the driver's side wheel well and feel for a box."

Adad walked around to the back of the van and put his hand and arm up into the wheel well and felt for an object.

Sargon said, "Now yank it out of the van."

Adad pulled it out.

"Now walk over to the tree trunk and smash the box against the tree until it is broken into many pieces."

Adad did, and at that second the tracking image on Seacrest, Williams, and Dobias computers disappeared.

CHAPTER 106

Springfield, St. Patrick Catholic Church

SHERIFF JIM WHITTLES AND MAJOR Omid Rahimi met outside St. Patrick Church in Springfield about 11:30 Sunday morning. They were dressed in their finest dress uniforms along with representatives from most of the police departments around the state, all there to honor the service and ultimate sacrifice that Sergeant Jerry Kelly had made for his fellow officers, his community, and his nation.

The inside of the church was full to the point that there was no place left to stand inside, and people were standing outside just to be part of the memorial service for the fallen hero. Only two people who were there truly understood how important the sacrifice Jerry Kelly had made for his country was. As the two men stood at the back of the church, they could hear the priest read the letters of condolences from state, local, and national leaders. The letter from President Nathan Jordan was especially moving in its praise for Kelly's bravery and the sacrifice he had made.

The whole ceremony took about twenty minutes, and after the service, there was a reception at the parish center just across the street. Whittles was designated to stand next to Jerry's wife, Helen, in the receiving line, and the children were too small to be part of the line, so they were kept occupied by friends and relatives. Whittles decided that Helen needed to sit down because the stream of well-wishers was so long, he felt Helen was going to be exhausted. He arranged for a chair to be brought up for Helen to sit and greet people. It took almost two hours for all the people who wanted to wish Helen well and thank her for her husband's service to pass by; by the time it ended, Helen hands hurt, her back ached, and she was concerned about her children. She had not seen them in several hours, and she worried about whether or not they were okay. Helen walked to the serving table with Whittles and told him how overwhelmed she was at the turnout for her husband.

Whittles didn't know what to say to her, other than to say that his office would always be there for her, and should she need anything, never to hesitate to call him. Whittles stayed with Helen until she was ready to go home and then he gave Helen a big bear hug and a kiss on the cheek and helped her into her car and waved to her as the car drove out of sight.

As Whittles turned around, there was Omid in his dress blues looking at his cell phone. "I could use a drink," the sheriff said, sighing.

Omid said, "Based on what I just got from Brown, I will join you."

"What did you hear?"

"Let's get out of the range of other people."

They both got in Whittles car and drove off to his house. Megan had sent Rahimi the results of the fingerprints on the AK-47.

"So were they able to identify the prints?"

"Yes. They were Mike Ridley's. Not Michael's, Mike's."

Whittles hit the brakes. "That means at least Mike Ridley is still in town or near Springfield." They pulled into Whittles driveway and went into the house.

"What'll you have?"

"Do you have a cold beer?"

"Light or full-bodied?"

"I'll take full strength, if you please, because I just got *more* info from Brown."

"Hold on until I get you the Bud." He opened the fridge and walked to the living room to hand the beer to Omid.

"What is the rest of the news?"

"The bullet we dug out of the wall in the bank. Brown says it isn't from the rifle we recovered."

"So are you saying that the shot came from the same vicinity from a different rifle, but that the rifle we found was a plant?"

"It looks that way."

"Then Mike Ridley may *not* be in town as I originally thought." The sheriff took a long draw of his Jack Daniels. "Then who took the shot at Mary and why?"

CHAPTER 107

The Warehouse in Syria

MORDECAI RETURNED FROM TOWN BUT was not able to find his contact. He concluded that it was too early; he was expecting the bomb to come much later. As he walked through the door, Sargon told him that Adad and Jaiari were on the way to ZanJan for the night and were expected to be there late the next afternoon.

"They want to talk with you to tell you what they were able to see in the new bomb." Sargon called the number, and Adad answered. "Before we get started talking to Mordecai, can you explain to both of us what we did at the pull off?"

"When you were packing the van, a GPS homing device was hidden without your knowledge so that we could track your movements. It occurred to me that if we were getting the signal, then perhaps other people might also be following your movements. I decided that you were on your way home, and I didn't need the tracking device anymore, so I decided to have you get rid of it, and you did. Now let's move on to the new bomb."

Mordecai asked, "In general, what can you tell me about the bomb?"

Jaiari responded. "On the outside, the case looks the same, and when you open the case, it actually looks like the new system is smaller than the old. We told them we wanted something more powerful than the old bomb, and they told us that the new bomb was three to five times more powerful. The lab people told us that the explosive they were going to use to replace the TNT was called Octanitrocubane. They said it was more stable than TNT, which was used in the old bombs. We asked about power, and they said that the range of contamination on this bomb was three to five times greater. The radiological material comes from spent power plant fuel that is encased in a lead cylinder. The lead keeps the radiation from leaking out and is easily disintegrated with the power of the blast. With a more powerful explosive taking up less space, they told us that they could put more radioactive material in the bomb."

"Is there anything else they said was different in the new bomb?"

Both men thought for a moment, and they said the only other thing they could think of was that the wiring was more modern, and the detonator could be cell phone activated. Mordecai thanked them very much and said he was looking forward to seeing them the next day.

After he hung up, Mordecai said to Sargon, "A very strange thing happened while I was in town. I went out of town toward the meeting site I had set up with Ishtar, and just as I came round the bend and approached the barn, the door opened and hit me and knocked me down. As I looked up, a very attractive woman came around the door with a look of horror on her face. I think she must have thought she had killed me. She quickly came to my aid and was very apologetic; she helped me up and brushed me off. She offered to take me back to the village and find me a doctor. I told her I was fine, just a little startled. Then she asked to buy me a glass of wine instead."

Mordecai sat down, thinking about his encounter at the barn. "I said that I needed to meet somebody, but I could meet her in an hour in the village at the café off the town square. She asked again if I was all right, and she kept brushing me off. I said I needed to leave, and I asked her, 'By the way, why were you in the barn?'

"She replied that she was in her last year of university, and her major was architecture, and she was doing her last paper on old buildings and when she saw this barn, she had to see the inside. 'Is this your barn?' she asked. 'I'm sorry, I didn't know whom to ask in the village who owned it, but I didn't harm it.' I told her I didn't own it and that I was sure the owner wouldn't mind. She still seemed rattled, and she asked again whether I was okay, and I replied yes. She asked again, 'Are we meeting in an hour?' I said I'd try. I don't know why, but it felt strange I just couldn't figure out whether it was good strange or bad strange, but she was pretty, and I wanted to see her again."

Captain Oppenheimer was listening to the conversation, and he now knew what explosive and nuclear material was used in the bomb. He sent a text message to Dobias to forward to Seacrest. He wondered whether the woman in the barn was one of his team and whether she was working him to try to get close enough to attach the GPS. He decided that after he had sent the text to Nava and John, he would send one to Lt. Hassen and arrange a meeting to talk about what to do if, in fact, the person whom Mordecai had met was indeed Lt. Hassen.

He texted: *Meet me on the road north out of town in thirty minutes and bring your smile.*

CHAPTER 108

Viktor Antipova, the Money behind the Plot

S EACREST HAD A CALL HOLDING from Harold Wellington from Interpol. He picked up the phone and apologized for leaving him on hold, explaining that he had been on the phone with Frank Williams.

Wellington said, "Old boy, I have a story to tell you about Viktor Antipova. He was the president, chairman, and principal shareholder of Antipova Oil, a Russian oil and gas exploration company with drilling interests all over Russia and many of the old Soviet Union satellite countries. His personal net worth is projected to be in the unknown billions. Before the breakup of the old Soviet Union, he was responsible for the non-missile-based nuclear weapons. When the old government crumbled, he took control of thousands of these weapons and had them transferred to warehouses under his control. When the first major oil fields were discovered in Russia, he was able to sell some of his inventory on the black market to raise money to begin to buy oil leases.

"His company began to drill for, and found, vast amounts of oil and gas. The money he made on the current oil finds allowed him to buy more oil leases, and he built a juggernaut that propelled his company into being one of the largest non-Middle East oil companies in the world. Viktor has used his current income from oil and gas sales to expand into other business opportunities and in turn increased his net worth, making him one of the richest men in the world. It has been said about Antipova that he has a thirst for money and that his thirst maybe unquenchable. He was never married, but can be seen every night out on the town with a beautiful young woman. Rumors have abounded that he has several illegitimate children whom he supports."

"What else does he do with his money?"

"He has been known to provide funds to rebels for the overthrow of governments in exchange for drilling rights in the country. He funds the rebels and gets the oil for free until the next rebels come in and want to overthrow that government. The rumor now going around is that he is trying to corner the oil market."

Seacrest said, "You've got to be kidding! With the oil market so large, how could anyone get control?"

"I'm not saying he wants to buy all the oil in the world; he wants to control a great deal of the current supply. The word is that through many of his companies he has been buying oil futures. For a small amount of money, actually cents on the dollar, you can buy control of a large quantity of oil for a period of time."

"So how do you make money in this business?"

"Excellent question. The short answer is leverage. You can buy a futures contract, the contract gives you the right to buy a thousand barrels of oil, let's say for $105 a barrel. The cost of the future in our example is fifty seven hundred dollars. So for less than $6,000, per contract you control a around $400,000 worth of crude oil. So the leverage is $400,000 divided by $6,000 or 67 times. Now take someone like our Russian: he can spend millions of dollars buying futures. So let's suppose something really bad happens in America, say, like 9/11. The price of oil could go to $200 a barrel. You could exercise your contract and take deliver of the oil and then sell it or you could sell your futures contract. The profit in our example, our six thousand dollar investments, turns into $400,000 a profit, if we own one thousand barrels of oil. In this illustration the profit is 6,600 percent if the price doubles. We heard that in London and in New York our Russian is a very big buyer of longer maturity futures in both West Texas and Brent crude oil, so he is betting that something really bad is going to happen somewhere, and he stands to make hundreds of millions of dollars, if not billions."

"If he has made a huge bet, and it doesn't work, can he lose his fortune?"

"He could lose a great deal of money, but my guess is he is trying to hedge his bets by creating or supporting the group to make it happen. He will try to interrupt the world oil supply and make his futures worth another fortune. One other thing, old chap. He didn't have any legitimate children, but he does have a nephew, Oleg Barbolio, whom he took in as a small child when his parents were killed in a tragic car accident. We think Oleg has worked for his uncle's oil business for many years, and he has a graduate degree in petroleum engineering from Stanford University in the States. But, here is the difficult part: we have no idea where he is at the moment.

"According to Interpol, the last place he showed up was in San Francisco. Unless he left the US in a nontraditional way, we have every reason to believe that he is still in the US."

While they were talking, Seacrest looked up Oleg's passport file, and it showed, just as Harold said, that he had come into San Francisco, but there was no record that he had ever left the country. "Thanks, Harold, for all the help." After he hung up, he remembered his thought about it being an easy way to get into the country along the Canadian border; could it be just as easy to escape the same way?

CHAPTER 109

Warehouse in Syria

ADAD AND JAIARI CALLED SARGON when they thought they were one hour away from the warehouse. Sargon called Mordecai and Oleg to tell them that the van would be at the warehouse within the hour, and he would need their help in unloading the shipment.

Just before Hassen went to meet Mordecai, she had a brief meeting with Oppenheimer in the woods just north of the village. She told David that she had come flying out of a barn at the south end of the village and she opened the door on Mordecai and knocked him down. When she went around the door to see what she knocked down she was flabbergasted to see Mordecai on the ground. She didn't have the GPS with her, so she arranged to meet him for drinks at the café near the center of town.

Oppenheimer asked her whether she had gotten his last name, and she said, "Yes, when I apologized, I said, 'I'm sorry, but I don't know your name,' and he said, 'Mordecai Hagal.' I said, 'my name is Hadar Hassen.'" After she told him her real name she wondered, *"should I have given him my real name? I didn't have a hidden identity so what else could I have done?"*

Nice to meet you, and I'll see you again in an hour.' Mordecai said he had to meet somebody and might be late, but I said, 'You'll make it, you'll make it.'"

"It would be very hard to say no to you, and you know it."

She smiled at Oppenheimer and reminded him of what he had said at the staging area: *by any means possible.* "I got the means, and they made it happen."

"You said that he was going to meet somebody; did that happen?"

"I don't know because I didn't want to hang around and arouse suspicion. I will ask him when we meet whether he met his friend." Hadar told Oppenheimer what Mordecai was wearing, and she wanted to know where he thought the best place was to put the GPS on Mordecai; Oppenheimer suggested on his back below the shoulder blade. "If you put it on the front, it might easily be discovered because we more often meet people head-on than approaching them from behind. Below the shoulder blade will locate it below the line of sight, and having it to the side it will make it less likely to be noticed by Mordecai when he takes off his jacket or puts it on."

"You have different colors for the GPS?" Think about what he was wearing when you met and take a couple different colors with you."

"Yes. Good idea to bring different colors because he may not wear the same jacket that he had on when I knocked him down."

Hadar looked at the device when she got back to the hotel, and it had a small hook pin like a fish hook.

"When you greet him, give him a slight hug, but enough of a hug that he can feel you pressing against him. When you lean into him, bring your left hand around and place it on his back and drop it down and attach the GPS. The approach should be innocent enough, but sexually distracting. Sit down, have some wine and cheese, and try to get him to tell you whom he was trying to meet. If you see he is uncomfortable talking about the person he was going to meet, back off. Hadar, I realize that you were not trained to be a spy, but you do have the brains and the assets to do very well. Call me after you're done. One last suggestion: if at any time you are afraid, get up and leave. We do not know who or what this guy really is, so there is no need for you to put yourself in danger.

"It also might be a good idea that you have a backup or two who could step in and rescue you. Their job is to play the boyfriend, and so you work out a signal for help, and your teammate will come and take you away. No fuss and no bother, just get out."

Hadar nodded, nervous but brave.

CHAPTER 110

Frank Williams's Office

WILLIAMS WAS PREPARING FOR HIS briefing with the president; the meeting was scheduled for four o'clock that afternoon. He was in his conference room working with Baker and his assistant Marie on handouts for the president. Frank had just heard from Dobias of Mossad that they had identified Mordecai Hagal as one of the terrorists. Hagal was born and raised in New York City and was first in his class at MIT in nuclear engineering. He was recruited by Israel to come and work in their nuclear program. The report on Hagal was that he became disenchanted with what he was doing and got involved with antigovernment protests. About six months ago he vanished, until the pictures of him in Syria with the rest of the terrorist team showed up.

"We know that Adad Assad is another member and was the driver of the cargo van that went to Iran with the first bomb. Adad is a successful businessman and for reasons not known to us, got involved with the leader whose identity is still unknown to us. We know nothing about the other person who was in the van with Adad that went to Iran. The last person in a leadership position may be Russian. We think he may be related to the Russian oil and gas billionaire Viktor Antipova, who Interpol believes has a very significant amount of money invested in long oil futures. The leader of the group is still unknown to us, but from what we can gather, he has a strong but gentle hand on the group.

"Michael Ridley's girlfriend was shot at in the bank where she works, and the fingerprints on the rifle were those of Michael's father, but the bullet dug out of the wall didn't come from the rifle that was found, so it appears that someone was trying to mislead us about the father. Michael has an identical twin, Ishtar, who recently flew to Amman, Jordan. At least we think it was Ishtar; it could have been Michael. Mary Murphy has been sleeping with both men but apparently doesn't know that there are two different twins.

"Seacrest thinks that if they are going to use the bombs against us, they will come in through Canada. And the biggest question still unanswered is *where* will they use them? Mossad has two teams on the ground and one with a listening device trained on the warehouse, so if we are lucky we can hear what they want to bomb. The president is going to ask: should we take them out now?"

Baker responded to Williams's question. "They have both bombs in one place, so with a tactical, long-range air strike from one of our carriers in the Mediterranean, we could destroy the whole terrorist cell, their bombs, their buildings and all the people. We would have to notify Mossad that they would need to get their people out of the area and get as far away as possible very quickly."

Williams responded, "Some would consider this an act of war against Syria, and the damage of the secondary explosions spreading the nuclear matter all over that part of Syria would be hard to explain to the world."

Baker suggested that he tell the president that they have to wait and see what they plan to do and where they take the bombs. "My guess is that the bombs will both be set up with cell phone detonation capabilities, and so an assault to try to capture the bombs could force the terrorists to set them off. You might want to say to the president that we are between a rock and a hard place on this one. We can't ask our friends in Israel to take them out because it would be seen as an attack on Syria, and the entire Muslim world would rise up and unite against Israel."

"Sir, it just doesn't appear that we have any real options. We have to wait until the bombs arrive on American soil to do anything. Unfortunately, we just have to wait."

CHAPTER III

Café off the Village Square

HADAR SET HER TEAM OF rescuers in position and changed into something much more revealing. She hoped that the way she looked would distract Mordecai enough that she could attach the GPS; her teammates thought she would have no problem. She waits away from the café to let him arrive first so she can see what he is wearing to pick the right color GPS to attach. She looked all around the square, and she spotted him coming into it past the bakery. He walked across the square and headed to the café. He picked a table that looked out into the square so he could see her coming.

She waited a few moments and saw that he was fidgety and decided to walk into the square directly toward him.

He spotted her and couldn't take his eyes off her. She had dark hair that fell just below her shoulders—long enough to lie on her ample, high breasts. She was wearing a sweater, buttoned from the bottom, over a blouse that was unbuttoned two buttons from the top, accentuating her form. When she was about twenty feet away, Mordecai leaped from his chair like a racehorse out of the starting gate. She walked over to him and opened her left arm to bring him into her, and he responded willingly; when he caressed her, she attached the GPS and left her hand on his shoulder for a moment while they walked the short distance to the table.

They both went to sit down, and Mordecai held the chair for her, and she said, "Quite the gentleman!"

They sat down, and he called over the waiter and asked Hadar what she would like to drink, and she said, "White." He told the waiter, "A bottle of white with hard, crusty bread and an assortment of cheeses."

Hadar said to him, "Again, I apologize about the barn door, and this is on me."

Mordecai said, "No, thank you for coming and looking so gorgeous, and I insist, this is on me."

While they were waiting, Hadar asked, "Did you find your friend?"

Mordecai, still mesmerized by her looks, wasn't paying attention. Distractedly, he replied, "No, not today. I guess I got the dates mixed up. I'll call him later."

"So you know what I do besides knocking people down with barn doors. What do you do for a living?"

Mordecai replied, "I'm a nuclear engineer. I'm just here on a little vacation."

"And are you enjoying yourself?"

He responded, "I am now, thanks to you." The waiter brought their food and bottle of wine, and Hadar was trying to figure out what to do next while the waiter was setting up the table.

"Is your friend an engineer too?"

"You mean the one I was looking for? No, he is a salesman of sorts."

"Could you pour me some wine, please?"

Mordecai said, "I'm sorry," and poured her some wine, gave her a plate, and offered her some bread and cheese. "Enough about me. You said that you were just finishing university in architecture. What would like to design after you graduate?"

"I have been thinking about that a great deal, and I think I want to go to the American West, maybe Texas, and learn how to build adobe houses and then translate that construction approach to building homes in Africa for the poor."

Mordecai responded, "That's amazing." Just then his phone rang, and he had a text message: *It's here.*

Mordecai stood abruptly. "I have to leave; something has come up unexpectedly."

Hassen asked, "Is somebody hurt?"

He replied, "No, just something that I have to attend to right away. I'm sorry I have to leave. Can we meet again and finish our conversation?"

"I would very much like to continue the conversation, but I don't know how much longer I'll be here. Can I give you a call?"

"No, but if I have time I will give you a call. Can I have your number?"

She wrote it down and gave it to him and said good-bye with a light kiss on the cheek, and she pressed her right breast into his chest, saying, "I really hope to see you again."

CHAPTER 112

Welcome Home

As hard as it was for Mordecai to leave Hadar, he knew he had to get back to the warehouse just outside of town. The walk from the center of the village to the warehouse was about twenty minutes. As he made the turn off the main road to the lane that led to the warehouse, all he could think about was the image of Hadar walking across the village square and then the last kiss and her firm breast in his chest. He knew that he had to get that image out of his mind and concentrate on the work at hand. As he turned the corner of the lane, he could see the warehouse and Assad's cargo van parked outside the loading dock door. He saw Sargon, Adad, Jaiari, and Oleg standing at the back of the van just about to open the back door.

He walked up to them and gave each of them a huge hug of welcome. Sargon opened the roll-up metal door with the chain winch, and when the door was fully open, he made sure the path to the workbench was clear. Sargon went outside and opened the back door, and they began to uncover the bomb. When all the boxes were clear of the bomb, the four of them slowly slid the bomb out the back of the van. It reminded Oleg of the way they took the coffins out of the hearse for his parents' funeral. They slowly turned and moved into the warehouse and placed the bomb on the worktable.

Oleg remarked that it seemed lighter than the other bomb, and the other three agreed. Once the bomb was in place, Sargon closed the door by pulling the chain as fast as he could and walked over to the rest of his team. The five of them walked upstairs and sat at the table as they had so many times before. Sargon said, "The next step is for Mordecai to go over the new bomb and see what he needs to make the bomb equal to or better than the Iranian bomb. I want Jaiari and Oleg to assist in any way they can."

Mordecai said that he had a contact that he believed could get what he needed to make the conversion.

Sargon nodded, pleased. "But before we go there, I know that all of you have been talking about what we should do with these bombs, and we will have time to hear each of your plans, but for right now we need to think about how to get them to the United States."

Jaiari spoke up and said, "I don't know what the rest of you have come up with, but I think Adad has a great solution to the problem."

"Adad let us hear your plan."

"Well, it is very simple for most of the way. In my business I collect from my customer's unwanted computers, printers, fax machines, and copiers as a service. They give them to me to dispose of them for their companies. I have a business relationship with a company in Canada that buys the used equipment from me and rebuilds it and sells this equipment to Third-World countries at a very handsome profit. I collect this equipment over time, and when I have a full container, I ship it to this company in Canada. We could hide the bombs in the storage container, and when it is off-loaded in Canada, we pick up the bombs at the recycling company. If the government wants to scan the cargo container, they will see all kind of signals and will not be able to distinguish our bombs from the rest of the equipment. We pick up the bombs and cross the border into the United States and place our bombs in just the rights spots to bring down America."

Sargon was very pleased with what Adad had come up with but asks the team, "Does anybody have an alternative suggestion? Any objections?"

The Brotherhood all seemed to agree that this was a good plan and nodded their assent.

"So I want Adad to begin to plan the route to the harbor and how we get our cargo on—and, just as important—off the boat. Then I want him to look for a place in Canada that we can cross into the United States and back without being detected. When he has completed his plan, and he is ready, he will lay it out for us so we can understand exactly how we are going to do this and what role each of us will play.

"I know that Mordecai is itching to get a look at the Iranian bomb, so Adad and Jaiari, you have had a long day, and I need both of you to get a good night's rest. Tomorrow morning we will start with a session of your ideas.

"I do want to set some ground rules: each of you will have whatever amount of time you need to present your option. You will do so without interruption, and after you have completed your pitches, then comes a very important part. The other four of us will ask you questions about your plan, and you must be in a position to defend what you want to do. It is my hope that through this approach we will come out of these discussions with the most destructive use of these bombs."

Chapter 113

The Brotherhood's Warehouse

Sargon had Mordecai and Oleg working together on the bomb, but Mordecai was the one in charge. He walked over to the table where the bomb was placed. The case had two straps that came over the top, and the package looked like an old-fashioned briefcase with straps and buckles, but many times longer. Mordecai was unfastening the straps but thinking about unbuttoning those buttons on Hadar instead. He thought to himself, *"enough about the girl. You have work to do."*

He pulled back the straps, which were attached to the top of the case, and then lifted the front panel and folded it back toward the table. Now he could see the entire bomb's components. The bottom half held the explosives, and the top half was divided into two sections, one for the nuclear material and the other section for the detonating equipment. As he examined the components, he asked Oleg to write down the names that he could identify so he could call Ishtar later that night and find out how long it would take him to get the equipment he needed.

Mordecai called over to Sargon to come to the workbench. When

Sargon arrived, Mordecai showed him the bomb and how it worked and then said, "The only thing we can use from the old bomb is the nuclear material, but we will need more and the case."

"What do we do with the existing explosive? If we let it warm, aren't we taking a high risk?"

"Yes, but I have an idea: we can, while the explosive is cold, break it down into smaller pieces, which we can sell to the rebels and let them get rid of them for us. So I will start disassembling the bomb tomorrow morning, and perhaps Jaiari can find out tonight how to contact the rebels to get rid of the explosives. When I start to rebuild the bomb, I will use the same approach in that everything will be attached to a motherboard and slipped into the suitcase, so if we have to, we can take out the bomb and leave the case behind, especially if we want the bomb to be less conspicuous.

"I'm going to call Ishtar in a few minutes and find out how long before he can get me what I need. I doubt he will have it here tomorrow—more likely in two to three days—so I will have time for the discussions in the morning. I don't want to start taking the bomb apart until I know we have a place for the explosives. I would hate to have all of our work be destroyed by a heat wave."

Oppenheimer had been listening to the conversation and knew that the bombs were going to leave for Canada and that Mordecai would most likely start disassembling the bomb the next day. He needed to get ahold of Hadar and tell her that she needed one of her men to pose as a rebel leader who wanted to buy the explosives.

He said, "You have a picture of Jaiari to send to all your people, and all of you need to be on the lookout when he comes to the village. I want you to stay out of sight, just in case Mordecai wants to meet again."

She shuddered at the thought and just then her phone rang.

CHAPTER 114

The Village

Jaiari walked into the village and went into a local bar for a drink. He had one, then he had another and, his confidence up, he turned to the bartender and said, "I hear that there is a rebel group around here somewhere. I heard there was a big explosion a few nights ago that lit up the sky."

"I saw that too. It was really bright."

"Do you know how someone might get in contact with the rebels?"

"We don't get many rebels in here, but the next time I see one, I'll let him know." Two members of Hassen team were in the bar, and two more were outside the back door. The two men inside the bar approached Jaiari and said they had overheard his conversation with the bartender, and they knew someone who might be of help. They would be happy to make the introduction, and they asked Jaiari to join them and they would take him to the rebel leader.

Jaiari and the two men walked out the back door, and when the door was closed, two other men grabbed Jaiari and put a hood over his head and shoulders and took him down through the alley into an abandoned store. Sitting at a table was another of Hassen team dressed like a rebel leader with sunglasses and a Shemagh scarf. "I have been told you might have some stuff for sale that goes big boom, is that true?"

With the hood off his head, Jaiari said, "I might."

"How much do you have?"

"Enough to make a really *big* boom."

"Can you be more specific?"

"Possibly twenty-four half-pound blocks of TNT."

The rebel leader said, "Very nice. How much do you want?"

"How about 57,000 Syrian pounds per block, and I'll give you a deal. I'll let you have the twenty-four for 1.3 million Syrian pounds."

The rebel leader said, "Deal," but he didn't know where he was going to get the money. He said, "I will meet you in the village square at the fountain in three days with the money."

Jaiari agreed and said, "I will take you to the explosives when I see the money."

The team members put the hood on Jaiari, led him down the alley, and then released him into the street.

CHAPTER 115

The Café—Back to the Buttons

MORDECAI HAD NOTHING TO DO until morning, and it was still somewhat early, so he pulled out the note and looked at Hassen's cell phone number. Her image as she walked into the village square was still in his mind. He asked himself why he was so attracted to this woman; yes, she was gorgeous, but he had dated other gorgeous women. For some reason, this one had just knocked the wind out of his sails. He dialed her number, and it rang three times, and he thought she was out, but on the fourth ring she answered.

Hadar knew it was he from the caller ID, but she asked, "Who is this?"

"It's Mordecai, from the café."

She paused and said, "We never finished our wine and cheese."

"Would you like to have dinner?"

She said that she had already eaten but that they could have dessert. They arranged to meet in twenty minutes at the café.

She quickly got up and tried to figure out what to wear that would attract and distract him. She had a semi sheer blouse with a shawl for a cover-up and snug-fitting jeans. She combed her hair, put on some bright-red lipstick, and headed toward the café. Mordecai was waiting for her, and she looked fabulous when she walked up to the table. He pulled back her chair, and the waiter brought over the dessert menu. She decided on baklava, and he ordered cookies and coffee with milk.

As she was eating her dessert, she commented, "You had to leave so abruptly last time; is everything all right?"

He responded, "Everything is great and especially great since I have a chance to see you again."

"You're too kind, but it is good to see you too. How much longer do you think you will be here?"

Mordecai replied, "I'm not sure, but probably a week or so longer."

"And your friend, when do you expect him?"

Mordecai was so infatuated with her that he had forgotten to call Ishtar. He turned to her and said, "I have to make a lengthy phone call; once again I have to leave."

She looked at him and asked, "Are you sure you just don't want to be around me for any length of time?"

"Absolutely, and you are the reason I forgot about the call."

"I think that is a compliment."

Mordecai smiled and told her he hoped to meet again soon, and for longer.

Meanwhile, Jaiari was very proud of himself as he walked back to the warehouse. He strode through the door and saw Sargon and Oleg putting more ice on the bomb and commented, "You won't have to be doing that much longer; I just made a deal with the rebels to buy our explosives for 1.3 million Syrian pounds. If Mordecai can get it out and cut it into one-half-pound blocks by Wednesday, we will have the money and be rid of the explosives."

"Great job! How did you find them?"

"I went into the village and stopped by the local bar and ordered a couple of drinks and struck up a conversation with the bartender. He didn't know how to get in touch with the rebels, but a few minutes later, two men came over and said they could take me to the rebel leader. We went out the back door, and two more rebels grabbed me and put a large hood over my head and shoulders and took me to their leader. I have to admit, I was really scared, but in the end I was okay. I was concerned that they would take the explosives and not pay, so I said we would meet in the village square and after I see the money, I would take them to the explosives."

"Excellent idea, but what if they have more men?"

"I guess that is a risk I have to take."

CHAPTER 116

Meeting Day

MORDECAI FINALLY MADE CONTACT WITH Ishtar and gave him his shopping list. Ishtar said it would take three days to get the things he needed; he also told Mordecai that it was going to be expensive, estimating that it might cost as much as 500,000 American dollars. Mordecai replied that that should not be a problem. As he walked through the village square, he thought about the two times he had had to leave Hadar; he was disappointed and already wanted to see her again. But for now all his attention had to be focused on the meetings and then the bomb, when the parts arrived.

He was the last to return to the warehouse, but even he arrived before the time that Sargon wanted to start the meeting. They all went upstairs and checked the ice around the bomb, just to make sure it was sufficiently covered. They all sat down at the same seats they had used in the past.

Sargon invited them to have some coffee and some fruit and then he said, "Let's get started. We will take as long as necessary to complete the process; however, Mordecai has told me that the parts necessary to build our bomb will be here in three days, and once he starts it will be very difficult for him to stop. So when we have completed all the presentations and to the best of our ability answered the questions, we will make the decision by a Majority vote what the target or targets will be and who will be in charge of completing the project. Keep in mind that we only have two bombs and that means we will have two teams of two men each. Any questions?"

"What if we can't agree on the target?"

Sargon replied, "Then I will make the target decision. Now I have asked Mordecai to go first."

Mordecai stood and said that he had listened to Oleg's presentation and was very interested in hearing the other two. "If Adad's and Jaiari's ideas are as creative as Oleg's, we will be in for a difficult time in making the decision. First, I think you need some background on the process so you will have a better appreciation for the beauty of my plan." He then told the story of the Centralia, Pennsylvania, and the coal fire to the group.

"My attack plan will only take one bomb, so that if somebody has an idea for a single bomb use, then with the two combined we can really do a lot of damage. The city of New York no longer has any coal-fired generating stations, but across the river in Jersey City, Public Service Electric and Gas (PSEG) has a coal, natural gas, and oil-fired power generating station at Duffield and Van Keuren Avenue. This power plant has an inventory of coal; in fact, it has over 50,000 tons on-site. When PSEG wants to use coal to fire the plant, it has belt conveyors in a concrete enclosure and electric feeders that draw from the bottom of the pile to fill the belts that go to the plant to fire the boilers that generate steam to turn the turbines that generate the electricity.

"Coal needs to be at 871 degrees to start the burning process effectively, so we will plant our bomb at the bottom of the pile. You may recall that I said they could run several different fuels. They want this flexibility to burn the least expensive fuel to generate electricity. If they are running natural gas, because it is less expensive than coal, the coal pile sits waiting. When the plant is not running coal, we will break into the plant and go down into the conveyor tunnel and install the bomb. It should fit in the opening were the coal comes out of the pile when the feeders are used to fill the conveyor belt. The concrete tunnel under the pile of coal will intensify the initial explosion almost like a funnel. The energy of the bomb will be pushed against the concrete walls of the tunnel and finding no way to escape through the walls, the power will take the path of least resistance and be forced up. I'm not expecting our little Mt. St. Helens to encircle the globe, but I do believe it could have an impact on at least a third of the eastern United States, which could impact as many as seventy-five million people."

"Do you think people will want to stay in New York City? How could the government accommodate the millions of people who will want to be relocated out of harm's way very quickly?"

"They can't! It will be chaos for years. So what do you think will happen to the largest metropolitan population in the United States? If New York becomes a ghost town, what happens to the capital market and the banking system in the United States? If I may, I would like to take you all outside and show you the power of what one bomb could do."

Sargon nodded, happy with Mordecai's plan so far.

They all went outside to the orange grove, and Mordecai showed them the site where the trees were sheared off at the ground. Mordecai said, "Gentlemen, you can see the significant amount of destruction that took place here, and it was all done with one *drop* of explosive—slightly more than the head of a pin. Keep in mind that the new bomb will be three to five times as destructive. One drop of the new explosive could take out this entire citrus grove; that is how powerful it is compared to the old bomb. Now imagine that you have *ten pounds* of this explosive. America will be devastated, the city of New York will be gone, and millions of people will be dislocated. Most important, I believe the will of America will be broken, never to recover."

With that, they started to walk back to the warehouse for the question session.

Adad asked, "Because the power plant is so close to the river, can they put out the fire with fireboats?"

"Excellent question. No, they will not be able to get close enough to the fire with the fireboats because of the high level of radiation, perhaps for years after the coal fire burns out. Due to the intensity of the radioactive material, it will be years before they will want to approach the plant."

Jaiari asked, "You said the bomb is going to be at the bottom of the coal pile; what is the possibility that when they start the belt that they destroy the bomb?"

"That is clearly a risk; the torque in the belt when it starts could chop up the bomb, making it useless. Perhaps we could place the bomb and immediately detonate it."

Oleg said, "We want to set off the bomb with a cell phone; is the signal strong enough to penetrate the concrete walls of the tunnel and the coal pile?"

"That clearly has to be looked at. Two factors would be the thickness of the concrete and whether it has reinforcing steel in the walls, since both would have an impact on the strength of the signal. We could possibly add a signal booster to compensate for the pile of coal and the thickness of the walls."

Sargon said, "I will ask only one question, and all of you must be prepared to answer the question. My question, Mordecai, and to each of you, is on a scale of one to ten, what do you think your chances of success are in destroying America with your project? Mordecai says his point value is seven. After all the presentations have been made, I want each of you to vote on what idea you think has the best chance of success. This vote will be on a secret-ballot basis, and I will hold the results until we arrive in America."

CHAPTER 117

The Warehouse, Adad Speaks

SARGON SAID, "WITH THAT OUT of the way, Adad, it's your floor."

"If we wanted to attack America, I think we should attack the Internet. Hypothetically, companies and individuals store all of their data on servers, and more and more the operating software for business and governments in America resides in the servers. America is totally dependent of the reliability of the servers to get access to their systems or their data.

"The technology is changing so fast that the expense in keeping up to date with the latest developments can be prohibitive from a cost standpoint, except for the largest companies. The demand for storage is growing exponentially. Two years ago Facebook had ten thousand servers, and just recently they are up to thirty thousand. You may have seen the ads for the blade servers; imagine thirty thousand of those in one place.

"If we can knock out two Major data storage farms, perhaps we can shut down the Internet for all of America. Microsoft has a storage farm near Chicago, and Hewlett Packard has facilities in San Antonio. The Chicago operation for Microsoft has at least 300,000 servers on-site, and it takes three substations alone to power that operation. This one facility is ten times larger than the entire Facebook server facility.

"Currently in America they have over seven thousand server farms to process the data, but a new approach is developing quickly. This new approach is called the cloud. The cloud allows customers to store their data on a cloud system. Hewlett Packard, the largest computer maker in the world, is, through the expansion of their cloud storage program, consolidating and concentrating all of its cloud operations by replacing eighty-five data centers across the world with six in the US. I think that several big companies will increase the size of their server farms to keep up with the exponential growth in data and the need to store it. The big will get larger and larger, and smaller ones will be closed, because they can't compete, The fact that Hewlett Packard is consolidating eighty-five centers into six is proof of my concept of concentration.

"One dirty bomb at the Microsoft facility will take out the power substations and contaminate the substations, and access to the 300,000 servers will be shut down forever. At the same time, we use the other bomb at the HP data center in San Antonio, and we shut down one site of the HP data storage. With the fallout from the dirty bomb, you could not change out any of the servers in either location, and while it might be true that some of the capacity could be transferred to some of the other centers, trying to move all the data might prove to be impossible. Without power you can't get to the data on the server. It will all have a domino effect.

"Banks, insurance companies, capital markets, can't open and process transactions because they can't clear transactions. UPS and FedEx can't fly their planes because the programs that would build their flight plans don't work; the software is in the data center. For that matter, no commercial airplanes will fly, and most likely no military planes will fly because they need the Internet to monitor flight plans and paths. And all of those UPS brown trucks and the FedEx vans go nowhere because the computers can't read the bar codes on the packages, so nothing gets picked up or delivered.

"The impact would be devastating: think about taking the computer out of a government, business, school, or home and how do you think America could function? One other thought: with the loss of hundreds of thousands of servers, the remaining part of the Internet would eventually collapse under the weight of the missing capacity.

"If we use our two dirty bombs correctly, we could close down the Internet. When the last domino falls, we will have shut down the Internet and America by proxy. So one bomb is placed in the middle power substation in Chicago. The range of the bombs will take out the other two substations and would devastate an area of between five to eighteen miles around the plants, taking out most of the city of Chicago, though unfortunately a considerable amount of the energy would be dispersed over Lake Michigan. It would be years before anybody would risk their life to go to the plants. I would do the same with San Antonio: put the bomb in a car, park it in the visitors parking lot and detonate the bomb; the building and all the servers are gone, and for five to eighteen miles, the city of San Antonio will disappear.

"Without the Internet, America will decline very rapidly; we could spend hours talking about the ramifications and the trickle-down effects of the destruction of the Internet. But for now what are your questions?"

Oleg commented, "You said that the fall of the Internet in America could spill over into other countries; with the shutting down of the Internet in the United States, is it possible because of the interconnection on a global basis that you could destroy the Internet globally? Is there a way to confine the destruction to the United States or North America? Adad, is there a way to isolate America from the rest of the world?"

"Not that I know of. To be quite honest, we could bring down the whole world, in fact."

Jaiari said, "What about picking just one city? If you didn't destroy San Antonio, would the rest of the world be spared?"

"If I had to choose one, I would take Chicago. As to your question about San Antonio, I think based on what I'm able to learn, San Antonio is the center for North America. If I'm wrong, then we would have blown up a city and gained nothing more than destroying a city and affected Internet service somewhere in the world."

Mordecai asked, "You say that Chicago has at least 300,000 servers in place and yet you also say that there are over 7,000 server installations around the country. What percentage does the 300,000 represent of the total number of servers?"

"Sources suggest that one in five Americans have computers, so America has sixty million computers, and while 300,000 seems like a small percentage, that number includes all the ones in your house, at the office, in schools, and libraries. I think the telling comparison is Facebook, with 30,000 and Microsoft with 300,000 in one center. It impossible for me to know what the percentage of servers this one facility has, but I believe it is the largest concentration in the industry. If we adopt my plan, it is simple to execute and will be effective in shutting down America for years to come."

Sargon said, "Adad, thank you, and men, think about how you would score this project. I would score it an eight."

Outside in the citrus grove, Oppenheimer had been listening to all the presentations and had had a difficult time keeping up with his notes, but the ideas so far had been devastating. Was what the three of them proposed possible? Could it really happen? Could an idea from one of these men do what Osama bin Laden and his fellow terrorists had never been able to do in all their attempts? Had terrorism moved to a new level—one that would use nuclear weapons to achieve an objective, regardless of the cost of human lives and the destruction of countries and cities?

Could the success of an attack on America mean that other terrorists would be emboldened to attack his country and would do so very quickly, because America wouldn't be able to help? Would the government of Israel use its 300 nuclear weapons to knock out Iran and all the other countries it believed had missiles pointed at it? *At what cost to the world?* David asked himself. *Will we start World War III!*

He must find a way to communicate all these plans to Seacrest and Dobias, for even the ones they did not choose must be added into the protection equation. Maybe they would not choose to go after the Internet, but someone else just might try to bring it down. As Oppenheimer thought about the possible ramifications of the options presented so far, he thought that one result would be a less connected world and a world where more countries would be more focused on dealing with the needs of their people, perhaps not interfering with other nations.

He briefly thought, *No doubt that the world would be different without the Internet, but might it also be better?* My score would be a 7.

Chapter 118

The Warehouse—Oleg's Time to Shine

O LEG, ITCHING TO TALK ABOUT his true love, oil, began his pitch. "Energy is the blood of growth and prosperity in America. If Americans can't get gas for their cars at a cheap price, they panic, as they did in 1973 when OPEC decided to slow down the flow of crude oil to the United States. I want to bring back that sense of hopelessness in America, and I think I know how to do it with two bombs. If you look at a map of the network of these pipelines, you will find a very high concentration of pipelines in Texas and Louisiana. The largest oil refinery in America is located in Texas, and the largest transportation network carrying crude, finished product like gasoline, jet fuel, and natural gas is located in Louisiana. In fact this single site carries 25 percent of the petroleum product moved in the United States."

Oleg went on to explain the contamination process, along with the natural gas threat that America would face. "So let's assume that we set off a dirty bomb in these two places. Soon, the president would have to shut down production in the Gulf and other offshore drilling areas because there would be no place to store the crude and no place that could process the oversupply of crude. The chairman of the Securities and Exchange Commission would strongly suggest to the president that he close the market indefinitely. The chairman of the Federal Reserve Board would also strongly suggest to the president that he close the bank indefinitely. The president would be forced to say, 'My fellow Americans, we have a grave situation that will cause us to make great sacrifice,' and thus, without the blood of oil and gas, America would wither and die."

Mordecai interrupted. "How can we be sure that the bombs will take out the sites?"

"The high concentrations of the refinery sites are well within the minimal capacity of the bomb. With a destructive range of five to fifteen miles, all the refinery sites would collapse and be covered with radioactive material. The metal would be covered with the radioactive material and the heat intensity of the bomb would melt the fittings, valves, and pipes, allowing the fires to be fed by the natural gas and finished oil products in the pipelines and storage tanks.

"In the case of site two, the oil and gas pipelines from the Gulf of Mexico come up out of the gulf, and raw oil and natural gas is channeled into pipelines and storage tanks. All of this would be set on fire, and until they could get to the five thousand drilling platforms to shut down the pumping, the fire would be reaching enormous heights and spreading nuclear material far and wide, and depending on the wind speed and direction, drilling platforms in the Gulf could be contaminated."

Adad wondered, "Given that both places you propose are located near water— in fact, the one in Louisiana is at the water's edge, couldn't the Coast Guard just bring fireboats up and put out the fire?"

"Like with the proposal of coal fires in New Jersey, the intensity of the heat from the massive fires and the high level of radiation would not allow them to get close enough to do anything about the fires. The American government would have to starve the fire by shutting down drilling platforms in the Gulf. As for the pipelines in Texas, they would have to look for shutoff valves many miles away from the refineries. In shutting the valves, they would be cutting off supply to the northern part of America."

Jaiari said, "So the refineries are destroyed, but can't the other 130 or so refineries just pick up the slack and increase capacity while new refineries are being built?"

"Excellent question. How long does it take to build a refinery? Answer: two or three years. Next question: where does America get the crude to refine if the pipelines are shut because of nuclear contamination? They buy it in the open market and send money to countries that may be like OPEC and change the flow. But my guess is that OPEC countries would not bring their tankers into America for fear of contamination, as I said before. The outcome would be much higher prices, and the more it costs for energy in the United States, the poorer America becomes. My score is a ten."

Sargon said, "With all the presentations complete, I think we need to take a day and think about our scoring. I want to thank all of you for excellent work, and I think *all* the plans could bring America down. I suggest we all go to town for a drink. But, before we leave, let me make one more point: you may have read recently about the underwear bombs that al-Qaeda is trying to develop to bring down airplanes. The American government infiltrated the group developing the bomb and brought a prototype back to America, and they have already adjusted their airport security to detect these bombs. This is an example of not learning from your past mistakes and why we spent the time in the beginning trying to figure out what mistakes al-Qaeda made in its attacks against the United States. It is clear to me that al-Qaeda is stupid, in that they still think that bringing down one aircraft will bring down America. They clearly do not understand that we are in a different world and that blind faith will not get the result we all want: the destruction of America, *forever.*"

CHAPTER 119

The Warehouse—Oppenheimer Gets a Closer Look

OPPENHEIMER HAD LISTENED WITH GREAT interest to the last idea from Oleg, and he believed that Oleg had made the most compelling case. With the terrorists leaving for drinks and dinner, he weighed the chances of getting close enough to the warehouse to get some pictures of the new bomb. He asked his men to tell him when all five had left the warehouse and were well out of sight, and after about ten minutes, he got the all-clear.

"Do we have someone who can see the entrance of the lane where they will have to turn in returning to the warehouse?"

He got the message that he was covered, and he slowly approached the warehouse. David was about 200 yards from the warehouse when he asked, "Has anybody seen the security guard? Did he go with the group to celebrate?"

Nobody could place the security guard, so David had to be very careful.

He said to his second in command, "If something should happen to me, you must at all cost get this information to Mossad and Dobias; he will know what to do with it."

As Oppenheimer approached the warehouse, he picked up a few handfuls of large pebbles that he would use to see whether anybody was in the warehouse. He was in the grove and about fifty yards from the warehouse. He tossed a few pebbles against the window. He made three advances, and still no guard at the window; now he was about ten yards from the window. He threw a larger handful of pebbles against the wall, and just as he was ready to move to the window, he saw the guard heading for the door.

Oppenheimer quickly retreated under the cover of an orange tree when the door swung open, and the guard came out with a rifle in his hand, looking as if he were ready to shoot anything that moved. Oppenheimer held his breath and didn't move as the guard walked around the warehouse and started into the grove toward him. Just then one of the team members threw some pebbles around the other side of the house, and the noise of the impact of the pebbles distracted the guard to turn back to the warehouse and away from Oppenheimer, who took a deep breath and thought, *Thank you Lord*, but no pictures today.

Oppenheimer returned to his team and sent Oleg's plan to Mossad. Nava had by now had a chance to study the other three plans briefly and had forwarded them to Seacrest and Williams. When he received the final plan and the pronouncement from Sargon that the objective would not be disclosed until they arrived in the United States, Nava had a horrible thought: *"is it possible that they know that we are listening?"*

CHAPTER 120

Williams's Office

WILLIAMS HAD CALLED BAKER TO his office for a couple of reasons. First, he had to brief the president on the four possible scenarios and what action he thought the president needed to take to protect the country. He ran them by Baker first.

"We can send in FBI agents and Marines to set up perimeters around all the facilities to intercept the bombers. We would have to place people in New York, Chicago, and San Antonio. The fourth place is not specified and could be any point along the Gulf coast. We know the Texas shoreline is 624 miles long, and the Louisiana shoreline is about 400 miles, and we have about 35 percent of all our refineries along the Gulf coast.

"This is an impossible task; if the effective range of the bombs is five to eighteen miles, we would have to cordon off all of Manhattan and parts of New Jersey, Brooklyn, and Queens. A bomb exploded within the effective range could accomplish a great deal of what they want to do, even if it doesn't go off at ground zero. We can protect the power plant in Jersey City, but the rest can't be protected. If a bomb goes off four miles from the server farm in Chicago, it may not take out the power plants, but the magnetic effect from the bomb will scramble the storage disks. Our best choice is to try to intercept them at the border. We know how the bombs are going to be shipped; we just don't know when or how long they will wait to cross the border."

CHAPTER 121

The Warehouse

THE NEXT MORNING, MORDECAI UNPACKED the old bomb from the ice and, with help from Oleg, set it on the table. They undid the straps, opened the top, folded down the front, and carefully slid the bomb out of the case. The first thing he had to do was disconnect the TNT from the detonator. He traced the wire to the blasting caps and removed each one carefully. The blasting caps themselves could explode if a spark set them off.

Once the caps were removed, he carefully removed the TNT from the bomb platform. He set aside the rest of the bomb and worked on the TNT. He used a very sharp knife to cut the twelve sticks into twenty-four half-pound sticks of TNT, carefully wrapped each stick in brown paper and wound it with masking tape, and carefully put them into a cooler and packed them with ice. Once that was done, Mordecai told Oleg to take the cooler and set it in a dark place, away from sunlight, and to bring over the other cooler. Oleg brought him the cooler, and he wrapped the blasting caps and cord in the same brown paper and put them in the cooler and packed them with ice. He called Jaiari over and told him, "These are the two coolers that contain the explosives and cord you are selling to the rebels tomorrow. Keep them in a cool, dark place and covered with ice before you go tomorrow to collect your money."

Mordecai went back to the old bomb and took out the nuclear material and set it under the table. Next, he stripped away everything else on the platform, and he was ready for the new material. Now all he could do was wait, and while he did, he thought about how he might be able to see Hadar one last time. He thought that he might give her a call, but he looked at his watch, and it was after two a.m.; he had been working on the old bomb for over sixteen hours, with no food and nothing to drink and only a few bathroom breaks. It was too late to call her, and he could hardly walk because he had been standing so long. He decided to walk, albeit very slowly, to the cot and lie down to rest. The new parts would be there sometime the next day, and he needed to be very sharp to make the new bomb; it might take at least two more sixteen-hour days to finish the work.

While Mordecai was sleeping, Oppenheimer contacted Dobias and said that he was not getting anything new, and the vote was in the morning, but nobody would know the outcome until the terrorists reached America. It had become more apparent that Israel was not a target, so there was not much else he could do; should he report back to base? He proposed to leave Hadar and a few members of her team in the village, just in case Mordecai contacted her, so she could learn where they were going. He wanted to deploy his men to the three ports in Syria to see whether they could find out what shipping line Adad used and when the next ship to Canada would be.

Dobias eventually came back and said, "There are four ports in Syria: Tatrous, Banias, Lattakia, and Borj Islam. You have twelve people on your team?"

"Yes, but I will take eight from Lt. Hassen's team; that would give us five people per port."

"I agree; we need to try to find out what boat. When do you want to redeploy?"

Oppenheimer asked Dobias to report the move to Seacrest and Williams and said, "I will redeploy my men tonight, sir."

"Be careful: the ports are very different from hiding under an orange tree."

CHAPTER 122

The Warehouse and Redeployment

I N THE MORNING, MORDECAI RECEIVED a text message from Ishtar that he would be in the village by noon, and he wanted to know where Mordecai could come and meet him to take him to the warehouse? Mordecai texted back: *Find the abandon barn south of town about a mile out side of town and meet me there, at noon.* It was 8:30, and he wondered whether it was too early to call Hadar. This might be the last chance he had to see her, as he was probably leaving in two days, depending on his progress, so he called her, and after several rings, a sleepy-sounding, but fully awake Hadar answered the phone. She said, "Hello, who is this?"

"Mordecai."

In a more excited voice, she said, "Oh hi, how are you?"

"I'm busy, but I have a break; would you like to have breakfast?"

She arranged to see him in an hour and hung up. Oppenheimer was in her room working with her, and they were trying to decide who she wanted to keep with her and who should go with Oppenheimer.

She looked into Oppenheimer eyes and knew what he wanted. She wanted it too, but there wasn't enough time; her team would be arriving shortly. Sure enough, there was soon a knock at the door, and she looked through the peephole to see the first arrivals of her team. Within five minutes they were all in the room, and Oppenheimer spoke.

"I will need eight of you to go with me to the seaports to try to find out what boat they're taking, where it will sail to, and when it will depart with the bombs. The other three will stay with Lt. Hassen to try to gain as much information as possible on the Brotherhood. I need three of the people who met with Jaiari to stay, especially the one who played the chief, and I have for you the money to pay for the explosives. In addition to your other duties, you are to protect Lt. Hassen. Any questions?"

"Sir, how much longer do you think we will be here?"

"Probably three to five days, perhaps less. Let's get moving; those of you who are going with me, we will assemble in the trees north of town at one o'clock."

The men left the room in groups, and when they had all gone, Oppenheimer took Hadar in his arms and gave her a long and passionate kiss and reminded her of his promise at the beginning of this mission. Only this time, the kiss felt different: he was kissing her, but she was not kissing him. What was different? And why was it different?

Chapter 123

Springfield

When Sheriff Jim Whittles and Major Omid Rahimi returned to St. Patrick's Church so Omid could get his car, waiting on the front steps was John Bowman, Mike and Mary Ridley's neighbor. Bowman, Sheriff Whittles brother-in-law, extended his hand and introduced himself to Omid.

Whittles explained, "He lives down the street from the Ridley house, and I think he and my sister had as much contact with the Ridleys as anyone in Springfield. Shall we all go someplace and get a cup of coffee?"

"Let me think: Sunday afternoon, not a lot of places open, but how about Susie's?"

Whittles said, "That will work, and won't be busy this time of day."

Bowman decided to follow them to Susie's, and soon they met at the front door and walked in, the sheriff and the Major in dress uniforms, so it made for a dramatic sight, though there was only one person at the counter, so there were not many people to impress.

"We'll take the booth in the back and please bring us three black coffees and some cream and sugar, thank you." The three men, all of them large, tried to squeeze into the booth, and Whittles said, "Let's use that table over there. It will be more comfortable. They must have built that booth for skinny teenagers, not for us."

They sat down comfortably at the table, and their waitress, whose nametag said "Beth," asked whether they wanted anything else. The sheriff said, "No, thank you."

After taking a sip of his coffee, Omid said to John, "Sheriff Whittles tells me that you work for the state's attorney?"

"Yes, I'm a special investigator for fraud against the government. I work all over trying to find people who are defrauding the state and in turn sometimes the federal government. Recently I have been reviewing the construction contracts and the construction of some pipelines south of here. I don't want to bore you with a bunch of details, but when you lay a natural gas or oil pipeline, the pipe connections have to be welded and X-rayed to make sure the pipes will not come apart and leak under pressure. I have to check the welds and the X-rays to make sure they match."

"You check every weld?"

"Not possible," Bowman replied, "so I do random checks. But you don't want to hear about that; you want to talk about Mike and Mary and Michael Ridley."

"Yes, sir, I do. Do you know where Mike Ridley worked?"

Bowman replied, "I think it was …" He paused, clearly drawing a blank, and then said, "For the life of me, I can't remember ever talking about work with him. So to answer your question, no, Major, I don't know where he worked."

"You live next door to somebody for eighteen years, and you don't know where he worked?"

"Sarah might know. You can ask her."

"Did Mary work outside the house?"

"Not that I recall."

"Was Michael born in Springfield?"

"No, he was adopted as a baby. I think he was about six months old when they brought him home. I think it was one of those foreign adoptions, and I think they were gone at least a month when they went to get Michael."

"Did you ever hear what country they adopted Michael from?"

"No I never heard. I thought it rude to ask."

"What can you tell me about Michael?"

"Michael was always well behaved; sometimes I wish my two were as well behaved as Michael. He was an excellent student in school, exceptional in science. I think he won several science fairs in high school. He didn't play sports very much. I think he was on a T-ball team I coached when he was a little boy, but I could tell he didn't like it, so he moved on. He was always respectful, and, to the best of my knowledge, he was never in trouble with the law. Still, we were a bit surprised that he got the scholarship to UC Berkeley."

"Why were you surprised?"

"We all knew he was very smart but never understood why a West Coast school, so far away from Springfield, had offered him a free ride. We figured he would go to MIT."

"Did he get an offer from MIT?"

"Not that I'm aware of. You see, all of them kept to themselves. So we didn't know a great deal about them. Mike Ridley, all those years, never had a job, so how did he adopt a child and pay all his bills?"

"We would like to know the answer to that question ourselves," Omid remarked, frowning into his coffee cup.

CHAPTER 124

Syria, the Café and the Warehouse

MORDECAI WAS SITTING AT THE table anticipating Hadar arrival; it was 9:30, and she was not there. By 9:45 he was growing nervous that she would not show, but as he looked at the fountain, he caught a glimpse of her coming across the square. His heart and other things started to pound with the excitement of seeing her. She was wearing very tight jeans, a turtleneck sweater, and a windbreaker. She walked toward the table, and Mordecai stood up to greet her.

She walked over and planted a great big kiss on his lips, and he kissed her back as hard as she had kissed him. They broke apart and then sat down to take a breath. Hadar remembered Oppenheimer kiss that morning and compared it to the one she had just experienced. She had only been with Mordecai twice, but she knew she felt something very special.

Mordecai didn't know what to say for a moment. He finally said, "That was fantastic; can you imagine what the sex would be like?" Then he apologized for the outburst. Hadar blushed and looked down and said, "I was wondering the same thing."

"You were going to America to study; how soon would you be there?"

Hadar responded, "Probably in a week or two—why?"

"I will be there myself in maybe two to three weeks; are you still thinking about going to Texas?"

"Do you know where you are going?"

"Not yet; I still have to work out the details. Will your cell phone work in the United States?"

She says yes; it is a global phone.

"Well, if I know where you are, and if I'm around, I would love to come and see you and see what we can make happen. Would you like that?"

"Yes, very much."

Mordecai left Hadar after breakfast, telling her he would probably not have time to see her before they both left, but he was hopeful they could see each other in America. The kiss good-bye was as passionate as the one saying hello, and confirmed, at least in his mind, that he had to have her.

But for now he knew he must walk to the barn outside of town where he was to meet Ishtar, and he forced his mind to focus on the layout of the bomb, not of Hadar. Mordecai knew that he needed to get this done quickly so they could all be on their way to their meeting with destiny. He approached the lane where the barn was, and he saw Ishtar, but as he looked again, he saw *two* Ishtar's.

He went over to the pair of them and laughingly asked, "Which one is the real Ishtar?"

The real Ishtar, with a smile on his face, reached out and gave Mordecai a hug, saying, "I want you to meet my twin brother, Michael; he is here from America. He is here to help us build the bomb. I have all the components in my car on the other side of the barn. So let's get this thing built."

They went around the barn and hopped into the car and headed to the warehouse. In the car Mordecai talked about the other members of the team and some of their plans about how to use the bombs. Ishtar asked, "How are you going to get the bomb out of Syria?"

"Adad's plan is to put them on the ship carrying all of his used equipment to Canada and then into the United States."

"That is going to be difficult. First, you have to get the bombs through that rebel fighting in the port cities. You never know on any given day who is in control of the ports. You might want to consider shipping them through Port Aqaba, in Jordan, instead. The port is safer and more stable and then we can get them on a smaller boat to an oil platform in the Gulf and then off-load them to a boat going to the mainland and avoid customs."

Mordecai said, "I like that a lot better," and Ishtar said, "I can send my brother Michael to shepherd the bombs."

As they turned down the lane, Mordecai said, "Let me go in and prepare the team for you, and later today, when we take a break, we can talk about sending the bombs through Jordan." They pulled the car up to the loading dock, and Mordecai got out and went inside to tell Sargon that the bomb parts were there, and his friends who were supplying the parts were going to help him build the bomb.

"Can you trust these people?"

"They could be asking the same question about trust of you. In many countries of the world they would be put in prison or to death for what they are doing for us."

Sargon called the rest of the team and told them about the people who were coming in to help them build the bomb and said that they could be trusted. "They are risking their lives to help us." Mordecai went out and brought in Ishtar and Michael; he laughed at the expressions on the rest of their faces when they saw the twins.

The greetings over, the twins went back outside and brought in the materials for the bomb. They set all of it on the workbench and began to unpack it; placing it in the order they thought they would use it.

Mordecai reached under the worktable and brought out the old platform and said, "We have to fit everything on the platform so it can fit in the existing case. Now that we have more hands, the building process will go faster. Then we might be able to leave for the port as early as tomorrow."

CHAPTER 125

Williams's Office

WILLIAMS GOT OFF THE PHONE with Dobias after being told that Mossad was sending a team to the ports in Syria to find out when Assad would be sending his next shipment to Canada.

"As soon as we get the details, we will send them to you."

"If it is possible to somehow mark or get the container number that the bombs will be placed in, that would be extremely helpful. They will want the name of the ship and when it is scheduled to depart, and what port in Canada will be its destination."

"We will do our best."

Williams understood that the way it worked was that the transport company would pick up the container at Assad's complex and then take it dockside to off-load it, so it would just sit there waiting to be loaded, which could take hours or days. "The tricky part will be the type of ship that will carry the container, because if we mark it on the top and one side, it is possible that the markings could be covered up by other containers."

Dobias had said that they would do the best they could, watching the container being loaded so as to gain as much information on its location as possible. Nava had explained that, depending on the shipping company, they would load the cargo based on number sequence, so they would start with one and go up, and when they unloaded, they would also unload in sequence. "The container that is picked up at Assad's warehouse will have a number on the side that has the doors. We need the number, and if we can, we need to mark the top and one side."

Williams called in Baker to discuss what to do about the bombs. Baker arrived, and they met in Williams's conference room. On the wall was a large map of the North Atlantic and the Mediterranean Sea. "We can't let these bombs get into Canada, much less the United States, so we are going to have to intercept them at sea. I think we should use Navy Seals, and we need two teams on two subs. The question is, should we intercept in the Mediterranean or the Atlantic?"

Baker thought for a while and finally said, "We should wait until they get into the Atlantic."

Williams agreed. "You need to get in touch with the Department of Defense and get the wheels in motion to secure the assets we will need right away. Looking at the route maps, it should take about three days to clear the Mediterranean and perhaps as much as six days to cross the Atlantic. We need to get the teams and the sub out in the next twenty-four hours. Any questions?"

"Sir, we are to board and take only the bombs? And what about casualties?"

Williams paused for a moment. "We are trying to save millions of lives, but if I have to sacrifice a few for the many, then I can live with that. We need to tell the Seals that the fewer casualties, the better. We must allow them to defend their lives, but we don't have to kill unless it is either them or us."

Baker asked, "To whom do you want this operation to report?"

"For now, to me, but I will talk about this with the president and his team today; if there is any change in reporting, I will let you know. I want you to plan to board the ship in the middle of the Atlantic. If we have trouble boarding the ship, I will want the subs to sink the ship and send the bombs to the ocean floor. I will also review this part of the plan with the president, and I'll let you know his orders."

CHAPTER 126

Syria—Time to Play Rebel Chief

Mordecai, Ishtar, and Michael had been working almost nonstop on assembling the bomb. They had made great progress, and Mordecai told Sargon that they thought, unless they ran into trouble, that the bomb would be finished by midafternoon the following day. Mordecai looked at his watch and saw that the time Jaiari was supposed to meet with the rebels was fast approaching. Mordecai called out to Sargon, "I need a break, so could we talk about something before Jaiari heads out?"

Sargon said, "Yes," so he called the team to come upstairs. They all went upstairs and left Ishtar and Michael downstairs working on the bomb.

"Go ahead."

Mordecai began, "We have all put in a great deal of work on the plan, and we hope that we can achieve our goals. I just want to call to your attention some of the risks that I think we are taking in transporting the bomb the way Adad has suggested. Adad, I'm not being critical of your suggestion, and, under other circumstances, I truly believe your idea would be an excellent one. But today, between here and the ports, most of the country is practically in civil war. We are taking a great risk trusting that we can get these two bombs through all the turmoil and get them safely on board a ship bound for Canada. Then we have to clear Canadian customs, which I believe we will clear without problems. Then we have to get around the even more difficult customs of the United States.

"Ishtar came up with another suggestion, which I believe deserves just as much vetting as the process of targeting our bombs. He suggests we take the bombs through Jordan on a ship headed for the Bahamas. We unload the bombs in the Bahamas and transfer them to a charter that takes them to a drilling platform in the Gulf of Mexico. When the crew changes, the bombs will be off-loaded with baggage to the work shuttle and back to the mainland, where we will collect the bombs. We will pick up the bombs and then meet in Houston and decide how we want to use the bombs. By using this approach, we will reduce the chances of getting caught and increase the chances of getting the bombs into the United States. I think we should all think about this overnight, and we can discuss it again tomorrow after I have finished the bomb." Sargon turned to the group and said, "And we will also take our votes tomorrow, agreed?"

The men agreed easily.

Jaiari said, "It is time to go." So he put on his jacket and sunglasses and headed for the barn where he would deposit the TNT and fuses and, he hoped, return with enough cash to pay for the shipping of the bomb.

About two hours later, Jaiari returned to the warehouse with 1.3 million pounds and a big smile on his face.

"Did you have any trouble?"

"Not really, I asked for the money and told them where the TNT and fuses could be found. I said, 'Leave one of your men with me, and if you do not return within thirty minutes, he can kill me, but I will have the woods full of my men, and if they don't hear from me within the thirty minutes, they will start shooting both at the barn and here.' So they went to the barn, and I'm sure they were looking around for my men. It was dark, and sometimes fear makes shadows where none exist. But they got their TNT, and I got the money, and I thanked them for doing business, and I walked out with this heavy load of money."

Everybody congratulated Jaiari for taking the risk, delivering the goods, and collecting the money.

After celebrating Jaiari's safe return, Mordecai, Ishtar, and Michael continued working through most of the night on completing the bomb. They went to sleep at about four in the morning and were awake by seven to start working on it again. Throughout the night, Mordecai talked a lot with both Ishtar and Michael.

The first thing he wanted to know was how Michael got his name when his brother's name was something as un-American as Ishtar. They responded that they had found out years ago that they had been born of Jordanian parents who were very poor. They could not take care of two babies, so they gave one to the orphanage. It was very hard to do, and later they regretted their decision and went back to the orphanage to get their son, but he was gone. Their mother told Ishtar later that it was about three months after their birth when they went back to get his brother. It was then that they found out that the owner of the orphanage was a crook and had sold their son, Ishtar's brother, to a baby broker. They learned that a man and woman who lived in Springfield, Texas, had adopted their child.

The parents never had the money to go to America and find their child, but their other son, Ishtar, was smart, and when he grew up, he got a job that took him to America. He was living on the West Coast, in Berkeley, and was trying to get information on Michael. He subscribed to the local Springfield paper, and when he saw that Michael was coming to Berkeley, he sent him a letter telling him the whole story and inviting Michael to contact him when he came to school. Michael called Ishtar the day he arrived, and they met that night. Ishtar tried to answer all Michael's questions as best he could.

After a while Ishtar told Michael of his business of exporting items and asked Michael whether he wanted to join him in his business. "If things work out, you will be able to go to Jordan and meet our mother, as our father has passed away." Michael wanted to know how soon he could go. "We have to get my partners to trust you, but my guess is at least a year."

Michael asked, "What about school?"

"It is your choice; one or the other, but you can't do both."

"Plus, I have a girlfriend back home. What about her?"

"Well, she can come here if you are in school, and nothing will change. If you join me, she can come here, but she can't know about me for at least six months; I need to feel that I can trust her. If you are traveling on company business, then I can stand in for you; she will never know the difference."

So Michael told his brother, "I'm in," and they had been working together ever since.

After much talking and sweating and soldering, at about one o'clock in the afternoon, Mordecai announced to Sargon, "It's done."

CHAPTER 127

Which Way to Go

THE BOMB WAS DONE, AND now it was time for a very important meeting, so Sargon called for all the team members to meet upstairs. They all walked up the stairs knowing that they were about to make a commitment to do something no other people or nation had ever done: conquer America. Sargon started off the discussion.

"Whatever we decide, whatever we accomplish, it is because of the brains in this room. When we first met, I called you my think-tank, and you have shown that I picked the best brains I could to help me on this mission. Thank you all. Now, first we have to choose between the two ways presented to get these bombs out of Syria. You all know the choices; do any of you have any questions on either way out?"

No hands in the air, nobody spoke up.

"Then let's vote on which way out. All in favor of the port in Jordan raise your hands."

Sargon and three of the four raised their hands. "Jordan it is, so Mordecai, bring in your friend Ishtar."

Mordecai called downstairs for Ishtar and Michael to come up. Michael and Ishtar were excited that the group had selected their plan. Ishtar told them of his contacts all along the way. He thought that Michael and Mordecai should take the freighter from Jordan to Nassau, and at that point Ishtar would join them on the charter out of Nassau to the well block number 103892 by using the Global Unique Well Identifier (GUWI). At that point, Mordecai and Ishtar would off-load the bombs. They would time their departure from Nassau to the arrival of the shift change, so the bombs could be transferred, and Ishtar and Mordecai would have time to get back to Nassau and fly to the destination point. From there they would meet and select the site or sites they were about to vote on.

"We expect it to take probably ten days for the bombs to reach the US, so let's all make our travel plans on different flights to arrive in Houston, Texas ten days from now, and allowing for travel changes. We will want to trigger our bombs to go off two weeks from today."

Everybody agreed again and then the voting began. Sargon instructed them: "Just put one letter on the paper: A for Adad, M for Mordecai, O for Oleg, and finally J for Jaiari. If there is a tie, I will break the tie with my vote. Mark your papers and pass them to me; I will reveal the target or targets in Houston. Now let's load the bombs and be on our way."

CHAPTER 128

The Port in Jordan

MORDECAI, MICHAEL, AND ISHTAR WERE in the car with two bombs on their way to Port Aqaba, in Jordan. Mordecai asked, "Why this port?"

Ishtar responded, "This is the port we use for most of our shipping activities when we want to bring stuff into the Middle East; we have connections with all the people who run the port, so we can get anything in or out of the port."

"And why do you use the Nassau, Bahamas, ports?"

"Because we have a great many connections in that port, and we can also get almost anything in or out that we want. We have used the rig drop-off and pickup many, many times. I will go in and make passage for two of us and then we will check our baggage. I will keep one suitcase in my room, and Mordecai will keep the other. I'm sorry, brother, but twins will cause more grief than we need, so I want you to fly to Houston in about a week and we will meet you there."

Michael protested, but he reluctantly understood and agreed.

Ishtar said, "The boat will sail in about twelve hours, so we'll check in first and then find you a nice hotel and have a great meal."

Michael said, "Sounds like a plan."

Ishtar confirmed the reservation he made for the two rooms. "This is not an ocean liner; it is in fact a cargo ship, probably much like the one Adad uses, but the accommodations are very comfortable. We will be well fed and have a comfortable seven-day voyage to Nassau. Everything is set."

And so they moved into their cabins, locked the doors, and in about two hours they had found Michael a great place to stay. They ate a good meal together, and Ishtar said good-bye to Michael. Before he left, Ishtar gave his brother a huge bear hug and said, "I love you, and I'll see you in about a week."

The two terrorists due to set sail headed back to their boat and the cabins and had a drink while leaning on the rail. Ishtar looked out at the ocean and commented on how beautiful it was, and Mordecai looked out and could only think about how beautiful Hadar was: would he ever see her again, and would he ever unbutton those buttons?

Chapter 129

Williams's Office

WILLIAMS HAD TWO SUBMARINES AND two Navy Seal teams cruising around the North Atlantic waiting to intercept the boat coming from Syria. Williams had been on the phone constantly with Dobias, who in turn had been on the phone with Oppenheimer, and none of his team had reported seeing Adad's van or any manifest of any ship in all the ports in Syria carrying anything from Assad. The team member who was watching Assad's warehouse saw the container, but nothing had been put in it for days.

Williams called in Baker to talk about what was going on. "The bombs can't just vanish off the face of the earth; so where the hell are they? It's been seven days and nothing. I have to tell the president that we have lost track of the bombs, and we have no intelligence about where they might be at this moment."

Oppenheimer had sent Hadar and her team back to the warehouse, but she reported back: nothing there, and no sign of where they were headed.

Williams left the office and headed home to his wife, Ellen. He got home, and Ellen was fixing dinner. Frank walked into the kitchen and put his arms around her to give her a gentle hug, and she moved his hands up to her breasts, but he dropped them to her waist and said, "We need to talk." He took her hand, and they walked outside and sat on the couch on the patio. He turned to her and looked her in the eyes, and she knew something was very wrong. As tears came to his eyes, he told her that the United States was going to be attacked by terrorists with two powerful dirty bombs and, although he and the government had tried the best they could, they could no longer stop it from happening.

"We don't know where it is going to take place or when, but they are coming." Ellen took him in her arms and said, "We will do the best we can. America always comes back from adversity."

I hope so, Williams thought, *but perhaps not this time*. He wanted to run, but he didn't know where to go, so he just stayed in his wife's arms, the safest place he knew.

Chapter 130

Houston, Texas

It had been about ten days since the Brotherhood left Syria, and by text message they had decided to meet at the Houston Galleria outside Macy's North at five o'clock.

The team started arriving one by one, and they waited for Sargon to arrive. Mordecai looked down the escalator and saw Sargon coming up to greet them. They shook hands and walked over to the side of the entrance of Macy's, where there was space, and it was away from the traffic going into the store.

Sargon opened the envelope with the four votes, and it was unanimous for O: Oleg's oil plan. They left the mall and headed down to their cars.

"Each of you will travel in one car. The car with the bomb will be the one that we leave behind; when you are clear of the blast, at a preset time, you will dial the cell phone number for your bomb. The way the bombs are programmed, they will not explode until the cell phone calls the detonator of the bomb."

Mordecai and Adad were ready to head south with their bomb, and

Oleg and Jaiari were packing to head east toward New Orleans with theirs. "We know what to do and how we are going to plant the bombs; you are taking your cars as close as you can to the target. The other car will come in and pick you up and then get away as fast as you can. On your approach, Mordecai has built his bomb so it can be taken out of its case, so it will be easy to get out if you feel you need to do so, but I think the bombs will be fine in the cars. The bomb from Iran will be too difficult to get out of the case, so we will leave it in place. If, as you approach your target, you see an opportunity to get your bomb closer to your target's ground zero, then take that opportunity. If not, then leave it in the car and get the car as close to the target as you can. Any questions?"

"Where do we meet afterward?"

"If we survive, we meet back here as soon as possible after the attack. It may take days or even weeks, but let's keep in contact by text."

"What about the twins?"

"I'm going to assign one each to the car that is carrying the bomb. I want Michael to go with the team going south, and Ishtar with the team going east. If there are no other questions, then be on your way and be proud of what you are about to do. You men will be the first people in the world to conquer America."

Chapter 131

En Route

THE TWO TEAMS STARTED OUT for their targets. The southbound team took less than an hour to get to theirs. The eastbound team would take almost seven hours to reach its target, and both teams would spend the night in their target cities. The first bomb would go off at noon the next day. The second bomb would go off twelve hours later, at midnight. The drive to the targets was somber, and not much talking was going on. The radio was on, but that was about it; they were very quiet. They knew that something serious was going to happen: people would die, and lives would be changed forever.

The next morning John Bowman was getting ready to go to the pipeline project south and decided to take his dog, Chandler, with him in the car. Chandler was a great dog; he went in the grass at the side of the road when they stopped, and, while it would be a long day for both of them, they could go down and back in one day, and Chandler would be company for Bowman. He finally got everything he needed packed in the car, but by now he was about an hour late, so he got on the road at nine. Traffic was light when he hit Houston about eleven thirty. John got through and was on his way south, when about twelve o'clock he saw a great fireball in the sky.

Shortly afterward, traffic started backing up, so he turned on the car radio, and he heard an emergency alert broadcast over the radio to move away from Texas City. The radio stations stopped their music and reported that the town of Texas City, Texas, had been destroyed by a nuclear explosion, and it was not safe to go anywhere near Texas City. The Department of Homeland Security was doing everything they could to evacuate the survivors, and they were advising not to panic. They suggested that if you were on the road toward Texas City you should turn around and go north.

John Bowman called his wife and asked whether she had heard the news, and she said that she had; they had closed the schools and sent everybody home. They had closed all the state and city offices and sent those people home to be with their families. She reported that the president was expected to address the nation later that day.

"We will just have to wait and see what he says about how bad it is. I'm trying to turn around and get home as soon as I can; I just don't know how long it will take, but I see a service area ahead, so I'm going to pull off and get a full tank of gas and something to eat. I'll call you every hour or so and let you know what is happening."

"John, please be careful."

"I will, and I love you. Don't worry. It will be all right."

John got his gas, but there was a long line, and the food was disappearing off the shelves very quickly. He was able to get a few things to take with him for himself and Chandler to snack on while they were heading home. He began driving again and felt a lot better on the highway than in the service area. As Bowman headed home, he saw the same yellow trucks with the flashing, brilliant, orange lights he saw the night when all this had started, and the Ridleys had disappeared, only this time the flashing lights were bouncing on all the cars trying to escape whatever has had just happened in Texas City.

He heard on the radio that the president would address the nation at around eleven thirty. He was still a long way from home. An hour later he looked at his watch, and it was eleven thirty, and no president. He looked again, and it was now close to midnight, and the announcer finally said, "The president of the United States …"

CHAPTER 132

The End of America

Broadcasting from the Oval Office, the president said, "My fellow Americans—"

The radio crackled. "We interrupt the president: there is a report of a second nuclear bomb exploding in—"

The radio went dead.